WAKING in RUINS

Volume One of *The Continental Divide*

Alanson Rand

Acknowledgments

Special thanks to Joey Clark, Debbie Witt, and Cathy Rathbun for pointing out when I was making no sense.

Editor: Timothy Stead

Rose Island Press LLC
www.roseislandpress.com
info@roseislandpress.com

ISBN (print edition): 978-1-946843-01-2

Also by Alanson Rand:

The Continental Divide

Waking in Ruins

Anarchista

The American Main

Wednesday's Children

Eighteen Hells

The Year of Endings

A Drive with Auntie (coming 2021)

East to Eden

The Shores of Distant Time

<u>KEY FIGURES IN THE REVOLUTION OF 2043</u>

Victoria Lang, MD, Human Trials Director for Chalys Pharmaceuticals
Ada Lang, her daughter
Jonas Deming, MD, Staff Physician, St. Elizabeth's Hospital
Emil Horscht, MD, Professor of Clinical Virology, Johns Hopkins University
Tommy Talbott, MD, Deputy Inspector General, Food & Drug Administration
Mae Esteban, MD, Surgeon General of the United States

Krista Warner, author of *The Rake*
Edify Stanton, a respiratory care nurse
Arista Molle, a television journalist

William Gibbon, President of the United States
Gabriel Cheyn, Vice President of the United States
Marcus Grimes, Chief of Staff for Gabriel Cheyn
Noah Hayborn, Speaker of the House

<u>National Security Forces</u>
Bob Downs, Watcher
Raphael Vinola, Deputy Watcher
Philip Cochon, Day Chief – Intelligence
Ari Stein, Night Chief – Intelligence
Sara Hogue, Day Chief – Tactical Operations
Tom Riddick, Night Chief – Tactical Operations
Hideki Buta, Day Chief – Acquisition
Peter Mochyn, Day Chief – Cybermeasures

PROLOGUE

Pelican Point
Angel Island, California
October 19, 2069

"Heroes," she says, blowing a plume of smoke into the air. "What a crock of shit."

"I'm not saying it's true. It's just that everybody believes that passionate Activist heroes ignited a grassroots revolution and took down an atrophied and evil government. They don't want the truth."

"That's because the truth isn't as dramatic as that damn movie, Boog." She stubs out her cigarette and sits back in the chair with a sigh. "You can tell them how it really happened, but they won't listen. History's already written."

The war was only twenty-six years ago, so it's premature to say its history is etched into the memorial stones. Most people believe that dauntless, rock-jawed Activist armies fought the Continental Divide, the war that sundered the United States into today's Seven Nations. I thought they needed to know the truth: The real engine of the revolution was desperation, dumb luck, and improbable coincidence, all fueled by fantastical bullshit. And if it wasn't for the magnificent might of that bullshit, the Archangelists would have won, and we'd all be speaking English now. Well, you get my point.

But while I might convince readers of that, I was less sure that anybody would accept that the beloved Anarchistas were mere humans. Superheroes sell books, not girls running and hiding, so I wondered if writing this story was a waste of time. I often questioned that when I was sitting on a cramped plane to get to yet another interview, and I was tempted to ditch this project and work on my tan instead. After all, I'm Californian. I have priorities.

Nonetheless, I needed to write the real history. The war is an obsession I've had since childhood, and I couldn't walk away from telling the tale. I needed to finish this book no matter how many people said it was futile.

Relieved that I've resolved those doubts, I sit back in my wicker chair and look across the water. Fog blankets the bay, and San Francisco floats on the magical white cloud, freed from gravity's burden, as does Yerba Buena Island. If you stared at them long enough, the islands seemed to drift with the tides.

As a child, I'd loved those days when this magic came to visit, and I'd sit here on the west porch and soak it in. But I always sat here alone; Mom hated these fogs because of the memories they brought, and she'd stay in her room with the curtains drawn until it burned off, as she was doing right now. After talking to her these past few weeks, I now understand why she fears the fog. I would if I'd experienced the horrors she had.

The Bay's resplendence is absorbing, and we sit in comfortable silence for a few minutes. We're quiet because we're exhausted from finishing her oral history today, an effort that occupied an entire week.

"So you're all headed down to Yerba Buena tonight?" she asks.

"She always sends a hundred paper lanterns to Heaven on the anniversary. She hasn't missed a year yet, and she won't today, either. Why don't you ever go with us?"

"Bagpipes make me cry."

"Right. Now, the real reason?"

"Listen, Boog, I tried pretty hard to get off that damned rock, and it feels wrong to go back. Is that good enough for you?" Her eyes flash like she's going to unload on me, but it passes quickly. "Bad memories there. You know, your mom and I were almost killed on that island."

"You were with the 184th Infantry then, right?"

"What was left of them." She looks away so I can't see her expression. "I don't know why she likes to relive that night."

"She doesn't. She's honoring his last request, that's all, and she'll do it till she dies. Besides, the place is beautiful."

"I couldn't say. I was only there once, and it was nighttime. I don't remember it." She turns to me with a smile. "Old people and their memories. It's all true what they say."

She's not that old, and her memory is flawless. Over the past week, she's recalled two months of her life in fine detail, and those months passed twenty-six years ago. And age doesn't bother her; like many of her peers, I think she fancies becoming old. For a long time, she didn't think she'd get the chance.

She lights another cigarette and watches her cloud drift off the porch to join the fog tendrils. "Now that was an awful day."

"I can only imagine. So much ended on October 19th. The world nearly ended." I turn in my seat to see her face. "So what was it like? To make history, I mean."

She scrunches up her face as if the answer is unpleasant, although I can't imagine why it should be. "Well, we didn't know we were making history. It wasn't the way historians make it now, all noble and full of purpose and grand intentions. We were just doing what we needed to, which was trying to outrun the virus and save our asses. I didn't feel heroic or anything."

Now that she's given me the opening, I ask the question I've never had answered to my satisfaction. "So how *did* it feel? For all you've told me, you've avoided describing what it felt like to be there."

She stubs out her cigarette. I always want to tell her to cut down on the damn things, but she'd just flatten me if I tried. Besides, I know I'd get the same answer Mom gives me: I should have died forty times already, I'm living in the bonus round now, and I'll damned well enjoy it.

I suspect that she's not afraid of harm because nothing frightens this generation. Mom once told me that she'd had the fright scared right out of her during the war, and I'd thought it was a glib turn of phrase at the time. Now I think it was a profound insight. This casual disregard of fear is almost universal among the two hundred survivors I'd interviewed for the book.

I'd gone to considerable lengths to get their histories: I'd driven across the States to Sagebrush, to the Free Cities, and then to New America, which was a story in itself. I flew to Havana, and even to China to interview the crew of the *Guang Shenzhen*; while they were on history's stage for only half an hour, I wanted to know their story. Almost all those survivors treat fear as something too insignificant to acknowledge, which I suspect is because their experiences during the war make today's troubles seem pale.

Exposing how the characters reacted to the revolution's unforeseen horrors is critical to making the history come alive, though, so I asked every survivor to describe the experience of war. And every one changed the subject.

"How did it feel?" She clears her throat. "You wouldn't understand. You had to be there."

"Why not try?"

She fidgets in her chair and finds a new position. "It's hard to describe. It was like everything, all at once. Words don't convey it. I mean, how does cotton candy taste? In words?

"Everything was extreme. Live or die, fight or flee, win or lose, love or hate…you get the idea. It was always one extreme or the other.

"And everything was intense. I feared intensely, loved intensely, fought intensely, lived intensely, knowing I could die any moment.

"How did it feel? It was exhausting. I don't know how else to describe it."

"But I need to describe it. I don't want to write another dry history of the dead. Every time you write about the revolution, you end up focusing on atrocities – the RVE Initiative, Economic Selection, and so on – that have been analyzed and rectally probed till they're not interesting. I don't want to write another catalog of death. I want to explore the life of the time and how it triumphed in a world of constantly evolving terror. I want to convey how it felt to escape the jaws of the beast, not recite dates and locations and megadeaths."

She rubs her temples, which means she's becoming aggravated and impatient again. "Try this. Imagine feeling so tired and scared that killing yourself becomes attractive."

I close my eyes and try, but that one's beyond me. "Nope. I can't do that."

"It's good you can't." She looks away and is silent for some time, and then she takes a long sip of water. "Boog, I want to keep the past in the past. I don't want to waste what life I have left recalling it. It's over, but I think you're coming close to worshipping it."

"I'm just immersing myself in the time so I can write."

"Uh-huh. Sure you are."

A pair of deer emerges from the tree line, and we watch them graze until they saunter into the fog. She turns and looks at me earnestly. "This is a beautiful time, a beautiful place." She barks a bitter laugh and shakes her head. "I suppose you could even call it Eden."

"No, I'd rather not. Please."

"But this is your time, and you should live fully in it. Take my advice – let the past go and stop trying to live in it." She looks over the bay, and a distant expression settles on her face. "Trust me. You wouldn't have wanted to be there."

THE PHYSICIAN

Day 1
Wednesday night, August 19, 2043
Klean Koal Arena, Newark, New Jersey

The guard had some hang-up about dying. Michael had been strangling him for over two minutes, but he still flailed at Michael's chest and tried to struggle from his grasp. He wondered if the man had an iron windpipe.

"Look, bud, I've got a schedule to keep here," Michael said. "This is a clockwork operation. Give it up already." The guard wriggled even more and struck Michael on the side of the head. The blow was weak, but Michael was done with drama. He released his grip on the man's throat, grabbed the side of his head, and broke his neck. The guard dropped to the floor and lay still.

"Finally," he whispered, wriggling his fingers to see if they'd been affected by the crude manual kill. He hadn't wanted to risk his sense of touch, but the guard had walked into the arena's mechanical room just as he was deploying his gear. Operational security was paramount in this mission, and a guard's life wasn't.

He stepped over the body and opened the duct access door, and the air inside ruffled his short brown hair. It smelled fresh and clean, which was a rare sensation these days, and he sighed at the thought of breathing the choking mixture of coal smoke and fog outside after he finished placing the device.

What we've done to Eden, he thought. He was old enough to remember when people breathed the outdoor air without masks, and he could recognize neighbors walking on his street. Now everybody wore a blue surgical mask – were they his neighbors, or were they murderers and mullahs? He couldn't tell anymore.

The duct was pumping air into the empty arena beyond the wall. He turned his face into the stream and savored the coolness; not only was it brutally hot outside, but he was also in the throes of a viral sweat.

He was probably infected with RVE already – which was no surprise since the weaponized Ellesmere virus was highly transmissible – but since he was vaccinated, the sweat was merely an annoyance. While a high fever was harmless, though, running a hundred-plus fever on a hundred-plus day made him uncomfortable. More importantly, it weakened his situational awareness, a dangerous thing at such a mission-critical point.

Grunting, he rolled his black case to the duct door and opened the lid to check the fragile glass virus cylinders and the aerosolizing nozzles. After slipping on thick cotton gloves, he lifted them from their foam niches and laid them gently on a blanket inside the duct.

He climbed in, the metal popping and groaning under his weight as he arranged his tools and equipment. Once all was in order, he began the task he'd trained for weeks to execute.

He shivered in the cool air, and he spread his arms and released his fever heat into the stream. After this mission, he'd enjoy a monthlong vacation at the Guantanamo Bay beach house, where it was supposed to be cooler than New Jersey. He closed his eyes and imagined chilling in the pool all day, only coming out at night for a little R&R.

After eleven minutes of work, his task was almost complete. He paused a moment and prayed, which he always did when he was distressed; wielding the sword of the Archangel was an honor, but it was also a sad and terrible duty. Nevertheless, he willed himself to be strong. Bounteous good would arise once Man stopped despoiling God's Earthly Heaven.

He drew a deep breath and made the sign of the cross over his chest, and then he pressed the black button on top of the device and confirmed that two red lights were blinking. Being careful to avoid disturbing it, he climbed out of the duct and closed the hatch behind him. He immediately began roasting again.

Looking at the guard, he sighed and wiped his brow; the death had to appear accidental, so his work was incomplete. He dragged the corpse onto the catwalk over the event floor, broke the railing, and kicked it over the edge.

He looked at the body sprawled a hundred feet below, admiring the blood spatter for a moment, and then tossed the dead man a jaunty salute.

THE COLLAPSE OF THE UNION began a week later. On that steamy August morning, a weary physician faced the seemingly inconsequential choice of whether to go to work or get plastered. She couldn't know that the moment she parked her car at St. Elizabeth's Hospital, she'd trigger a cataclysmic chain of events that would rip apart the United States in seventy-six harrowing days.

Dr. Victoria Lang drove slowly through the lot in front of the Administration Building searching for her favorite parking space. She had compelling reasons to ditch work: First, a mountain of soul-crushingly tedious FDA paperwork sat on her tiny desk at the hospital, and second, the heat and humidity were intolerable. Her top was already soaked through, and the air conditioning was turned up to maximum.

She found the space and tapped her finger on the steering wheel, thinking that a few umbrella drinks at a breezy Eastern Shore marina would be delightful after two days of double shifts. However, the prospect of doing twice the work tomorrow was too depressing to contemplate. She pulled in and turned off the engine.

Her satnav display said she was in front of the Administration Building, but she couldn't tell; the fug was so thick today that she couldn't see past her hood ornament.

She'd never seen weather so awful. Temperatures on the East Coast hadn't dipped below a hundred degrees since June, and the air conditioners were using so much electricity that the power plants were operating beyond capacity. Their coal smoke melded with the moist air and formed a noxious fog so dense that even the hurricanes couldn't disperse it.

She coughed in anticipation of breathing the stuff; while her face mask filtered out the airborne soot, it couldn't neutralize the acids in the fug that damaged the lungs. It wouldn't be long before the physician became the patient.

Looking at her face in the mirror, she resolved yet again to get out of St. Elizabeth's before the ever-present scowl froze on her face. Her short blonde hair and brown eyes looked perfect, though, and she was grateful that St. E's hadn't aged them yet.

She reached into her bag and felt for the soft cloth cup of her face mask. As her fingers closed around it, her tablet chirped and the screen displayed the name of an old classmate from Johns Hopkins, Dr. Jonas Deming, who was a staff physician in Infectious Diseases.

She struggled to put on a happier expression, tapped the tablet, and watched his face shimmer onto the screen. "Hey, Tori!"

"Yo, Jo, how are you?"

"Ahh, I'm up to my neck in shit, but it was up to my eyeballs yesterday. Things are looking up, I guess. How are you doing?"

"I'm depressed. I have a day of deadly dull Chalys paperwork to do."

"My sad, sad prima donna! Why don't you ditch all that wealth and comfort, Oh-So-Mighty Human Trials Director, and join me here, do some real medicine for a change?"

Victoria snorted. "What I do is real medicine, bubba. Remember that the next time you administer a Chalys drug."

"Okay, you got me there. Look, lemme take you away from that boring paperwork for a while. I've got a problem you can help me with."

"A patient?" she asked. "I only do drug testing, Jonas. I don't have practice privileges here."

He laughed. "You're worried about the formalities in this sewer? Gimme a break. But we can keep it informal if you want. I just need an outside opinion. I've got a case here that's driving me up the wall."

"Hmm. What makes you think I can help?"

"Well, the case is probably viral."

"Call in a virologist for a consult. Really, Jonas, that's the protocol."

"It is, yeah." Frustration appeared at the corners of his mouth. "But I can't get any virologists to come to this cesspool. It'd be easier to get the Pope to drop his drawers in a whorehouse."

"So…?"

"So everyone knows you've got a virus fetish. You're better than most virologists I know anyway." Victoria gave Deming's image an exaggerated frown. "Or you could sit over in the Scream Factory, listen to people die, do boring paperwork, miss seeing my handsome face, ignore this compelling viral enigma…"

She laughed. "All right. I can spare a few minutes for a consult. Where are you today?"

"First floor, Infectives Building. See you in, say, fifteen minutes?"

"Sure. See you then." She slipped on her mask, and after taking a final breath of clean air, she opened the car door and climbed out. The sting of the fug immediately made her eyes water.

She walked to the Administration Building and turned toward the center of the campus and the Infectives Unit. After ten minutes of stumbling past small buildings she could barely see through the fug, she spotted a sign for the Infectives Building. She turned down a sidewalk and found an old Victorian mansion that had been converted into a patient unit.

The tired woman behind the reception desk directed her to the three-room isolation unit at the rear of the building. Victoria walked down a winding corridor that creaked and sagged as she walked; patients loitered in the hall, watching her walk by as if she might dispense hope, a cure, or just a kind word. She slipped her mask back on her face.

Every building at St. Elizabeth's was crowded and noisy, every corner stank, and every inch was filthy, but the hospital escaped punishment because it was the only place to dump the unhealthy poor. Those who couldn't afford Wellness Corp's health insurance ended up in a place like this or as dead stiffers in the gutter.

The indigents said this was better treatment than none. *Sure, just not much better than none,* she thought, squirting a stream of sanitizer into her hands. *It's best to avoid being poor in this town.*

After a few turns, she reached the Isolation Unit and spotted a tall, gangly man talking to a nurse. He turned as she entered, and then his face broke into a broad smile.

Jonas hugged her, and they walked to a dictation desk in an alcove. He pulled out two wooden chairs, offered her one, and then turned his chair around and sat, crossing his arms over the seat back. "Okay, Tori, this is a weird one. I've got a patient, John Durant, came in Monday presenting flu symptoms. I've tried three different courses of antivirals on him, and there's been no effect whatsoever. In fact, his condition is degrading."

"Hmm. What makes you think this is viral?"

"Look at his chart yourself." He pulled a thick tan folder off the desk, shook a dead fly off, and handed it to her. She flipped through the pages and then stopped, her eyes wide.

"He's been running a fever of 104 degrees for four days straight?"

"Yep. Can't bring it down no matter what, and believe me, we're trying."

"How's he surviving that?"

"He's healthy otherwise. Some mild emphysema in his left lung, that's all."

"That's pretty common these days," she said to herself as she paged through the chart again. "I'm getting it, too, despite wearing a face mask. This damned fug is terrible." She scanned the rest of the chart and then looked up with unfocused eyes. "None of the usual virus swabs came up positive, and one of them should have. I wonder if we have a mutation here, something new that's resistant to all the antivirals you've pumped into this guy. Have you done any bloodwork?"

"Well, I have. The lab lost the samples the first time, so yesterday I sent a new set down."

"Did they identify the virus?"

He gave her a wide, lopsided smile and shrugged. "Nope, but they said he's pregnant."

She laughed. "Well, that would be historic."

"Hell, maybe he *is* pregnant. I don't care. Him and his fetus will be dead in a week if I can't bring that fever down."

"Sooner than that, Jo, sooner than that." She drummed her fingers on the chart, lost in thought. "I can take blood samples back to my lab and try to identify and challenge the pathogen. Maybe I can find a drug that's effective against it in a controlled environment. That's all I can do."

"I'd appreciate that, Tori, I really would. I'm getting frustrated shooting in the dark."

"Okay. Draw me ten cc's of blood, and I'll work it and let you know. I'll also send the results to Mae. And Horscht, too, in case he can shed some light."

His face soured. "*That* prick?"

"That prick might help. Isn't that what you want?"

"Well, yeah…" He waved to a passing nurse and asked her to draw Durant's blood.

"If this is a mutation, though, we'll need to know his contact history. There'll be an epidemiological follow-up."

"I've already taken his history. Durant works as a janitor at a sports arena in northern New Jersey. Friday morning, he left to visit his brother in

Anacostia for a week. Soon after he arrived, he began experiencing flu-like symptoms. He treated himself with over-the-counter meds for two days but only saw a worsening of his condition. He was admitted Monday afternoon with a fever of 104 degrees."

Victoria frowned. "A full history would list his known associates and incidental contacts, patterns of travel, and so forth. What you have won't be enough, Jonas. You need to get more from him, and you need to do it before he strokes. After four days of elevated temperature, that's the immediate danger, not the infection."

Deming ran his fingers through his unkempt brown hair. "Yeah, but that's all I can get outta him. He's Haitian, and English is like a distant second language to him. I need someone who can speak French to get all the details. How am I gonna get an interpreter to come to this shithole?"

"No need. I speak French."

"Really?"

"Fluently. I was stationed in Cherbourg for a year after med school. By the way, you should isolate him until we understand this virus more."

"I *can't* isolate him. There's another patient in with him, a lungbutter case – you know, pneumonia, bronchitis, the whole nine yards – and I've got no place to put him except out on the porch. Hell, we're at the point where we might as well do that and let the poor guy die." He shook his head. "I can put a gown and mask order on the room and curtain off Durant, but isolation ain't happening."

"That won't be enough, Jonas. You know that."

Deming gave her a broad but weary smile. "Welcome to St. E's, where substandard is the new standard! Always Aiming Lower! That should be our motto."

"Well, that's in your hands, Jo. You don't have much to work with here." She walked to a nearby closet and rummaged inside. "Where do you keep the moon suits?"

Deming laughed. "You've gotta be kidding. You're lucky we even have gowns."

"All right. I'll just keep my distance and hope for the best." She put on a gown, mask, and booties, and snapped on a pair of latex examination gloves. "I'll go talk to him now."

"Room Nine," he said.

VICTORIA TAPPED ON THE DOOR and walked into Room Nine. A lean, brown-skinned man in his twenties lay on a bed near the door, and she saw the feet of the lungbutter case past the divider curtain. A nurse fussed around Durant's right arm. Victoria passed her to sit in the chair beside his bed as the nurse drew the blood sample.

She sat and then jumped up; a large chip of dirty plaster lay on the chair, matching a hole in the ceiling. Scowling, she swept it to the floor with the chart and then turned her attention back to Durant.

She introduced herself, and he replied in a voice so weak that she needed to lean close to hear him. She felt his body heat as she did; she didn't need a thermometer to know that the man was dangerously feverish. His almond-shaped, golden eyes were sunken and dull, radiating agony the way his body radiated heat.

For the next half hour, he answered her questions with as much strength as he could muster. He said that he rarely left his small apartment in Elizabeth, New Jersey; he worked the second janitorial shift at Klean Koal Arena six nights a week and spent the rest of his time either commuting or in his apartment playing the piano.

She tapped a pen against her lips as she listened to his history. As reclusive as he was, John Durant wouldn't normally be exposed to community infections. He most likely caught the bug at Klean Koal Arena – a venue that held twenty-four thousand people.

BACK AT CHALYS PHARMACEUTICALS, Victoria unlocked the door to her small lab and sat in front of one of her two protein modelers. She opened a transparent plastic box underneath it, slipped her hands into the attached gloves, and then withdrew a small amount of Durant's blood and deposited it into the machine's preparation slot.

The imaging process would take a few minutes, so she pulled her tablet from her purse and composed a message to Dr. Emil Horscht at Johns Hopkins Medical School. He'd been her virology professor during her first school year, but when the coronavirus pandemic struck America in March of '20, he'd persuaded his star student to join his team and research treatments for the disease. They'd worked together for five months, spending seven days a week and sixteen hours a day in the lab, testing antigens on the SARS-CoV-2 virus and laying the groundwork for scores of antiviral treatments. He was still obsessed with tracking emerging viruses, and he'd want to know about this one – if he didn't already.

She wrote down the details of the Durant case and set the tablet aside. Weariness overcame her, and she fell into a light doze that shattered when the protein modeler chimed.

The image on the screen was full of sub-cellular debris, and she searched through the clutter for half an hour to find the virus. Once she did, she zoomed in.

The virus was tiny, measuring only seventy nanometers. It was smaller than a coronavirus virion but looked similar, like a sphere adorned with suction cups. Unlike a coronavirus, though, it was asymmetrical – one side was deeply indented, and a dense cluster of protein spikes filled the cavity.

She'd never seen such an unusual virus form, so she captured an image of it and attached it to Dr. Horscht's message. She also sent a copy to Mae Esteban, another classmate from Johns Hopkins. Mae, more a politician than a physician, had risen faster than anyone in her class to become the Surgeon General. Although she didn't have Horscht's pulse on the world of emerging viruses, she had more power to act if necessary.

Sitting back in the chair, she examined the screen image. It might be another exotic virus that had bubbled out of the melting Arctic permafrost, a bug that humankind hadn't seen for a thousand years, which could explain why none of the antiviral treatments worked against it.

The rising sea levels and famines brought on by climate change weren't the real danger to humanity – it was the ancient bugs that Arctic warming was re-introducing to the world, bugs for which no living creature had immunity. She decided to cross-check the exotics archive and search for a match.

The search would require a detailed model, so she set the first modeler to analyze the virus's protein shell and produce a three-dimensional image. She lined up eight Petri dishes with growth medium in her second modeler's glovebox and then placed a drop of Durant's blood on each one.

After that, she reached into her small refrigerator for a rack of experimental antiviral agents. She applied ones that hadn't been tried on Durant into the first seven dishes, but she introduced the mysterious drug Recombin, which she'd been testing for months, into the eighth. She knew that the Recombin virus was genomically engineered, and she suspected it was a virophage – a virus that killed other viruses – but she didn't know what bug it was built to attack. After testing Recombin against other viruses forty-seven times with no positive result, though, she expected the same this time.

She stood, turned off the lights, and locked the lab. It usually took twelve hours for any reliable results, and there was no point in staying. She'd have useful information tomorrow.

After she left her office, she realized that she'd forgotten her tablet but decided to leave it there. A quiet evening would be nice for a change.

THE EMERGENT

Day 9
Thursday morning, August 27, 2043
Chalys Pharmaceuticals, Fort Washington, Maryland

Victoria unlocked the door to her lab, curious to see what her virus challenge had produced overnight. She sat at the counter and clicked on the protein modeler's monitor, and then she scrolled through the results until the graphs of the live-virus count appeared, which showed the percentage of live virus particles remaining in the sample.

As she scrolled through the charts, she reached over, tapped her tablet on, and saw nineteen messages from Dr. Horscht asking her to contact him. She raised an eyebrow. Emil never panicked; if his pants were on fire, he'd grab a ruler and measure the flames to decide if taking them off was warranted.

She tapped the tablet to return his call. He picked up on the first ring and bellowed in his deep German baritone as his jowly face materialized on her screen. "Victoria! At last! Have you been on a mountaintop? Why have you not returned my calls?"

"Umm…a problem with my battery. It's fixed now."

"This is grave, what you have sent me, young Victoria, very grave. Are you still in good health? Have you been exposed to this virus? Prophylaxis! Remember! It saves lives, perhaps your own!"

She was still scrolling through the live-virus charts; so far, the antiviral drugs had been ineffective. "Emil, slowly please. What are you talking about?"

"This photograph you have sent me. I have seen this virus. It appeared last week in three hospitals in New Jersey and one in New York, and we have recorded two thousand suspected cases already. It is a novel virus with pandemic potential, and it is a grave development that it is already in Washington. Grave!"

"I believe that the patient may have acquired it in New Jersey at an arena. I interviewed him myself. He's probably the only case here, Emil."

"All the patients report that they were at that very same arena. Klean Koal Arena, last Thursday evening, monster truck rally. Your patient must remain the only case there, Victoria. Prophylaxis, isolation, containment. Do you remember? This is what you must do first. Then you must trace and quarantine his contacts."

"We're doing our best. And yes, before you say it, we'll do even better. So what is this bug? Do you know anything about it?"

"It is not an *insect*. It is a virion-phase virus."

She rolled her eyes and willed herself to be calm. "What do you know about this virus?"

"We know nothing about it. The response in New Jersey is disorganized, and that is being gracious. CDC has taken charge, and all they have done is assign two epidemiologists to the case. Two! It should be a hundred! Useless, absolutely useless, Victoria. Perhaps when everyone comes back from summer vacation, they will take it more seriously. We should ask this virus to wait for a more convenient time, no?"

She scrolled through to the next chart and started to feel like she was drilling a dry well. While Dr. Horscht continued to rant about the CDC's incompetence, she scrolled the last chart into view and froze when she saw the blinking text at the bottom of the screen:

LIVE VIRUS PARTICLE COUNT: 0.0 PER CC

She scanned the data in the table: Recombin, the cure for which there was no disease, had eradicated the New Jersey virus in less than four hours.

She gazed at the data and tried to make sense of what she knew. She'd stolen the Recombin samples back in April, but the virus it was designed to kill had been unknown before last week – except that Chalys had to have known about it because their bioengineers would have needed a sample to build such a powerful virophage. Then they'd developed a huge supply of Recombin well before the virus emerged and didn't let anyone know it existed.

She tried to find a believable reason for Chalys to do that, all the time suppressing a growing tide of panic.

HORSCHT YELLED, "Victoria! Are you all right?"

She blinked her eyes a few times and looked down at the tablet. "I'm sorry?"

"You have been staring like a stupid person for more than two minutes. Completely unresponsive. Are you well? Do you need assistance?"

"Uhh…yeah, no, I'm fine. Look, something just came up. I'll call you back, all right, thanks, bye." She tapped the tablet off, threw it on the counter, and then scrutinized the data again. "I did something wrong," she said. "There must be some mistake."

She sterilized the modeler and repeated the preparations for Recombin she'd performed last night. She tapped again on the screen and ordered an accelerated process, and the modeler began to hum and whir.

After the work was underway, she walked to a small sample refrigerator across the lab and reached into the space behind it. She pulled out a three-inch-thick packet of paper, which was a collection of manifests, production reports, lab notes, and tests on Recombin. For more than an hour, she scanned it for anything that might contradict her conclusion, but it only made more sense when she was done: Recombin was built specifically to combat the New Jersey virus.

The modeler chirped and displayed the live-virus counts, which were already dropping. Recombin was wiping out the virus again.

She swore and thumped the counter with her fist, causing the blood vial in the glovebox to roll toward her. She saw the name 'Durant' written on it in marker, and then she ran across the room to the refrigerator, snatched a bottle of Recombin from inside, and bolted from the lab.

VICTORIA PULLED INTO THE ADMINISTRATION LOT and squealed to a stop. Without even putting on her mask, she jumped out and sprinted across the campus to the Infectives Building.

She burst through the double doors to the Isolation Unit. Dr. Deming was leaving Room Nine, holding the door open for a young nurse carrying a tray of vials. "Jonas! How is Durant?"

Deming waved for her to come closer and replied in a weak, hoarse voice. "Not good, I'm afraid." He leaned against the corridor wall.

"How are you feeling?" Alarmed, she looked at his sunken eyes and held her hand to his forehead, which was dangerously hot.

"Just a little warm, thassall. I can keep going if they'll fix this air conditioning. There's nothing you can do for Durant, though. You might as well go on back. Thanks for your help, Tori."

"Still, I'll gown up and check in on him. Why don't you lie down?"

Deming waved her away. "I'm fine, fine, don't worry about me," he said, pulling a chart from a wall rack. She watched him walk into the next room, unsteady on his feet, and then she ran to the gown cart and donned a mask, gown, cap, and booties.

She pushed open the door to Room Nine. Durant, his chest heaving and caked in thin blood, was thrashing on the bed. Red droplets speckled the curtain and the walls.

"Nurse, restrain him before he hurts himself," Victoria said. The nurse tightened a strap on his left wrist and then leaned across him to grab his right. Victoria took a seat and observed Durant's condition: He was bleeding from his eyes and nose, and blood dribbled down his chin and across the sheets. He turned to Victoria and whispered, *"Vomissure…Je dégueulerai…"*

Victoria jumped to her feet and reached for the nurse. "Get back! He's going to –" Durant suddenly sat up and vomited, coating the nurse's head and shoulder with blood and ragged gray-pink flecks of tissue. She screamed and reached for her eyes with bloody gloves.

"It's in my eyes!" the nurse wailed. "His blood is in –"

"Don't touch them!" Victoria hurried to the other side of the curtain and disconnected the oxygen hose from the respiratory patient, and then she ran to the head of the bed and began to push it. Slowly, the heavy bed started to move.

"What can I do?" asked the nurse, who was pressed against the wall.

"Nothing! Help me get this patient outta here now! Come on!"

The nurse snapped off her gloves and ran around the foot of Durant's bed, nearly slipping on the bloody floor. "Okay, I got this end," she said. "You had the brake on. Let's go. Just watch the blood on the floor! Push!"

Victoria shoved the bed toward the door.

"There's nothing we can do?" the nurse asked, looking at Durant.

"That was his stomach lining you got sprayed with. There's nothing to save now. We need to contain this, and the first thing is to get this guy out. Second thing is to get you cleaned off."

"Do you think I just got what he has?" the nurse asked, her brown eyes wide in fear.

Definitely, thought Victoria. "Maybe not," she said, and then she slipped on a slick of blood and banged her chin against the bed frame. As she got up, Durant coughed and sprayed her and the patient with a thin mist of infected blood. She shoved the bed again, but the patient's catheter hose caught on the doorknob; he moaned as the catheter pulled out of him, and a bag of urine slung under the bed dropped to the floor and broke open. Durant grunted and collapsed back on the bloody sheets.

"Shit! What else can go wrong? Hold up a sec." Victoria wrangled the hose free of the handle, and as she did, she heard a soft thump from the hall outside.

"Dr. Deming just collapsed," said the nurse, looking at the commotion.

"Tell everyone to stay back! Don't touch him!" yelled Victoria as she pushed the bed through the doorway and hooked the door closed with her foot. They pushed the bed to the side, and she pointed to the nurse. "Wash your eyes now!" She turned to the people standing in the corridor. "The rest of you, pull those patients out of those rooms and get them past the containment doors! Then get out and don't open those doors till I say so!"

The staff stood still and glanced at each other until the nurse unleashed a barrage of venomous Spanish. They began to mill around, and Victoria yelled, "Now, dammit!" They rushed into the rooms, and in less than five minutes, the suite beyond the double doors was empty. Victoria and the nurse stayed behind with Deming and the old man in the bed.

THE QUIET WAS DISTURBING after the commotion of the previous fifteen minutes, and Victoria and the nurse stood in the corridor waiting for something else to happen. After a few uneventful minutes passed, they stripped off their gowns and then washed their hands and faces. The nurse stayed behind to rinse her eyes again, while Victoria knelt next to Deming.

The side of his head was bruised, but he was uninjured otherwise. The nurse arrived at her side with a thermometer, held it to his forehead, and whistled. "Hundred and four. Seems to be the magic number around here lately."

"We need to cool him down," Victoria said.

"Does no good. With Durant, the more we tried to lower his temperature, the more we stressed him. Just leave him be for now."

Victoria thought for a few seconds. "It makes no difference in the end, does it?"

The nurse shook her head. "Nothing works with this bug. Do you think he has it?"

Victoria nodded.

The nurse walked to the refrigerator, pulled out two soft drinks, and handed one to Victoria. They popped open the cans and sat on the yellowed linoleum floor, their backs against the desk of the nurse's station.

"What's your name?" asked Victoria.

"Plunkett," she said. "Sharilah Plunkett."

"Sharilah. That's a pretty name." She held out her hand. "Victoria Lang. Call me Tori."

Plunkett shook her hand. "You a doctor?"

Victoria nodded. "I run the drug tests for Chalys. I'm a friend of Jonas. I usually work over at Terminals, but I came here to help out this morning." Victoria glanced at the bloody door of Room Nine. "I didn't expect this."

Plunkett laughed bitterly. "I thought the worst thing I'd see today was a full bedpan."

They sat without speaking for several minutes and sipped their drinks. The air conditioning stopped with a rattle and a sigh, and the air began to feel close and warm. Without the white noise, they heard a babble of voices outside the double doors and then the *rikking* sound of paper tape being peeled. The doors shook as workers taped the gaps.

"Well, we're on our own now," said Plunkett. "This sucks."

"Well said." Victoria watched Deming for a few moments and pursed her lips. "Sharilah, this isn't the time for deception. Whatever Durant has, we have it now, too."

Plunkett looked into her lap and nodded. "I know. This is a death sentence, isn't it?" She sat quietly for a few moments and shuddered. "Durant was eaten from the inside out. I'd rather be euthanized than go through…well, that." She nodded at the closed door of Room Nine.

Victoria nodded. "I would too. But there's another possibility. Do you know what a virophage is?"

Plunkett shook her head.

Victoria pulled a Cryogenie from her coat pocket and opened the small refrigerated case. "A virophage is a virus that attacks other viruses." She handed a bottle of Recombin to her. "This virophage attacks the virus that made Durant sick. *In vitro*, it's one hundred percent effective. *In vivo*, I have no idea what it'll do. It's never been tested in humans, as far as I know. We could administer this to ourselves, and it would probably help, but it's an unknown risk."

"Dunno about you, but I've got no choice here. Nothing else we tried helped Durant."

"There may be side effects. It's a gamble. I can't make any guarantees."

A soft, wet sucking sound came from Room Nine and then stopped. She turned to Victoria, and her eyes, young and frightened moments ago, now seemed older and harder. "Screw the side effects. It's the effects that scare me." She pulled up the sleeve of her scrubs.

Victoria walked to the back of the nurse's station and returned with three syringes. She uncapped one, filled it with Recombin, and then jabbed the needle into Plunkett's arm and depressed the plunger.

"Damn, that hurts. What is that, ice? My fingers are tingling."

"Sorry." Victoria removed the syringe, capped it, and then handed another to Plunkett. "At least you get the chance to get me back."

"Going down together, huh? Okay. Let's hope this stuff of yours works, or we're both screwed." She jabbed the syringe into Victoria's arm. "Hey, guess what?"

"Mmm?"

"We just made medical history!"

"Yeah." Victoria snorted. "Not the way I'd always hoped to, though. But I guess the old saying is true – some people are born to greatness..."

"...and some get greatness barfed all over their face?"

They laughed for a moment, but then the uncomfortable silence grew again. "I can still feel that shit on my skin. It's driving me nuts," said Plunkett.

"Why don't you go shower? Just help me with Jonas first." Victoria prepared another syringe while Plunkett raised Deming's head and rested it on a rolled blanket. Victoria tried to pull off his lab coat, but he was unwieldy for a thin man, so she cut the sleeve off and injected him. He stirred at the sudden pain and began to mumble, but he was still deep in a fevered semi-consciousness and soon became quiet again.

They walked around the small hallway and attended to details; Plunkett plugged the old respiratory patient's oxygen tubes into a wall outlet, while Victoria scrawled QUARANTINE on two pieces of paper and taped them to the windows of the double doors. However, the staff on the other side retreated when Victoria approached the doors, so they already knew to stay away. Near the front entrance, she spotted hospital security guards huddled in a discussion.

Victoria returned to the nurse's station and leaned against the counter, and Plunkett joined her. "So now what?"

"We wait for the virophage to work, I suppose," said Victoria.

"How long?"

"Three hours, fifty-four minutes," said Victoria.

"Could you be more specific?" She looked at the clock. "Guess I have time to take that shower." She walked to a nearby closet and pulled out a red biohazard bag. "I'm bagging these scrubs. You oughta shower too."

"When you're done. I'll handle things here in the meantime."

After she heard the locker room door close, Victoria sat on the floor in front of the nurse's station again so she could see both Deming and the double doors. She leaned her head back against the desk and considered her next steps; however, she'd blundered into a minefield and wasn't sure any steps were safe.

On the drive to St. E's, she'd called Simon Rance, the CEO of Chalys Pharmaceuticals, and demanded to know why they'd made a secret vaccine. Instead of answering, he'd invited her to his house for dinner that night to discuss the matter further.

That was the last thing she'd do. Back in March, the breast cancer viral treatment her team had developed, Amulette, was beginning production. However, the engineer building the new bioreactors discovered that they'd suddenly been switched to producing Recombin instead. He went to Rance's house for a dinnertime chat about the switchover – and the next day he was gone, supposedly transferred to Georgia. She wrote and called him, hoping to learn why Amulette production had been suspended, but he never replied.

She'd wondered what happened at that dinner, but she suspected that he'd walked blindly into a trap – and now that she'd just done the same, she might not have long to live.

She felt a flash of panic, and her pulse began to race. But panic wouldn't help her escape this trap, and she forced her mind to focus on the facts.

First, thousands of people had suddenly caught a novel virus in a New Jersey arena. Transmission never occurred that rapidly with natural viruses – but it did when a weaponized virus was released. That meant that the virus release was an intentional act.

Second, Chalys had known that the virus would be released, but they'd done nothing to prevent it. They hadn't warned the CDC about the threat, nor had they shared what they knew about the bug – and they had to know everything because they'd engineered a virophage to attack it.

Third, Chalys had made three hundred million doses of that virophage but never acknowledged its existence – and may have even killed a man to keep it secret. They were planning to restrict the vaccine's distribution, and since they hadn't made enough to vaccinate the entire population, they also weren't planning to protect everyone.

Widespread, agonizing death was in America's immediate future. For some reason she couldn't imagine, that was Chalys' plan.

It wouldn't be long before Chalys or its co-conspirators tried to kill her, maybe only hours or days. All she could think to do was to pick up her daughter, drive to Canada that night, and send the entire packet of notes to someone else so they could continue the battle.

That someone was Krista Warner at *The Rake*. The dauntless journalist thrived on upsetting the Washington status quo – just the year before, she'd written a blistering exposé of Congresswoman Rosen's bizarre personal life, forcing her to resign in utter and abject disgrace. With all the evidence Victoria could give her, Warner would unravel this conspiracy and bring down international condemnation on Chalys.

The more she planned her escape, though, the more she despised herself for considering it. Running was for cowards, and she'd always been a fighter.

And this was a battle she could win because Chalys wouldn't expect her to fight. It would confuse her opponents and give her control of the engagement, and she could use that brief time to get the Deputy Inspector

General of the FDA to begin his investigation. Once in motion, the FDA machinery was unstoppable, and it wouldn't relent until it uncovered what Chalys and its co-conspirators were really doing.

She rubbed her temples to ward off a growing tension headache, but it had no effect. Pressing her thumbs into the tops of her eye sockets, she concentrated on the dull pain until her worries began to fade.

Through the windows of the double doors, concerned and curious eyes peeked over blue masks. Blood smeared the door to Room Nine, and a stream of it trickled into the corridor.

Lying by the wall, Deming snored softly. She listened to the incessant beeping of an alarm in Room Nine, which was loud in the quiet hall, and then rested her head against the desk and said to the empty room, "I will *not* worry about what I should have done better. I can't change the past, and I won't let my mistakes weaken me."

She closed her eyes and hoped her mistakes didn't kill her first.

THE DAUNTLESS JOURNALIST

Day 12
Sunday, August 30, 2043
3120 L Street NW, Washington, DC

Krista Warner sniffed the sulfurous air and wrinkled her nose. Her eyes were already watering from the acidic mist, and she wiped her tears with the sleeve of her hoodie.

The fug's soupiness was legendary this morning; the sun was trying, and barely succeeding, to penetrate the greasy yellow haze blanketing the city. She lit a cigarette and exhaled a long plume into the miasma. It disappeared in four seconds, close to a record low.

However, the pollution had a mesmerizing beauty; the haze cast a glowing, golden aura around the buildings up on M Street and the trees across the canal. The old oaks were still alive, despite the acid assault Man waged on them. It reaffirmed her faith that the Life Force was strong, strong enough to endure even the fug.

Stepping back from the balcony's edge, she picked up her patio chair and tapped off the night's soot. She settled into it, upended her coffee tankard, and held her hand out at arm's length: It didn't shake at all, meaning her brown blood-cell count was perilously low. That accounted for her lack of motivation.

She was out of ideas. Writing a pithy and punchy post about the worsening air was the first and only item on her list, but the fug's toxicity was an unsanctioned fact; the Media Regulatory Commission's sanctioned fact was that the air quality was the best ever and getting better every day. Contradicting the dreaded Sanctioned Fact directly would earn her an expensive fine. The most she could do was report her personal experience with the fug, but her caffeine-deprived brain couldn't find a clever way to do that.

If she slipped up and got smacked with another fine, she'd be fighting the alley cats for the mice. There was a good chance of that, too – she was fined so regularly that the MRC probably had some bitter, ancient crone reading her posts and waiting to pounce on every mistake.

"Now you'd be lettin your imagination run away with you again, wouldn't you, Miss Kellen? They're not *all* out to get you." She licked the last drops of coffee out of her cup. "Just most of 'em."

As she watched the fug dancing around the treetops across the canal, she rubbed her temples. It was best to play it safe, she decided, and work up another pointless, snarky post instead. Or maybe a hard-hitting article on puppies and kittens.

A thick, oily fug cloud slouched toward her from up the canal, and fug that thick would rot her lungs instantly. She stubbed out her cigarette and walked back into her apartment for a breath of fresh air.

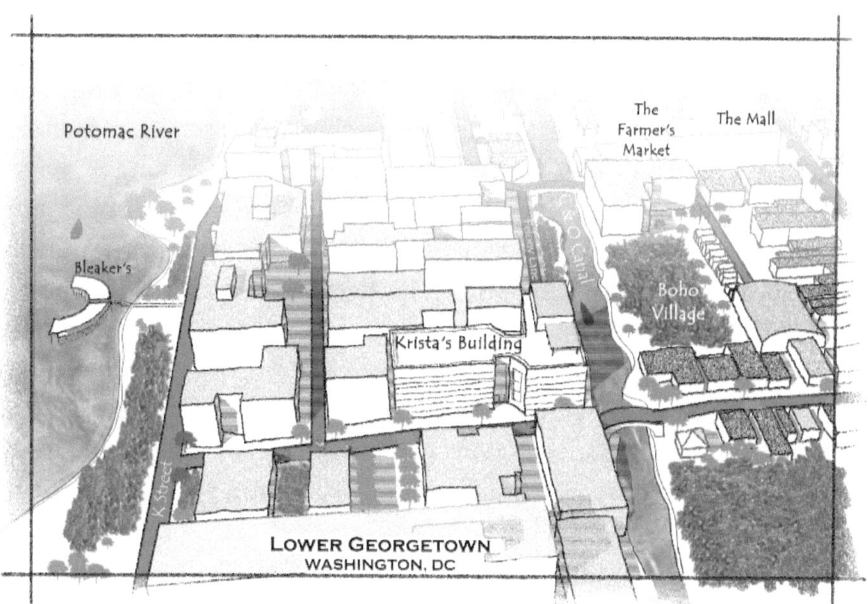

Sitting atop an office building and overlooking the Chesapeake and Ohio Canal, the remodeled machinery penthouse had been a welcome sanctuary from Washington's madness for the past four years. Sometimes, though, she wondered if too much safety and seclusion were healthy; the cage that kept the mad world out also kept her in.

The concrete walls seemed to absorb her life energy today, though, and a shiver of loneliness ran through her as she listened to the soft whistle of the air purifier. Shaking off the feeling, she started walking to the study – and then froze in place. Something had just rattled in her upstairs bedroom.

She grabbed the pepper spray from her hoodie pocket and crept up the stairs. When she reached the bedroom door, she held the spray can out and kicked the door open like a TV show cop.

The room was empty. Tiptoeing to her bed, she reached for the ruffle but then stopped: The dust bunnies lived under there, and she wasn't sure she could face them in her agitated state. As she was stepping back, a lampshade on her nightstand trembled in the erratic breeze from an air diffuser and rattled against the wall.

She sagged against the door. "Jaysus, you're gettin far away in the head, kiddo." With a disgusted huff, she screwed the shade tighter and then turned her sound system volume up to banish any more fictional intruders.

She bopped down the steps to the study beneath the bedroom, the High Hyenas wailing in her ears, and then sank into her large office chair. As she settled in, the air purifiers started to strain and the ribbon on the air register dropped. Looking through the window, she saw the oily fug cloud lurking around her air intake. She needed to change the scrubber filters again, and it would be a mess because she'd put it off for so long.

But she could put it off even longer, so she logged in to her blog, flexed her fingers, and began to draft a story about Vice President Gabriel Cheyn. She'd heard a rumor from someone on his demoralized staff, who openly called themselves the Cheyn Gang even around the boss, that Cheyn had killed and devoured a staffer the previous week during a fit of Napoleonic rage. She worked the story for an hour, trying to turn it into something witty and entertaining, but the task was impossible. The benighted girl hadn't actually been consumed; she'd merely run home to Vermont, scared witless by the irascible VPOTUS.

Even Krista couldn't fudge the truth enough to make the story readable since Cheyn's tantrums were common knowledge. She glared at the screen for a few minutes, and once she started wishing the staffer had sent photos of bones in the bottom of Cheyn's toilet, she posted it on *Midnight Sun* as an anonymous Witness and flopped back in her chair.

Her audience wanted the fearless truth-to-power brand she'd cultivated, not the vacuous sleaze-slinging of *DC Confidential.* However, she was descending to their level fast. She was seriously considering changing the name of her blog from *The Rake* to something that better described her work, like *The Turd Collector*.

"You'll be a common gossip columnist soon, kiddo," she said to the empty room. "Now what happened to the girl who wanted to change the world? Where'd she go?"

She sipped her coffee and sighed; her goal of speaking truth to power had been crushed long ago by the relentless and indifferent DC political machine. Instead, she'd settled for spinning salacious stories to keep her numbed and apathetic audience clicking on her site.

They expected her to play the muckraker, but sometimes she couldn't find enough real scandal to fill eight posts a day, every day, and keep her reputation hot. When that happened, she fabricated the stories, and sometimes she actually wrote the headline first and the story after. That bothered her, but not because she was lying – she was a beacon of rectitude by the standards of post-truth Washington – but because she'd always found distinguishing between reality and fantasy difficult. Blurring the line even more was dangerous.

She needed to find a better career than being a frustrated and crappy writer, or worse, becoming a news entertainer instead of a real journalist. Sometimes she wondered if that's why the MRC gave her a reporting license. Maybe they knew she'd never amount to much.

HELEN HARDIN RIPPED THE FILTER OFF her cigarette and dangled it from her wrinkled lips. It wasn't even eleven in the morning, and she'd polished off her first pack already. She needed the crutch. Keeping track of her ninety-one journalists nationwide was a hard job without plenty of nicotine to grease the neural pathways.

She squinted through the smoke at a picture of a huge, bright red truck with three doors on a side: the new '40 Silverback, which was even bigger than last year's model. With twelve cylinders, nine seats, and the carbon output of a small city, it was the ultimate symbol of wealthy indifference. She blew a kiss at the picture. "Oh yeah, darlin, maybe today you'll be mine."

Helen was four thousand dollars short of buying the truck for cash. If she went over the top today, she was going down to the dealership to drive her baby off the lot. She didn't even need a ride – she'd roll her little wheezing Hugo into the trunk and drop it off at the junkyard on the way home.

Maybe one of her opinion-analysis journalists would slip up and report something the newsfeeds hadn't, and she could levy a $10,000 unsanctioned news-reporting fine. Even better, maybe one would challenge a sanctioned fact and she could earn a sweet $25,000 fine, but those were rare. Since she split the fines forty-sixty with the Media Regulatory Commission, though, she only needed to find some unsanctioned news to buy her baby.

She blew a greasy cloud of smoke at the 'No Smoking' sign above her desk, and the new guy two desks over coughed. "Helen Hardin's an institution here, honey. Get used to it," she growled. "Nobody's gonna touch me."

She kissed her finger and touched it to her framed picture of President John Clune. It was his inauguration photograph, and it showed him at his best – the wavy black hair and the piercing blue eyes exuding the confidence of the new guard. Leaning back in the chair, she recalled the reign of the straight-talking, no-nonsense Idaho agribillionaire who'd promised to end the Washington gridlock sapping America's spirit. "Now that was a leader. He knew what to do after the Detroit Riots of '26 – ban all broadcast news, replace it with the MRC newsfeeds, and allow only airheads and idiots to post on the Internet. He saw that the real problem was the facts, so he changed the truth. That was bold. That was a real man. I wish he were still around to straighten us all out now."

"Did you say something?" the woman in the next cubicle asked.

"Mind your own business, shitwhistle," she said. "If I wanted to hear an asshole, I woulda farted."

She scanned her journalist activity screen, but Krista Warner hadn't posted yet this morning. She was puzzled why Warner continued to work under the MRC – she was fined nearly once a month and had to be going bankrupt, but the woman never seemed to understand the rules. Since the MRC only licensed the most scatterbrained journalists, she'd probably spotted something shiny and forgot them. Or maybe she didn't mind paying the fines because MRC credentials made her a Serious Journalist.

If she worked on the SatNet, she'd have no regulation at all, but those fever swamps were full of liars and fantasists. Everyone who posted on it was suspect. Her sources would dry up because she wouldn't be considered a credible journalist there; nobody believed any SatNet site except for the Canadian news aggregator *Midnight Sun*.

Everyone at the MRC suspected that Warner was also a *Midnight Sun* Witness although nobody had ever confirmed it. Maybe she'd report for them full-time after the MRC bankrupted her, but Helen didn't care; all she wanted from her was one more fine.

Preferably today.

KRISTA PACED HER LIVING ROOM. She'd thought about taking a stroll out in the world, but her pulse began to race when she walked to the elevator. That meant she was still in a withdrawal cycle, and it would have to be an indoors day.

She needed to post something by noon to keep her audience from wandering off, but her creative flow was logjammed. The scrubber filter needed changing, but she still wasn't in the mood. She kicked a pillow across the carpet, revealing an orphaned sock, and decided to wash her laundry.

She grabbed the laundry basket and patrolled the house, corralling stray socks from the potted plants and panties from the couch cushions, even reaching behind the toilet and snagging the bra that got stuck there months before. Whistling, she toted the overflowing basket to the laundry room, filled the clothes washer, and tapped the control screen on the Swedish high-tech machine.

It flickered and turned blue, displaying a cryptic message sprinkled with the slashy O's and dotty A's the Swedes adored. She punched the screen a few more times, and Nordic gibberish scrolled across while the washer bleeped a dirge of disappointment. She banged her head against the wall and then yanked the cord from the outlet; the damned thing would speak English again after a day without power. She had enough panties to last her that long.

She stomped to her study and threw herself into the chair. Out of morbid curiosity, she clicked on a newsfeed, but it said everything was fabulous in the American Paradise: The ex-employed weren't starving, and people weren't keeling over in the streets or choking on the noxious air. "Right, and feckin giggling unicorns soar across the sky and fart sparkly rainbows," she muttered as she changed the channel. The other newsfeeds were painting the same sunny picture, though.

She finally clicked on *Midnight Sun* and found the real news. They reported that the US unemployment rate had fallen below ten percent for the first time in ten years, and corks had popped off champagne bottles in Washington and New York. However, a Witness wrote that unemployment was only dropping because people were giving up on looking for jobs.

Writing about America's plummeting industrial employment would be journalistic suicide, though, because it would bore the hell out of her ADD-afflicted readers. She moved on to the next article.

China and India had lodged a formal complaint with the United Nations about America's increasing smokestack emissions, which were raising global temperatures so fast that some scientists were warning of impending human extinction. They were calling for the Arabs and Persians to end their sixteen-year oil embargo so America could wean itself from coal, but that call would land on deaf ears again. The Persians still held a grudge for the Persian Regional Conflict, and she expected the ill will to last a thousand more years.

But old wars were boring too. She scrolled down the page a bit more and found something interesting: The Soviet Bloc had released their new ICBM targeting assignments, and they'd assigned thirty warheads to the Washington area, more than any American city.

The Reds were only flexing their muscles – for now. The United States was rapidly building a first-strike advantage, and the Navy's new Lancet hypersonic stealth missile would soon give the American president the ability to strike anywhere with impunity. This growing threat was destabilizing Russia and the other fifteen Soviet Bloc nations, and the chances of a Red preemptive nuclear strike were climbing daily.

However, the mushroom cloud came with a silver lining: With thirty warheads targeting Washington, she'd be the first to know that nuclear war had broken out. Her Armageddon would last a fraction of a second, and she wouldn't have to wander through a post-nuclear wasteland.

The United States was clearly provoking a nuclear confrontation. A few months before, Hollywood released a movie called *Mushrooms over Moscow* depicting the American Navy's unstoppable power. The final scene showed the submarine *Patrick Henry* launching its missiles and reducing

Moscow to radioactive rubble, all in morbid and lavish detail – for no other reason except that the submarine's commander had the guts and patriotism to blow away the Reds when the politicians didn't.

She'd written that the movie was nothing more than an inversion of *Dr. Strangelove* with Gen. Jack Ripper as the hero. The next week, her site traffic dropped nearly to zero, which she suspected was the MRC's way of punishing her for pissing off Gabriel Cheyn. That had chilled her even more than the gory movie.

Despite getting slammed by the MRC, she was thinking of taking on the arms race once more, this time comparing chief executive penis length to the number of warheads under his control. However, the research would be daunting: She'd have to discover whether President Gibbon and Premier Rutskoy were foot-longs or bun-lengths, which wouldn't be public knowledge.

She smiled and sipped her coffee. "Why bother? All I've got to say is they're both hung like a moose. What guy would dispute that? Omigod, this'll be great!" A belly laugh erupted from nowhere, and coffee squirted out of her nose, down her sweatshirt, and across her desk. She reached for some tissues and rubbed her aching chest until the fit passed. "*Throw Weight!* It's the perfect title for it. I've got to write this!"

The threat of nuclear Armageddon would get her readers clicking, but she couldn't imagine yet how to write it without getting impaled on the horns of Unsanctioned News and Sanctioned Fact.

She took a few notes and then picked up the remote. While whistling the catchy new jingle from Civil Defense, *Duck and Cover*, she searched for *Molle's Hill.*

Arista Molle was the NewsHub Political Affairs Channel's foremost talking head, who moderated an eight-hour-long, walk-in talking opportunity for the elected inmates of Capitol Hill. Her studio was off the Rotunda, so she often had a surplus of politicians looking for free airtime. New ground was rarely broken on her show because Molle was as smart as a houseplant – in fact, her producer once told Krista that if Arista were any stupider, he'd have to water her – but that put her on par with the politicians she interviewed. Since the pols weren't under the MRC's claw, though, they sometimes let slip some interesting nuggets. And if they didn't, Krista enjoyed watching morons pontificate to imbeciles.

Arista was wearing a stylishly short brunette wig and minimal makeup. The look said *Fuck with me and I'll eat your dog,* which meant there might be straight talk today.

Settling deeper into her chair, Krista watched Arista pretend she was intelligent and incisive, an incredible act that she faked every weekday and Sunday. She passed the time waiting for something interesting to happen by making a gun of her fingers, scoring a few direct hits on Arista's airy head, and imagining it deflating. The fun wore off after a few minutes, though, and she dozed, only waking when paleo-liberal Senator Ezra Schuler started shouting and banging his shoe on the table:

> Molle: Please, Senator, this is a new table.
>
> Schuler: Why won't anybody listen? Are you even paying attention?
>
> Molle: Well, no, right now I'm thinking about how I can get those dents out. This is synthetic wood. It doesn't exactly grow on trees.
>
> Schuler: To hell with the table! The country's heading for the brink, and we're whistling our way to doom!
>
> Molle: I can't whistle, so I'll be safe.
>
> Schuler: It was a metaphor! For the love of all that's holy…maybe the issues are so complex that nobody understands the problem, so I'll explain it to you in the simplest terms. If you can get it, anybody can.
>
> Molle: If you put your shoe back on, I'll give it my best.
>
> Schuler: All right…okay, happy now? Listen, it's simple. If California recalls its tenpez coins back to their state, the dollar will lose the support of the gold currency and become virtually worthless overnight. The government will be broke in thirty days, and government assistance will end.
>
> Molle: That sounds bad.
>
> Schuler: It's a disaster! Forty percent of this country is either elderly or unemployed, and they rely on government assistance to survive. And don't expect our Corporate-American friends to chip in and help the people they put out of work. Oh, no, we get to care for the

obsoleted they don't want anymore. And what do you think the starving poor will do when we can't fulfill our promises?

Molle: Somebody should do something about this.

Schuler: I knew you weren't listening. That's why I'm so agitated. I talked to the vice president's office to see how they plan to respond, and they stonewalled me. Vice President Cheyn said I shouldn't worry because his staff has a contingency plan. But when I asked what it was, he wouldn't say. I think we all need to know how Gabriel Cheyn plans to stave off an economic apocalypse. He owes it to the American public to tell us this majestic and mysterious plan of his, if he even has one. I wouldn't put it past him to spin a good yarn just to shut me up.

Krista sat up in her chair, waiting to hear his plan of action, but Schuler only settled into a familiar liberal drone on class equality and economic justice. No matter how many shoes the last remaining progressives banged on American Democracy's table, though, the Haves would always be dining at it while the Have Nots waited below for whatever crumbs fell off. It had been that way all her life and wouldn't change.

Nevertheless, he'd made sense of rumors she'd heard in recent weeks, and she felt a story in it. She decrypted her secure mail and scrolled through the messages from her sources.

The story's first thread was easy to find. Her source in the Sacramento State House had confirmed only the week before that the State Senate was quietly debating a proposal to make California's gold tenpez the state's only legal currency. If that passed, Californians would have to buy tenpez with their dollars, eventually removing the gold from circulation outside the state.

The second thread came from an aide on the Hill, who'd reported that Congress couldn't find the funds to finance the government. Corporate-American tax revenues had plummeted fifty percent since the 31st Amendment exempted corporations from taxes, and Congress was burning through bond money to compensate. But if the Treasury couldn't sell bonds, the flow of borrowed dollars would stop.

The third thread took an hour to find. The message came from a Treasury accountant, which she ignored at first because it contained numbers and financial jargon, and such things made her mind retreat into its safe space. However, this time she forced herself to read it to the end.

He was concerned that the next bond auction might fail. Although he didn't say why, she didn't need a financier to tell her that no investors would buy bonds denominated in worthless dollars, which would happen if California's tenpez recall passed.

And then something worse than economic apocalypse might follow. The last time bond auctions failed, after the coronavirus pandemic in the early 20's, unemployment soared to twenty-five percent. The government shipped pallets of freshly printed dollars to the Corporate-Americans as a stimulus, but at the same time they cut aid even more to the cities.

The Corporate-Americans pocketed the cash and delivered not a single new job while the city economies augured into the ground. By 2024, the urban population had had enough, and Rust Belt cities exploded into uncontrollable riots that lasted for months until, after more than a year, the National Security Forces brought them to heel. America lost entire cities during The Troubles: Detroit, Flint, Gary, Toledo, and Akron were reduced to rubble, their populations relocated to God-knows-where.

All that would avert this disaster was a mysterious Administration plan – one that might or might not exist.

She sent the messages to a wall monitor. Picking up her tapstones and clicking along to the infectious rhythms of Ebolaband, she studied them, looking for the links between the three messages and letting the story come to her.

Twenty minutes later, it did. She untied her long auburn hair and then flexed her fingers and unfolded her tablet. "You wanted some meat? Well, you got it."

The Rake
August 30, 2043

THE GREAT FORTY-EIGHT

Can you recite all the state capitals? No? Well, it'll be easier soon

So I'll be running down to the store to get some blue markers, but I've got a question first: Which star on the flag is California's, and which is West Virginia's? Or should I wait till the new flags come out? Whatcha think?

Oh, I should back up, right. Well, I was watching my Sunday shows and figured out that we'll be a nation of forty-eight states soon. I think the America we've known is toast, so I'll need a new flag.

The revelation came to me during *Molle's Hill.* Senator Ezra Schuler (D-Paleozoic Era) was ranting again about the end of the world, but for the first time in this century, the man was right.

Here's how I think the end times might arrive: California will call its gold tenpez home, making the dollar worth even less, so we won't be able to borrow money from anybody but complete suckers, and *voila!* the economy goes right down the crapper. From what my sources tell me, it could unravel by Christmas.

If this happens, of course, we common folk will take the brunt. Think things are tough now? Double poverty, unemployment, and homelessness, throw in a dash of urban unrest and a jigger of Federal brutality, and you'll get the picture. Take my advice and turtle if you can. What's coming our way will rattle your bones, and nobody can stop it.

We'll blame California for wanting their own gold back, and while it might feel satisfying to flick boogers at the Left Coast, it won't lessen the challenge ahead. All we can do is hope we survive this storm.

The Fifty United States won't survive together, though. We're not the nation we once were, and it's time to accept that the United States can't fight the enemy anymore. We've capitulated – not to the fearsome armies of the Reds or the Nazis, but to insurmountable debt and the infinite greed of our moneyed class.

America willingly mortgaged itself to the Corporate-Americans at Shylock rates, who won't hesitate to kneecap Miss Liberty if she doesn't pay the vig. But who would have thought the banks and the corporations would be the real threat to democracy, not the Reds? We learned too late that the enemy within usually delivers the kill shot.

I think we're past the tipping point now. We've sold off most of the national parks (including the Shasta National Forest, which turned out to have a bazillion tons of gold underneath it – and does California thank us for that?) so now if we can't find dupes to buy our Treasury Bills, the government has nothing left to sell to raise its operating funds. (Memo to Treasury: Try selling T-Bills by lottery! Or those scratch-off cards you get at the convenience store! There's a market you can tap!)

The Administration says they have a super-secret magic trick to avert the coming apocalypse. Uh-huh, right. All they can do now is ask the Corporate-Americans for our money back, which they won't do unless we sell them a share of the government – and if we do, they'll start cutting out the dead wood to make the USA a leaner, more efficient machine.

Let's face it: There are too many of us, and some have got to go. We need to downsize the country for the greater good. Maybe we should take a lesson from the Corporate-Americans and pink-slip a few states! I recommend that we start small – let's pink-slip Deadwood, South Dakota! Really, aren't they asking for it?

California's already gotten the message that our ship of state is taking on water, and they're acknowledging what we already know but won't say out loud: They don't need to go down with America. California has become less reliant on us with each passing year, and it's made them stronger; they've traded with only a handful of states since the passage of the Hate States Act, but the Pacific Rim Partnership more than made up for the loss. Now they have the world's fourth-largest economy, and they did it without us.

So all of us, let's sing a hearty *Auld Lang Syne* for the Golden State! It's time to say goodbye, just like we did with West Virginia.

Whuh? When did that happen? C'mon, people, weren't you paying attention? Let's have a show of hands – who knew that the Wevvies stopped using the dollar five years ago and switched to a barter economy? Who knew they turned their back on America and went their own way?

Nobody? I thought so. But I bet you'd notice if California went its own way, right? Especially if you've got to trade a pound of dollars for a pound of bread.

But we shouldn't resent them. California just grew up and left home, which is a *(sniff)* normal and natural thing for a child to do, and honestly, isn't it best for them? (Of course, I won't mention that a painful and drawn-out death is also normal and natural, and that would be *our* fate. But I wouldn't want to be a buzzkill.)

Like a child who's finally matured, though, shouldn't we be happy to see California succeed? If we're nice to them, they might send us a little something at Christmas.

The Great Forty-Eight. It rhymes! It's a slogan with legs, I tell ya.

-KLW

CAGES

Day 13
Monday afternoon, August 31, 2043
St. Elizabeth's Hospital for the Indigent, Washington, DC

Victoria Lang opened the door into the third-floor Cancer Care Unit in the Terminals Building and stopped at the reception counter. A variety of cheap chairs was scattered along the hall, and in them were patients in varying states of distress or neglect. She suspected that a few were dead.

"Good afternoon, Dr. Lang," said the volunteer at the desk. "Dr. Talbott hasn't arrived yet, but the proctors are at the nurse's station."

"Thanks," Victoria muttered.

She turned in to the nurse's station, a small space with a counter and two chairs. The walls and ceiling shed peeling flakes of green paint and a single flickering fluorescent lamp buzzed above. Two young FDA proctors leaned against the far wall and flipped through charts.

Patients in the drug trials at St. Elizabeth's were tested with terminal-phase medications, for which they received a modest payment, about the value of a small home. In return, they agreed to the study's rules, which meant that those in the control group would receive no treatment for their terminal condition, while the other half would receive the experimental drug, which wasn't guaranteed to work.

The studies once were performed in destitute Third World countries, but after the passing of the Pharmaceutical Innovation Act, they were in-sourced back to America. Politicians and civic leaders applauded the Corporate-Americans for putting America back to work.

Even though the studies were unethical, she was glad she didn't have to drag her daughter to China or South Africa anymore. It had only destabilized the child's life even more than the divorce, and all they'd gotten in return was a worthless fluency in Mandarin and Zulu.

After ten minutes, the portly figure and flushed face of Dr. Tommy Talbott, the FDA's Deputy Inspector General, appeared in the doorway, and the group set out to see the first patient.

"Tori, everyone's talking about your run-in with that new virus last week," Talbott said as they walked down the corridor. "How are you feeling?"

"Just a bit tired, and I'm still itchy from the decontamination scrubdown."

"I hear you used a new wonder drug. Saved a few lives and became the hero of the day," he said.

"Yes. I'd like to tell you about that."

"And I'd like to hear, but I have to finish these reviews first. I'm way behind schedule today." Dr. Talbott read the notes on his tablet and frowned. "Now, I've noticed a few anomalies."

"Oh, yes," said Victoria. "I have, too, believe me."

THE GROUP MOVED FROM ROOM TO ROOM examining the remaining patients in the study. Chalys was testing a new viral treatment for chronic leukemia, which the FDA would reject because it was utterly ineffective – the treated and the untreated were dying at the same rate. Victoria wasn't concerned about her trial passing the FDA protocol audit, though. She owned Tommy Talbott, and he hadn't failed her yet. However, her impatience with the dog-and-pony show was building.

After two long hours, her back and feet were sore, and she was delighted when the last case wrapped up early. After the group shook hands and promised meeting updates, she pulled Talbott aside.

"Tommy," she said, "I need about a half hour of your time to advise me on a critical issue."

"Hmm. Since when do you need anybody's advice, Tori? Now this is intriguing." He scrutinized her over his eyeglass frames. "Critical, you say? Personally? Professionally?"

"Professionally. I need to talk to you as the Deputy Inspector General, not as a clinical investigator."

"Now my curiosity is aroused, lass. It must be about this wonder drug of yours. How will I be able to refuse?"

"It's impossible to resist me, Tommy. I'm too charismatic," she said with a weary smile. "Can you squeeze me in today?"

"I have two more trial audits this afternoon. My schedule's packed." He ran his hands through his thinning gray hair as if he might find more time lurking there. "I'll tell you what. Meet me at six o'clock tomorrow up in the fifth-floor doctor's lounge. I can go home a bit late. In fact, I might even miss the evening rush hour."

Victoria smiled. "Thanks, Tommy. I appreciate it. This is important."

He patted her shoulder. "I'll see you then."

VICTORIA WALKED TO THE DOCTOR'S LOUNGE. She needed to massage her tired feet and stretch away the tension that had built up in her back and neck.

She couldn't relieve the tension in her mind as easily because the prospect of what might lie ahead was hard to escape. The path of exposure didn't frighten her – it was the right thing to do – but waiting to act was exhausting. And she had to endure another day of waiting and another sleepless, tortured night.

Scowling, she maneuvered through the obstacles in the third-floor corridor and broke into a brisk commander-on-deck stride.

THE HOSPITAL WAS A VICTORIAN HELLHOLE, but the fifth-floor doctor's lounge was a slice of heaven. It had to be, or no doctor would bother to practice at St. Elizabeth's. The hospital's designers had created a space with soft lighting and colors, and with a thick, plush carpet to absorb noise; large chairs lined the outer walls, and many faced windows with a view of Washington on clear days.

Fortunately, the masseur was on duty in his little alcove near the buffet, and he massaged the kinks out of Victoria's back and neck. Feeling revived, she slipped her paper mail from a wall slot, made a sandwich from the buffet and grabbed a bottle of water, and then collapsed into a leather chair by the window.

She gazed at the gauzy landscape beyond the glass. As the environmentally aware Archangelists gained more political power, the air pollution actually worsened. While they lobbied for closing the coal-fired generating plants causing it, the Arkies hadn't shut them down even though they controlled Congress.

Another mystery in a tapestry of mysteries, she thought as she rubbed her temples, but the real mystery was how she'd endure the next day.

She took a cup of coffee from a passing waiter, sat back in the soft chair, and flipped through her mail. She smiled at the insincere marriage proposal from Jonas and then turned to the autopsy report on John Durant.

His internal organs had been infected by a virus – the report didn't identify which – and the bug had dissolved them. The damage was irreversible, and he couldn't have been saved no matter what she'd done.

She touched the bump on her right arm and hoped that the Recombin was still working.

VICTORIA OPENED THE DOOR to the north stairwell, the only one descending to the tunnel level. The stair treads were dangerously fractured concrete that could give way any second, and she stepped carefully down them.

She heard wailing from the fourth floor and tried to ignore it. The Terminals Building was a depressing place at its best, but the fourth floor was where they warehoused the incurables; sometimes their pain was managed but usually not. The floor was the worst in the entire hospital.

Reaching the ground level, she opened a rusted door set into the landing wall and descended the stairs beyond to the tunnel level two floors below. She yanked at the iron door at the bottom, which opened with its customary groan, and then stepped into a dimly lit concrete tunnel clogged with outmoded equipment.

She'd been working at St. Elizabeth's for eight years and had learned the tunnel layout early on. She learned fast, because while the Terminals Building was the third largest in the forty-building complex, it had the smallest parking lot. The walk from a remote surface lot was long and perhaps even an asphyxiation hazard; parking at Administration and walking underground was the most practical solution.

The tunnels were forgotten, confusing, and frightening, and few people knew they even existed. They weren't even mapped or shown on any of the hospital's plans, so she'd had to learn by trial and error how to navigate them. As she approached a T-intersection, she knew to walk through the door ahead because the tunnels that ran right and left led to dark dead ends.

The old iron door she faced was a patchwork of rust and flaking paint held together by rivets. She pulled it open to the creaking protest of unoiled hinges and walked into a smaller corridor lined with similar iron doors on both sides. A single fluorescent lamp illuminated its hundred-foot length. It smelled of rot, wet plaster, and fear; the damp air was thick and close, laced with sharp undertones of mold and rat feces. Stalactites reached from the ceiling, and seepage dripping off them filled foul puddles on the floor.

She'd heard the rumors about the infamous Cages, where the dangerously insane had been housed a century and a half ago. They were once full, with each six- by ten-foot cell housing three inmates. Warehousing the insane was the most shameful act St. Elizabeth's had performed in its asylum days, and it was an episode of history that everyone wished would be forgotten.

They were now empty and disused, but their history was embedded in the stains and scratches on the deteriorating plaster walls. The scratches were the most chilling part of the Cages – deep gouges made by inmates who desperately wanted to escape, and whose only tools were fingernails.

Some who knew about the tunnels whispered rumors that ghosts, vengeful demons, and even the undead stalked this place. She didn't fear any of that. The dead were just dead; as for supernatural threats, she had enough natural threats to keep her occupied. And if the undead wanted her attention, they could damned well make an appointment like everyone else.

By carefully stepping around the fallen plaster and rusted fragments of the cage doors, she reached the far end without dirtying her shoes. She opened the door there, made a left and then a right, and climbed a short concrete stair. At the top, she opened the door into the lobby of the Administration Building.

"Afternoon, Dr. Lang," said Roscoe, the withered, wrinkled guard defending the entrance from the barbarian hordes.

"Afternoon, Roscoe. How are you doing this fine, sunny day?"

"It's sunny?" Roscoe peered out the window. "Yeah, well, I s'pose that's sunshine."

"Why don't we pretend it is?"

"You got it, ma'am," Roscoe said. "Make sure you don't catch a tan out there! There's some fearsome rays out there, girl!"

"I'll take precautions, big guy. See you tomorrow!" She pulled out her mask, strapped it on, and opened the door.

VICTORIA WALKED DOWN THE MARBLE STEPS to the front lot. She'd parked about fifty feet to the left of the wooden bench, but she couldn't see her car and tapped her remote. Lights flashed in the fug, further away than she remembered.

She heard cracks of gunfire in the distance and flinched. The weapons sounded like small-caliber semi-automatics, probably one of the CheapShots the Mal-Marts sold. The Metro Police didn't try to control the bloodshed in Southeast Washington, and she suspected that the powers running the District were letting natural selection drain the gene pool so they wouldn't have to feed, educate, or rehabilitate the poor and the desperate. The Powers That Be were Archangelists, though, and she wasn't sure they'd do something so openly Darwinist.

She shook her head and tried to banish the contradiction from her mind. Trying to make sense of religious snapcases was asking for trouble, and she didn't need to ask. Trouble came to her free and unbidden.

Her sports coupe, a bright red '42 Bicep Sixty-Six, took shape in the fug ahead. After ensuring no muggers were lurking in the backseat, she climbed in and turned the scrubbers to the highest setting. Having clean cabin air was one of the two reasons she'd chosen this car; the other feature was the heads-up radar display on the windshield that showed the location, direction, and speed of all vehicles within fifty feet. That was valuable when visibility was often less than that, and the radar had already saved her from a few accidents in the brief time she'd owned the car.

Her right hand trembled as she reached for the stereo, and when she tried to still the shaking, it became even worse. She needed a sedative. Another unmedicated day of this stress would crush her.

She turned on relaxing ambient music, laid her head back against the headrest, and closed her eyes. After a few minutes, feeling recharged, she drove through the south gate and turned onto the Suitland Parkway. Gunshots cracked from both sides behind her as she glided south, and she hunched deeper in her seat until she cleared the combat zone.

When she arrived home, she planned to sneak in a comfy-chair nap before the evening squabble with her daughter Ada. It was inevitable because she was playing hooky again, arguing that she'd rather work on some time-travel theory than yawn through the eleventh grade. But life was more than physics, and Victoria had to tell her she was returning to school whether she wanted to or not.

But she didn't have to tell her now. She had more immediate problems to contend with, namely that she'd need to leave Washington for a while to avoid getting drawn into the political vortex resulting from exposing Chalys' virus conspiracy. However, this would leave nobody to watch over her daughter. It would have been easier if Ada attended the Naval Academy Science Camp the following week as she'd planned, but she'd said this morning that she wasn't going anymore. Victoria needed an alternative fast because someone had to watch her. It would be unwise to leave Ada alone to contemplate the cosmos, or worse, build some diabolical machine.

She decided to ask Tommy Talbott to take her next week, and then she'd force Ada back to school, somehow, after Tommy took over the Chalys investigation and relieved the pressure on her. She breathed a long sigh – another squabble had been averted, which was a rare accomplishment these days.

She drove up the long driveway to the garage and tapped the door opener. The doors parted with a hiss of pressurized air, blowing away the thin coat of soot in front of them, and she drove in. She turned off the car, giving the dust in the garage time to settle.

Taking a deep breath, she climbed out and walked into the kitchen.

VICTORIA SMELLED CIGARETTE SMOKE. She bit back her anger, regretting that she hadn't fought harder years ago, although she *had* resisted when she first discovered the girl was smoking. Hoping deprivation would work, she'd locked her cigarettes in a desk drawer with a supposedly unpickable lock, but Ada picked it hours later. After that, they had a mother-daughter chat.

Victoria assumed Ada was following the fashion of her non-devout Archangelist peers, who smoked like coal trains straining to climb a hill, but Ada's reason stunned her: She said that she'd found a friend who smoked, and she didn't want to seem like a freak. She then asked Victoria respectfully for her permission even though she didn't need it.

Ada had never had a real, human friend before, so Victoria limited her to three a day and hoped she'd grow out of the phase before the foul habit killed her. However, like everything else Ada did, it soon spun out of control, and Victoria had to settle for just banning smoking in the house.

In retrospect, she should have seen Ada's unruliness as a warning years ago and acted to control it. She hadn't fully understood Ada's capabilities back then, though; if she had, she never would have given her the keys to the Chalys Creation Lab the following summer. That was the tragic mistake that ruined their lives.

She recalled the terrifying night when Ada had been arrested. Reaching into a cabinet for her favorite whiskey, she pushed back on the ugly memory; she wouldn't relive that night for any reason. It had destroyed the bond between them, and they'd never recovered from the experience.

She opened the bottle and let out a shaky sigh. The truth was that she'd sent their relationship into a spiral, however inadvertently, and she needed to own that failure.

Leaning against the kitchen table and sipping her whiskey, she remembered awakening from narcotic darkness the day after Ada's capture, lying on a cot in a bedroom whose door had no handle and whose windows wouldn't open. Through the glass, she saw the dusty, blazing Wyoming prairie stretching to the horizon, its monotony broken only by patches of tumbleweeds.

Disoriented and angry, she'd spat a poisonous accusation at Ada when she awakened: Their lives had been wrecked now, and it was all because Ada was a monster who couldn't control her impulses. She hadn't meant it, but their bond had begun its slow decay as soon as the words left her mouth.

Shortly after, the gray men arrived and finished the wrecking job Victoria started. She fought for Ada but couldn't win, and she realized that all she could do was negotiate the best deal for her. And negotiate she did, for three long and draining weeks, until she knew she could get nothing better.

The silver thread that connected them was strong on the day she signed Ada's future away, and the twisting and withering of her daughter's soul felt like it was happening inside her.

Ada sat in a simmering quiet on the trip back, and she erupted as soon as they walked into the kitchen. The arguments hadn't stopped for four years. Victoria wanted to call a truce and explain that she wasn't mad at her; in fact, she was immensely proud and loved her far more than she loved herself. A truce was impossible, though, because it required all Victoria's energy to control her temper, and she had none left to bridge the growing gulf between them. Over the years, the arguments had become a habit neither could break.

She set her drink down and prepared to walk upstairs for the inevitable argument, but she didn't have the heart for it. Ada deserved her peace too. Sighing again, she refilled her glass and sat at the kitchen table.

AN AIR OF SUBSTANCE

Day 13
Monday afternoon, August 31, 2043
3120 L Street NW, Washington, DC

Krista Warner had spent much of the afternoon cleaning up the mess of her website and needed a break. She walked to the railing, lit a cigarette, and exhaled a plume of smoke into the fug; this time it was gone in less than four seconds. She had to change the scrubber filters, or the filthy air might seep into her apartment.

She walked to the side of her penthouse, twisted the latches on a hatch, and stepped into the old air shaft that housed her air scrubber. After closing the door, she pulled her full-face respirator from a bag and slipped it over her head, and then she opened the bottom door of the scrubber to let the black soot fall through the metal grate into the shaft below. It was six stories high and could take plenty of dirt before it needed cleaning.

Next, she opened the filter access door. Three filters were lined up inside, each designed to remove different contaminants. The installer had cautioned her not to touch the americium filter without wearing gloves; after changing it a dozen times bare-handed, she learned that the thing was radioactive. It was furry with black soot, though, so it was doing its job.

She planted one foot on the air shaft's ladder to get enough leverage to pull out the filters. This part of the job she feared the most because she'd fall six stories if she slipped. After awkward contortion and ample swearing, she removed the filters, tossed them through the hole, and heard them hit bottom seconds later. They could only be discarded legally in Nevada, so the shaft was the only place for them.

She sometimes had nightmares of radioactive soot-golems climbing from the air shaft and chasing her through the apartment. Living alone could be unsettling, especially at night when she was the only person in the entire building. At times like that, she wished she'd been born without intellect or imagination like Arista Molle.

MINUTES LATER, Krista was singing in the shower. It had been a busy day and she was exhausted. She usually only worked for four hours, but she'd been wrestling her balky servers today since she rolled out of bed.

She stepped from the shower, wrapped a towel around her hair, and lifted her breasts to dry underneath. For some time, she'd wanted to take on the Creationists in an article, and Intelligent Design was good material for a gratifying smackdown.

Cupping her breasts in her hands, she looked in the mirror. *Okay, tell me how these things were Intelligently Designed. Why hang ten pounds of meat right off the front so they get in the way of everything and make my back sore? How come the fool didn't build in an underwire while he was at it?* She pulled the towel off her hair and began combing it. *And ass hair. Show me the sense in that. I'd love to hear that argument.*

Dressed in only her bra, she walked to the balcony door and peered at the dark purple sky. She hadn't eaten since sunrise, but she couldn't cook after a grueling day of techie labor. Nobody could deliver to her apartment, but a nearby Ethiopian restaurant served what she wanted.

She had to go out into the world eventually anyway, and Ethiopian food was a good excuse. She shrugged on a Georgetown University hoodie over the light sweatpants she typically wore and then laced up a pair of athletic shoes. At twenty-seven, the tall, befreckled redhead could still be mistaken for a student, and the clothing made her effectively invisible to the public. Everybody ignored Georgetown students.

At a table by the elevator, she squirted Alkaliniment into her hands and spread a thin layer over her face. She always followed the ritual before she left because the lotion neutralized the fug's skin-damaging acids. Even though the stuff was expensive, avoiding a stubborn rash was worth it.

She pressed the call button for the freight elevator and waited for the red light over the door to illuminate. The elevator creaked to her floor, and she pulled apart the up-down inner door, stepped in, and punched the button for the loading dock. The dock was her front door: Her penthouse originally housed machinery, not people, so the passenger elevator didn't rise to her floor. She hoped the building never caught fire because the elevator was the only way in or out.

As soon as she stepped on the dock, her chest and throat constricted, and her back muscles knotted. It was partly because Felony Lane was outside the gate, which would make any reasonable person tense, but also because there'd be so many people out there. However, she needed to go out. She'd been in her apartment for far too long, which only reinforced her withdrawal cycles.

But she wasn't in a hurry, so she sat on the dock's edge and lit up. It was a terrible thing to do – especially in predominantly Archangelist Washington, which tolerated smoking only slightly more than the microwaving of kittens – but if she didn't do it, she would have chain-sawed a dozen people by now. She watched her cloud drift away and recalled the advice of her current psychiatrist, who constantly told her that she needed to desensitize herself to life's challenges to find happiness. He'd given her a list of trite mantras to help her, but he'd laughed when she told him that smoking heavily soothed her nerves far better than any of them. That meant it was time to shop for a new shrink.

Curdled yellow light leaked through the slats of the loading bay grille from a lamp outside. She glared through the gate at the drifting fug beyond, finished her mantras, and then stubbed out her cigarette. Pulling on her mask, she walked down a short flight of concrete stairs to the deserted loading bay floor.

When she passed a roll-up metal door on her left, she tried to pull it up. Her car and valuables were stored in the room beyond, so she always made sure the door was locked. She continued walking to the grille, pulled out her pepper spray, and laid her palm on the biometric lockpad. The grille rattled open.

She strolled along Felony Lane and through the swirling fug toward Wisconsin Avenue. The lane, officially named L Street NW, was a narrow band of cobblestones and patched asphalt bordered by a tall, rough crowd of weeds on the canal side and a row of old, empty brick warehouses on the other. Since it was unlit, Felony Lane could be dangerous at night, and sober pedestrians avoided it. Even some gangs feared it and kept away, but not enough to make it safe.

She'd only walked a few more steps when she stopped and peered into the weeds. A stiffer lay in the shadows by the canal, an old gray-haired man, flabby and well dressed. She'd never seen an upper class stiffer here because they had health insurance and could die in a hospital. The Ranks didn't, and they were who she usually found in the weeds.

Her pulse began to pound in her ears, and she recited another mantra her shrink had taught her. "You're a dead thing and you can't hurt me. You're post-human litter, the spent wrapper of a human being, and you can't hurt me."

Papers fluttered from a leather portfolio at the man's feet, and she knelt to collect them. Squinting in the dim light, she read one letter which said he was an attorney for Klean Koal Arena in New Jersey. She gathered more papers, but they were covered with legal gibberish. "Felony Lane's no place for the gentler class to hang around in, friend. But I guess you've figured that out already, eh?"

She sidled around the ring of weeds to see his face. His white particulate mask was soaked in blood, and looking closer, she noticed that his head was lying in a pool of dark liquid. His eyes were open, and she saw something she'd never seen in her life – tears of thin red blood ran down his cheeks.

"Mugged by a feckin Baser looking for Rock money, I'll bet. Must have clobbered you pretty hard to make your eyes bleed." That meant she was crouching in a crime scene, though, and she dropped the papers and opened her tablet. The city's stiffer collection schedule didn't show this one yet, so she noted the location and sent a new pickup request to Sanitation. They'd collect the body and report the suspicious death to the police.

She continued walking and had to tag another before she reached Wisconsin Avenue.

THE RESTAURANT WAS ONLY THREE BLOCKS AWAY, a distance she typically covered in ten minutes, but thousands of people were clogging the artery of the sidewalk.

She placed her order and sat by the window to watch the corpuscles of humanity pulse by. The waiter arrived a few minutes later, and she devoured the meal.

In an after-dinner glow, she ventured back out onto M Street. She'd just started to cross the street when a car screeched and swerved around her, leaving in its wake the twin stinks of cheap alcohol and profanity. She made it across alive and strolled down the street, checking out the gorgeous, indulgent stuff filling the windows.

The crowds bumped and jostled her, and seeking refuge, she hurried into a large concourse between the two hulking Victorian buildings forming Georgetown's shopping center. The crowds thinned enough that she could look at the windows in peace; the fug formed a corona around the fake gas lamps and spun a precious bubble of privacy around her.

She shopped more windows in the golden lambent light, sauntering down the concourse and savoring her solitude, astonished to find that the high-end clothing was now priced in tenpez. One gold tenpez was worth just over a thousand dollars, and durable items such as houses and cars were priced in gold, while disposable items like food were priced in dollars. The strange hybrid of currencies kept inflation under control, at least as long as California allowed their gold to circulate. All the same, clothing wasn't durable, especially the fashion clothing she saw in the windows.

Shrugging, she moved to the next window, took a quick glance, and stopped and looked again. In the center of the window, a child's mannequin wore a wide, floppy sunhat colored bubblegum pink with purple ribbons and glittery butterflies. The shop had installed a fan in the window, and when the breeze wafted across the ribbons, the shiny butterflies twinkled merrily and took flight. She imagined it on Spring's head; smiling, she recalled all the times the little BoHo girl had brightened her gloomy days over the years. She deserved this treat and more.

However, the store had closed for the night, so she moved on to her favorite place in the District. The space opened onto a long, narrow square, partly paved in cobblestone, and the old farmers' market occupied the far side at a bend in the canal. A lacy, arched cast-iron canopy bathed in a hundred coats of green paint covered most of the market, with a cracked wired-glass skylight and the occasional lamp illuminating the broad stone walkway below. To her, it was one of the most beautiful parts of Washington, overlooking the serene canal and far removed from the city's noise. It sometimes still sold farm goods, but it always offered light entertainment for the genteel of Georgetown, performed by itinerant BoHo artists and musicians who merely asked for the scraps from Georgetown's table.

She looked for the street artist's stall where he usually set up by the canal wall, but he hadn't come that night. That meant she wouldn't find

Spring either, so she walked over to the shopping center wall to see what was going on. There, she found a group of street performers and watched their magic acts, comedy, and dance for a delightful half hour. The infusion of life was welcome after eight days sequestered in her apartment, and she drew a chest-filling breath for the first time in weeks.

She bought a waffle, took a bite, and then held her arm straight out: Her hand barely shook, so she could drink more coffee. She snaked through the crowd to her favorite coffee stand, where they roasted the beans so black that they could only be seen in full daylight, and even then she had to squint. After getting a large cup, she stopped to watch a mime perform the Invisible Wall, his face a mask of comic alarm as his hands patted at the air. In the thick fug, though, he appeared no different from any other citizen of the District trying to navigate the miasmic city.

She leaned toward him. "Hey, Marcel, lemme give you a hint, wouldja? The Invisible Wall only works when the air's invisible, boyo. You look like everybody else, just with more makeup."

His eyes narrowed and he glared at her, but his mouth kept its inane smile.

"Bet that whiteface keeps the acid rash off, huh, Marcel? At least you've got that."

"Fuck off, I'm working," Marcel said without moving his lips.

"Hey, you're good! Get into ventriloquism!" She dropped a coin into the man's hat. "But thanks, Marcel! You've given me an idea for a good article!"

After another hour of wandering, she started home, her mind mulling over a snarky post that even the Crone couldn't fine her for.

The Rake
August 31, 2043

AN AIR OF SUBSTANCE
The soot falls like black snowflakes, and the air is thick with grief over the sun's demise

Maybe that was too dramatic. Actually, I like our fuggy air.

It's got moxie. It's got grit. It won't back down. This is American air. Hooyah!

I like that when I drop my coffee cup, it takes a full ten seconds to reach the ground. I've saved a fortune in dishes already.

I like that I can feel myself breathing now. What a wonder! I'd always taken that for granted!

Either our choking air is the result of vast governmental ineptitude, or it's all part of a super-secret government conspiracy to kill us all. Now, I vote for this being an evil plot, not only because I believe our government can't be *that* inept, but because it's a more intriguing notion (and I get so bored at times).

The Persian Regional Conflict was a masterstroke of political manipulation, finding a way to cut off our supply of foreign oil, forcing us to build coal plants burning All-American Klean Koal, AND turning us against the ~~ragheads~~ People of Persian Persuasion all in one tidy little war. Mandating that eighty percent of all cars be totally electric by 2035 and creating an impossible strain on the electrical grid was another deft maneuver, one that was definitely NOT financed by Klean Koal. Nosiree, bub. Nuh-uh.

And what end did this evil plan seek to achieve? Was it to asphyxiate us by firing up plants that belch hundreds of tons of toxic hydrocarbons an hour and corrode any living tissue they touch? Or was it to choke us to death with this fug before we reach retirement age so we don't collect Social Security? It's no secret that our government thinks the nation would be better off with fewer of us in it, and one could argue that this is just one facet of an extermination strategy, one less obvious than getting blown away by federal Ironshirts on a Detroit street.

But I don't think so. That's too obvious for the minds that steer our ~~clownocracy~~ great nation. No, I think the government has blanketed us with fug for another reason.

I think it's to put the mimes out of business.

Oh, so you laugh? Do you know how hard it is to get rid of a mime? Once they latch onto you with those beady black eyes, they'll stick like a skunk-stank, leering all the time with those creepy painted grins. I, for one, am glad the government has taken decisive action.

Really, that's my hypothesis.

Okay, you can stop laughing. It's getting awkward now.

-KLW

DISPATCHES

Molle's Hill
NewsHub Political Affairs Channel
Broadcast Transcript of August 31, 2043

Molle: I'm here today with Surgeon General Mae Esteban, and our topic is the New York virus that's garnered so much attention in recent days. General, should we worry?

Esteban: Please, Arista, call me Mae or Dr. Esteban.

Molle: Sorry, Mae, the uniform and the medals confused –

Esteban: It happens all the time, Arista.

Molle: This New York virus has everyone concerned. Can you shed some light on what it is and how our government is responding?

Esteban: All we know at this point is that this particular virus has never been seen. This virus may be in a class of its own. At this time, we're calling this new class Neovirus.

The Centers for Disease Control has been working around the clock with the samples collected from New York to determine what response we can develop.

It's a highly communicative virus, but the reported symptoms are mild. Of the nine-hundred-plus cases confirmed in the New York metro area, we've suffered only six deaths from this Neovirus.

Molle: Are your teams working on a vaccine?

Esteban: They are, but please understand that vaccines are time-consuming to test and develop, even with well-studied viruses. With a new class of virus, a vaccine may take more time to develop. We're optimistic about the chances of engineering one, though.

Molle: What are the symptoms of this disease?

Esteban: The virus creates a vigorous immune response in the body which is dangerous for some populations. This could be a threat to children and the elderly, who often have immature or compromised immune systems.

Molle: Will last year's flu shot provide any immunity, Mae?

Esteban: I'm sorry, no. This isn't an influenza virus.

Molle: It sounds troubling indeed, Mae, but I'm reassured knowing our medical warriors are hard at work finding an answer to this plague.

Esteban: Plague is bacterial, and this is a virus. But it may become pandemic, as I'm sure you meant.

Molle: Yes, that's what I was alluding to, Mae. What is the likelihood of a pandemic?

Esteban: Disturbingly high, I'm afraid. This virus aerosolizes easily and remains viable in the air for hours. Not only that, the infected can shed virus long before they present symptoms of illness. This results in an extremely high rate of transmission, with a tentative R-naught of ten. This means that each infected person can transmit it to ten others. We've notified the World Health Organization, and they're studying the New York samples to see if they can offer any guidance.

Molle: Now, I've heard so much about this new Dickson P95 mask. With this virus floating around, it's a great idea for everyone to stock up on some, wouldn't you agree?

Esteban: Neovirus measures seventy nanometers, and a P95 only filters out particles three hundred nanometers and larger, so an aerosolized virus would pass through like it was driving into the Lincoln Tunnel –

Molle: Making it the perfect mask for this crisis! And the good news is that they're available in stores near you! Plenty in stock for everyone! The Dickson P95 mask!

Esteban: The only effective means of avoiding transmission is to avoid contact with the infected. I advise against relying –

Molle: Thanks for coming and enlightening us, General.

Midnight Sun
News Post of August 31, 2043

NEW YORK CITY GREETS VIRUS WITH A YAWN

Our Witness on the Upper West Side of Manhattan reports indifference at the prospect of an epidemic:

"Y'know, we hear this shit all the time. Nobody gets all worked up over some tiny bug anymore. It's the people you gotta watch out for. If you can keep from gettin screwed over, everything else is just small beer, know what I mean?

"We've seen worse, believe me. I was here back in '20 when that coronavirus hit. Everybody ended up gettin it, even if you were in a fuckin lockdown. I spent three months binge-watching cop shows, and it turns out I had it but didn't get symptoms. But I had a ton of COVID antibodies, so I was immune all along. What a waste of time that was.

"So why get agita tryin not to catch it? Sure, there'll be body bags like last time, but it's not worth gettin all kung-flu and hidin under the bed again. This'll burn out like that one did, and life will go on.

"Still, this bug's a lot faster than that coronavirus. I heard it on the street and the subway today, everybody blowin and sneezin. Everybody's gonna get this one too. But y'know, you can't ever avoid it, not in a city like New York."

UNKNOWN UNKNOWNS

Day 14
Tuesday afternoon, September 1, 2043
Chalys Pharmaceuticals, Fort Washington, Maryland

Victoria Lang sat at her cherrywood desk and viewed the vast 800-acre Chalys complex beyond the window. In the distance, barely visible through the fug, mists and vapors arose from stainless steel pipes sprouting from the long, low buildings where the drugs were manufactured.

She turned from the window and resumed clearing her desk. An aluminum briefcase sat in the center; she opened it and placed her favorite pen and pencil set inside, followed by a framed photograph of Ada.

Sitting back in her chair, she looked at another framed picture, which was her wedding portrait. Even after seventeen years, she remembered why she married the man.

She shrugged and dropped the photograph into her briefcase, and then crossed the office to her private lab. Her two protein modelers still displayed the results of the testing she'd performed since April. Chalys might break in and erase her evidence, but it also might not occur to them that she'd done all the work here. The modelers would make unimpeachable witnesses if they didn't wipe them clean, but she had plenty of other evidence if they did.

Ada had loved her lab; she had such a natural affinity for lab work that she'd learned how to model a complex virus when she was only eight. *She'll get a lab of her own someday*, Victoria thought, *but she won't see this one again.* She turned off the light and deadbolted the door.

At the wet bar, she pulled aside a bottle of whiskey. A flat, silver aluminum case sat behind it, six inches long by four inches wide, with a cord snaking to a wall outlet. She turned it over and checked the battery indicator. It glowed green, showing that the little refrigerator was good for at least a month, and she only needed to keep the samples cool for a day or two.

She turned it back over and checked the seal light, which was also green. She rotated two small thumbscrews on the front side; the lid hissed as she opened it, and frigid air escaped the Cryogenie.

Inside, six fifty-milliliter vials of Recombin dated April 5, 2043 rested in padded neoprene niches. Each held a clear liquid, and each was still sealed with plastic security caps. She closed the lid and turned the thumbscrews until the seal light turned green again, and then she slipped it into a padded pocket built into the briefcase lid.

Returning to her desk, she placed the four packets of documents she'd prepared into the briefcase, closed it, and spun the combination dials.

After looking at her office one last time, she left and locked the door behind her.

VICTORIA PULLED INTO THE DRIVEWAY and honked the horn. A minute later, she honked again, and a petite teen girl ran from around the back of the house, her long blonde hair flowing behind and a leather bookbag swinging from her shoulder. She slid on the driveway soot and bumped into the car door, and then she opened it and let a cloud of fine black grime into the car. Ada jumped in, reeking of cigarette smoke, and Victoria turned the scrubbers to high.

In appearance, they were almost identical. They had the same dark eyes, upturned nose, and softly angular face, and Victoria had even worn her hair the same way in high school – loose and long, wild and wavy. On the inside, though, they were completely different. Where Victoria sought the cool comfort of linear thought, Ada thrived on chaos and intensity. Although she'd never said so, Ada sometimes seemed like an alien to her.

Perhaps reading her mother's mind, Ada rolled her eyes and raised her hand in a Vulcan salute. "Greetings, Earthling?"

"Clever." Victoria glared through the windshield, clamping down on her irritation. "Just buckle in, and don't be a wiseass with me today."

VICTORIA ARRIVED at the Administration Building lot at 5:50 PM. She parked in her favorite spot, leaving the engine running to keep the scrubbers working. The fug was much worse up here because the wind had shifted and the smoke from St. Elizabeth's coal-fired power plant billowed over them. The plant was always belching smoke; the outdoor air quality was so poor that it needed to burn tons of coal each day to keep the air inside the hospital cool and clean. Tonight, the atmospheric miasma was almost palpable, with visibility less than five feet.

"Ada, I need you to listen and do exactly what I say. Do you understand?" Ada nodded in agreement. "I have a meeting at six o'clock up in the Terminals Building. It should take no more than an hour. What I'm going to do there is...well, controversial." She unlocked her briefcase, pulled out two packets of documents, and then locked it again and placed it on Ada's lap. "You stay here and watch this briefcase. Understood? That's your job. Don't leave the car, don't open the door, don't leave this briefcase. It has things I need, and I'm trusting you to watch it. It's my bargaining chip."

"Okay, got it. You don't have to say it over and over."

"I just know you, and I know you'll interpret it the way you want, but look, this briefcase never leaves your hand."

"Aye-aye, Commander." Ada flipped a salute.

Victoria was silent for a minute as she ran down her mental checklist. Finally, she said, "Now give me your cigarettes and lighter. That way you won't leave the car."

Ada opened her mouth to complain, but she shut it with a snap when she saw her mother's annoyed expression. She reached into her bookbag and handed over the contraband, and Victoria slid it into a pocket of her suit jacket.

"I'll be back around seven. Be good, okay? Love you."

VICTORIA NAVIGATED THE TUNNELS and arrived at the doctors' lounge at 6:00 PM. The place was deserted, so she reached behind the wet bar and filled a plastic cup to the brim with her favorite whiskey. She sipped, wishing the masseur was still there to loosen her tight neck muscles.

Talbott opened the door ten minutes later. "Tori," he said, wrapping her arms around her. He kissed her and tightened his embrace, and she ran her arms up his back and pressed her hips into his as he weaved his fingers through her cropped hair. She reminded herself that it was just another business kiss. Nevertheless, she decided to give Talbott just a minute more, and then they'd have to talk shop.

"Tommy..."

"Tori, you should come out to the Eastern Shore again some weekend. It's been so long since we had time together."

"Maybe. Okay, I promise, yes, once this all blows over."

"Mmm, your crisis, I forgot." He pantomimed putting a hat on his head. "Okay, my Deputy Inspector General cap is on. What's so all-fired important?"

They sat in leather armchairs by the window, and she handed a document packet to Talbott and laid the other on her lap. "Before we start, I need to know that you'll back me up. I want your promise that you'll stand by me, and so will the FDA."

"What are you talking about?"

"I'm lodging a whistleblower complaint that'll blast Chalys and multiple government officials out of the water, and lots of big names will go to jail when this is over. I need you to submit the complaint to the House Oversight Committee before Chalys can mobilize."

Talbott raised an eyebrow and stood. "Sometimes you scare me, child." He walked to the baristomat and poured a large cup of coffee. Taking a sip, he returned to his seat. "If I was a cautious and circumspect man – and that I am – I'd demand to have more of the facts in hand before I made any promises. But I know you, and if you're bothered, there's a good reason." He took a sip of his coffee. "I promise you my full personal support, and to the extent I can deliver it, the support of the FDA and HHS. But whether the FDA plays along is a question, and I make no guarantees."

"Thanks," she said.

"Now stop being mysterious and get on with it. I'm an old man. I could croak any minute."

She laughed and then drew a deep breath. Life would never be the same if she told her story, but the road back to normalcy had closed days ago. Her only choice was to take the road forward and face its unknowable unknowns.

"So give me the complaint specifics. What are you all worked up about?" he said.

She looked into his eyes. "Genocide."

ADA THUNDERED THROUGH SUB-NUCLEONIC SPACE astride two fast mesons, her hands gripping their glowing orange coronas. She squinted into the purple glow of the plutonium nucleus she was orbiting and waved to her friends below – tiny quarks and tinier demiquarks, gauge bosons and leptons, and unnamed sub-nucleonic particles that only she knew existed. Some days these particles were the only friends she had, and most days they were the only friends she could count on.

Her fast mesons found a road, a silvery neutrino swarm that disappeared over the plutonium nucleus' horizon, and they put on speed. Blac Sacrament began her favorite road song, *Blastsphere,* and she gave the mesons a sharp kick. They sped faster, and then even faster, until she was approaching lightspeed and the neutrinos became bright silver slashes across the black sky. Far ahead, she spotted the greenish auras of the Kinesis Termina, beyond which matter, space, and time were one, and her heart pounded along with Blind Billy's bass...

Something buzzed in her pants pocket, and she opened her eyes. She'd wanted to bust through the Termina during this dream and find what lay beyond, but she didn't make it yet again. She unfolded her tablet and frowned at the screen: The buzz was only to alert her that it was seven o'clock.

Her mother should have returned. She peered into the fug, and then a kill-me-now craving wrapped around the base of her skull and squeezed. In desperation, she groped into the depths of her bookbag for her spare cigarettes and lighter, and her fingers closed around a pack of the Turkish delights in seconds. "Kamelles, baby! Jubilations!" she whispered to the empty car.

She dropped the earbuds into their case and slid everything into her bookbag, and then remembering her mother's instructions, she heaved the heavy aluminum briefcase from the driver's seat. She reached for the N100 respirator her mother insisted she wear outside but then stopped; it filtered out more oxygen than soot and left a ring of sweat zits on her face. Besides, she'd only be gone for a few minutes.

She opened the door and pulled a long, thin cigarette from her pack. Her feet were numb, as was the spot on her right arm where her mother had injected her with some sort of vaccine this morning. A little walk to get the blood circulating wouldn't hurt.

As she walked away from the car, she realized that the fug was denser than she'd thought. She aimed for the familiar lights of the Administration Building entrance and the vague shadow of a tree trunk, and the outlines of a bench appeared a few steps later.

"Double jubilations!" She windmilled her arm, struck a silent chord on her air guitar, and then rammed her shin into a bicycle rack. She hopped to the bench and sat, trying to find comfort on the hard wood, and set the briefcase and bookbag beside her. However, as she rubbed her shin, she realized that she couldn't see the car. She didn't know how to get back and had left the keys behind, so she couldn't flash the remote to find it.

She lit up and wondered what to do. It would be hard to explain why she'd gotten lost – unless she did something weird and told her mother the truth.

TALBOTT LOOKED AT THE DOCUMENT pack in his lap as if it might explode any second; his face was ashen, his features sagged, and his eyes were sad and watery. "How'd you discover all this, Tori? Did you have someone inside Building 32?"

"That's what raised my suspicions. I *should* have had someone inside Building 32, but I didn't."

"I'm not following, sorry."

"All right, I'll try to slow down. In March, we were configuring the four live-virus lines in Building 32 to produce Amulette."

"The breast cancer drug we tested here two years ago."

"The breast cancer *cure*, Tommy. We were using a new continuous-tube bioreactor system to produce it because demand would be high, and we brought in our best viroculture process engineer to make it work. He worked on it day and night, and by mid-March, he'd completed the equipment reconfiguration and calibration and was ready for the first live-run testing of the system. Then on March 21, he was gone, never showed for work, and Ada told me his daughter wasn't showing up in class either. I drove over to his house, and it was empty. Like he was never there.

"So I started asking around, and that's when the lies started. Dave Eggie said he suffered a nervous breakdown, Tom Connors said he requested a transfer out west, Lev Chakra said he was on a sabbatical. I finally worked my way up to Simon Rance on the day Durant died."

"I know him well. He's an El...excuse me." He coughed into his hand and took a quick sip of coffee. "He's an elegant man."

"Elegant? Maybe an elegant liar, like most Arkies. Rance told me the engineer had been transferred to our Ashford plant in Georgia, which is ridiculous, Tommy. Ashford is an automated pill mill. Fort Washington's the only virus production line in the country besides the Army labs. Why would a viroculture process engineer go to a pill press? And what's even more suspicious is that suspending production of Amulette cost Chalys at least ten billion dollars. The worldwide projected first-year revenue for Amulette is forty billion dollars, Tommy. *Forty billion dollars.*"

He whistled. "I'm in the wrong business."

"Anyway, I started looking for my own answers after he disappeared. I discovered that Building 32 was a real beehive of activity, and it was also completely locked down. Even *I* couldn't get in, and I have unrestricted access to every Chalys facility."

"How'd you get the April Recombin samples, then? I imagine security would've been high there," he asked, looking away. "You couldn't do this alone. You would've needed the cooperation of someone on the inside."

She laughed. "Oh, I got help all right. I couldn't get on the production floor, so I just walked to the loading dock where they had boxes ready to ship, thanked the NSF officer on watch for his patriotic service, and gave him two tenpez for a cup of coffee."

"He walked one way, and you walked the other with the Recombin?"

"An entire box. Twenty-four vials."

"Oh, God. Such a simple way to breach security."

"I got to work analyzing and modeling it right away, but I didn't make any breakthroughs till I proved this week that it was designed for Neovirus. And that's what led me here."

Talbott stood and refilled his cup at the baristomat, and then he ambled back, deep in thought, and settled his bulk into the chair. "The Director himself gave me an in-depth briefing this morning, and at first it seemed like Recombin was a convenient miracle."

"Exactly!" She emptied her water bottle and threw it into the trash. "Okay, now you've validated my point. You thought Recombin was a convenient miracle, so you had your doubts too."

"Tori, one doesn't want to scrutinize miracles sometimes."

"There are no miracles, Tommy."

His eyes narrowed. "You should watch that kind of talk."

"You've never been religious. You don't believe that Arkie tripe either."

"For the record, I do, and so should you." He rubbed his eyes with trembling hands. "Listen, as Deputy Inspector General, I have to say this, Tori – let this go. You have nothing but raw data in here, which isn't enough evidence to call this credible whistleblowing."

"I have a ream of evidence!" She pulled the packet from her lap and paged through it. "Recombin is an exquisitely engineered virophage. The capsid is so complex that it took me two days to model it. Look." She held up a brightly colored image of a helical object. "It would've taken at least six months to engineer this work of art, and that's assuming the team had a sample of Neovirus to work with from the beginning. That means that someone knew that Neovirus would be released into the population. Not only that, I have the sample and production logs that prove Recombin was in full production long before the virus appeared, and that production stopped well short of the amount needed to treat everyone. That doesn't make my argument credible?"

"Please, I have but a rudimentary knowledge of virology. Show me some mercy and stop waving that techie mumbo-jumbo in my face." He drew a long breath and said, "Be honest with yourself. If I take this to Congress, you'll get outed no matter how hard I try to conceal your identity, and then the political machine will destroy you in a matter of days. You'll never get a chance to make any argument or present any evidence." He held up his packet. "This won't prevent that, and I advise you, as a friend and as a colleague, to not pursue this."

"I *have* to pursue it! For chrissakes, we're talking genocide, Tommy!"

"So you assume!"

"Assume? I never assume anything, and you know that. And I think the evidence is sufficient to intercede and stop this conspiracy. Besides, whether or not the bogies come after me doesn't scare me. I have lawyers and lots of offshore cash, and it's a fight I'll win. Stopping this tragedy is my immediate goal, and this is where I need your help as DIG."

"Yes, yes, but if what you say is true…" He held up his hands. "This is huge. This is political. This is beyond a mere DIG."

"I'm sorry, but you're the only one I could bring this to. You're the only one in the FDA or HHS I trust to stop this madness now." She leaned toward him, trying to see his face. "What's wrong, Tommy? This is your job."

"This is tantamount to urinating on a third rail, Tori. Chalys is a corporation, and Corporate-Americans are virtually untouchable to begin with, and President Gibbon himself sits on the board of this one. There'd be repercussions up and down the food chain if I took this to the House Oversight Committee."

"What the hell happened to you? You're like a completely different person. Look, we could be in the opening stages of a genocidal biowar, and the government and our own medical-pharmaceutical complex are the enemies. How bad does it need to get before you'll do something?"

He looked up, his eyes brightening. "Maybe we should compromise. Why don't you just let me run a discreet investigation? That way I can guarantee it won't get swept under the rug, and I could keep you off the radar too."

"Because this has to stop now! A discreet investigation would cost lives, maybe thousands, maybe millions!" She jumped to her feet, paced to the window, and gazed through it for a few moments. "Okay, let's forget idealism and be practical. What's your downside for acting? How much trouble can you get into? Once this information goes public, the outcry will be enough to protect you. Chalys will take the fall, and this entire operation will be exposed and stopped. You'll be a hero. They'll make a statue of you."

"You're right. They'll probably bronze me for this." He rubbed his eyes as if trying to wipe away a vision. "Honestly, Tori, I thought you were more realistic. You know this game won't play out that way."

"So it won't be easy. Damn it, it's time to man up and do what's right regardless of the circumstances! Don't you understand what's going on?"

"I do…"

"Then would you stop worrying about your own ass? Do you think I'm worrying about mine all that much? I'm throwing away all I've worked for because it's the right thing to do!"

"Don't push me, Tori, please. I need to handle this delicately. You don't understand the stakes."

She turned to face him. "When did you become such a pussy?"

"Don't make me do this. I beg you, please, Tori..."

"It's Dr. Lang to you! Only friends call me Tori!" She threw the packet against the window and cracked the pane. "All I'm asking is that you be half the man I'm being, Dr. Talbott!"

He jumped out of the chair. "Get a grip! I just can't change the world to satisfy you! No man, or half-man, could do that!"

"You're flaking out on me?"

"No, I'm not. I'm saying that tilting at the Chalys windmill, without even the merest iota of conclusive evidence, will produce consequences I can't control. I'm asking you to use reason, perhaps consider alternatives."

"Alternatives? You want alternatives?" She leaned forward until their noses almost touched and then spoke in a low voice. "Okay, Tommy, here's my Plan B: If you won't help me, then I'll take all those protocol audits you helped me falsify –"

"You wouldn't!"

"– and give them to Director Plover, and right after that, I'll have a chat with Marsha about what we've really been doing at your cottage all those weekends –"

"You're getting out of control, Dr. Lang!"

"– and I won't stop there. I'll send this entire package to *The Rake* and get the story out myself while you're still calling divorce lawyers. Warner would publish this. She's under the protection of the MRC. And *she's* not afraid for her damned job."

"It's not my job I'm afraid for, it's my life!"

"Good, because that's Plan C," she said. "And you'll really hate Plan D."

He stepped back, his mouth moving as if to speak.

"You need testosterone therapy, Tommy, you know that? You're afraid of every little thing anymore."

He shook his head and paced the room as Victoria turned to the windows and looked at the dusky fug. He stopped at the bar, poured a tall drink, and leaned back against the bar. "Listen, I just can't do anything with this material. I need more to work with. Can't you give me something that's not so circumstantial?"

"I have everything in that packet, and it's conclusive, Tommy. I have everything that proves what Chalys did and all the engineering notes on how to reproduce the virophage. I have the original Recombin samples too, and you can have them if you promise to act. If not, then I'm switching to Plan B. I don't have a choice. You do."

"Do you have the samples with you now?" He glanced around the room.

"They're down in my car. I'll get them if you promise to stop this."

He finished his drink and dropped the cup on the bar. "I wish you hadn't forced the issue. I wish you'd let me handle it. You've always been so headstrong, maybe too headstrong for your own good." He took a deep breath and exhaled slowly. "I can't do this alone. I need to call Director Plover and bring him into this. He may have better strategies up his sleeve than I do."

He pulled his tablet from his pocket and looked at the screen with a scowl. "Of course, I can't get a decent signal. Stay here. I'll be back in a moment."

VICTORIA GRABBED A BOTTLE of chilled water from the buffet, collapsed into a chair, and rubbed her neck. The Recombin problem was out of her hands at last, but she didn't feel relieved.

Her tablet rang, and she swiped the incoming call icon.

"Mom?"

"Hey, honey," she said with tired cheer.

"You know it's like nearly eight o'clock?"

She glanced at the wall clock. "We'll be done soon, I promise. Just hang on a few minutes more. Do you still have my briefcase?"

"Sure. Do you need it now?"

"No, not now. I'll be done in a few minutes. See you soon." She clicked off the call and settled back into the chair, savoring the coldness of the water as it slid down her raspy throat. As she raised the bottle to sip some more, though, she was jolted by an awful realization: Tommy Talbott used the same voice service she did.

She pulled out her tablet, and it showed a strong voice signal. "Fool. Naïve fool!" she whispered.

She ran from the room and down the corridor toward the north stair. As she turned the corner, the south door squeaked, and she pressed her body against the wall. In the dome mirror on the wall above, she saw several figures stalking to the doctor's lounge with their pistols drawn.

Once they entered the room, she opened the door quietly and ran down the stairs.

BOB DOWNS STOOD MOTIONLESS on his podium and observed the activity in the Domestic Intelligence Command's Watch Room. He stifled a yawn, loosened his stiff tunic collar, and looked around the room.

Tactical Operations was frenetic. The quadrant chief, Sara Hogue, was twirling her fingers through her short brown ponytail. She was entitled to be anxious: The Syllogic Engine had identified a bounty of Pre-Emergents in the Northeast, and she had seventy Executive and Technical teams in the field working on dissident redaction.

Redaction, Red Action: No matter how one used the word, it fit the task, he thought. He turned to Acquisition, which analyzed images captured from millions of ground-based cameras – on highways, in ATM's and webcams, in stores and offices – as well as high resolution imagery from the aging Keyholes in orbit and the unmanned Blackeye airships floating sixteen miles above the ground. Buta, the quadrant chief, serenely scanned the images on the Wall above him.

He checked the Cybermeasures quadrant, where Mochyn and his team were hunched over their keyboards. Their screens showed the NSA digital intelligence stream, a river of voice, email, and social media datapoints gathered by the TRIPWIRE and PRISMUS systems. It was gibberish to him, so he turned to Intelligence. This was the heart of the Watch Room, but also the quietest quadrant, because all Cochon and his team did was think. They were busy, so he reviewed the aerial images on the Wall.

He wiggled his toes and discovered that his right foot was numb, as it usually was by the eleventh hour of his Watch. Another yawn rose inside, and he was fighting the urge when Cochon snapped him back to full alert. "Incoming Redaction Order, sir! Emergency priority!"

Downs wheeled to Intelligence. "Authority?"

"FDA through VPOTUS, sir."

"Cheyn's approved it?"

"Yes, sir."

"Location?"

"St. Elizabeth's Hospital, Terminals Building, fifth floor."

Downs turned to Tactical. "Hogue, what Executive teams are available?"

Hogue scanned the monitor. "Three in the area. Executives Four, Eight, and Nine. All assigned, sir."

"Move them in now. Give me an ETA when you have it. Cochon, what's our target?"

"Victoria Lang, 39, Caucasian, female, 5 feet 4 inches, 136 pounds, blonde hair and brown eyes, sir." A picture and history appeared on the Wall.

"Pass that on to the teams. Site activity status?"

"Hospital security is searching the fifth floor, sir. They're reporting that they can't locate her."

"So this target knows she's under pursuit," Downs said. "Searching the fifth floor is pointless, but tell them to do it again. I need them out of my way. We'll concentrate police assets at the event perimeter, which is where we'll probably catch her. Call Metro Police and get them moving. And give me an aerial photo of the hospital."

A detailed overhead view of the hospital complex appeared on the Wall. Downs scanned it for a second and said, "Tell Metro to seal the exits. The compound is fenced, so she'll be heading for a gate. We'll need six units."

"Yes, sir. Contacting them now," said Hogue.

"Buta, surveillance?"

"The Blackeyes are fugged out, and the Keyhole is out of range," the Acquisitions chief said. "No eyes in that building, sir. I'm tapping grounds cameras, but they're all fugged up too. It's really thick up there tonight. I'm monitoring wireless voice through the NSA feed, but that's all the input I'm getting."

"ETA on Executives Four is six minutes. Executives Nine will be onsite a minute later and Executives Eight five minutes later, sir," said Hogue.

"Acknowledged. Buta, get me more visuals. There's got to be something inside the building, an ATM or whatever. Find it and acquire it before the first Executives get there. We're not sending them in blind."

"Metro Police will be onsite in three minutes with six units, sir," said Hogue.

"Get me plans of those buildings!"

"Working on it, sir," said Cochon.

Downs scanned the monitors on the Wall. It had been a while since they'd had a good hunt, so this might be a decent night after all.

VICTORIA RAN DOWN THE STAIRCASE hoping the decrepit concrete treads would support her one last time.

When she reached the fourth floor, she yanked open the door and then jammed her fingers in her ears, trying to block the cacophony of moans from the terminal wards. She strode to a supply room, threw open the door, and slammed it behind her, but the wailing still filtered through. She pressed her palms to her temples and pushed hard; she needed to think if she didn't want to join the ranks of the dying.

She breathed deeply and forced the growing terror away from her conscious mind. She reached into her mind for a calm theta state, but panic pulsed and refused to release its grip. Her heart pounded in time to the wails of the dying, and then she realized that she'd never leave the hospital grounds alive.

With a small cry, she stumbled to the counter, groped into an overhead cabinet, and pulled out a shrink-wrapped tray. She clawed through the plastic wrap and pulled out a chromed scalpel. Her pulse pounding in her ears, she closed her eyes and pushed the blade into the skin of her left forearm. Her eyes flew open and she gasped. She pulled the blade through the skin, raising a thin, wavering line of blood as her hand trembled.

She flung the scalpel to the floor and threw her head back against the door, teeth clamped, concentrating on the pain until all she knew was an agony that eclipsed all else. Time passed oddly, measured by thudding heartbeats and not seconds, but the pain subsided a few minutes later and she drew a slow, deep breath. Her mind was clear again.

As she watched blood pulse down her arm and onto the floor, reason returned – she'd accidentally nicked a blood vessel and needed to close the incision fast. She rummaged through the drawers and found an old surgical stapler that didn't look sterile, but it was better than nothing. Gritting her teeth, she shot the staples into her skin and stopped the bleeding.

Wrapping gauze around her arm, she looked around the small room, which seemed ordinary again and uncolored by panic. She continued to wrap her arm and assessed the tactical situation: Those men upstairs weren't going to arrest her but kill her; she'd walked into a trap and couldn't simply walk out; Tommy had betrayed her and the police would swarm the hospital in minutes; and it would be pointless to fight them.

Evasion was her only option, but she needed a weapon in case she became trapped. She also needed a way to get off the campus unnoticed because the police would be watching her car.

She searched the cabinet drawers and the instrument bin but found nothing that would make an effective weapon. Frustrated, she slammed the drawers and closed her eyes.

A plan took shape in her mind – a dangerous plan, but one that would work, a plan that maximized her advantages and threw the opposing force into chaos. She'd be in control for the entire operation, and as she'd learned from SEAL Team Six when she was stationed at Coronado, a controlled operation was always winnable. Relief coursed through her, followed by new confidence and energy.

And she realized that the weapon she needed was there on the back wall. She walked to the medcart and opened a drawer filled with vials and syringes. Her fingers shook as she turned the vials over, and she examined each until she found sodium thiopental, a potent sedative. She grabbed six syringes, filled them, and then recapped them all and dropped them into her right coat pocket.

She turned to leave – there was no time to waste, and she needed to be mobile before her pursuers organized – but then another thought occurred to her. She returned to the medcart and opened more drawers until she found the mercy box; she broke open the cheap camlock on its heavy black lid and saw more rows of vials.

Over-preparation never kills, but under-preparation always does. Commander Dolan had said that a thousand times to his SEALs, and it was wise advice to follow tonight. She filled six more syringes with pancuronium bromide and dropped them into her left pocket.

Slowly, she opened the door a crack and checked the corridor for police. The area looked clear, and she ran to the north stair and then down to the ground floor. She burst through the rusted door on the landing, sending it clanging against the wall, and descended one more floor to the basement level above the tunnels. Hospital orderlies trudged down the hall, and she slipped into the flow.

Trying to appear calm and unconcerned, she continued down the corridor to a closet door. She slipped into the closet and then crept to the opposite door, which opened into the clean supply room.

Banks of stainless-steel cart washers lined the far wall. In front of them, a technician was assembling trays of instruments – a female about her height and weight. She closed her eyes and calculated: Six cc's of sodium thiopental would put her out for hours.

The woman wore a glossy brown chin-length bob without a hair out of place, which had to be a wig. Victoria decided to use that as a disguise later. She was playing loud music that would cover the sound of an approach, and the door was already open to one of the cart cleaning rooms. The breaks were going in her favor.

Victoria pulled a syringe from her right pocket. She deadbolted the door to the corridor, slipped off her shoes and jacket, and then opened the door and walked in.

Creeping on tiptoes, she traversed the twenty feet between them silently. The technician was sorting sterilized instruments from the autoclaves on the counter; between her attention to her task and the music, Victoria approached unnoticed.

She grasped the technician's forehead, pulled it back sharply, and jabbed the syringe into the soft tissue at the front of her neck. The technician struggled and tried to cry out, but Victoria held her tight; in seconds, the sedative took effect and her movements slowed and weakened. She lost consciousness a minute later.

Victoria waited until she was limp and lowered her to the floor. She removed the woman's lab coat, checked the pockets, and found car keys, which meant that the ignition wasn't biometric and she could start it. Her identification showed that her name was Lusa d'Abruzzo and that she had a parking permit for Staff Lot 6, the one by the power plant.

That was perfect because she could only escape St. Elizabeth's through the power plant. No road connected it to Lot 6, though, so Victoria would have to make her own. She hoped Lusa had kept up her insurance payments.

She loosened the clips from Lusa's wig and removed it; the woman's scalp was wet, as was the inside of the wig. Choking back her revulsion, Victoria placed it on her head and noticed her reflection in the cart washer's polished metal wall.

She looked good as a brunette; it brought out the brown of her eyes. Giving her reflection a half smile, she shrugged on the lab coat and then grabbed Lusa under the armpits and dragged her into an empty cart-washing room. She propped her against the wall, closed the door, and locked it.

Victoria picked up the technician's tablet, which also wasn't biometric, and dialed Ada's number as she cleaned up the evidence of the scuffle. She tried to remember her Zulu; if someone were listening in, she'd make it hard for them.

Ada answered the phone and started to talk, but Victoria interrupted her. "*Intombi,* don't answer me in English."

Ada paused as she switched languages. "Hey, *inkosikazi,* why the bush lingo? Are you –"

"Get out of the car and take my briefcase with you. Now!"

"I'm not in the car."

"Why aren't you in…never mind. Where are you?"

Ada paused a second. "Just sitting on a bench, that's all."

"The one by Administration? Good. Now head for the building, and when you come to the sidewalk, make a left. Keep walking till you see some old stairs. Follow them all the way down till they end at the power plant. I'll be there in about ten minutes. Do *not* make a sound, do *not* stop, do *not* let anyone see you. Understand?"

"Got it. Hey, what's going on? Are you in trouble? I see lights moving in the parking lot now where the car should be. Are they after you or –"

"I'm in it deep, and so are you. Once we're out of this, we'll talk, but right now you need to get moving."

"Hospital security confirms that she isn't on the fifth floor, sir," Cochon said.

"I knew that five minutes ago," Downs said. "It's never that easy. Any voice intercepts?"

"Yes, sir, but they sound like routine conversations. Only one voice call from the hospital contained strong verbal stress cues, but I believe it was being spoken in Xhosa or Zulu. We have no automatic translators for that, but I could call State and see if they can find a human translator."

"How long will that take?"

"Unknown, sir."

"Forget it. We'll be toe-tagging this woman in ten or fifteen minutes." Downs pursed his lips and considered how to use his scarce assets best. "Have hospital security send everyone available to Terminals and start a top-down search. They might flush her out. Have them check the roof too."

"Metro found her car, sir, a '42 Bicep Sixty-Six," said Hogue.

"And she wouldn't be in it, I suppose?"

"No, sir. The car is empty, but it's still running."

"FDA says there should be something in the car," Downs said. "Search it, put a locator on it, and post two officers there in case she returns. Location?"

"Lot 1, Administration Building."

"Map that." A blue dot flashed on the aerial image. "Why did she park all the way across the campus? Why walk that far? And why leave a luxury car running in the most crime-ridden part of town?"

"Executives Four is onsite, sir," said Hogue.

"Send them to Terminals and have them track from behind. And send two Metro officers to Administration. I want to know why she parked there."

VICTORIA LEFT THE CLEAN ROOM and rejoined the flow of workers in the basement corridor. Lusa's lab coat was perfect camouflage down here, and none of the orderlies paid attention to her.

To get to Lot 6 without attracting attention or passing a guard station, she needed to descend to the tunnel level and walk to the Physical Plant Building, which was near the power plant and the parking lot. She tried to remember the layout of the tunnels and recalled some going that way, but she'd never used them. All she could do was to try one, see where it led, and hope she was right.

As she neared the north stair, she spotted two hospital security guards ahead in the corridor: One had just opened a door and was inspecting a supply closet, and the other was checking the identification badges of the staff. She wrapped her right hand around a syringe in her pocket, placed her fingernail on the cap, and hid behind a large orderly in front of her.

The man walked forward a few paces, but the guard, a well-built man with high-and-tight sandy hair, held up a hand and stopped him. Victoria pegged him as the Standard American Skinhead Model, Brain Optional. He bellowed, "You seen a woman down here, short blonde hair, prob'ly in a hurry?"

The orderly shook his head.

"You even speak English, chili shitter?"

The orderly shook his head again, which gave her an idea. She tried to recall her high school Italian lessons and began silently mouthing the basic tourist questions the teacher had drilled into her.

The guard gave up trying to communicate. With a disgusted snort, he lifted the linen on the orderly's cart, glimpsed what the bottom compartment held, and then turned his head away and squeezed his eyes shut. He waved the orderly on weakly.

Victoria smiled. *Now you know why it's called a morgue cart, idiot.* She moved up in line, and the guard checked her identification card and asked if she'd seen a woman with short blonde hair.

"Mi scusi. Dov'è si mangia bene?" She furrowed her brow and tried to appear clueless.

"Christ, it's like the fuckin UN down here!"

"Dov'è il bagno, per favore? Devo andare in bagno."

He looked at her identification card again and sneered. "A fuckin wop. Awright, just move on." He waved her by.

"Dovresti imparare italiano, finocchio!" she sang as she sauntered to the stairwell door. Once it closed behind her, she ran down a level to the tunnels, trying to recall the way to the Physical Plant Building.

"The guard in Administration says there's a network of tunnels connecting the buildings, sir," said Cochon. He worked his monitor furiously, tapping at icons and links.

"She could be down there," Downs said. "Hogue, ETA on Executives Nine?"

"Less than one minute, sir."

"Send them down into that tunnel from the Administration Building and try to head her off. Maybe she'll go back to her car. But why was the car running? Did she come alone?"

"Reportedly, sir. The initiator of the Redaction Order says he spent nearly two hours alone with her before he called it in. She has a daughter, but school records show she's attending a Science Camp at Annapolis until September 9."

"Understood. Once this is done, we need a conference on why we keep getting these Emergents with no warning. We didn't see the Scranton Bomber coming, either, and I don't like being forced to react."

"The Syllogic Engine may be inhibited by data overdensity," Cochon said. "As Dr. Hallowell predicted, we're capturing more data than the Engine can process, causing the AI modules to fail at discriminating between relevant and irrelevant information. Its effectiveness is diminishing."

"I'll set up a meeting with IT," Downs said. "Where's the map of those tunnels?"

"There are none, sir. They date back to the late nineteenth century and were built without plans."

"Pass that on to the teams. They should know what they're getting into. Buta, how about some visuals?"

Buta turned to Downs and shrugged with a dejected look.

VICTORIA WAS LOST. She'd turned right down the corridor outside the Cages because she'd seen light at the end, but it had deteriorated into a dark chute full of rubble. She was about to turn back and admit defeat when she found a side corridor and saw faint light in the distance.

After weaving through furniture blocking the way, she reached the light – and discovered that she was in front of the door she'd seen a few minutes before. She'd just gone full circle.

Opening the riveted door quietly, this time she decided to make a left at the other end. She crunched through the cracked plaster and had walked as far as the third cell when the door at the far end of the hallway creaked.

She stopped short and squinted down the dim corridor. A man's beefy hand pushed open the door, and the muzzle of a small-caliber automatic rifle poked through the opening. She backed into a cage whose door had fallen off long ago. The wet, sour smell of decaying concrete was stronger, but the cage was in near-total darkness.

Plaster crunched as footsteps approached. The man sounded like he was sacrificing stealth for speed, meaning she could safely run the other way once he passed. In case he was searching the cells, she shrugged off the white lab coat and hung it out of sight on an iron bar jutting from the wall. Her navy blue suit now made her almost invisible in the darkness.

The footsteps sounded closer, and she heard a *skishing* sound as plaster skidded across the floor. She watched him pass by, a tall and well-muscled man in a gray T-shirt, black camouflage pants, and black nylon boots, carrying an assault rifle in one hand. He had a combat knife strapped to his thigh, a sidearm holstered on his hip, and was wearing a two-way headset. That was all – he was lightly armed and rigged only for quick and brutal physical action.

He tapped a finger to his headset and called, "Nine Alpha, Nine Alpha?" and then repeated the call a few seconds later. With a snort, he pulled off the headset and looked left and right, and then into the cage where she was hiding. Apparently finding nothing, he moved on a few steps.

Then he stopped and turned his head from side to side; she saw his profile, his nostrils flaring as his senses sought the prey. Her nose twitched from a sudden, coppery tang of blood, and she covered her wounded arm with her hand so he wouldn't smell it.

He stood motionless, sniffing the air, and her pulse raced as she realized that she might have to fight an armed manhunter. Her fingers trembling, she reached into her coat pocket and grasped a syringe of pancuronium bromide – if injected into a vein, it would stop his breathing in ten seconds. It was risky to use, not just because one accidental jab could kill her, but also because ten seconds was an eternity in close-quarters combat.

Holding the syringe in her fist, she pressed her body even closer to the concrete wall. The man crouched and closed his eyes for a moment, and then he looked into her cage. Snorting like he was disappointed, he stood and retraced his steps past the opening to her cage. Just as she felt a rush of relief, she heard the soft sibilance of a combat knife sliding from its sheath and a quiet tap as he rested the assault rifle on the floor. She pictured him holding his knife high against his chest, preparing to strike.

On the other side of the wall, Victoria struck the same pose armed only with the syringe.

"We've lost contact with Executives Nine, sir. The signal blanked when they went down into the tunnels. They won't be able to communicate with each other, either, or the communications will be degraded if they can," said Hogue.

"God be with them, then. They're on their own. Status on Executives Four?"

"Ground floor, Terminals Building. Executives Eight reports they're onsite, sir."

"Good. Send them into the tunnels from the Terminals side. Warn them that they'll go silent once they're in." Downs knew she was in the tunnels because that's where he would have gone if he were being hunted. But as a trained Executive, he could escape such a trap, and Victoria Lang was a middle-aged physician who couldn't, not unless she was a superhero. This hunt would be over soon.

He just hoped it wouldn't be over too soon.

ADA WALKED ALONG THE UNDERGROWTH as close to the side of the stairs as possible. She'd narrowly missed a group of men running her way a few minutes earlier, so she wanted to be able to jump into the bushes for cover if she needed to. It would slow her progress, but her mother would wait. She smiled as an image of The Commander came to mind, sitting in her car and glancing at the clock every two seconds.

I'm dead, Victoria thought. *He's waiting to strike, and I'm dead when he does.* She tried to suppress the rising panic by taking deep, quiet breaths, but it wasn't working.

She dug her fingernails into her arm wound until the pain cleared her mind. As the panic receded, her mind kicked into action. She held several tactical advantages – he had to enter through the doorway, he was unsure where she was, and he'd be blind in the darkness. He'd have his knife in his hand because the walls were concrete, and any gunshot would ricochet.

He'd attack with a high downward slash at first, hoping to cut her neck or chest, which would leave him vulnerable below the waist.

The door opening was to her right, so she palmed the syringe in her left hand and placed her thumb on the plunger. She shifted most of her weight to her right foot, freeing the left leg to propel her turn, and then listened for his move.

Ten seconds, fifteen, twenty...she couldn't hold this position much longer. With the toe of her shoe, she found a small piece of plaster and kicked it to the back of the cell.

Outside, a boot turned on plaster dust, and she quietly swung her left leg around while sinking into a low crouch and extending her left arm with the syringe pointing out. He came through the opening at the same time, his blade flashing over her head and slicing only at the darkness. The syringe pierced the femoral artery in his left thigh, and she pushed the plunger hard as the backstroke of his knife strike caught her wig and sent it flying against the wall.

She jumped to the back of the cell and started counting the seconds. Hearing her move, he leaped in her direction, his body blocking the hazy light from the corridor. She rolled across the floor toward him, and he tripped and hit the concrete floor hard.

She huddled by the doorway, holding the empty syringe in front of her, praying for the critical ten seconds to pass, and coiled for a last, desperate counterstrike if necessary. Once her mental count hit ten, though, the sound of his breathing stopped.

Capping the used syringe, she rose to her feet. She slipped his pistol from its holster and walloped him on the skull, hoping to spare him from four minutes of mortal terror as he tried to coax his paralyzed lungs to draw air.

She dusted off her suit jacket and then pulled the lab coat down from the iron bar. Laughing shakily, she leaned back against the wall and clutched her arms around her chest.

SHE STUMBLED DOWN ANOTHER DARK CORRIDOR, picking a path through the debris and trying to match her location with the campus layout above. She'd need to make a right somewhere soon to get to the Physical Plant Building – if it even connected to this corridor.

Suddenly, a pile of furniture collapsed and hit the floor behind her. She froze and heard the scuffling of boots some distance away; another killer was now pursuing her, and she'd be trapped if this route turned out to be a dead-end. She pulled the pistol from her pocket and moved forward in the darkness, probing the wall and praying to find an exit.

As she ran her hands along the wall, her fingers found the frame of an iron door to her right. She pulled the handle, and a loud screech echoed through the hallway as the door slowly opened. Somewhere behind her, she heard the killer's feet skidding across plaster as he turned toward the sound.

Time had run out. She spun on the balls of her feet, pulled the pistol into position, and fired three glancing rounds into the right wall, three into the ceiling, and three into the left wall, spinning a deadly lacework of concrete chips and high-powered hollow points which ricocheted down the long concrete tunnel. She jumped behind the door just as two rounds slammed into it, showering her shoulders with rusty flakes.

Once the bullets stopped zinging past, she listened for sounds of movement; a man groaned somewhere in the darkness down the corridor, but she heard nothing else. She ran through the doorway, slammed the door shut with a clang, and slid its rusted latch into place.

A narrow hallway filled with boxes stretched before her, and a dim light illuminated a large room at the end. She ran toward it and soon skittered into a workspace with papers strewn across desks.

The dark room appeared empty. She ran to stairs at the far end and bounded up them to the first door she found. It opened after a few hard kicks, and then she stepped into the outside world for the first time in two horrific hours.

The power plant's smokestack glowed red in the fug, marking where the car would be, and she set off in that direction. As she neared Lot 6, she reached into the lab coat pocket for the keys and fumbled for the remote, stabbing at the buttons. A yellow light flashed ahead, and she skidded on a thin coat of soot and headed for it.

The smokestack for the hospital power plant towered above the lot, its red collision lights blinking and its mouth spewing red embers and black smoke. Directly under the plume, a small car sat with its hazard lights flashing. Victoria felt a sense of relief that evaporated the instant she realized what it was: a little white Hugo, the worst car ever to wear a license plate. Not only that, it was ancient.

She slid into the stinking cabin and turned the ignition key, and the engine rattled to life asthmatically and threatened to stall. As it warmed up, she climbed out and checked the rusted chain-link fence separating the lot from the power plant. It was set into the top of a steep, ivy-covered slope that ended at the base of the generating building fifty feet below.

She jumped back in and cinched her seat belt tight. With a silent prayer, she backed the little car up – and then she rammed the shifter into gear and drove through the fence.

ADA WAS SITTING ON THE BOTTOM STEP of the concrete stairs when she heard metal twanging on the hill above. Something was moving in the darkness and making a sound like fabric being torn, but the fug obscured her vision. She heard a metallic crunch and then the whine of an engine. As she stepped back into the shrubs, a car with ivy vines entwined in the grille slalomed around the corner of the building and rattled to a stop beside her.

The passenger window creaked as it rolled down. "Ada?" her mother called.

She scooped up the briefcase and ran to the car. A minute later, they drove through the open gate of the power plant and into freedom.

AMERICANS WORE JACKBOOTS THEN

Day 15
Wednesday afternoon, September 2, 2043
3120 L Street NW, Washington, DC

Krista pressed the extra buzz button on her baristomat a few times. It was time to review the trust accounting, and there wasn't enough caffeine in Colombia to make that tolerable. The task shouldn't have been difficult – her only assets were a building and a car – but the accountants made a simple task anguishing. They even expected her to understand math.

She slumped into her chair, set the mug on the table, and opened the long spreadsheet. *Thank god they don't know that all the trust's gold is sitting under my car seat,* she thought. *They'd tack another eight pages on.*

She'd stolen the gold from her mother's trust years before to keep her adoptive father, Warren Warner, from spending her inheritance on himself. An image of him flashed into her mind, and she suppressed her irritation and focused on the spreadsheet. After a few minutes of futile brainwork, she scrolled to the last page to see the final total. The number was black, which she figured was good, so she signed the sheet and sent it off. Before she could distract her mind with something else, though, her anger flared again.

However, this happened every month, and she knew what to do. Relaxing her shoulder muscles, she took deep breaths and entered her calm space. *I am in harmony with good stuff. I am water in a mountain stream. I am water burbling serenely over rocks rounded by eons of water burbling serenely over rocks, water grinding the stones to dust in mindless and destructive obedience to gravity...*

She opened her eyes and blinked a few times. Trying a different tack, she envisioned a blank movie screen – and then she saw Warren Warner's fat mottled face and beady eyes on it, looking like a mutant raisin scone brought to life.

Her kumbaya shattered, and she slammed her fists on the table so hard that her coffee cup bounced off. Growling, she jumped up from the chair, stalked to the balcony and paced its edges, scared the pigeons off the roof and chain-smoked, but her anger wouldn't dissipate. Cursing her temper, she strode back into her apartment to drown it in coffee. Passing her sagging green rain barrel on the way, she cocked her leg back and kicked the thing with all her might.

The barrel was full of water and hard as granite, and her left big toe went numb, promising unbearable pain to follow. Cradling her foot in her hands, she pogoed to a nearby column and leaned against it, making a frustrated sound that was part grumble and part roar.

She hobbled away and tried to walk it off, making a prison-yard circuit of the balcony and swearing under her breath the entire time.

KRISTA TRIED TO HURRY through the shower because she'd forgotten that she was chaperoning her best friend Liza's Christian Renewal Day Bash class trip. The Bash was an informal party for elementary school students who didn't get the day off for the Renewal Ceremony like every Archangelist over the age of twelve.

The Ceremony wasn't complicated – the faithful dropped a tenpez in the tray and were dunked – but since almost every working adult in the capital area was an Archangelist, the Ceremony had to be repeated millions of times in a day. Experience showed that allowing children to play in the baptismal waters delayed an already-slow process.

And on their bonanza day, the Church tolerated no obstacles on the way to the offerings basket. Faith Corporation, the parent company of the Archangelic Church of the Son of Christ, received almost ninety percent of their income on Renewal Day. In the previous year, that amounted to thirty-two billion dollars.

Thus, the little ones went to school on everybody else's day off. Because that made even eight-year-olds surly, Liza was taking her class to the National Museum of American History. She agreed to go along because the museum was hosting an exhibit she wanted to see.

She hadn't known how angry she'd be, though, and was tempted to call and cancel. However, she needed a break from her ghosts for a few hours. If she stayed in this place, in this murderous mood, she'd go crazy.

THE SCHOOL BUS GLIDED TO A STOP in the West Mall parking lot two hours later. Krista helped Liza funnel the children into an irregular throng and herd them toward the museum.

The crowd reached Madison Avenue and waited until the street sweeper passed. Legend said that the robotic sweepers had eaten children, which was almost plausible because their safety sensors often clogged with soot. She doubted it was true, but Liza didn't want to chance anything and kept the kids far away.

They had practical reasons to avoid the sweepers too. The machines were solar powered and would sometimes blow soot off the panels with compressed air. She'd once seen a man on M Street walk through a cloud of it, and he'd come out looking like a vaudevillian in blackface.

They'd arrived early to allow time for the security screening. Krista suspected there was an unspoken reason for the screenings: They kept the gropers and lechers off the streets and at a place where someone could watch them. True to her suspicions, the guards patted down Liza with extreme thoroughness – she was blonde and bosomy, clearly the defining characteristics of a hardened terrorist. They patted Krista down almost as thoroughly, which strangely pleased her.

The throng headed for the Wonders of American Animation cartoon exhibit. The prime attraction was a special screening of *The World's Tiniest Violin,* the animated feature that had won the 2042 Best Picture Award. She'd heard the buzz about the touching story of a tiny, broken violin being repaired by an Archangelist minister and then becoming a part of God's heavenly orchestra.

She'd never been tempted to see it. The plot sounded too much like *Rudolph the Red-Nosed Arkie,* and stories where someone had no self-worth until the big guys said so always turned her off. However, the kids would love it, and it would show them how the Archangelist hegemony expected them to conform as they matured. It would also give her more than an hour to satisfy her morbid curiosity with President Clune, the billionaire populist who'd nearly destroyed the nation.

She limped through the crowds to the East Wing. At the exhibit's entrance, metal letters arching over a wrought-iron gate spelled 'AMERICAN FASCISM 2025-2029,' which she thought was overly dramatic. President Clune and his ilk hadn't been fascists; they'd merely packaged autocracy in the American flag and called it patriotism. And most of the country had fallen for it.

America's autocratic period was her enduring obsession mainly because she'd never learned why Clune wrecked his own nation – and her life along with it. The Troubles that he caused were like an earthquake occurring in the night and waking the next morning to find a world inexplicably in ruins. She'd spent much of her adult life trying to understand why.

All she remembered of the time was that her mother would sometimes watch TV and mutter that the world was going to hell, but Krista hadn't understood. As she matured, she learned that Clune had been a monster and that his policies had orphaned her, to be sold like so much meat to the Warners so they could pillage her inheritance.

Turning a corner, she arrived at the display she'd come to see and saw a crowd around it. She pretty-girl-smiled her way to the front to see the star attraction, but they were just a simple pair of chromed handcuffs, ordinary and common, an inadequate vessel for the meaning they carried. She'd envisioned them as manacles fashioned from the coarsest pig iron.

The next case showed the noose. The display told the bare facts of Clune's demise a month after leaving office: He was caught with child pornography in Arkansas, tried, convicted, and hanged in three days. It didn't mention how biased the trial was – the jurors were all Archangelist men with young teen daughters, for example – but nobody cared. Clune was guilty of far worse, and he'd earned a short drop and a sudden stop long before.

Someone jostled her arm, and a brief spasm of panic gripped her when she realized that she was in a crowd. Seeking a less-congested area, she wandered into an empty alcove holding a tall glass cabinet with a National Security Forces Ironshirt armorsuit inside. It changed color as she approached; the woven ballistic fabric holding the armor plates cast a slight sheen that looked reddish from one angle and dark gray from another, almost like freshly milled iron.

The thing was frightening even with nobody inside. What chilled her more, though, was that the fabric was scratched and ripped, and the dark gray visored helmet was melted. It had been there.

What would it have been like? she thought. *What would it have been like to see thousands of these suits, filled with the murderous NSF Ironshirts, marching in a line down Gratiot Avenue behind the unwilling Michigan National Guard? Would I have resisted too as they cleared the Detroit streets through a pall of smoke from the doomed, burning downtown? Would I have fought beside the Antifas as the Ironshirts herded the poor and the hungry to the trains for resettlement to become wretched Transportees and never be seen again? Would I have thrown Molotov cocktails at the ranks of the NSF like the anti-fascists? What would it have been like?*

She shivered; the image would have given Hitler a boner. *And I was sitting on the floor playing with dolls while it happened. God, I wish I'd been there. I wish I could have done something.*

She left the alcove and wandered into a room with displays about First Detroit and Second Detroit, the major riots of the time. A massive bronze plaque dominated the wall, listing the names of those killed during Clune's suppressions of the city in '25 and '26.

First Detroit felled three thousand people, mostly young men, but the nation's leaders had been less concerned about the death toll than the rebellion of a major city. Resolving that such an insurrection would never happen again, Congress passed the Domestic Tranquility Act after the smoke cleared and formed the National Security Forces to enforce it. Directed by the Domestic Intelligence Command, they were charged with suppressing violent dissent using whatever force they deemed necessary.

The new agency understood that its unwritten mission was to preserve the government's power. When Detroit's voters threw out its city government after the first riot and elected an Antifa mayor and council, the NSF reacted with alarm. When the new government openly criticized their benefactor Clune and demanded a complete repeal of the Domestic Tranquility Act, the NSF decided they had to go.

In a closed-door session with the House Domestic Tranquility Committee, they proposed that any anti-fascist gathering the NSF believed could turn violent should be classified as criminal domestic terrorism. The committee agreed, thus sealing Detroit's fate.

When riots struck the city again in August '26, the NSF used its new authority to crush the troublesome Antifas. As a result, Second Detroit was far bloodier, and the body count topped eight thousand. The rebellions in Cleveland, Flint, Akron, and Toledo ended almost as violently.

Although the plaque was immense, she thought it needed to be even larger because it named only the eleven thousand dead of the riots. The Troubles had affected many more. The Transportees' names weren't on it, and they reportedly numbered in the millions; her name or her mother's weren't on it, either. They were victims of Clune's brutality as much as any who'd gotten an NSF slug in the back.

She edged around the plaque and arrived at the last display, which ended with Second Detroit. Puzzled, she glanced around the corner to see if it continued, but it didn't. She stood with her hands on her hips, glaring at the empty wall. In her mind, it should have shown how the NSF amplified autocracy into fascism after Second Detroit.

She knew exactly how they'd done it. Dr. Bill Hallowell, the NSF's former Chief Technologist, detailed their ruthless grasp of power on a SatNet blog three years after he resigned. As a young teen, Krista spent long nights reading the eight-part *mea culpa* until she'd memorized Hallowell's confession.

Hallowell had bared everything. His greatest regret was attending a sci-fi convention in San Diego in 1998, where he met a young writer who was adapting a story for the big screen and wanted to bounce a few ideas off the esteemed Dr. Hallowell, Nobel Prize winner and resident genius at Advanced Heuristics. The writer wanted to update an old story about a future where a trio of psychics predicted crime, and it being the nineties, he wondered if a computer could do the same thing. Dozens of ideas at once swarmed Hallowell's mind, and he grabbed a marker and began sketching out the first design of the Syllogic Engine on the conference center walls.

The befuddled writer understood none of the scribbles and reused the psychic angle for his screenplay. The movie was a smashing success, but Hallowell was still developing his prototype of the Engine for years after. In 2026, he finished the tool that would give the NSF absolute power. He regretted it instantly.

Using a massively parallel supercomputer array powered by dual artificial-intelligence modules – and drawing from the NSF's extensive database of government records, phone taps, digital communications, and social posts – the Engine distilled a human's spirit and life experience into numbers and then modeled an individual's belief structure. From this, the computer's AI prediction module extrapolated an individual's future reaction to varied sociopolitical pressures; an adversarial AI module challenged those results and highlighted their flaws. By alternately querying the artificial intelligences, the Engine revised and perfected its threat model.

The Syllogic Engine was terrifyingly accurate. Within a month of its unveiling, the NSF could find domestic terrorists before they lit their first fuse, and a fearful Congress embraced the new crime-fighting tool. In 2027, they declared incipient terrorism a capital crime and set the NSF loose on the so-called Pre-Emergents. The freedom that patriots fought so hard for disappeared overnight, and Americans learned fast to keep their opinions to themselves.

The NSF also learned fast. In a subjugated society where they could read the heart and soul of every American using a wireless connection, they didn't need the brutal Ironshirts. They could grab greater control by unleashing the Syllogic Engine on America's law enforcement and intelligence agencies instead.

Within months, the NSF collected so much incriminating evidence that they gained the fearful allegiance of even the local police departments, giving them a stranglehold on the flow of domestic intelligence. By the end of 2027, nobody dared to question the National Security Forces, not even members of Congress.

A troubled quiet settled over the land as Americans realized that they'd found peace by sacrificing their few remaining civil liberties. Over time, though, they accepted the price of domestic tranquility, and Americans ambled into the future forgetting they'd once been free.

However, Dr. Hallowell forgot nothing, and neither did the NSF, who issued a rare Citizen's Apprehension Directive – popularly known as the Snuff Order – for the capture of Hallowell and the SatNet bloggers who'd published his story. Hallowell ran into the safe, deep shadows of urban America, but the bloggers were killed within days.

She sighed and leaned against the plaque. She'd always wanted to meet this man, her idol through the bleak and angry teen years, but Hallowell had gone insane upon hearing of the bloggers' deaths. If the SatNet rumors were true, he now lived in the sewers of Washington and preached anarchy to the rats. While she'd love to interview him, she wouldn't walk through the stinking tunnels of underground Washington to find the man.

A mob of teens slouched around the corner, and she tingled with panic and backed into a different hall lined with wall displays about the PASS Act. Mercifully, the place was empty and quiet, and she exhaled her tension away and read the panels.

Before the Domestic Tranquility Act's passage, a conference of state governors had asked the Federal government to settle the country's increasingly discontent rank and file. Congress and President Clune worked the problem and finally concluded that working-class jobs would never return.

It was time for an outside-the-box solution. Their idea: Reduce the number of unemployed by making it easier for the distressed populace to kill itself. Their brilliant tool was the PASS Act of 2026, which removed all restrictions on the sale of tobacco, alcohol, marijuana, and guns. It intended that if this cancer or that cirrhosis didn't thin the herd, the downtrodden could always find relief at the business end of a bong or a pistol.

She leaned against the wall and recalled the day when the Act took effect. Using money she'd saved for weeks, she bought a pack at the corner bodega and hustled to Union Square. That first cigarette tasted horrible, but she didn't care. It made her feel tougher and less like a vulnerable child, which was important to a young girl growing up in a city that routinely destroyed capable adults.

She didn't feel tough for long, though. Remembering what happened a year later, a familiar queasiness twisted her gut.

The hot evening at Union Square, feeding the pigeons, and then the car on 14th Street swerving drunkenly. Mom's hand lets go of mine, and then my head is ringing and I hear the cries and shocked murmur of a crowd, the cloppita-cloppita of police horses and the faraway wail of sirens. My bodyguard calls for Miss Kellen, and then he's standing over me, crying. Seth's strong arms lift me and take me away from my dying mother forever.

She closed her eyes and stepped back, trying to banish the memory, but it still hurt as if it had happened yesterday, not sixteen years before. She practiced her yogic breathing exercises and recited the idiotic mantras, and she was able to move on after a few minutes.

That Congress passed a bill giving the right to buy distilled spirits to anyone with a driver's license – and lowered the national driving age to fifteen – enraged her to the point of verbal incoherence. Her own government had sent random bolts of drunken destruction throughout the country, and one of those bolts had landed on New York's Union Square on the night of May 18, 2027. It had changed her life forever.

Her anger was boiling higher with each panel she read, so she left the hall and moved into the next room before she erupted into Tourette's-grade profanity. Photographs of politicians dotted the walls of this room, and one showed a young Gabriel Cheyn.

He'd been handsome back when he was Clune's National Security Advisor, and even when she was his history student ten years later. Still, she'd seen enough of his face and moved to the next photos, which depicted the administration of President Rieke, Clune's successor.

She recalled Sam Rieke's appearance at the MRC Correspondent's Dinner back in '40, four years after he'd left office. He shocked the crowd with a string of off-color one-liners nobody expected from a strait-laced Archangelist, but that made the jokes even funnier. After his speech, he sat at her table and spent the rest of dinner ogling her breasts.

When he invited her to after-dinner coffee up in his suite, she was shocked. She knew her ample bustline could open doors – sometimes literally – but never expected it to earn a presidential invitation. Nevertheless, it was her opportunity to interview an ex-president, and she decided to risk a post-executive grope.

They sat on his balcony and watched the twinkling lights of Washington. To her surprise, he remained a perfect gentleman throughout. He *had* only wanted to talk, and he told her a fascinating story under the condition that she'd never publish a word of it.

He'd never expected to become president. Before 2028, he was only a business manager for the Archangelic Church of the Son of Christ. He worked directly with The Profit Joseph, whom Arkies believed was the son of Jesus.

Back then, the unknown Yale MBA was reorganizing the church into a corporate franchise model. Early in his career, Rieke realized that the schizophrenic Archangelist doctrine could power a successful business model in a deeply polarized America. The Profit loved his ideas and gave him carte blanche to sell as many franchises as the religion market could bear.

The Archangelist faith had always been powered by a Frankenstein of extreme and contradictory beliefs that had long kept them a laughingstock. However, since the Great Correction had decimated the skeptical middle class, Rieke saw how the Archangelists could consolidate the power bases they'd built at the nation's political poles and cover the Earth like kudzu after a spring rain.

His business model was so simple that Rieke was shocked nobody had already exploited it. America's extreme political right and left had more in common with each other than the reasonable political center; both despised political centrists as weak and rudderless, and both longed for a strongman to pound the ideological impurities out of the infidels. The extremists' fanatical energy and deep pockets could be mined by convincing them that The Profit Joseph was that strongman.

All Rieke needed to do was fuse the opposing ideologies. He began by reworking the Archangelist catechism into a furious diatribe against the timid and small-minded, which at the same time exhorted men of passion and imagination to work together and lead the world back to Godliness. In Rieke's clever construction, tiptoeing through the tulips of an unblemished and pure Eden could only be achieved by reducing the bloated government to something so small that it could be drowned in a toilet, and vice versa. Since both the far right and left had abandoned reason long before, they'd never see that this fantasy was impossible to realize.

To prevent pesky realities from corroding their faith, Rieke borrowed three innovations from the Neo-Nazi template. First, no Archangelist could discuss what happened in the temple under the penalty of excommunication. Second, members could only get their news from the local temple's Internet portal, which promised to deliver the True Story. Third, Rieke carefully engineered that True Story to scare the flock into donating every cent they had.

It worked better than Rieke expected, but he didn't get the chance to stay with his program. In 2027, The Profit called him to East Texarkana for a new assignment: to rescue the country from the madness of John Clune.

The Profit agreed with the government that the biggest problem facing America was a plethora of Americans, but the damage Clune had wrought thinning the herd appalled him. He'd potholed the economy with his Rust Belt war and purged Arkies with the NSF's crackdown on Pre-Emergents, but then he'd picked a fight with Persia that accomplished nothing except to deprive the country of foreign oil. Corporate America was suffering under his presidency, and The Profit intended to end the madness and mount a third-party challenge to Clune's reelection. Rieke begged off at first, arguing that he worked calculators and not caucuses, and that the Church would be better represented by someone who hadn't been a lifelong atheist. The Profit was adamant, though, and Rieke threw his hat into the ring.

Krista remembered his campaign fondly. It was the only thing that made her laugh in the dismal year of '28, an unnatural and almost comical political display the pundits dubbed 'simultaneously hysterical and historical.' He had plenty of cash thanks to Corporate America, but Rieke's platform was confused and contradictory. That was summarized perfectly by his campaign slogan: There's Gotta Be a Better Way.

In an ordinary year, he would have been ridiculed into obscurity, but the 2028 presidential debate proved it was no ordinary year. On the stage to Rieke's right, the robustly paranoid John Wilson Clune yelled, "LAW AND ORDER! LAW AND ORDER!" and demanded that voters give him four more years so he could finish crushing his imagined enemies. Even his rabid mouth-breather base changed the channel then, incapable of admitting that their idol had descended into the malignant monkey stage of madness.

To his left, the brilliant, compassionate, but quadriplegic Democratic candidate sprawled across his wheelchair and drooled down his tie, unable to respond except by blinking his eyes. In that august company, Rieke seemed wiser and more redoubtable than Lincoln. He won with three-quarters of the popular vote.

Rieke went to work fast. On his first day, he ordered American forces out of the Persian Gulf and disbanded the Domestic Operations Command of the NSF and their reviled Ironshirts.

On the second day, he began remaking America in the Archangelist image, starting with the federal institutions and bureaucracies Clune had wrecked. He fired the staff of the NSF's Domestic Intelligence Command, the FBI, and the NSA, which were packed with corrupt Clune appointees, and replaced them with loyal Arkies. He then reached into to every Federal agency and even America's boardrooms. A year later, though, his makeover hit the immovable object called Congress, having managed to get the Republican Senate and Democratic House to finally agree on something – to reject every initiative the upstart third-party president proposed and crush his political movement.

Rieke gave as good as he got: For the next seven years, he said Washington "saw more Vitos than a Sicilian trattoria on Mafia Night." Krista got the joke a minute later as she was sipping coffee, and she snorted it all over her thousand dollar dress. Mortified that she'd disgraced herself before an ex-president, she muttered her apologies and started to leave, but Rieke chuckled and said the coffee stain was a badge of honor; he'd worked with humorless Arkies for decades, and one of his jokes earning a coffee-snorting belly laugh was long overdue. He told his aide to send her over a new dress in the morning and then continued his story.

Congress retaliated for his vetoes by shutting the government down so often that it stopped making the news. Rieke closed the entire National Park System in return, paralyzing much of Washington. But nobody cared, and he sold most of the parks to mining companies for operating cash a few years later.

Despite the political theatrics, America settled into a welcome *Pax Archangelica* during his two terms, relieved to see normal political squabbles and not constant destruction, death, and disease. The Arkies exploited this peace to weaken the failing American empire and begin building a theocratic one.

Many critics later charged that Rieke had been an ineffective president, but he changed America fundamentally if quietly by the time he left office. Nearly every house of worship in the nation was Archangelist or affiliated with them in some way, and most Corporate-American boardrooms were stocked with Archangelist directors. In much of the East, a jobseeker needed an Archangelist ID to land a decent position, and workers flocked to bend their knee at Arkie temples. Without much fanfare, the Arkies had grabbed every lever of power in the country.

Three hours later, his Secret Service escort interrupted him, and he stood and apologized that they couldn't continue their talk. After he said goodbye, he kissed her hand longer than proper manners allowed, sending her pulse racing. For weeks after, she kept her tablet in her hand day and night, hoping he'd call, but they never spoke again.

She still remembered his soft, laughing brown eyes, his aura of power and confidence, his strong jaw and full lips. Picturing those lips, she leaned against the wall, savoring the climate of her imagination – hot, humid, with a chance of reckless desire – but then another gaggle of teens burst into the room.

She scurried across the main hall into the Model Gallery, a large room with before-and-after models of the Rust Belt cities that had been the NSF's battlegrounds. She stopped at the Cleveland model first.

The starving, disadvantaged districts of the city had rioted in the summer of 2026, and the models showed the result of the NSF suppression effort. While the before-2026 model was a hodge-podge expanse of city and concrete, the after-2026 model showed a wide greenbelt surrounding the downtown. That area was razed after the NSF had subdued and removed the Transportees, and the city elders decided to plant a forest there instead of looking at the ring of blasted city.

The suburbs shunned Cleveland, but it bounced back unexpectedly. The sturdy and practical survivors converted the tall office towers into small businesses, and they filled quickly with a mix of humble uses: Homes sat next to workshops, offices beside small factories, stores by warehouses. The city thrived, and an earthy and alternative culture grew. In one of her posts, she'd dubbed the city 'The World's Tallest Village,' and the city council had had that painted on all their welcome signs. She'd mounted a picture of one on her study wall.

The transformation of Cleveland was a marvel. As urban renewal went, it was a smashing success, and all it had required was the forced removal of almost a million urban poor and the illegal expropriation of their property.

She walked to the Detroit models. The city's experience was harsher because the population had been far more desperate, and the riots of 2025 and 2026 laid waste to most of it.

Detroit was abandoned after with the hope that Nature would reclaim it and spare humanity the trouble of tearing it down. Nature hadn't wanted it, but Klean Koal had. They'd pushed the ruins back with bulldozers, creating an embankment of fifty-foot-high rubble dikes around their four new power plants.

Now, nearly twenty years later, all that remained of the once-vital city was a model in a museum.

Well, Clune did promise he'd turn Detroit into a model city, she said to herself. *He just didn't say how.* She tried to suppress a giggle but failed.

A stern-looking matron threw her a sharp look. "Do you find something amusing, Miss?"

At least he didn't turn us into model citizens. Thank Jaysus for that, eh? A horsey laugh escaped her mouth that echoed through the somber hall. Eyebrows rose across the room and portly men harrumphed. She couldn't stop laughing, though, and she backed out of the hall.

KRISTA LIMPED INTO A BULLPEN on the Mall side, where the smokers went to satisfy their addictions without enduring another security grope on the way back. "You're really losing it," she muttered. "You're having another Away in the Head day, kiddo. Maybe you should start doing drugs."

She imagined a soft, drug-addled life, happily wasting away in a cozy Oriental den, but decided that would never work out. Being a credible drug addict involved using needles, which was the worst of the dozen or so phobias she had.

She gazed across the Mall at the twisted, egg-shaped iron frame of the new National Museum of the Corporate-American. It was barely visible through the fug, but that was a blessing. Even the corporations that had funded its construction thought the building was ugly.

She was mulling over a snarky post on Corporate-Americans as noble savages – the article had to involve pinstriped loincloths, but she couldn't work it in – when Liza appeared at her side. "The kids drive me insane sometimes," she said, pulling a Cannabliss inhaler from her purse. "I love them to death, but it's so noisy in there." She sucked so hard on the toke's mouthpiece that the little gizmo whistled and bubbled in protest, and then she exhaled a thin plume of THC vapor and sighed. "That's better. So next month we're going to the opening of the Corporate-American Museum, do you want to come? Great, so after the movie, I was thinking we could take the kids to see the American Fascism exhibit, I know they're a little young for the topic and I didn't prepare a lesson plan but they'll get this in the fifth grade, an introduction would be good, and anyway, the exhibit is only here for the next month, so it'd be enriching..."

Krista leaned back against the fence and looked up at the sky.

DOWNS WALKED INTO THE WATCH ROOM, his hair still damp from his Renewal. "Status, Cochon?"

"West Virginia Border Control confirms that a white '29 Hugo registered to Lusa d'Abruzzo entered the state at 0131 hours, sir."

"And are they complying with the Compact?"

"Yes, sir. They issued a seven-day sanctuary. It expires next Wednesday at 0227 hours."

Downs looked up at the Wall, a small smile playing across his face. They'd have Lang soon because she'd driven into a trap – there were only eight westerly exits from West Virginia, and the National Security Forces covered each one.

They caught eighty-six percent of refugees at the border, with the remaining fourteen percent probably being murdered by the locals. Most West Virginians were desperately poor, and the fugitives often carried substantial amounts of cash or gold, making them irresistible targets. Downs wasn't disturbed by that intrusion onto his turf, but he wished the hillbillies would report their kills so he could close his files. "Status of the chokepoints, Hogue?" he asked.

"We have twenty-two Special Activity Groups deployed, sir, providing full coverage to all eight chokepoints."

"Pass on that information to the Groups and let them know we anticipate a flight window from early Tuesday to early Wednesday."

Downs scowled at the mention of the Special Activity Groups. They were simple, crude tools, nothing more than a fast truck with six armed brutes who could chase another car and capture the occupants. They were worlds apart from Executives, who were all MMU graduates.

They were the elite – only one in four candidates were chosen for Executive training in their senior year of the Applied Political Science program, and of those, sixty percent washed out. Downs knew this because he'd been one of those culled.

He'd excelled in his Field Practicum but contracted a rare mutation of the Rubella virus in November of his senior year. Although he recovered fully, the illness left him nearsighted, and Executives needed perfect vision. He refused the corrective eye surgery MMU offered, so they ejected him from the Practicum.

Another man might have become bitter, but Downs had felt joy. He'd felt God's guiding hand steering him from his errant course and placing him where he could serve the Lord better. God had known that Downs would be needed now – at this time, on this podium – to complete his holy mission.

Like many Archangelists, Downs yearned for a return to Eden. As a child in Morningwater, Oklahoma, he'd seen the farming machines torturing the land day and night, plying it with foul chemicals so the unworthy multitudes could feed. Once harvested, the exhausted soil was ripped, furrowed, and re-seeded immediately. Downs swore that he heard it weep at night.

When he was twelve, he visited an Archangelist temple in Austin, Texas, and was enraptured by their promise that the Earth could be returned to a vestal state of Eden. He converted to Archangelism and soon found an ideological home among the Second Creationists, a group within the Church that wasn't just yearning for an Earthly Eden but working to make it reality. When he turned twenty-one, they named him an Elder of the Second Creation, and like many of his peers, God placed him in a position of power and influence.

He knew that God had put him here so he could steer Gabriel Cheyn at the dawn of the Second Creation. So he and his fellow Elders could cleanse the Earth of the weak, the impure, the heretics, and the Others. So the Earth could heal, and the Archangelists could multiply upon it as God intended.

Cheyn, the disciple of his demented god Clune, had his secular agenda and believed he was saving American democracy for future generations. However, Downs knew that it was the last secular agenda American politics would embrace. Ever since Clune's reign, the Church had been working to end the madness that a faithless America bred.

He smiled an invisible smile. *How will Gabriel Cheyn react,* he mused, *when he discovers that thirty of the thirty-seven Working Group members are Elders? That Marcus Grimes, his trusted counselor, is an Elder? That the RVE Initiative only happened because it fit the Elders' agenda?*

Perhaps Satan would tell Cheyn all about it, he thought. Satan enjoyed that sort of mischief.

THE PIECE THAT DOESN'T FIT

Day 17
Friday morning, September 4, 2043
3120 L Street NW, Washington, DC

Krista sat in a patio chair and examined her swollen toe, wondering if she'd broken it. She took a puff, let out a disgusted plume, and limped to the railing.

Hurricane Willa had blown away the fug, and she could see across the canal to the stone wall lining the towpath. Beyond it, a scraggly urban forest concealed the BoHo camp. By squinting, she found the gray triangles of their tents hidden under the gray-green shrubs.

She spotted a smudge of pink, which suddenly vanished and then burst through the undergrowth. Spring ran to the high stone wall and waved at the balcony far above, and Krista's gloom cloud lifted an inch or two as she waved back. She was eight or nine, and Krista was convinced she was related to the pastel artist at the farmer's market: The girl stuck to his side whenever Krista saw them together, as a child would stay with a parent, and she had his olive complexion, dark eyes, and beautiful dark curly hair that flowed to her shoulders.

The land the BoHos camped on belonged to the Park Service, but park rangers rarely ventured there as it was only accessible by foot. Tucked back as far as they were, the BoHo village was invisible to everyone except her. Nevertheless, the rangers swept through periodically with dog teams because the BoHos were trespassing on Federal land.

She knew many of the rangers, and they were mellow guys. Even more importantly, they always had potent coffee down at the Canal House, and she'd hang out with them on chilly winter days. She learned over coffee that the raiding orders came from Archangelists in the Interior Department.

The Arkies couldn't stand the BoHos. Not only were they Others, that group that the Church leadership had marginalized; they were also ex-employed, and unlike the rest of that benighted class, they refused to slink away and hide their destitution. In fact, the BoHos flaunted it every night at the Farmer's Market. For these transgressions, the Arkies labeled them Vessels of Incipient Evil.

The Arkies would label her the same if they ever saw her write. Left-handedness was also an Incipient Evil: The Profit Joseph himself had decreed so after he'd learned that the Latin word for 'left' was 'sinister.' The Arkie devout even trained their left-handed children to use only their right to avoid the stigma of being branded an Other. She grinned at her left hand, certain that the Incipient Evil was in her middle finger. It sometimes even spoke on its own.

The Arkies had strange core beliefs, but they'd started out strange. They covered up their origins, but she recalled some dirt on the founder that her Church sources had leaked: Mother Mary Ann Christ was actually Maryann Heilmann, who'd been a deep-discount street prostitute from East Texarkana until she'd found Jesus one glorious day.

According to the Archangelic legend, Jesus met the Virgin Mary Ann in a fallow field north of East Texarkana. He revealed that he'd chosen her to bear the Grandson of God, the Mortal Archangel who would re-create Eden – and the next day she discovered she was pregnant.

According to her sources, however, Mary Ann's conception wasn't quite immaculate – she'd simply lost her packet of contraceptive patches and continued to turn tricks, so it was unsurprising she'd conceived so fast. Nonetheless, she claimed the pregnancy was an Act of God.

In Mary Ann's defense, she didn't know much about reproductive biology. She suffered from profound learning disabilities and had dropped out of school in the seventh grade, at the age of fifteen, to explore opportunities in prostitution.

When the boy was born, she gave him a name she believed befitted the Grandson of God: The Profit Joseph. Krista knew that was the actual spelling on the birth certificate because she'd seen a stolen copy of it.

The Archangelists claimed that was how Jesus spelled 'Prophet', and anyone who said otherwise was a heretic. Eventually, they had the change added to the dictionaries, making it official. She was often tempted to write an exposé on the Arkies because their material was so rich – it was pure absurdist comedy, and she wouldn't even have to think before writing. All she'd have to do was report, and it would be hilarious.

But that was a story she wouldn't write. The religion was a fabrication and even had a false prophet, but they cared for their own. That was important in a lonely and disconnected world, and she refused to attack them for having a few quirks.

The Arkies were weird, but she was certain that they were harmless.

SHE WALKED OUT OF THE LOADING BAY and down Felony Lane to Wisconsin, this time in daylight. Proud of her boldness, she swung her tankard as she limped up to the coffee shop to meet Liza.

She stopped once to tag a stiffer in the alley – another homicide, with bloody tears like the one she'd found a few days before – but it didn't bother her because the day was nearly fugless. Real sunshine and shadow graced the city, and everything appeared three-dimensional for once.

Shopkeepers were removing the soot from their sidewalks, most of them pushing it into the gutter to avoid stirring it up. One woman was even hosing down the walk, which was illegal. The EPA had banned the practice years before when tests showed that the soot was carcinogenic. As defenders of the public health, they passed a regulation: They forbade washing the gunk down the storm drains so it wouldn't harm the fish.

Krista walked through a swirling cloud of disturbed soot, caught some in her throat, and barked a harsh cough. She berated herself for forgetting her face mask again and walked on.

After a few more steps, she emerged from the soot cloud and spotted Liza in front of Bad to the Bean, their favorite buzz hole. The coffee shop was crowded, but a few seats were still open. A blue haze filled the dark, tin-ceilinged room, almost as thick as the murmur of many low voices; the room was huge and held a hundred people or more, and every one came here to talk. She loved the *noir* feel of it, and the avant-garde funk was so thick that she wanted to wear a beret every time she came.

They swiped their paytabs across a baristomat machine on the counter and ordered their coffee – a small Mach Schell for Liza and a full tankard of Achtung for Krista – and then sat in comfy chairs by the window. Liza said, "Every time we meet, you've got a huge mug in your hand."

"I'm atoning." Krista siphoned the cooler coffee off the top of the tankard.

"For what?" Liza asked.

"For the mortal sin of being drowsy while the sun is up," said Krista, smiling. "Actually, I turn into a beast if I don't keep my caffeine level high. You sure don't want to see me like that."

Liza looked away and sighed. "I wish I didn't have to go back to school next week. I'd love to have a long break like when teachers had the entire summer off." She sucked hard on her Cannabliss toke, and her eyes brightened when the pharmaceutical-grade THC tickled her brainstem. "Ahh, that sends the pouties away. I wonder what it'd be like to have two whole months off. Wow, the things I could do!"

"You'd also be getting paid for two months less," Krista said, and Liza wrinkled her nose in disgust.

"So how's Ed?" Liza asked. "You two still seeing each other?"

Krista didn't want to talk about Ed Stanton and their weird relationship. She wasn't sure he loved her, but he loved everyone else, so he had to love her too – and that was as much sense as she could make of his feelings.

To make it worse, she didn't know if she loved him as much as his ability to thrive in this abnormal world, although she wasn't sure about that, either. The previous week at Bleaker's, he'd ordered an African meal that turned out to be breaded dung. She'd asked the server if it was a sick joke, and he'd snapped into high snotmode as only waiters and certain European monarchs can.

It's good that Ed stopped me from mashing the feckin plate into that waiter's pompous face and then telling off the chef. But did he actually have to eat the stuff just to get along? I want to get along too, but I was hoping for a more sanitary answer than eating whatever shit –

Liza snapped her fingers. "Krista? You in there?"

"Right, right, just reminiscing. We're on and off, here and there. He was promoted to nursing supervisor. Respiratory Care Unit, too."

"Fantastic! I hear they're hopping over there," Liza exclaimed.

"Now it's hard to see him, though. He's got this banjaxed schedule – sixty hours one week, then twenty hours the next but all on third shift," Krista said. "And you?"

Liza began a detailed account of her love life. Krista lost the thread of the chatter after a few minutes and her mind wandered again.

She pictured Ed, Liza, Krista, and Washington as if they were pieces of a three-dimensional puzzle. No matter how she tried to fit Krista into the puzzle, though, she needed to break off a piece of her personality to fit in. It didn't bother her – she knew something would need to give – but what piece would she sacrifice?

She felt an empty spot grow inside her, and grabbing the cup, she gulped coffee to fill it. Her fingernails began to itch, which was a bad sign when drinking Achtung. She gazed over Liza's shoulder at the throngs of people clogging the street.

Why fight fitting in? I'm not happy doing what I do. Writing just keeps me from feeling bad. One day I'll lose my edge and become a has-been, then I won't even have the snark, and then somebody will find my bones in my apartment after the stink gets too thick. Maybe I should just marry Ed, give up on the whole reality gig, live in his world of cotton-candy clouds and lollipop trees –

"So do you think I should?" Liza asked.

Damn! "You should do what you want," Krista answered, hoping that Liza hadn't just asked if she should slaughter her students. She added quickly, "How's things at school?"

Liza began talking about her work as if Krista wasn't there.

I've got to remember to take those ADHD drugs Dr. Abramovitz gave me. Why do I keep forgetting?

She scanned the room as Liza defiled some standardized testing requirement. *Am I the only one here with natural hair? I know that all these femmes wearing wigs are buzzed to stubble underneath. Everything's so fake here. It looks like a coffee shop at a Hollywood sound stage, but take the wigs off, and it'd look like the coffee shop at Auschwitz.* Krista shuddered. *Now that was a gruesome image. Where does that crap come from –*

"Krista?" Liza said.

Damn it! I was away with the fairies again! "Hmm?" she answered.

"Didn't you hear me? Do you want to go?" Liza asked.

"Oh, sorry. Where again?" She looked back at Liza and saw her wearing a vexed expression with her lips wrapped around her pink toke again. "I'm sorry, I just didn't catch that."

"The National Tranquility Center, next Tuesday. This is the last year the class can go. The Domestic Intelligence Command only gives tours to third grade and below, so I can't put it off till next year and I need a chaperone on the bus since Imelda will be in Baltimore. You weren't listening, were you?"

"Just woolgathering, Liza," Krista said. "The coffee hasn't kicked in yet. See, that's why I drink so much of it. I'd go catatonic without it, that I would."

"Well? Want to go? I'd appreciate it and I think you'd love it!" Liza chirped.

"Sure, sure, I'd love to see what the National Security Forces are up to these days. You know how curious I am about anything related to Clune." She leaned toward Liza and said in a hushed voice, "And I could use a little DIC!"

"Well, I know a guy, he's clean –"

Krista's face soured. "It was a joke, Liza! You know, Domestic Intelligence Command – D-I-C?"

Liza sucked on her toke, her eyebrows furrowed, and then said, "Well, now that you explain it, it's really very funny."

THE BLIGHT AT THE END OF THE TUNNEL

Day 18
Saturday afternoon, September 5, 2043
Clarkston, West Virginia

"Betcha got money. Y'all look like ya got some. Got more'n ya need."

Victoria backed down the street, a row of empty swaybacked houses to one side and parked cars to the other. "I don't feel threatened by your behavior," she said to the approaching man.

"Don't fuckin care, lady," he said.

"You should," she said. She handed the briefcase and the hanger holding her clean suit to Ada. "Honey, I need you to get out of the way, okay?"

"Mom?" Ada backed up as well.

"Just do what I say, please?" She eyed the emaciated, ponytailed man and the black iron pipe in his right hand. He was tapping it on the slate sidewalk as if she might overlook such an obvious weapon. It was insulting.

"Sure look like a lady, an all the ladies got money. I need money. Yer gonna gimme some, right?"

"Sure, why not? I have tons of cash. C'mon over here. I'll give you all you want."

"I want a lot."

"Well, just you c'mon over, then."

"Oh, I'll be comin, lady, count on that." He laughed wickedly and tapped the pipe hard against an iron railing, making a dull clang and releasing a shower of rust.

Victoria needed him to come two steps closer, but more importantly, she needed him to start his strike with the pipe. It was in his right hand, so the first thing he'd do was to shift his weight to his left foot. Once he committed to the move, she'd hook that knee, deliver a quick palm strike to the bridge of his nose, and he'd be flat on his back in two seconds. She wasn't sure if she'd break his neck once he was down or just hurt him, but she still had plenty of time to decide.

"Gonna like this, an I think you will too. We gonna have a big little party."

"I know I'm going to like it."

He moved a step closer, and she decided to stun him and run. She didn't want Ada to witness her killing a man; their relationship was under enough stress already.

He stepped closer and shifted his weight to his left foot, and she also shifted to her left and prepared for the quick turn and the palm strike, and then she –

A police horn squawked and a door slammed. "Gudammit, Johnson, din't we just talk about this? Y'all got an attention problem or somethin, dumfuck?" A potbellied police officer wearing sergeant's stripes walked between the parked cars from the street. "When they made you, they just poured a ton a stupid into that mold, din't they?"

"We was just talkin, Jimmy."

"With a pipe in yer hands? The fuck?" He placed his hand on Johnson's chest and shoved him to the ground. "I oughta tase ya and see if that'll set that little brain a-tickin agin. This keeps happenin, an I don't think yer gettin the message."

"Jimmy, Jimmy..." Johnson held up his hands and cringed.

"Aww, shit, I'll just tase ya anyway. I'm outta ideas." Before he finished the sentence, Johnson was on his feet and running. The sergeant yelled, "This happens agin an you'll be wipin asses out at the asylum the resta yer life!"

"Thanks for intervening, Sergeant," said Victoria.

He turned around. "Y'all still here? Doncha have the common sense to run?"

"I'm sorry."

"Don't be sorry, just stay off the damn street. You fugees drive the dumfucks crazy, an it just makes 'em get their stupid on. Shit, rollin one a you's like winnin the damn lottery, so do me a favor an get off the street or just get the hell outta my town, okay?" He waddled back to his car. "I got too much to do already. Don't need no fugee shit too."

VICTORIA HAD PARKED EIGHT BLOCKS AWAY, and getting off the streets wasn't quick or easy. She'd wanted to make the walk to the dry cleaner as long as possible because they'd been going stir-crazy in the hotel.

Walking through downtown Clarkston was like watching a video clip from olden times – the windows, the cars, the people, and their clothes were all a shade of gray or black. What little color she did see was desperate and drained.

Almost like me, she thought, wondering how she and West Virginia had ended up in such despair. She had happy memories of growing up in Monongah, which was less than an hour away.

Never once in her sixteen years there had she felt threatened. The townsfolk had been her only family; after her mother's death in childbirth, they took the responsibility of raising her. Coarse but kind, rough but wise, they knew that all the place could offer was serenity and security, and violence was unknown inside the village borders. Had somebody like Johnson walked down Monongah's Traction Avenue with a weapon, a dozen men would have been watching him through their gun sights.

Victoria smiled, recalling those she'd known and loved there. And they'd loved her in return: Monongah saw that gifted Victoria wouldn't stay among them forever, and like good friends, they didn't try to hold her back.

After Johns Hopkins Medical School accepted her application, they bought her a car. Every fender was a different color, and it burned more oil than gas, but they set her free to find a better future. The state chipped in too, giving her money to cover college costs the Navy wouldn't.

Then she arrived at Johns Hopkins, and her optimism evaporated: The elites instantly shunned the scrawny, chain-smoking Navy girl with the funny accent. Before long, some were even calling her Hicktoria Twang to her face.

She reined in her rage, although it required all her restraint. Instead, she bade her imperfect childhood farewell and set out to perfect her adulthood, and it worked – by her senior year, she'd dropped every troublesome West Virginia mannerism and placed second in her class behind the prodigy Mae Esteban. And half of Monongah bused to Baltimore to see her graduate.

Clarkston felt like an alien world in comparison. It didn't belong on the same planet as Monongah, and these gray people couldn't be the same species as the proud Mountaineers who'd raised her.

As they walked back to the car, she looked at the small stores lining the main street. Most had chalkboards nailed by their doors listing what the proprietors were willing to take in trade. Sometimes the barterboards listed odd items – 'Girls Dress, Size 4 Pink' was scrawled on one – but the first item on the list was usually 'Coal'. People on the street carried nylon mesh bags filled with the black rock, which meant they were shopping.

Strange contraptions chugged down the street. They appeared to be pickup trucks with large barrels and a confusion of pipes filling the rear bed; Ada, who was more mechanically inclined, guessed they used coal-powered steam engines because each of the pickups had two stacks, one belching black smoke and the other puffs of white steam.

Drivers behind the steamers didn't seem to mind getting sprayed with hot ash and enveloped in foul smoke, but then everyone here was indifferent to the world around them. The people of Clarkston looked worn out and resentful, but she didn't believe they'd be so apathetic that they wouldn't stop violence. While Johnson was menacing her and Ada, the passersby had merely detoured into the street to pass the altercation.

"That guy was proof zombies exist," Ada said. "You should've given that stupervo a shovel upside the head."

"I don't need tools, honey," Victoria said.

"But how'd he figure out we're refugees? We've gone profundo incognito, cheap Mal-Mart duds and everything like everyone else. I mean, I'm even wearing freakin polyester, which is already coming apart. What's this stuff made of, Chinesium? Jeez, how much lower do I have to go?"

"The briefcase is a giveaway. They can also tell because our hair and skin have been cared for. Most folks here don't know that hair stylists and dermatologists even exist. Their idea of hair styling is Mom running a clipper over their heads on the back porch. Skin care is washing your face with soap."

"You know a lot about this place for somebody who grew up in Baltimore."

Victoria looked away. "I know a guy from here. He told me."

"Okay. So should I rub coal dust in my hair or something to fit in?"

"Try not to be a snob. They're doing what they can with extraordinarily little. That doesn't make them inferior."

"I'm not being a snob. I just don't want any more attention."

"We'll just leave so we don't have to try to blend in." Victoria watched a passing family trudge by. "It's impossible."

"Oh, yeah? Watch." Ada's mouth went slack, and her eyes became lifeless and dull. "Unghh..."

"What are you doing?"

"It's my zombie face. Gimme a minute and I might even be able to drool."

"Stop it. Your face might get stuck that way."

"But I look like a local, don't I?"

"Too much. You're scaring me now. Please stop."

They passed a bakery they'd visited the previous day, and Ada grabbed Victoria's arm. "Hey, can we get some more of those butter cookies?"

"Ada, I don't want you to fill up with that garbage. It's just pure fat and sugar, for God's sake."

ADA STUFFED ANOTHER GREASY GOLDEN COOKIE into her mouth. "How can you eat so much junk food?" Victoria asked.

"This is *pure* junk food. You said it yourself, it's made from pure fat and sugar."

"Sure. Pure garbage is what it is. That kind of diet will just leach the minerals from your bones and make you fat as a cow. It'll kill you."

"I could live on it, really I could," protested Ada.

"Diabetes by the time you're sixteen, acne untreatable by modern medicine, nutritional deficiencies of every order, stunted skeletal development. What kind of life is that?"

"A divine one." She tripped over an upturned sidewalk stone and bobbled the box, trying not to spill the precious treats.

They reached the parking lot, and the Hugo was still there, as Victoria expected. The car had been a true junker to start with, and her trip down the hill at the power plant had only pounded more character into its already beaten face: The bumper hung at an angle, the radiator grille was twisted, and one of the headlights was shattered. Her college jalopy had looked better on the day she'd sent it to the junkyard.

She reached under the passenger seat and removed the pistol. "If we ever walk these streets again, I'm bringing this," Victoria said.

"Lemme see that."

"Oh, no. It's a dangerous weapon, honey."

Ada looked up at the ceiling and rolled her eyes. "If you're so freakin concerned about my safety, why'd you –"

"We agreed that we'd never talk about that, didn't we?"

"What*ever.*" Ada zipped her fingers across her lips. "Okay, so will you ever tell me how you ended up with that big black gun, like out of nowhere?"

Victoria shook her head and laid the pistol on her lap. Turning the key, she cranked the starter until the engine sputtered to life, which it might not do much longer. It coughed a cloud of blue smoke every time she started it now.

"And will you ever tell me why we're driving this piece of sh…crap? Will you ever tell me anything about what's going on?"

"Of course I will," Victoria said. "Just not right now."

"Right. You'll wait till I'm all grown up, when I'm like forty and my boobs are hanging down to my knees." Ada scowled through the side window, and Victoria slammed the car into gear with more force than she intended, causing the little car to buck as she backed out of the space. Ada shot her a sidelong glance and saw that she'd angered her again. "Okay, I'm sorry. That was really rude, I know."

"Mmm."

They drove out of town in uncomfortable silence, up to the hills surrounding Clarkston and past the glowing slagheaps of the coal mines. The acrid, dusty smell of smoldering high-sulfur coal permeated the air inside the car even though the windows were closed.

The heaps glowed a sinister blue at night; during the day, they looked like mountains of gravel, scattered across the land like the playthings of long-vanished giant toddlers. At night, they transformed into ghostly pyres, the pressure from tons of slag igniting the coal at the bottom. They flickered in the distance and spun green and yellow auroras throughout the fug.

Such a mountain loomed across the road from their hotel, a stately Victorian mansion from gentler times. A cluster of small children, some as young as six or seven, was scaling the heap and dragging nylon net bags behind them. Burnable coal was buried in the slagheaps, and although it was dangerous, collecting it was something young children could do for a struggling family. Coal lying on the heap was money waiting for harvest.

VICTORIA DECIDED NOT TO TEMPT THE LOCALS and stayed at the hotel for dinner. They dined with the proprietor, a polite and proper white-haired woman who blithely double-charged them because they were refugees.

After dinner, they strolled along the deep lemonade porch and found painted wicker chairs facing the supernaturally flaring slagheap across the road. Soft, flickering blue light lit the porch's beadboard and fretwork. The lightshow was hypnotic, and they sat and watched it for some time.

Victoria wished she had her tablet so she could plan the trip ahead, but both hers and Ada's had been stolen from the hotel room on the first day. They should have been safe because even the lowest idiot knew that Advanced Heuristics tablets wouldn't work without an authorized user's palmprint.

She didn't care about losing the devices as much as losing the original copies of her test results. Now the only evidence she had was secreted in her briefcase. All her carefully constructed layers of redundancy had been stripped, and with them went her credibility – and their safety.

"Mom, when can we get outta here?"

"Soon, honey."

"Can you tell me what's going on now? I know you don't wanna talk about it and all, but I'm starting to freak. This whole thing is so off-planet. That guy, this place, St. Elizabeth's…I mean, this is like t-minus-creepy and counting."

"Hunh?"

"This is getting weird."

"Oh, well, that's an understatement. It *is* like a different planet here." Victoria stood and walked to the railing; she poked at the delicate fretwork near the porch roof and discovered that it was held together only by paint. "I want you to understand that this is difficult for me." She leaned against the railing and turned to Ada. "You deserve to know what's going on, but I have a duty as your mother as well."

"If you tell me I'm not old enough again, Mom, I'll scream."

"Then please don't scream, but that's exactly the problem."

"Mom…"

Victoria held up her hand. "Adulthood will come soon enough. I just want you to enjoy your childhood while you still can."

"That rocket blasted off the pad years ago. All I've got left are the scorch marks."

"But that was in the past. We're here now, and it doesn't matter. You'll be sixteen soon, and that's a magical age full of dreams, honey. Is it so much to ask –"

"You were in med school when you were sixteen! Who are you to preach?"

"And I regret it," Victoria said. "I was ready intellectually, but I wasn't emotionally. I didn't adapt well."

"Holy sh…holy crap! Are you admitting you made a mistake?"

"Yes. I made a mistake. As you did five years ago. And like I moved beyond my errors, you can move beyond yours."

Ada fidgeted in her seat. "Stop pretending, Mom. I can only dream of having dreams now."

"I did my best in Wyoming!"

"You wrecked everything in Bumfuck Wyoming! Give it up already!"

"I refuse to give up, honey. We've faced some challenges, but I believe you can still have a childhood and mature into a whole and happy adult."

Ada snorted, reaching into her bookbag for a pack of cigarettes.

"I wish you wouldn't do that."

"There's a lot of things I wish for too."

"You really should quit. It's not that hard."

"Coming from a lifelong non-smoker, that's weird advice. I'll give it all the consideration it deserves." She lit a cigarette and blew a long plume in her mother's direction.

Victoria wrinkled her nose and turned away. "You're under a lot of stress, so I won't make an issue of this, but don't think it'll always be this way." She crossed her arms and studied the flaking paint on the wall, and they remained in a tense and uncomfortable silence until Ada stubbed out her cigarette.

"Okay. Now tell me the truth," Ada said. "You owe me that much."

Victoria drew a long breath and sat in the chair beside her. "I can't tell you everything, okay? Please respect that."

"You'll only tell me what you want anyway, so go ahead." She gazed at the flickering lights. "You're in control. You'll make sure I never win."

Victoria bit her lip and glared at the slag mountain. After a minute, her irritation faded enough that she could speak calmly. "I found out something bad was happening, and I thought I could stop it. I asked a person I trusted for help, but he betrayed me. I was naïve, but...well, I've never been good at reading people." She drew a slow breath and then looked directly at Ada. "I admit it. I made a mistake, and it was the worst mistake ever. I have evidence proving they were doing something bad, and they tried to stop me from revealing it at St. Elizabeth's. And they'll keep trying. Now my number one priority is to get us out of this trap, and number two is to give my evidence to somebody who won't drop it in the round file. That's all I can tell you now, honey."

"Like I couldn't figure most of that out on my own. So where are we going? Can you tell me that?"

"Sacramento. In California, out west."

"I know where it is, I mean, jeez." She turned away from the flickering lights and looked into her mother's eyes. "So you screwed the pooch, and we're never going home again, right? Nothing will ever be the same. It's all gone. You're taking me to California, and we'll never go back."

Victoria shook her head. "Things have changed forever. I'm so sorry this happened."

"And who is this *they* you keep talking about?" Ada asked.

"Bad people, honey. Powerful people. We'll need to avoid them, that's all, and we can do that."

"Bad people. What am I, like four or something?"

Victoria knew better than to respond and tapped her foot instead.

"Why are these *bad people* trying to kill you?"

"I didn't say they were trying to kill me, honey."

Ada jumped to her feet. "We left Washington at like a hundred miles an hour! You're running from them and you never run from a fight! That means you know they'll kill you if they get you! And me too! What you're saying sounds like the police and everybody else is after you and they'll put out a dragnet and find you unless we're invisible or something! And the shit's really –"

"Language!"

"Oh, shut it! The shit's really hit the fan if the only safe place we can go is California cuz that means the Federals are on your ass. Because freakin California is like another country now. Christ, what's in that briefcase? Plans for a megabomb?"

"I won't tell you." She stood and crossed her arms. "At least I can shelter you from that."

"Whatever it is, it's major shit, and the way we left Washington was like you had death all over you. If it was anything less, you'd just go back and fight. What did you do to get everybody so pissed...everything's gone, nothing's gonna be normal again...they could catch you, Mom, and I could be an orphan, and what do I do if you don't protect me...the Blues will take me away, or maybe even the Reds, and *that's* the end of the world, I'm so fucked..." She grabbed her pack and pulled a cigarette out with shaking fingers. "I knew it. I knew it..."

"Okay, okay, have a seat and calm down. Don't get upset."

"Calm down? What?"

"Shhh. Don't get upset. This is not the time."

"Yeah, it is! It really is!" She grabbed her lighter, and it fell from her trembling hand. "Oh, no, here it comes."

"A panic attack?"

Ada nodded, lit her cigarette, and exhaled a shaky cloud.

"I wish I had a benzodiazepine patch to interrupt this, but I left them in my medikit –"

"I don't need a zombie patch!"

"Okay, then we'll have to manage this together," Victoria said. "You have to stop feeding the panic, so first I want you to take a deep breath." Ada took a cheek-hollowing puff and inhaled down to her navel. "That's not what I meant!"

"I know, but it takes the edge off."

"It's just going to make it worse, and you...forget it. Listen to me – you need to face down this panic by using your head and not your heart. Our situation is serious, but we'll handle it. Use your head and you'll see that this isn't so difficult to overcome. Use your heart and the panic will get worse, trust me. Will you give that a try?"

Ada nodded silently and sat, and then she drew her knees up to her chin and wrapped her arms around them. "It's easing up already. I can feel it going."

"Good. This was a short one." Victoria wrapped an arm around her shoulder. "I wish I could make you see that I'm not an icicle, honey. I love you, and I only want the best for you. When we get to California, we can vent all you want, but until then, we need to keep cool and execute the plan. We won't have time for panic attacks. Deal?"

Ada gave a small nod. "Aye-aye, Commander." She turned away to watch the flickering blue light.

SCRAPING THE ICEBERG

Day 20
Monday morning, September 7, 2043
3120 L Street NW, Washington, DC

Early that morning, Krista leaned on the railing and looked across the canal. She breathed deep and caught a slight, sweet whiff of a linden tree.

Bright pink flashed through the trees, and then she saw Spring on the wall carrying a small bag. Within seconds, pigeons swarmed as she cast something about her feet; Krista couldn't tell if it was bread or seed, but the birds tucked into it even though Spring knelt to pet them. Everything was new and wonderful and innocent to her, and Krista wished the child's optimism were as infectious as that Neovirus.

When the bag was empty, the girl walked back under the canopy of trees. Krista sighed and trudged back to her studio.

AN HOUR LATER, blocked and frustrated again, she grabbed her tablet and brought up *Madame Ovary* on her sound system. She adored everything by the musician Keriana, and this was her favorite album, a twenty-eight-track magnum opus. The music soothed her and sometimes even cured her writer's block.

She walked around her living room, coffee cup in hand, as the music flowed. Closing her eyes, she lost herself in the harmonies as complex themes evolved with each passing track. She moved with the slow beat; she relaxed her neck and tilted her head back, and her long hair fell loose and swayed to the beat in counterpoint to her hips.

The vocals began on the third track, and she sang with Keriana, matching the pitch and tone perfectly. She sang along with the same passion, love, and yearning; she lamented and celebrated, loved and lost.

Madame Ovary was the eighth track on the album. By the time it started, Krista was a little girl again, lost and content in a world of sound. Her cares long gone, she undulated to the beat and sang her heart out.

After the last track faded out, Krista skipped around the channels and tried to find dance music. She found some lively Japanese Babydoll Pop and danced around the living room in her underwear until she could take no more.

Winded and sweaty, she flopped into her study chair and checked her mail. Nothing there engaged her except that her source from Treasury had written again: The Treasury Department hadn't scheduled debt auctions for the next three months, and he figured they didn't want to throw a party and have nobody show up. That currency crisis was getting closer to reality.

However, reporting that would earn her another fine, so she checked the newsfeeds and came across a disturbing interview on NewsHub's Science Channel about the Neovirus. The bug seemed especially nasty.

She'd never understood science, so everything the scientist said sounded like gibberish. He was a virologist from Johns Hopkins named Dr. Emil Horseshit, or something like that, who spoke the semi-English scientific lingo that always frustrated her in high school. However, he had to be smart; his forehead was so high that it looked like a drive-in theater screen. The interviewer struggled with the man to get him to speak in plain English, but still, the doctor's tone and body language showed he was alarmed more than his words.

The CDC couldn't confine it to the New York City metro area, and they'd shut down every activity and business inside a circle seventy-five miles from Times Square, which they called the Containment Ring. Since people could spread the virus without showing symptoms, the local health departments had ordered everybody to remain indoors. But in New York, they were doing the opposite.

The interviewer showed video clips of crowded festivals in the city parks, but she understood why they were partying. Even though she'd lived in New York only until she was eleven, she'd already absorbed the city mindset: I'm tough, and if you challenge me, I'll get even tougher. In such a hard place, that attitude sometimes made the difference between life and death. Spitting in the face of the virus made sense, at least to her.

However, Dr. Horseshit and the interviewer didn't understand it. They watched the videos in disbelief, and it *was* a foolish thing to do because Neovirus was hammering the city even harder than the coronavirus had in '20. Tens of thousands of cases had been confirmed, and probably ten times more were unconfirmed.

The young and the elderly were taking the brunt of the disease. Their immune systems couldn't fight the bug to a stalemate, and after the virus weakened them, it reproduced explosively in their intestines. Then the victims' insides liquefied into viral jelly, and they bled from their eyes, ears, nose, and mouth.

A tingle of panic sizzled through her and she sat bolt upright – the stiffers she'd found on Felony Lane had bled from the eyes. The virus was already in Washington. Worse, it was on her street.

KRISTA WALKED TO THE SMALL GROCERY STORE by the farmers' market to stock up before the panic hoarding started, but it was already picked over. There wasn't a shred of toilet paper or drop of milk in the entire store. She found two bags of pinto beans in the ethnic aisle, though, and she snatched them and checked out before anybody noticed.

On the way back, she glanced at the wall of an old warehouse a few hundred feet from her building. In the center of the wall's graffiti, she saw the letters "GX" scrawled in blue chalk. Trope had left a package for her on the SatNet.

She stopped walking and recalled his complicated chart of letters and colors. After a minute, she concluded that it was the correct code for a Monday and rubbed it off with her palm. It would be an entertaining night; Trope was always good for some scandal, and his cloak-and-dagger antics were a hoot.

In her apartment, she downloaded the file he'd left on his secure site and sat back in her chair as it decrypted. It took a while because she always downloaded certified originals of her research. It reinforced her credibility that she could prove her accusations in court.

Trope was one of her favorite sources but her most inconsistent one: Sometimes she wouldn't hear from him for months, and sometimes he contacted her once a week. She'd derived a few of her juiciest revelations from his work because people said the most shocking things in open spaces – and Trope was often watching and listening.

He was some sort of ex-spook who detested politicians, and he was superb at covert data tapping in public spaces, but she knew nothing about him besides that. She imagined that he was an extreme paranoiac too, as he insisted on ridiculous communication security.

The download was a twenty-three-minute video file with no text description. He never explained the point of his work, although it usually wasn't too hard to grasp, especially the time he'd filmed Representative Rosen energetically fellating an orangutan. Strangely, she'd never been sued for invading her privacy even though she'd been outrageously guilty.

The monitor chirped once the file decrypted, and she settled deep into her chair and started the playback. The contents were video clips date-stamped 2 February 43. Trope used excellent equipment, and from the video quality, he'd set up this shot in advance. It wasn't candid street pickup as he sometimes did. This was studio quality snoop.

The setting was Hains Point in East Potomac Park. National Airport was visible beyond the river levees, so Trope had been shooting from an elevated position across the Anacostia River. The image quality was astonishing: Even though he'd positioned his cameras miles away, the video showed minute details.

He focused the camera on two men in the distance and zoomed in. They were strolling the levee bike path and talking, but she couldn't make out their words. At the tip of Hains Point, they turned toward the camera, and she saw the faces of Vice President Gabriel Cheyn and his chief of staff, Marcus Grimes.

Krista knew Cheyn well; she'd taken two graduate history symposia he'd chaired at the University of Pennsylvania, where he'd been a professor. He was now sixty-three but still fit and handsome, and he still had the earnest demeanor that had won him so many hearts and minds. He was also an intellectual authority on many subjects, and most people accepted his opinions as fact, which was why the brainless Senator William Gibbon had chosen him as his running mate – Gibbon had been smart enough to know he wouldn't win the presidency without balancing the ticket's IQ. However, Cheyn needed him even more because Senator Gibbon neutralized the stink of John Wilson Clune that clung to Cheyn.

Gibbon had been one of the few senators who'd opposed Clune's jackboot tactics. He wasn't a fearsome opponent; he'd merely suggested that Clune shouldn't kill every peasant so someone would remain to wash the floors. Still, at a time when most senators were curled up under their desks hiding from Federal goons, Gibbon's mild opposition stood out as jut-jawed patriotism. That helped Americans forget that Cheyn had been Clune's National Security Advisor and had pushed for creating the National Security Forces after the first Detroit riots.

Since intellectual tasks bored Gibbon, Cheyn ran the Executive Branch, although he denied it. Krista once asked in a post if it was a coincidence that Gibbon rarely talked without Cheyn standing behind him, and she challenged the vice president to drink a glass of water the next time the president gave a speech. To date, he hadn't.

She watched the playback on her wall monitor. The tone of the conversation was clear from Cheyn's body language: He was lecturing, standing erect with his head high, and Grimes was the student receiving wisdom, with his hands clasped behind his back and his head bowed. Cheyn's face was grave, signifying a sober discussion.

A plane took off in the background and filled the audio with a ripping sound, but it faded after about thirty seconds. Trope focused the mike on Cheyn, and she could hear his words. "...clear lesson at this point, Marcus, that the Four Horsemen are humanity's greatest ally."

"Whoa, I've heard this before!" She paused the playback and unfolded her tablet. After scrolling through voice notes for ten minutes, she found the folder for a history lecture Dr. Cheyn had given. His voice came through the tablet's speakers: "War, Famine, Pestilence, and Death have all served to reduce the population to a level sustainable by the environment. Throughout recorded history, advances and innovations in art, science, and culture have followed a significant – if involuntary – reduction in the population. The Renaissance was a direct product of the Black Death, and were it not for the reallocation of resources among the few survivors, the sixteenth century would have been another period of Dark Ages squalor and despair. History gives us a clear lesson: The Four Horsemen of the Apocalypse have always been humanity's greatest ally."

"Why are you giving this old lecture to Grimes, boyo? Do you like hearing your own golden voice so much?" She picked up a pencil from the desk and tapped it against her teeth as she restarted the video.

No matter how intently she listened, though, only fragments of the conversation came through the noise after that. They talked about high unemployment, industrial realignment, diseases, advances in medicine, and reallocation of resources, but she couldn't decipher the primary topic of the discussion. It seemed like two old men deep in aimless conversation.

Near the end of the video, Cheyn stood and gazed to the east, his eyes heavy with sorrow, and she heard his next words clearly. "Like all losers of resource wars, Marcus, we will..." A yacht motored by, filling the audio with its engine growl. "...is not about who wins but who remains." He then sat on a bench facing away from the camera, and the video ended two minutes later.

She sat back in her chair and stared at the blank screen: Trope obviously thought this was important, but she couldn't understand why. "Thanks a lot, Trope," she said as she rubbed the bridge of her nose. "I just love solving your damned puzzles. I sure as hell do."

TRAPSPRING

Day 20
Monday evening, September 7, 2043
Eight miles west of Cadiz, Ohio

Victoria pushed the Hugo as hard as she could, but the little car refused to move any faster than forty-five miles an hour. Now that they were back in Federal territory, she needed to get off the highway and travel back roads. This part of Ohio looked abandoned – nothing but trees, the occasional decrepit shack, and empty pavement – and prying eyes wouldn't be able to see her as easily.

Once she put a few more miles between her and the border, they'd disappear.

"Acquisition! We have the d'Abruzzo vehicle. Exiting Weirton, West Virginia, moving west on Route 22 from Steubenville, Ohio. Keyhole out of range until 2055 hours and the Blackeye is fugged out, drones grounded due to weather," said Buta.

"A day earlier than I expected. Special Activity Groups rolling, Hogue?"

"I have Group Four moving, sir. They're positioned across from the Wheeling exit. I'll give an ETA when they have one. I approximate twenty minutes." Hogue thought a moment. "Sir, I recommend we move a backup into place."

Downs recalled the debacle at St. Elizabeth's. "I concur. Do it."

"Keyhole window is open in nine minutes, sir."

"Put it up when it is, Buta," said Downs.

ADA CLUTCHED HER STOMACH. "I need to go, mom."

"You went at the restaurant, didn't you?" Victoria asked.

"I did, but I need to go again. It was that sauerkraut."

"You should have ordered something without sauerkraut," said Victoria.

"Everything had sauerkraut on it! They put sauerkraut on their sauerkraut!" she said. "The ice cream had sauerkraut in it!"

"It did not."

Ada scowled and looked through the dirty car window. "I will never eat Pennsylvania Dutch food again in my life. Not ever."

"We're way out in the sticks here, honey. I don't think we can find a place for you to go. We could get off the road and try to find a restaurant, but I wouldn't count on that. Besides, it's best to stay anonymous. How long can you hold it?"

"It's like a five-megaton Code Brown."

"I guess that means you can't hold it long?"

Ada's intestines rumbled, and she clutched her stomach again.

"Well, keep an eye open for a rest area. But if we can stop, it has to be quick. We need to make time right now, okay?"

"I'll keep both eyes open!" Ada spotted a blue rest area sign a few minutes later. "There! It's just ahead!"

"Okay. Relax, we'll be there in a minute."

"One minute and forty-one seconds at this speed, but we can be there in a minute-ten if you'll go the freakin speed limit. It's the pedal on the right, Mom."

"I'm flooring it already! And you of all people shouldn't be lecturing me about my driving, young lady!"

Two minutes later, Victoria steered the wheezing Hugo onto the ramp, and then she coasted to a yellow brick building tucked into the trees between two parking lots. The entrance door was set into a greasy glass wall connecting two octagonal buildings, their walls adorned with colorful graffiti. Although theirs was the only vehicle in the parking lot, Victoria sensed that they were too exposed, with no place to hide and no way to spot an approaching enemy. However, Ada wasn't concerned. She leaped from the car and ran for the door.

"Wait! There might be someone in there!" Victoria called, but she was inside the lobby already, her bookbag thumping against her back as she ran past vending machines on the way to the restroom. Victoria climbed out and slipped on her suit jacket.

She pulled her briefcase from the backseat and walked across the cracked concrete into the lobby. The place was hard and built to endure human indifference, of which it had seen plenty – the tops of the vending machines were caked with greasy dust, the red floor tiles were cracked and stained, and the concrete block walls wore a painted patchwork of beiges where a worker had tried to cover up graffiti.

A sour, cheesy stink swarmed her, which was more than a smell in the air – it *was* the air. She pinched her nose and walked to the highway map, happy that she'd only have to endure the smell for a few minutes.

It showed that they were uncomfortably close to West Virginia, but at least they had the cover of night. The vending machines were stocked, which she hadn't expected in an unused rest stop in the middle of nowhere. She was rummaging in a pocket for change when Ada called from the women's room.

She pushed the door open and found a dingy, yellow-tiled room with five toilet stalls, two of which had doors. A single flickering fluorescent light lit the space, it hadn't seen a cleaning in months, and it stank like sewer gas.

"Whuzzup?" she asked in a cartoon voice, refusing to let go of her nose.

"There's no toilet paper in here. Is there anything out there?"

"No. There's just a hand dryer. Hold on, I'll check the men's room and see if they have any." She started to walk out but then felt the weight of the briefcase; the vaccine and the bioreactor plans it held made it too heavy to carry around for no good reason. She set it on the floor by Ada's stall and left for the men's room.

"Group Four is on-site, sir," Hogue said.

"Keyhole window is open, sir," Buta said. "We have the vehicle location."

Downs scrutinized the thermal images. "Where is she? In the car? In the building?"

"The car isn't running, sir. She's probably inside."

"Search the car and see if the materials are in it." Downs watched the spectral orange shapes of his men approach the car and disappear into it.

"Beginning search. So far, a box of cookies and a sidearm, nine millimeter, sir. Our issue. Possibly the same weapon Lang used to wound Nine Alpha," said Hogue. "Half the clip has been expended."

"Hmm. Can you get a visual confirmation of her location?"

Hogue talked to the group leader. "She's in the lobby, sir. She's entering the women's room and doesn't appear to be aware of our presence. No visible materials or containers on her person. Also, the car is empty. No vials or tubes or packages of documents."

"We need to recover those materials," Downs said, pacing. "She must have hidden them somewhere already, and we can't close this file until we find them. Instruct the Group to take her into custody. No firearms, hand weapons only. Injuries are acceptable, but she needs to be capable of withstanding cognitive modeling, so no head injuries. Repeat, no head injuries."

"Yes, sir."

"It'll be problematic to take her in an enclosed area. Tell them to find concealed positions outside on both sides of the entrances. Take her when she's at least ten feet clear." He watched the orange blotches of SAG Four moving along the side of the building. "Tell them to knock this target down fast. Take zero chances. Fast and dirty is the best strategy."

"The men's room doesn't have any either, honey," Victoria said. "I don't think anyone's been here for a while."

"What can I do?" Ada groaned. "I can't duck-walk out of here!"

"You may have to." Victoria turned the handle for the hot water, and brown liquid spurted into the cracked ceramic sink. It was cold. She tried the cold water with the same result. "Unless you want to wash up in cold water."

"I wish we hadn't thrown away those Mal-Mart duds. They were practically toilet paper anyway."

"True. Watch my briefcase, and I'll go out to the car and check if Lusa left any tissues or towels in the trunk. I'll be right back."

ON THE SATELLITE THERMAL IMAGES, the small orange spot of Victoria Lang appeared at the entrance. As it moved away from the building, two orange forms beside the entrance and two behind the car converged on her. The two forms at the building's other entrance ran around it.

She jumped to one side and the men followed. Two of them grabbed her, but she wriggled free. More men arrived and then, one by one, they fell to the ground and lay still. Downs watched in horror – less than a minute had elapsed, and half the team was disabled. "Hogue, the target is right in front of them! Tell them to take it down!"

"They're trying, sir."

"Not hard enough! What's their problem?"

Hogue pressed the headphones to her ears. "Too many voices, they're all yelling at once. Lots of confusion…can't pick it out…"

VICTORIA GRASPED THE LAST SYRINGE of paralytic in her fist and turned to keep each man in sight. They'd encircled her, which was a bad tactical move since it let her choose her targets. Because they were armed with only knives and nightsticks, she planned a quick combination of hand and weapon strikes.

Where are their pistols, though? she thought. *Why are they engaging in hand-to-hand with me? Are they that stupid?* However, she was grateful for their cluelessness. It had given her a chance to react to the surprise assault.

One man jabbed at her with his knife, and she resisted knocking it from his hand. Flaunting her superior skills only weakened her tactical advantages, although they should have realized she had hand-to-hand experience after she killed three of their teammates in less than a minute. Nevertheless, they were still intent on swarming her as if their size was the ultimate advantage.

She selected her targets – the bigger one, whom she'd named Draw, would get the syringe, and she swiveled around to make sure he was in the correct spot behind her. The two mouth-breathers in front were the ideal dupes for her feint. The one on the left, Feint One, would get Draw's knife in the abdomen. The one on the right, Feint Two, would get her personal attention after.

Victoria took a deep breath and centered her mind. When the mouth-breathers moved between her and the car, she glanced at it. Feint One grinned, unable to conceal his glee at deciphering her plan, and she tried to appear desperate. Suddenly, she bolted toward the car – and then stopped and crouched after one step. As she expected, Draw had run after her, and he stumbled over her body and hit the ground hard. Victoria jabbed the syringe into his shoulder blade with one hand and snatched his knife away with the other.

With a cross-body throw, she flung it at Feint One's abdomen, but the knife pierced his eye socket instead. Using his screams as a distraction, she jumped on her hands, cartwheeled over Draw, and kicked Feint Two in the face. She rolled into a fighting stance and wheeled to deliver a hand strike to his windpipe.

As she began her turn, though, Draw's hand reached up from the ground – and in his last act in life, he grabbed her ankle and pulled her to the ground.

"Hogue, did you find these men standing outside a seminary? Were they too mild-mannered to get in?" Downs pushed his glasses onto the bridge of his nose and glared at her. "Two minutes, six strong men. This should have been over long ago. How long till the backup gets there?"

"Three minutes, sir, approximately," Hogue said, consulting her monitor.

"We'll need them. Brief them that they'll be coming in hot."

The blotches circled each other on the screen. Lang tried to break the circle and run for her car, and after a confused moment of action, two men fell to the ground and lay still; only one man from SAG Four remained standing. Lang fell, and then he jumped on her, and their forms coalesced into a throbbing orange blotch that tumbled toward the car.

Then the SAG Four man stood and stepped back. The smaller form of Victoria Lang lay motionless on the pavement.

"Lang's unconscious, sir. Report following on the rest of the group," said Hogue. "Eye injury, non-fatal…one fatality…"

The screen went blank. "Keyhole window closed, sir," said Buta.

"Two...three...four fatalities, sir. Four of the six men are dead."

Downs stood stock still on the podium. "I want this Special Activity Group – what remains of it – put on suspension when they get back to the base. This was sloppy work. Six men, one unarmed woman –"

"Excuse me, sir, but it appears she *was* armed. They report that she injected them with something. It could be what she used at St. Elizabeth's."

"Irrelevant. This is sloppy work, and they should've taken her even if she was armed. It's what they're trained for. Suspend the survivors."

"Group Five is on-site, sir. Orders?" asked Hogue.

"Clean the mess up and take the surviving members of Four into custody. Return to base and take the injured to the infirmary."

"Instructions on Lang? We have a Redaction Order on her."

"I need her package first. Bring her here for cognitive modeling, if your men can control an unconscious woman. We'll execute her after she tells us where it is." With a faint tinge of respect, he added, "Besides, I want to talk to this one."

"Hell, I want to hire her," said Hogue.

DISPATCHES

Molle's Hill
NewsHub Political Affairs Channel
Broadcast Transcript of September 7, 2043

Molle: We're here again with Surgeon General Mae Esteban. How are you today, Mae?

Esteban: I'm fine, thank you.

Molle: General, would you fill us in on the latest developments with the New York virus?

Esteban: Arista, as you know, Neovirus has spread rapidly throughout the metropolitan New York area. From random tests we performed in New York, we've confirmed that this virus is transmitted efficiently long before symptoms manifest. Because of the pandemic potential, the Centers for Disease Control has imposed a quarantine on any movements in or out of this area, by air, sea, or land. We learned our lessons from the 2020 pandemics, and we intend to keep this disease completely contained until the vaccine is deployed.

Molle: The question on everyone's mind is when they can get the vaccine.

Esteban: It's already being distributed. There are limited quantities of Recombin – that's the name of this miracle vaccine, Arista – and our partners in the pharmaceutical industry are producing as much as they can, but there isn't enough yet to vaccinate the entire population. We've prioritized those communities within a radius of 75 to 125 miles from Times Square to receive the vaccine first, creating a firebreak of sorts. Obviously, the National Capital area will receive vaccine shipments on a first priority because we're coordinating our response to the disease from here.

Molle: It sounds like New York City is being abandoned.

Esteban: No, of course not. The vaccine is being distributed to first responders in the city as we speak. As more vaccine becomes available, more citizens will be vaccinated.

Molle: How is the vaccine production coming?

Esteban: We're all working day and night, Arista. We can't produce it any faster than we are.

Molle: There have been rumors – and they're only rumors since the news blackout was imposed in New York yesterday – that the virus has taken a lethal turn.

Esteban: The mortality rate is indeed rising as the disease dwells in the population, especially among the young and the elderly, because of this virus's unusual mechanism of action. It doesn't attack the host's body the way other viruses do. In the initial phase of the disease, it just stresses the body's immune system, which healthy adults can withstand. The young and the elderly cannot.

Unfortunately, we're also now seeing a more lethal phase develop after the initial fever, where viral growth amplifies and releases toxins inside the internal organs. This results in hemorrhagic –

Molle: Omigod! They get hemorrhoids too?

Esteban: I wish that was all they –

Molle: Because my friend just had a baby, and she got the worst hemorrhoids. She said it was like walking with a bag of marbles between her cheeks.

Esteban: You've misunderstood the term. You see, a hemorrhoid is a...there's a man behind the camera drawing his finger across his throat.

Molle: That's my producer telling me to pivot to another subject. General, informed sources say that Hackley's Brazilian Dingleberry Juice is effective at reducing the likelihood of contracting this disease, and Mack's Supermarkets just received a truckload at every one of its District stores! I'm getting a few bottles while I still can!

Esteban: (Clears throat).

Molle: Thanks for coming and giving us that update, General.

Midnight Sun
News Post of September 7, 2043

EXPERTS DOUBT EFFECTIVENESS OF CONTAINMENT MEASURES

We've discussed the effectiveness of the Containment Ring with epidemiological and public health experts in Vancouver, Canada, and their reactions range from puzzlement to stark disbelief. "A Containment Ring is a weak measure," says Gordon Ving of the University of the Upper Northwest. "It won't keep the contagion inside, but it'll ensure everyone catches the disease. I don't understand why they're using such a crude approach like containment when it's proven that social distancing measures, like closing all places of public assembly, keeping people indoors, and so on, are much more effective."

"It's also impossible to enforce the Ring," continues Ving. "Instead of some arbitrary radius where the border runs through the middle of a field, they should have chosen a defensible terrain feature. Put the border in the midst of a river or atop a mountain, and you might succeed at enforcement."

UNITED NATIONS ABANDONS MANHATTAN AS VIRUS SPREADS

Our Witness on the Upper West Side of Manhattan reports that the United Nations Complex is vacant. "I've lived here forty years, and I've never seen the place so dark. It's spooky. I've gotten used to seeing it lit up. But I don't blame them for looking out for Number One. Hey, at least they got out.

"This Containment Ring is the best thing to hit New York since Al Qaeda. Just stick us all in here so we can all go fuckin primate, yeah, that's totally *verkakte.*

"Like this fuckin Ring will really work. Everybody I know has a map of it, and they're figurin out where they can break through. And this vaccine. Everyone wants it, nobody's gettin it. Everyone's just pissed off, knowin they gotta wait. I know these people, and everybody in New York's got ADHD. You think they're just gonna stand around and wait like good little robots? I don't. They'll just start pushin and shovin their way to the front of the line, I mean, that's how you survive in this fuckin town, and it's not gonna be any different with the vaccine. It's gonna get ugly, I tell you, and it won't take long."

WATCHERS

Day 21
Tuesday morning, September 8, 2043
National Tranquility Center, Fort Belvoir, Virginia

Krista was growing uncomfortable as the school bus glided down Route 95 to Fort Belvoir. Not only were her shoes too tight and her skirt was riding up her thighs, but she'd missed her morning coffee and cigarettes. Her brain felt too big for her skull and her lungs too small for her chest, and the feeling was deepening with each passing mile.

As if to crown her discomfort, Liza stood beside her in the aisle and led the kids in a song, a loud and cacophonous kiddie karaoke that grated on her few ungrated nerves. With her fingers in her ears, she scanned the road ahead for the exit sign. She spotted it a few minutes later and thanked every god she could remember, even the weird Egyptian ones, and vowed to light up the instant her feet touched solid ground.

The bus rolled through a gate and hissed to a stop before a large glass building beside an obsessively manicured park, across which sat a row of small clapboard houses. Along the front of the building, identical gray sport utility vehicles were lined up. They were called Silverbacks, she remembered, the largest passenger car ever made.

Three metal towers bristling with antennae sprung from a small rise at the end of the lawn. In the clearing beyond them, she glimpsed the tops of satellite dishes, each pointing in a different direction. As she watched, one moved to a different position, and then another adjusted itself the same way.

A sturdy wooden sign on the sidewalk in front of the headquarters building declared NO SMOKING ON NTC CAMPUS. She groaned, and Liza darkened her mood even more by pulling out her Cannabliss and taking a surreptitious toke.

The crowd left the bus and assembled on the sidewalk in front of the building. She spotted blue-shirted men and women inside, talking and reading monitors or papers with a sense of urgency and purpose.

Liza corralled the children as they came off the bus, with Krista helping keep the crowd together. After a frantic effort, she herded the other outliers into a ragged cluster, and then the group surged toward the building and burst through the front doors with a spray of noise.

An oak reception desk sat beyond the doors. On the light blue wall behind it, gold letters spelled NATIONAL TRANQUILITY CENTER, and underneath, *Your Federal Friends!* Below that, a small plaque read:

DOMESTIC INTELLIGENCE COMMAND
NATIONAL SECURITY FORCES
DEPARTMENT OF INTERNAL SECURITY

Two muscular NSF officers stood at parade rest on either side of the desk and scrutinized the visitors. A young woman sat behind it – a fresh-scrubbed, guileless All-American girl wearing a robin's-egg blue golf shirt and khaki pants, the *après*-fascist uniform the NSF now wore instead of armorsuits. 'Annette' was embroidered on the shirt above a white 'E4.'

Krista eyed the numbers; according to the SatNet longbeards, the National Security Forces only had two A1's – the Watcher and the Deputy Watcher, the two people who saw everything America did and knew its deepest secrets. In Clune's day, they held the power of life and death over every citizen, but President Reike said he'd demoted them to high-powered intelligence analysts.

Annette walked around the desk, shouting above the din, "You must be Miss Wetmore from Roosevelt School!"

"Yes!" Liza yelled. She jammed two fingers in her mouth and whistled, and the din subsided. "Yes, I am. We're *so* looking forward to seeing your place!"

"Oh, so am I!" she gushed. "My name is Annette!"

The two women shook hands. "I'm just so delighted to meet you!" burbled Liza.

Annette ushered everyone into a small alcove off the lobby. The walls illuminated and images of eagles, spaceships, and the American flag crossfaded on them. Annette bent down to the kids' height and rested her hands on her knees. "Does anybody know what we do here at the National Tranquility Center?" she said.

"Keep us safe?" ventured a little girl in the front.

"Yes! We work day and night to keep you safe! But who do we keep you safe from?"

"Bad guys?" ventured the same girl. The rest of the class watched the spaceships.

"Baaad guys," Annette agreed. "But what does a bad guy look like?" The only reaction was that a small boy in the back picked his nose. "Right. Nobody knows what a bad guy looks like, do they? But we do. We find them and keep you safe."

"Mr. Applejack yelled at my dog yesterday. He scared me," said the nose picker.

"Well, I'll look right into that!" Annette peeped, and the boy brightened at the prospect of Applejack's imminent takedown. "We have to look very hard for the bad guys, but we're really lucky because we have so many cameras watching America. We have them orbiting in space, and now we even have blimps – great big balloons – floating over each big city and just bristling with cameras! Did you know that there's a surveillance camera for every person in the United States?"

The children shook their heads, but Krista surreptitiously searched the room for hidden lenses.

"Yes, they're all over! They're not only in space, but they're in your doorbell, your computer, your classroom, and every street corner! We watch them all, day and night. And we watch and listen to what the police and other agencies discover too, and we make sense of it. We find bad guys this way. And when we do, we send the police to catch them. And who knows why we do this?" Annette asked, holding her right hand up.

"Cuz you're our friends?" asked the girl in front.

"Right!" piped Annette. "We're your Federal Friends! Now, who wants to see where we do all this good work?" Annette asked.

"Me!" the innocent voices chorused.

ANNETTE CALLED AND CONFIRMED that the class was cleared to enter. Everybody handed over their tablets for safekeeping, and then the guards ushered the class through a pair of tall oak doors. Another All-American girl had already taken Annette's seat.

They walked down a long corridor. Krista spied for a coffee machine, or for dark state secrets, but all she found was a wall of office doors on one side and a large, darkened workspace with desks clustered into pods on the other. The people working there didn't wear the suburban-mild polo shirts but a gray uniform the color of approaching storm clouds, with a stiff tunic and a high collar.

After a long walk, they stopped at a curved glass wall, which was seamless except for a glass door in the center. An armed NSF officer stood beside it.

The circular room beyond the glass was two stories high and at least a hundred feet in diameter, with a row of large monitors filling the upper half of the space and glass-fronted meeting rooms below. Every surface in the room was flat gunmetal gray. The wall screens displayed aerial images of the major cities, and sometimes an image would flicker and zoom in on a building or a car. The screens cast the only light in the room except for small task lamps on each desk.

Fifty to sixty young men and women sat at curved desks arranged in concentric rings, watching and tapping desktop monitors and speaking into headsets. At times, workers facing her would gaze at the wall above. She assumed the monitors continued above the glass wall where she couldn't see.

In the center of the room, a trim, average-height man in a gray uniform stood on a raised podium, facing away from her with his hands clasped behind him. He watched the monitors and occasionally commented into a headset.

On the center monitor, the images changed to words:

WELCOME ROOSEVELT ELEMENTARY SCHOOL

The children cheered.

"This is the Watch Room, the heart of our little facility. This is where we watch the pictures from space," she said, pointing to the sky, "and from cameras on the ground too. There are so many, only our computers can count 'em!" She pointed to a towheaded boy in the front. "What's the largest number you know?"

"Ninety hundred," said the boy.

"I think there's more than even that!" Annette chirped. "And we watch each one. That's what the boys and girls in there are doing right now! Watching and listening for bad guys!"

Krista tuned out the canned babble since she was far more interested in seeing the fabled nerve center of the NSF. The SatNet conspiracy theorists said that this room was where all the surveillance input of US agencies came together to be processed and acted upon by the NSF.

The class moved on, but Krista stayed behind and studied the rarely seen nerve center. She glanced at the monitor showing Washington; underneath it, green letters blinked 'Blackeye 2'. The image was incredibly sharp and crisp, as good if not better than Trope's video, and the picture fascinated her despite being partly blocked by cloud cover. As she watched, the display changed from the overhead view to a rapid shuffle of images, flitting by almost too fast for the eye to see. However, she did make out a house and a parking lot.

She watched the images for a few seconds and then froze – she'd just seen a penthouse atop an office building, one with a red brick patio and a deformed green water barrel. She stood in place for a long moment with her eyes closed, replaying the image in her mind, and then opened her eyes and rechecked the monitor. It flicked through the images again a minute later – and she saw her apartment again, this time a slightly fuzzier image obscured by a denser bank of fug.

She turned slowly, seeing nothing but the pictures in her mind, and walked away to rejoin her class.

INSIDE THE WATCH ROOM, Downs glanced through the glass, and then he looked again to confirm what he'd seen. "Buta, display an image of Krista Warner on your monitor. Not the Wall."

"Yes, sir." The photograph appeared in the next instant.

"Current location?"

"In her apartment but unconfirmed. Only vehicles have exited her building today, sir."

"Perhaps you should look out in the hall."

Buta glanced up at the retreating figure, back at the monitor, and then up again. "That appears to be Warner, sir."

"She walked right in here. Why didn't our lobby cameras pick her up?"

"We've limited the Warner recognition area to Northwest Washington, sir. We're reducing the Syllogic Engine's computing demand per IT's latest guidance."

Downs snorted and leaned over Hogue's monitor. "Show me the nearest tech team we have to her apartment. Now."

Hogue's hands slid over the monitor. "None available, sir. They're all scheduled. The best chance we have is Tech Thirty-Two, who'll be coming in from Baltimore in...thirty to thirty-five minutes. It'll be tight."

"Mochyn? How long to tap her servers?"

"They're Advanced Heuristics Spinnakers, sir, with onboard Class Four AI. To tap those, the team would need to power down the units and clone the AI memory to another board wired with a hardware hack. I'd allow an hour once the team is inside the case, maybe two hours total to get in and out clean."

Downs did a quick calculation. "They might make it in time. Tell them to hurry. I'll delay her. Do it now."

SHE'D JUST REACHED THE REAR OF THE CLASS, which had gathered around the interactive displays. Some of the kids were flying toy models of the NSF's new Blackeye surveillance airships, which looked like shrunken versions of the pre-inferno *Hindenburg* minus the swastika.

Suddenly, she felt a prickling between her shoulder blades warning of a predator ready to strike, a feeling so potent that it pierced her distraction. She shivered and then heard a voice behind her. "Excuse me. Would you happen to be Krista Warner, by any chance?"

She turned and saw the man from the Watch Room. He was handsome in an ordinary way – he had brown hair and hazel eyes, fashionable eyeglasses perched on his aquiline nose, and was somewhere in his mid-thirties. He wore a stiff gray tunic devoid of any insignia except for a silver 'A1' pinned to his collar. "That I am," she said carefully.

The man smiled and held out his hand. "Bob Downs. It's a pleasure to meet you."

She shook his hand. "How may I help you, Mr. Downs?"

"Call me Bob, please. I'm the day supervisor in the Watch Room, and I happened to see you out here. Just thought I'd come and say hello. I read *The Rake* every day. Love your work."

"Really? I'd think you'd hate it. I haven't been kind to any of Clune's creations, rehabilitated or not."

"That's why I read it! You've got it so wrong!" Downs said. "It's funny stuff. I don't mean to be insulting, of course. It's just that you don't understand what we really do, which is all too common among the media. Would you allow me to prove that we're not the thugs from the days of President Clune? I'd love to clear the record."

"On the condition that I can use anything you say?"

"Absolutely," said Downs, holding up his hand as if being sworn in. "We have nothing to hide."

"On the further condition that you won't propagandize me like your bubbly pal Annette?" she asked, jerking a thumb over her shoulder.

Downs laughed. "She drinks too much coffee in the morning. But I'll be good. Scout's honor."

They walked side-by-side down a gray-carpeted corridor perpendicular to the one she'd taken from the lobby, and she pulled out her notepad and pen. "I've only got about half an hour before the bus returns. This needs to be brief."

"I won't be long," Downs said. "What we do here is simple, Miss Warner, and it's not the cloak and dagger stuff you and others believe. We monitor electronic surveillance captured by various governmental agencies and look for data alignments, and should we find a data, event, or image correlation, we notify the authority most responsible and appropriate for action in that jurisdiction. This enables us to coordinate the efforts of agencies from the FBI all the way down to local police departments, improving the efficiency of everyone participating in our program. In reality, we aren't the creepy spooks everyone thinks, but…computer geeks, I guess is the best term."

"That sounded like a prepared speech." She tapped her pen against her teeth. "So the NSF is now just a streamlined conduit for disseminating information? It's no longer the jackbooted brutes of the Detroit days?"

"Exactly," he said.

"Hmm. So how did the Federals, I mean the NSF, who shot National Guardsmen who refused to fire on rioters, transmogrify into this passive little club with the fluffy nickname of Federal Friends?" she asked.

"We never transmogrified, as you put it. The NSF was always comprised of two divisions: the Domestic Intelligence Command," he smiled and pointed to himself, "and the Domestic Operations Command. Sam Rieke disbanded the Operations Command, so we weren't magically transformed as much as amputated. All that remains of Operations is a lightly armed security force more like mall security guards than the Ironshirts, as they were commonly called."

"Like the muscle you've got out front?"

"Exactly. They're what's left of the Operations Command." He pointed right and they made a turn. "As for the Federal Friends nickname, some light-in-the-loafers marketing genius came up with that about ten years ago. They wanted to give us a friendlier feel, I suppose, and the kiddies just loved it. They love the little show we put on out there." He laughed. "I can't stand that nickname myself. It sounds like a line of plush toys."

"Maybe that nickname was created because a big lie is easier to sell than a small one?"

"That's a cynical thing to say. You've been in Washington too long."

"It's not cynical. It's a political tactic that's used all the time – the public will spot a small lie, but if you tell a big lie and repeat it often, they'll accept it as the truth. President Clune used this tactic to talk us into the Persian Regional Conflict."

"I'm sorry, but I'm not familiar with the concept."

"I'd expect our Federal Friends to know it by heart because Hitler came up with it."

"You're misinformed," he said. "Miss Warner, we find the truth here at the National Tranquility Center. Our job is to cut through the lies, big or small, and bring the liars to justice. We wouldn't *sell* any lies."

"Truth? Justice? What's next, the American Way?"

They approached a pair of large doors, one on each side of the corridor; the sign on both doors said:

COGNITIVE MAP MODELING
A-B LEVEL ACCESS ONLY

As they reached the door on the right, a man in a lab coat backed through it pulling a large stainless-steel machine with *'Mind's Eye III by Inquisite! Industries'* painted on the side in purple script. He crossed in front of them, muttering apologies, and pulled it through the opposite door.

"What's that machine for?" she asked.

Downs chuckled. "I have no idea, I really don't. There are so many gizmos around here that I can't keep track of them." He leaned toward her. "Don't tell anyone. I'm supposed to know."

She took out her notepad, wrote down the name of the machine, and then noticed Downs watch her writing with her left hand. Without thinking, she said, "Y'know, sometimes my left hand writes words that aren't even in my head!" Downs' eyebrows rose in alarm, and she wrinkled her nose. "Now isn't sinistrality the strangest thing?"

He gave her a look like an undertaker sizing the condemned for a coffin and then turned away quickly.

"You're an Arkie, aren't you?" she asked.

"My faith isn't your concern, Miss Warner. I'm sure there are more interesting things to write about."

"Oh, no. This is fascinating. Seeing me write with my left hand bothers you, so you must be a hard-core Arkie. I'll bet you were one of Rieke's Replacements. Did you start here in '29?"

"You're very observant. I joined the NSF in '31 as an Intelligence intern. And yes, I was appointed by President Rieke."

They walked past the double doors and continued down the corridor. "So, back to the Big Lie Principle," she said.

"Why do you keep implying that I'm not telling the truth?"

"Because you just lied. You admitted that this Federal Friends moniker is a fabrication."

"That's just marketing, Miss Warner. That's not a lie. It's an aspiration."

"If you *aspire* to be seen as open and friendly and huggable, that means you aren't. So what's the real NSF now? Has it ever changed from Clune's days, or was its real nature covered up by clever marketing? Are the Ironshirts really gone? Do you still disappear people like you did in the bad old days? Did you slip the iron fist into a fluffy glove so we'd all think we were safe, and your goons could do whatever they wanted?"

"I'm afraid I can't reveal details of our operations or our policies, Miss Warner," he said, glancing at a wall clock as they passed. "We have access to classified information streams, and I'd have to compromise them to answer your questions."

"Oh, here comes the national security shtick again."

"Didn't you read the sign on the door?"

She leaned against the wall and crossed her arms. "You aren't answering my questions. In fact, you're making a concerted effort to deflect them. I'm just getting the same propaganda that Annette would give me, just a more personal application."

"You seem to carry a lot of resentment."

"Cure me, Bobby. You don't have to divulge state secrets. Just give me the big picture."

"I don't know if I could. Our Utah facility captures over forty petabytes of data daily, and we have eight parallel supercomputers in the basement hosting the Syllogic Engine, which just makes sense of a fraction of it. The big data picture is beyond the comprehension of any single mind. But please trust me when I say we aren't surveilling everyone like the crazies believe. And when we do surveille, it's justified as being critical to the security of our nation," he said. "*Your* nation, Miss Warner, and *your* security as well. You're a direct beneficiary of the good we do here, not a victim of it."

"Ahh, so the computers are the real brains here?"

"Of course. As I said, no human mind could make the connections the Engine does, not with the vast amount of information it processes."

"What if the computers are wrong?"

"They aren't. Every anti-terrorist operation I've directed has been absolutely justified. Thousands of lives were saved and –"

"Prove it. Tell me what September 11th you prevented."

"Miss Warner..."

"Here it comes. You'll say I should just trust you because everything you do is some feckin secret. All right, forget it. Answer my first question instead. Is the NSF any different than it was in Clune's day? C'mon, Bobbaloo, just say yes or no."

"I don't have that authority." He turned and walked down the hall, and Krista fell into step beside him.

"Okay, answer this question, then – how do you force all the police departments to do your bidding?"

"If we find that field action is advisable, we forward the directive to the force most local and appropriate to the action required."

"And they just do what you say?"

"They're motivated to do what we recommend. Imagine if you were a police officer, and we notified you that there was a terrorist group building pipe bombs down the street. What would you do?"

She shook her head. "That's an extreme example. How do you get these agencies to comply when they're *not* motivated to?"

"They usually cooperate, Miss Warner. We're not their overlords. We all play for the same team."

"They *usually* cooperate. What do you do when they don't? Do you send your mall guards to talk to them?"

"This line of questioning is rather harsh, and it seems you have a preconceived notion in mind." He shook his head. "It's a notion so many share, unfortunately. The thugs of Detroit are just too strong an image for us to erase."

"Who runs you, then? Who directs you?"

"No one directs us. We operate independently, and since we make no decisions and take no action, no one needs to direct us. We're an information clearinghouse, Miss Warner, no more. We do nothing but assess and distribute intelligence."

"You really do nothing with all that power? You expect me to believe that?"

He stopped before a glass-walled office. "Why can't you accept the truth?"

"The truth? Okay, let's try that instead. Answer this question honestly." She looked into his eyes. "Are you watching my apartment?"

"Only if ya done sumthin naughty, Miz Warner," he said with homespun joviality. "You can tell me if you did. I'm *real* good with secrets."

Enunciating each word, she repeated, "Answer the question – are you watching my apartment?"

"No, Miss Warner, we're not," he said. "We're not the boogeyman under your bed."

A pair of men left the next office down the hall and turned in her direction. One of them, a medium-height man with an olive complexion, was saying, "…Lang is in Suite Seven, and we can't get her to cooperate, so we rolled in the Mapper –" The other man nudged him, and he stopped talking suddenly. "Bob?" he asked, tilting his head and looking from Downs to Krista and back.

"Raphael!" Downs said. "I'd like you to meet Krista Warner. I'm giving her a tour of our little shop."

"A tour…" He flashed a broad smile. "Of course! It's a pleasure to meet you, ma'am," Raphael said with a slight bow, holding out his hand.

She shook his hand and turned to the man behind Raphael. He was tall, well over six feet, with a muscular but lithe body like a predator built for strength and speed. He wore a tight-fitting gray T-shirt, black camouflage pants, and black ballistic nylon boots, and 'X-9A' was embroidered on his shirt in black. His left arm was clothed in bandages from his shoulder to his elbow. She held out her hand to the man and he took it; touching him, she felt the peculiar sensation of being simultaneously attracted and repulsed.

"Krista Warner," Raphael said. "Would you be the bloodsucking vampire of *The Rake*?"

She nodded and noticed that he wore the same rank on his collar as Downs. A tingle of panic danced along her spine as she realized that these were the NSF's two most powerful men.

"Ahh, our favorite Yellow Journalist! Then let me reintroduce myself. I'm AB Positive!" He laughed, and everyone joined in. "I read *The Rake* all the time!"

She smiled and nodded reflexively, surprised that her blog was so popular here. Intuition began scratching on the back door to her conscious mind.

"Well, if you'll excuse us, we're going to the dining room for coffee. It was a pleasure meeting you, Miss Warner." Raphael walked off, and in his wake, she imagined the smell of coffee – fresh ground – and her caffeine withdrawal headache deepened.

Downs cleared his throat, opened a door, and ushered her into a spacious corner office. He stood in front of his wall monitor and tapped on it, and she used the opportunity to scan the room. The office was large, but the only furnishings in it were a plain desk and two chairs. The floor was covered with gray carpet, and the light-gray walls were adorned with only a large wall monitor, a crucifix, and a few framed documents.

She watched him pull icons across the screen and then stifled a gasp, realizing that he'd recognized her – and she'd never allowed her photograph to be published. In fact, she hadn't been photographed since her college graduation and was rarely seen in public.

He tapped one last time on the monitor and pointed to a chair. "Please, have a seat. I apologize if we've gotten off on the wrong foot. Can we try again?"

She'd never discover the truth if she kept badgering him, so she bit back the indignant reply that came to her lips. "All right. This is a spare office, Mr. Downs. You must have an orderly mind."

"I hardly use this place. I'm in the Watch Room twelve hours a day, seven days a week. I do whatever administrative work I might have when I'm there."

"I'll bet that puts a crimp in your home life."

"I live here. My private quarters are just across The Green."

"Nevertheless, those are long hours."

"They'd be long hours for a job, Miss Warner, but not for a mission – and what I do is a mission I believe in completely." He grinned. "Now that I've said that, I know it makes me sound like a zealot. Honestly, the duty isn't hard, and twelve hours is easy to put in. Actually, I feel refreshed after my shift. I think the work frees my mind."

"I'll bet that sounds punchier in the original German."

"Sorry, I don't speak German."

"How odd. Anyway, what do you do for the DIC?"

"As I said, I'm the day supervisor, for lack of a better term. I observe what's happening, answer questions, and make decisions as needed. In the larger view, my function is to keep our operations fluid."

"Hmm," she said.

"Really, that's just a ten-dollar way of saying I stand around a lot."

"I'd like to know more about you personally, Mr. Downs, if you don't mind. Just for background." She stood and read the diplomas on the wall. "You graduated from MMU, I see."

"You figured that out already. Impressive."

Where a diploma usually conferred a Master of Arts or Master of Science, Downs' diploma conferred on him only the title of Master. She suppressed a shudder, imagining the man cracking a whip over a field of slaves. "MMU. North Texarkana, Arkansas. Now isn't that the one that's

$499.97 a credit, but you can get it at $399.88 during the doorbuster special?"

"Mal-Mart University isn't quite like that. The Mallon family endowed the university generously, and the funds were managed wisely to defray tuition costs. I simply couldn't have afforded any other college with the cost of tuition being so high. It was my only way out of Oklahoma, which isn't exactly the land of opportunity."

"And Arkansas is uptown?" she asked.

"Have you ever seen Oklahoma?"

"What was your major?" she asked, tapping her pen against the notepad.

"Applied Political Science. Most associates in the NSF are trained in that program."

"Specifically *for* the NSF, it seems, because the APS major is useless everywhere else in the country. I've heard about the curriculum for the program – no English, no arts, just lots of math, science, technology, and the mysterious 'Field Practicum' that takes up the entire senior year. Tell me, Mr. Downs, what is that?"

"It's just an introduction to how our education applies in the real world," he said carefully, "a transitional class from the ivory towers of academia to the field, that's all."

"Mmm. Wiretapping, videotaping, getting fitted for a black cloak, stuff like that, Bobby? Why is it that no graduate of that program talks about it?"

"Because it's just so danged technical and boring. There are no dark secrets there, trust me."

"You keep telling me to trust you, and in my sorry experience only people I shouldn't trust say that."

"It might be that I keep saying it because you obviously don't trust me, even though I've given you no reason to doubt me, and even though I've tried to be a patient and forthcoming host."

She sat slowly, locking him in his glare, her lips pursed and her color rising. "All right. You want to know why I don't trust you, boyo? You've lied to my face a few times already, and it doesn't bother you. You're a pathological liar."

Anger flashed briefly in his eyes, but then a tight smile crossed his face. He picked up a pen from his desk and said, "Please, say what's on your mind. Don't hold back on my account."

She leaned forward in her chair. "Oh, I forgot you went to MMU. The two syllables probably confused you. You're a liar. L-I-A-R." She leaned back in her chair, made an 'L' of her fingers, and thrust it into his face. "Let me know if I need to make it simpler, wouldja? I think I've got a crayon in my purse."

He clicked the pen some more and forced his smile wider. "Since I've already been convicted, would you do me the favor of telling me why you believe such nonsense?" She didn't respond but only continued to glare at him. "Please, Miss Warner, indulge my forensic curiosity."

"I asked if you were watching my apartment. You denied it. But when I was outside your fancy Watch Room, I saw a picture of my apartment flick by on one of your screens. Why are your feckin spy blimps watching my apartment?"

"Ahh." He sat back in his chair. "You think you saw your apartment during a Recognition Scan? You couldn't have. Only the computers use those, and they're nearly impossible for a human to see. They run at fifty frames a second."

"I know what I saw, and I saw it twice!"

Downs glanced at his desktop monitor for a few moments and then smiled. "Hmm, yes. Your apartment is near one of the most deadly streets in the District. It's known locally as Felony Lane, isn't it? And you're puzzled why we'd surveille this area?"

"Not that all your spying does anything. I find a feckin stiffer in the weeds every time I go out."

"From our records, you've reported nineteen so far this year, but that's no surprise. The Base-M trade is notoriously violent, and you live a block from the river, where the drugs usually come in."

"Or maybe it's because the NSF is so bloody incompetent. Maybe you oughta stop playing video games and get out and do one feckin positive thing, but instead you sit here and stroke your joysticks –"

"Miss Warner, crime's down because –"

"– and squirt your sticky fascist stuff all over the joint. I'm surprised you guys aren't all leaning back in your chairs and smoking cigarettes for all the wanking you do. Listen, why don't you stop spying on us and just admit you've all got a domination fetish? There's a shop in the mall called The Bishop's Secret, they've got all sorts of bondage toys in the window, you can be happy –"

"Enough!" He glared at her, clicking his pen so furiously that it burst and spurted ink on his trousers. Barely containing a growl, he dropped the pen into the trash and blotted ink from his pants with a tissue. "Okay, I get it now. I won't be baited by a paranoiac with a personal liberties hang-up –"

"Hey, Bubba, I'm not the only one who cherishes their personal liberty. Freedom's what America's all about. Maybe you've forgotten that."

"Freedom." He flung the inky tissue into the trash. "Don't worship the notion. Freedom has killed more Americans than all the terrorist acts worldwide."

"So Freedom was in those armorsuits, not Ironshirts? What about the people they shot on the Detroit streets? They died of Freedom Poisoning?"

"Exactly. Untethered freedom is toxic, and it poisons and paralyzes the body politic. It drains its vitality and suffocates it with delusions of an individuality that can never be sustained in a cooperative civilization. Advanced and enlightened cultures always limit freedom and liberty for the safety of their citizens. Those of us in influential positions work together to enforce those limits – and nobody works harder to choke off freedom than you."

"What!"

"Don't act like you're shocked, Miss Warner. You and your media ilk are central players in the restraint of freedom. Acting freely requires accurate and objective knowledge of the world, but hack journalists like you fabricate and perpetuate falsehoods that camouflage the truth and stifle curiosity. You distract your seven million readers with trivialities, you spoon-feed them lies day after day until only lies are the truth –"

"I do not!"

"I read your columns every evening. You must make up most of what you post. Tell me, do you write the headlines first and then compose the story to fit?"

Krista sank back in her seat and ran her fingers through her hair. "So I work the lowbrow beat. I've got to pump out eight stories a day just to keep the lights on, and I'm under the feckin MRC's claw the whole time. What choice have I got?"

"You don't have a choice. I don't, either. Nor did your parents, who were the first generation to realize that it was time to pull up stakes on American freedom. They willingly sacrificed your civil liberties for safety and order after the terrorist attacks in 2001."

She jumped to her feet and pointed a finger in his face. "Hey, don't be going on about my folks!"

"And Detroit proved them right. Detroit proved that wanton liberties like free speech and free assembly –"

"There was *nothing* right about Detroit, Downs!"

"Yes, there was. Detroit taught us we could only halt violence by redacting dissent before it gained critical mass, and that's what we do for the protection of –"

"Whoa, bucko. Is that why you're watching my apartment? You think I'm a dissenter? I'm some danger to your precious safety and order?" He started to speak but then clamped his lips together. "Answer me!" She planted one fist on his desk and the other on her hip. "You're spying on me, and I want to know why! Right now, and don't try to grease me anymore! I'm sick of it!"

He leaned over the desk until his face was only a foot away. "We are *not* spying on you. We have no reason to waste valuable resources on you. We're not interested in surveilling a self-absorbed basket case, and I certainly know *I'm* not."

She leaned even closer. "Well, thank the feckin Profit for that. The little whore-spawn might be watchin out for your fragile ego, eh? Maybe he's not the mental midget everybody says he is."

His hazel eyes seemed to turn a wintry gray, and a muscle twitched in his cheek. "Measure your words, Warner, or The Profit will measure them for you."

"Oh, fuck your fake prophet. And fuck you too, you two-bit Hitler wannabe." He stifled a gasp, and she stood back, leaving him leaning on the desk. "And you look like a bloody bellboy in that costume, boyo. At least the real Nazis had a proper sense of style." She straightened her skirt, clipped her pen to the notepad, and turned for the door. "I'll be taking my leave now, if it's no trouble. Or if it is."

Downs checked the time on his desk monitor. "Would you like some coffee, something to eat, perhaps? We have a nice dining room, usually only open to employees, but I can get you in." He paused, recalling something. "We have, umm, eight or nine varieties of coffee, all fresh-ground. My treat."

"Apparently there's something about 'goodbye' you don't understand, Mr. Downs. Maybe that stellar MMU education is failing you again."

"Umm...would you like a cook's tour of the facility? I promise it'll be entertaining," he said. "I can show you more of how we operate if you promise not to reveal it. I'm taking a risk by violating security directives, but I really do want to show that we're just regular folks doing a normal job."

"Why are you trying to keep me here?"

"I'm not. I'm just doing my job, even if the task is unpleasant."

"Oh, well, then I'll spare you the experience." She walked to the door.

"Wait, I have to accompany you," he said as he rose from the chair. "Please give me a moment." He walked to the wall monitor and began tapping a message.

"I don't do requests," she said, leaving the office.

He ran to catch her, and they walked down the corridor in tense silence. "Make a left here," he said at a crossing.

"But this isn't the way we came."

"This is a shorter route," Downs said.

They arrived at the lobby after a long walk and several turns. Downs opened the door and waited until Krista was through, and then, without a word, he closed it and returned into the NTC.

Liza called, "Krista! Where have you been?"

Krista retrieved her tablet and walked out of the building without answering. She stopped at the no-smoking sign and leaned against it, and then she lit a cigarette and blew a cloud at the building.

DOWNS RETURNED TO THE WATCH ROOM, and Cochon met him at the door. "The tech team got into a fender-bender, sir. They never made it to her apartment. By the way, you spilled ink on your –" Downs' face darkened and Cochon looked at the floor.

"I want to strangle that woman," Downs muttered as he stalked to the podium. "And take an hour doing it."

Cochon brightened. "Want me to request a redaction endorsement to her surveillance order?"

Downs scanned the Wall. "I don't want to owe Cheyn any favors, especially not right now," he said as the light of the monitors cast a kaleidoscope of colors across his face. "It wouldn't make sense anyway because we still need her as a stalking horse for Paparazzo. We need to drop Paparazzo in a deep hole as soon as possible. If he has the information I suspect, it absolutely cannot be allowed to go any further than him."

"I wish you'd tell me just what information we're trying to suppress, sir."

Downs nodded and lowered his voice. "We think Paparazzo recorded Cheyn out at Hains Point talking about the RVE Initiative. We spotted him and his cameras across the river, but he was gone when we got there. We're not sure how much he recorded or how much he knows, but if that conversation goes public, it could blow the entire Initiative wide open. We also believe that Warner is his media contact and that she can lead us to him."

"Are you sure she's merely a contact, sir?"

"Maybe not." Downs looked away, a muscle in his jaw twitching. "All the time we were talking, I felt that restless madness we've seen in the Emergents, that urge to destroy anything normal and ordered. It was like a heat, Cochon, like turning my face to the noonday sun."

"We *have* been missing more Emergents lately, sir. She could be another the Syllogic Engine failed to identify."

"Possibly," Downs said. "If so, she might not be the simpleton we assumed. She might be running Paparazzo instead of the other way around. Maybe she came here to observe our operations and gather intelligence."

"That would be bold." Cochon grimaced and let out a long breath. "And troubling for us. But once we get Paparazzo –"

"Request her redaction endorsement the instant we do, but that's for later. Right now, we're not getting closer to Paparazzo, and that'll change." Downs called his chiefs to attention. "Buta, Hogue, Mochyn. We've tried to get into the Warner apartment all this week and failed. We failed again today, and we had the opportunity. Suggestions?"

"Sir, if I may," said Cochon. "Warner's records show that she's agoraphobic. College psychiatric evaluations say she has variable cycles, meaning that she can often remain in her apartment for weeks without leaving. She appears to be in a withdrawal cycle now, where she typically doesn't leave the apartment for more than an hour. It makes her movements impossible to predict and prepare for."

"Except for today, we've had tech teams on call waiting for her to leave," said Hogue. "We had an opportunity last Wednesday when she was out of the apartment for four hours –"

"Last Wednesday was Christian Renewal Day, Miss Hogue," Downs said, an accusation of heresy in his voice.

"Understood, sir." Hogue found something interesting to examine on her monitor.

"We received the surveillance order at noon last Tuesday, and passive surveillance was in place six hours later," said Buta. "Eight grounds cameras have been running since then, and of course, we have Blackeye 2 on her when we get a break in the fug. When we can get the Keyhole, we use that for night surveillance. We also have two micro-drones tasked with following her in case she leaves her apartment."

"That's too passive," Downs said. "Perhaps we'll catch Paparazzo leaving material for Warner, but I doubt it. This fellow knows the craft. The only way we'll know what he's delivering to her is to see what's on those servers. And Cheyn wants Paparazzo yesterday. What options do we have?"

"Pull the fire alarm and go in then," suggested Buta.

"A seven-to-ten-minute window at best. Not enough to crack her servers."

"Sir, we have few options except to wait," said Cochon. "We can't risk spooking Paparazzo and having him go to ground."

"Yet we can't wait, or we may never get him." Downs paced the circumference of the podium. "We need to act. Hogue, can you make Executives Seventeen available on an open-ended basis?"

She consulted her monitor. "Starting Sunday, sir. They're our most under-utilized asset. But they're a little –"

"Sloppy. I know. But I have something messy planned for them anyway." He walked the perimeter again and then said, "The next time she goes out for an hour, we'll make sure she stays out for two. That's the only way we'll get a tech team inside. Make the arrangements, Hogue."

ORWELL GOT IT WRONG

Day 22
Wednesday morning, September 9, 2043
3120 L Street NW, Washington, DC

Krista slouched in her patio chair and watched Hurricane Xena's eyewall spin north. She emptied her cup and walked inside for a refill, but the skies had opened up again by the time she returned.

Running her hand through her hair, she collapsed into the chair with a groan. She should have been jackhammering after two large mugs of coffee, but the caffeine had failed to cut through her malaise. And the rain wasn't the only thing flattening her mood: She'd just been fined ten grand for reporting news in *The Great Forty-Eight* post, which always ruined her day. And now she knew that the NSF was watching her too.

She'd spent the entire evening checking every corner of her apartment for spy devices. Although she'd found nothing, she still felt their eyes on her.

Why they were watching was beyond her. How could a gossip columnist masquerading as a real journalist be a national security threat? What had she done to attract the NSF's attention?

I've done nothing wrong. I think I even pay my taxes, she thought, pulling her tablet from a hoodie pocket. *But if they can spy on me, I can spy on them.* Sheltering the tablet from the drifting rain, she tried to discover what Inquisite! Industries did. After an hour of surfing, all she learned was that Inquisite! only made specialized equipment for law enforcement. She tried to decipher the jargon about tomograms, tomographic reconstruction, and several other baffling terms, and eventually learned that they referred to a type of medical brain scanning.

What would they use a brain scanning device for? Well, what do they do at the NTC? They spy, and they must be using this machine to spy. Into someone's brain. She shivered in the chilly, moist air and pulled her sweater tight.

She lit a cigarette and gazed over the canal, letting her mind wander. *Why are they watching me, though? What have I got that the jackboots want?* She shivered again, pulled her legs up into the chair, and huddled into a ball. *Well, I'd better figure this out soon because I'm the only one who doesn't know what's going on. And I'm the one in their sights.*

The Rake
September 9, 2043

ORWELL GOT IT WRONG
It turns out that 1984 *was a documentary*

Yesterday, I earned a disconcerting honor. I had the full attention of Mr. Robert Downs, the National Security Forces Watcher and head honcho of the aptly-acronymed Domestic Intelligence Command, and may I say, it was an eye-opener.

I learned that the NSF is scrutinizing every move I make. Since their job is to control domestic terrorists, I've apparently been labeled as a rebel, which comes as quite the surprise to this humble scribe. Do they really think I'm making bombs in my basement or something? News flash – I don't even *have* a basement. (Well, I do, but it's six floors down and filled with strange and scary machines. I've only been there once, I swear.)

To untangle this colossal misunderstanding, I employed my fine-honed interviewing skills, subtly probing Downs' motivations and beliefs. And that's when I realized that lies flowed from this man's mouth as easily as dollar-store beer at a frat party kegger. Almost nothing he said was true, yet he revealed the truth in where he chose to lie: They're not our Federal Friends, but our Federal Enemies.

They're the Federals we remember and wish we could forget. The boogeyman we hoped would stay under the bed. The old NSF. Sure, their Ironshirts are long gone, and they don't shoot National Guardsmen in the back anymore, but we're totally f*cked if we celebrate that.

So they use different DIC moves now, and they slipped the iron fist into a fluffy glove. BFD. There's still something seriously ominous afoot, people, and we need to pay attention to it.

If you think I'm being paranoid, go down to the National Tranquility Center and talk to Call-Me-Bob yourself. He'd love to see you. (In fact, he loves to see you so much that he watches all you do with his spy cameras.)

All the time I was in his presence, I felt an Orwellian Gestapo vibe – that excruciating tension before the midnight knock on the door, the pause before the guillotine blade drops. But Orwell got one thing wrong: The villains we should fear aren't the faceless, malevolent autocrats serving The Machine, but the predators who act like they're your best buds, like all they truly want is what's best for you. They're far more dangerous because they look and sound like you and me.

But someday soon, they'll come for you and me. A domestic war is brewing, and it may have already started without us noticing or caring.

What's happened to America? Why do we allow predators to stalk us? Why do we let them calculate their kill strikes? When did we become so afraid of the shadows that we stopped looking into them?

If you can't answer those questions, answer this one: Will the kill shot feel any better if you don't see it coming?

-KLW

THE FARMER'S MARKET

Day 23
Thursday evening, September 10, 2043
3120 L Street NW, Washington, DC

Krista paced her living room. She'd been trying to make sense all day of what she'd learned at the NTC, but sense eluded her, and now it was evening. Her frustration was making it increasingly hard to think.

She stomped to her baristomat and held down the extra buzz button until the machine dripped out a dark and potent brew of brain juice. Sipping the coffee, she walked onto the balcony.

She forced herself to think objectively about her encounter at the NTC, and ideas soon coalesced in her mind. She opened her tablet and began to take notes but then sensed someone behind her; slowly, she grasped for the pepper spray in her pocket and then spun around, ready to ward off an attack.

Nobody was prowling the balcony, though. She checked every corner of her apartment again, but no spies lurked under the bed and no cameras whirred. Even so, she couldn't shake the feeling that someone was watching her.

Her tablet chirped as it received a wireless mail message. She read it and realized why she felt insecure – the security settings were set low on her tablet computer, and the NSF could tap into it. After scrolling through the menus for ten minutes, she found the security window and changed its settings to the highest level, and then discovered that the security blocked her from taking notes. With a disgusted huff, she pulled a paper notebook and pen from her pocket, sat in the balcony chair, and started to organize her thoughts the Stone Age way:

> The Federals are watching my home and probably a lot more than that. Why? Because of the Trope video. It's the only information I've received lately of any significance. Thanks to Trope, I know that the Administration is concerned about something involving the scarcity of resources, and maybe this thing is so massive that Cheyn needed to discuss it in historical terms. The NSF surveillance confirms that it's significant. What secret are they protecting?

She sat back, tapped her pen against her teeth, and let her thoughts flow. Minutes later, the conclusion sprang into her mind.

> It has to be that secret Administration plan Senator Schuler was talking about. If California recalls its gold tenpez, the economy's going to melt down, which would reduce the resources available for the rest – for who remains, as Cheyn said. Hunger and riots won't be far behind that disaster, and I'll bet that Cheyn wants to avoid that. He has some sort of plan to avoid the financial fallout, and that's what he's got to be talking about in the video. And the NSF is pissed that I know something about it. Why? How controversial can this mystery plan be? He's not planning to start World War III. He's just trying to fix a problem of too many people and too few resources.

She stood in the fug and sought the pattern connecting these thoughts. It came to her twenty minutes later. *I'll bet Cheyn's going to take over California or take its gold, or both. He's just going to grab their resources. That's got to be his mysterious rescue plan – he's going to start a civil war!*

KRISTA SHRUGGED ON HER HOODIE, pulled on her mask, and stabbed the elevator call button. Even though the virus might be floating around outside, she needed to get away from all the cameras she imagined in her apartment, or the seeds of paranoia would bloom and take over her mind. A trip to the farmer's market would cure her.

Instead of heading directly there, though, she turned at Wisconsin Avenue and walked toward the river. She needed to lose herself and her frustrations first, and Bleaker's was the perfect place.

When Wisconsin ended, she turned left and walked to the restaurant. She never turned right because Base-M dealers had infested the stinking slums at K Street's forsaken dead end, a foul place squeezed under the old freeway and bookended by a forever-leaking chemical plant and the city's trash incinerator. Walking there was begging for a mugging. She didn't want to end up with her head caved in and lying in the weeds of Felony Lane.

Two blocks later, she turned onto the bridge to Bleaker's. Its setting was the most dramatic of any restaurant in Washington: in the Potomac River, accessed only by footbridges and boats, much the way she imagined Venice had been. The brick and concrete building had once been a riverside office complex, but the tidal Potomac had risen after the Flash Thaw of '36 melted the glaciers and pushed the shoreline to the edge of K Street. The outlines of the grand plaza on the old waterfront were still visible at low tide, but the marsh grasses along the new shoreline usually obscured it.

She stopped at the top of the footbridge where it overlooked the river. The soft sweet scent of the reedy greensward below drifted by, mingling with the slight salty bite of the river air. Water lapped at the base of the tall concrete colonnade ten feet below; the small boat of a riverbottom fisherman poled along it, the bell on the bow tolling a flat and lonely sound. It glided into the fug and faded from sight, and then the fisherman called *Oyeh! Oyeh!* Other boats poled from the mist, passing the reeds crowding the rusted jets of the old plaza fountain, answering the call that a catch had been found.

She breathed in the complex river scents, releasing her tension with each breath, and blessed the Life Force for the abundant peace and beauty it offered – and then gunshots cracked down at the Baser's end of K Street. Police cars screeched around a corner and roared toward the shots, their sirens squawking and lights flashing. She ducked behind the bridge railing and jammed her fingers in her ears.

After a minute, she peeked over the rail. The police had stopped further down K Street, but she saw nobody at the end of the footbridge. She ran across the road, took a few shortcuts through alleys, and headed for the safety of the farmers' market.

On the way, she stopped at the grocery store on Wisconsin and found a solitary can of peas on the shelves. She checked every corner and nook, hoping to find someone to bring up food from the basement, but nobody was around. With a sigh, she walked to the auto-checkstand and scanned her meager prize. The monitor on the computer said the store would receive a shipment tomorrow, and she made a mental note to arrive before the mob cleaned out the place again.

With the peas in her hoodie pocket, she walked up Wisconsin to the mall and weaved through the crowds of shoppers to the children's store. She bought the hat in the window and tucked the brightly wrapped box under her arm, and again slipped through the mob until she found the rear entrance, which opened onto the square.

The market was always busy in the evening, filled with sellers and buyers, performers and observers. The fug had settled just above the gas lamps, casting a soft, shadowless glow across the old bricks.

The sound of steel drums tinkled in her ears. A BoHo reggae band was set up by the Wisconsin Avenue side, and they had the crowd hopping; some of the well-dressed onlookers were even dancing, an unusual and awkward thing to see in fastidiously proper Georgetown.

Even though *Fight for Your Life* was on, only a few people had stepped aside to follow the addictive show on their tablets. She knew why: Most didn't come here to see a TV show but to feel human and connected in a harsh and unmoored world. Once they left, alienation and isolation would grip them again, and they'd sigh as they remembered the human moments they'd shared. And the following week, they'd come back and happily make fools of themselves, and the BoHos would indulge them.

Still watching the reggae band, she backed up and bumped into a juggler, sending hard yellow balls bouncing everywhere. The kids chased them in delight.

She treated herself to a Belgian waffle from a street vendor – at twice the cost of the week before – and to put meat on her bones, she slathered it with whipped cream and chocolate syrup. After meandering through the throngs of merchants and eyeing their wares, she found the cast-iron canopy of the farmers' market, with the pastel artist's stall at the end facing the canal. He was sketching a portrait of a young boy, whose pinstripe-suited father stood to one side and watched the art take shape on the paper.

Spring peeked out from behind the artist's back, and her face brightened when she saw Krista. She skipped over and curtsied as if she were attending the King's court, and Krista waved her hand dismissively in the King's trademark gesture. The girl giggled and Krista caught the bug.

Spring noticed that Krista was hiding something behind her back. Krista turned as she tried to see around her, and before long, she was pirouetting wildly and getting dizzy. They fell to the cobblestones winded and flushed, and Krista handed her the prize.

Spring ripped the gift paper off and pulled out the pink beribboned hat. She turned it over in her hands and played with the butterflies, and then she looked up at Krista. She nodded, and Spring smiled and put the hat on. She jumped to her feet and twirled in her best fashion-model imitation, and the butterflies took flight.

Later, they walked to the edge of the canal and sat on the high stone wall, and they talked about the pressing issues of the day the way nine-year-old girls do.

CULTURAL CLEANSING

Day 24
Friday morning, September 11, 2043
3120 L Street NW, Washington, DC

Krista lounged in her chair, wearing the mess and funk of sleep. She was languid and thoughtful, and she watched the also-languid fug tendrils slide between the treetops across the canal. Nothing was in a hurry today.

Her mood had improved with a good night's sleep. She was now convinced her conclusions were correct – civil war with California or a resource grab was in America's near future. She'd considered the problem from every angle, but she saw no other conclusion: The Administration was laying the groundwork for war, or at least a major conflict, just like in the past.

Knowing that didn't frighten her as much as it had last night. However much the NSF might spy or intimidate, she was an MRC-credentialed journalist and was allowed to possess sensitive information. She was protected by law. They couldn't touch her.

In reality, Trope's video was a gift of relevant and valuable information, and she could write something worthy for once. She could become a real journalist and escape the suffocating orbit of gossip and guile plaguing her career. She could build a real future – at least, for as long as she had left – and all she needed to do was stand up to the Federals. How could she lose?

Nothing to lose and everything to gain, kiddo. What better deal can you get? She looked up at the northeast sky, where she imagined the spy blimp was watching, and flipped it a one-finger salute.

THAT NIGHT, she had another nightmare of radioactive soot-golems slinking up the old air shaft in filthy, choking silence, a crowd of them, five then ten then more, stumbling to her door in stutter-step like gray-black zombies, gathering silently at her window, their green-glowing americium eyes watching her through the glass, barking…her sleeping mind rebelled and ended the dream, but as she rose to wakefulness, the barking continued.

She sat up in bed in a sheen of sweat and listened. The dogs were barking across the canal, which meant that the Park Service was clearing out the BoHo village again.

The Rake
September 11, 2043

CULTURAL CLEANSING
Thank God our government has its priorities straight. It's not the toxic air that's killing us, it's the excess of culture

The Park Service raided a BoHo encampment in Georgetown last night, and it was a touch-and-go proposition for our doughty rangers. In the depths of night, as their unarmed opponent was sound asleep, and fortified only with automatic weapons, night-vision equipment, and trained attack dogs – they struck and emerged in glorious victory!

We should be proud of our boys in green! Because of their sacrifice, we may never again be assaulted in public places with music, performance art, street magic, and dancing. How I despised seeing luscious landscapes in pastel, unique handmade clothing, crafts made with love and skill!

But we of the upper class must sacrifice as well, and I know we'll all proudly bus our own tables after dining in tony restaurants. We'll happily wash our dishes after so we needn't suffer the blight of the Bohemian Homeless in our fine and fair city. Even though we never see their encampments, even though they live quietly and respectfully, demanding so little and giving so much – nay, even though they are no burden at all, they are a burden we shall not bear! Harrumph!

We don't need their popular culture sullying our filthy streets. We don't need their music and laughter to break the roar and din of the city's machines. We don't need the delight they bring to our constipated capital.

We're far too sober to suffer such tomfoolery. Humbug, say I!

-KLW

DISPATCHES

Midnight Sun
News Post of September 12, 2043

HAS THE CONTAINMENT RING FAILED?

Health officials outside the Ring say containment of the virus has failed, and Neovirus is believed to have spread as far south as Baltimore and as far west as Pittsburgh. Neovirus is also suspected in Boston, but there are no reports of the virus in Maine and New Hampshire, nor in the northern counties of New York State.

No reports of Neovirus have been received from Vermont, which closed its borders to all traffic in the early days of the crisis.

Health departments in the Pittsburgh area have imposed a twenty-four-hour curfew. Officials stress that avoiding interpersonal contact is the only practical means of stopping transmission.

A home-level quarantine will be enforced at sunset tonight. Anyone discovered outside their residence without Health Department identification or travel clearance will be detained and transported to local quarantine facilities being set up in area schools.

Food and water deliveries to homes will begin tomorrow, and a toll-free number has been set up for those needing assistance.

Additionally, all transportation hubs, including the international airport and all rail and bus stations, will close indefinitely at 8:00 PM local time tonight.

URBAN UNREST INTENSIFIES IN NEW JERSEY

Reports from our Witnesses indicate that conditions are degrading rapidly inside the Containment Ring as civil order breaks down. Our Witness in West Orange reports:

"I have a friend who works down in Newark, and he came up Springfield Avenue tonight. He saw looters running down the street with flat-screen TVs and other stuff, and the cops weren't even trying to stop them.

"Other people tell me they haven't seen any cops at all in Newark, and the crime is picking up. Now, the city's got a bad rep, for sure. They do this kinda thing down there sometimes. But this could be bad if it spreads, and nobody tries to stop it.

"I'll drive down there to see for myself. We're safe up here in West Orange, but I'd like to know just how bad it is. Maybe we'll have to bug out.

"I tried getting the vaccine today, but it turns out we're all Class Three, so we have to wait until the Ones and Twos get their shots. I don't know when we'll be getting it, if we ever do. We've kept the kids home from school and taped up the windows and stayed inside. We don't have enough food and water to stay here for long, though.

"I won't have time to report if this all goes south. The safety of my family comes first."

THE BLEEDING EDGE

Day 26
Sunday morning, September 13, 2043
3120 L Street NW, Washington, DC

Krista took a walk that morning to escape her personal prison again. She strolled over to the farmer's market, but it was empty except for a few artisans.

Spring wasn't there, which she'd expected because her village had been raided; she and the other BoHos were likely camping somewhere nearby, but they'd return in a day or two. They always did. Georgetown was too lucrative a market to ignore.

She sat on the canal wall and tried to relax, but it didn't work. Later, she stopped at the grocery store to pick up food, but it was closed; a sign on the door said they'd only reopen if they received a new shipment.

AS KRISTA RETURNED HOME, she noticed "GW" scrawled in red chalk on the warehouse wall, which was Trope's code to check his secure dropbox today.

Her mood darkened. She was still trying to puzzle through his last package, but it brought on a throbbing headache every time she tried.

She noticed a pile of rags in the weeds to her left. Suddenly, she smelled fresh-cut oranges, and then something wet slapped across her face. Sharp, pungent vapors stung her eyes and nose. Arms wrapped around her, pinning her arms to her sides. She tried to run, but her feet found nothing but air beneath them.

Then it seemed as if she was floating free in a gray world where short moments lasted forever.

SHE SMELLED DIRT AND URINE. Breaking a crust on her eyelids, she opened her eyes and saw that she was lying on her side with her hair over her face. Her eyelids closed by themselves; her brain felt like it was rolling around in her skull when they were open.

The feeling passed after some time, and she looked around without moving her head: She was lying in a clump of weeds, the air smelled like sour oranges, and trucks rumbled in the distance. She tried to turn and her brain perambulated again, but she refused to close her eyes this time.

She heard the lapping of water nearby and concluded she was lying in the weeds by the canal's edge. The tops of the old warehouse buildings across the alley took shape as her vision cleared, but the effort of looking exhausted her and she passed out.

KRISTA ROSE OUT OF UNCONSCIOUSNESS again. She was cold in some places, hot in others, and felt like she was lying in a sticky pool of lukewarm coffee. The shadows on the warehouses had vanished, so she'd been laying in one position for hours, and her arms and legs had gone numb. However, she could move them.

She rolled onto her back and lay still, flexing blood back into her limbs. With her left hand, she pulled the hair away from her face and then spat out dirt that had lodged in her mouth.

Raising her head even an inch made her brain take another walk. Instead, she turned it to each side. She saw only weeds on the right, so she looked to the left – and saw the dead gray face of a boy. His eyes were open in shock, and they stared at her as if imploring her for salvation. Blood tears tracked through the soot on his face, and his teeth were stained brown with blood.

She tried to scream, but her throat only managed a thin, dry wheeze.

AFTER HER HEART STOPPED THUDDING in her ears, Krista tried to sit up. Her brain gyrated, and an odd sensation washed over her as if she needed to vomit but couldn't be bothered. She dangled her head between her legs to calm her spinning brain and smelled urine again. A dark stain on her pants spread from between her legs and down her thighs; it smelled more like urine than blood, so she hadn't been raped. Lying defenseless on Felony Lane was asking for sexual assault, though. She needed to get moving.

With a grunt, she rolled onto her knees and saw more stains on the side of her pants: dry brown smudges and flecks of something like shredded pink tissue paper. The ground where she'd been lying was damp and covered with the same pinkish-gray flecks.

She struggled to her feet and stumbled to the alley. Her purse lay in the gutter, and she grabbed it and then staggered to the old warehouse's steps and sat. Feeling woozy and weak, and incapable of anything more, she rested her head in her hands and massaged her temples. Her mouth was as dry as baked sand and her tongue felt like it was two sizes too big, and worse, she tasted burned copper and dirt. She tried to spit but couldn't muster even a drop of saliva.

The wooziness passed soon, and she sat up and rested her head against the warehouse door. Across the alley, she saw the pile of rags that had been a boy, and next to him were the bloody, flattened weeds where she'd been lying.

She checked her purse. Nothing was missing; her wallet, cigarettes, and pepper spray were untouched. Looking inside the wallet, she discovered that her paytabs and cash were still there.

For a moment, she imagined reporting the assault to the police and then laughed at the absurd notion. Warmth spread between her legs as her bladder emptied again.

She sat for another few minutes to gather her energy and then rose unsteadily. The remaining hundred feet to the loading bay grille felt like a mile, and she had to steady herself against the warehouse walls to keep from falling.

Upstairs, she stumbled into the apartment and locked the elevator door, something she always forgot to do. She staggered into the bathroom, locked the door, and propped her dressing chair against the knob. Sitting on the toilet, she stared sightlessly at the locked door, and then she grabbed a cup and drank three glasses of water to soothe her parched throat.

She started the bath water and puzzled over possible motivations for the attack. If her assailant hadn't wanted money or sex, why did he attack her? A Baser would have taken both and killed her. A common thief would have clubbed her and stolen everything she had. Nobody would have mugged her with a knockout drug without taking something.

Then she realized that the assault *had* taken something: It had destroyed what little sense of security she'd had and left her feeling vulnerable and weak. She realized then who was behind it.

Bob Downs. The Federals had shown they were stronger, and that she'd never be safe from them. But why bother? Was flipping the bird at their spy blimp enough, and was Downs so thin-skinned that he needed to retaliate?

A critical piece of the puzzle was missing, just like with Trope's video. She remembered seeing Trope's signal just before the lights went out, but the spy and his antics would need to wait until she felt better.

She wrapped her robe around her waist, and armed with her pepper spray, she stepped onto the balcony. Gazing at the dark orange clouds in the dusk sky, she felt the answer to the puzzle in her subconscious mind. But she couldn't draw it out no matter how hard she tried.

She picked up her chair and tapped it clean, intending to sit, and then she threw it down and walked back inside. On legs that were still unsteady, she climbed the stairs to her bedroom to rest.

KRISTA AWOKE FEELING RESTED and saw it was already nighttime. She brewed a cup and walked onto the balcony.

As she mulled over yet another turn of events she couldn't understand, she became frustrated again, realizing that she'd been reduced to nothing more than a clueless, helpless victim. All she could do was to move forward with her work and see if it would shed light on what had happened.

However, she was vulnerable and needed a bodyguard to protect her now. She closed her eyes and envisioned the ideal one – a vast, quiet manslab like her mother's, Seth Poulsen. She smiled as a happy, warm tingle rose inside her.

She shook off the fantasy and decided to check the personal-security services tomorrow. Right now, she had work to do.

BACK IN HER STUDY, Krista sat behind the desk and worked on the latest Trope contact. She signed onto his SatNet site, downloaded the file, and let it decrypt.

She'd been groping for a handle on the story, trying to weave more into it given the bare threads she had, but she'd found nothing useful; a modern American civil war wasn't a subject of speculation by academics because nobody expected one. She'd resorted to reading an alternative history novel called *Civil War Redux* for color she could add. The author had labored to reenact the Civil War in modern times, but all the book proved was that it couldn't be the same as the original – a modern civil war would last only minutes, and the United States would win. California only had a highway patrol, not a military. It would be a slaughter.

That meant her conclusion was wrong. Subduing California and stealing their gold would be so easy that it wouldn't be a momentous historic event – and Cheyn had clearly seen himself at the center of history in Trope's video. She was beginning to doubt whether they were planning a California takeover in that meeting.

Her musing stopped abruptly when the computer chimed, signaling that the files were decrypted. The servers were running much slower than usual; the day before, she'd raised the security of her equipment to the highest level, which had to be slowing everything to half its normal speed. Since the hardware was acting strangely, she saved the files to her tablet instead of the servers in case the system crashed.

She opened the files and found a text attachment and ten video files. Trope had never sent text with his video before. Curious, she opened the text file first:

> KRISTA:
>
> IT'S ALL GONE DOWN AND THERE'S NO REASON TO STAY. GIVE ME A DAY TO GET OUT AND THEN YOU CAN USE ALL MY MATERIAL HOWEVER YOU WISH.
>
> WEST VIRGINIA IS PLEASANT THIS TIME OF YEAR. MAYBE I'LL SEE YOU THERE.
>
> TROPE.

"Aww, bloody hell," she groaned. "*What's* gone down? Why can't you just come out and say it?" She sat back in her chair, curling her lip. He gave her puzzles within puzzles but no way to decipher them.

With a frustrated snort, she tapped the playback icon and watched the videos. The one she'd seen earlier was there, as well as nine others she'd never viewed. These videos also contained audio, but it was unintelligible.

The locations were Fort McNair in seven cases and Hains Point in three, date-stamped and covering a period from late February to late April. Cheyn and Grimes were present in each video, but sometimes other people were too. A tall Army colonel named Grovenor appeared in four clips, and Director John Plover of the FDA and Judy Pill from the HHS appeared in two. Others were pictured, but she couldn't identify them.

Most of the unknowns were military, but they carried clues on their uniforms. She stopped the playback and zoomed in as far as she could. Trope's equipment was the best and the resolution was extremely high, and she could see their rank and other insignia: Except for Grovenor, they were lieutenant colonels, most wearing the caduceus of the Army Medical Corps. She made a list of the names on their uniforms, thinking that she might get an idea of what they were discussing if she could discover their identities.

Some meetings took place in high wind and rain, which was significant. It meant that Cheyn needed to discuss this subject outdoors and away from the Washington bureaucracy, irrespective of the weather, suggesting that they were conspiring to do something that would frighten the bureaucrats.

She settled deep into her chair, tucked her knees under her chin, and pulled out her notebook. Cheyn wouldn't need Army medical brass to take over California. And while that might be a politically disastrous move, the Executive Branch had both the power and the duty to subdue a rebellious state. He didn't need to skulk around in harsh weather to discuss it.

Tapping her pencil against her teeth, she mulled over what she knew and what she didn't. When she realized that she'd never learn what Cheyn was doing on her own, she decided to ask the world for help.

"Sir, we have activity on the Warner servers. A secure SatNet download, encrypted and certified originals, large files," said Mochyn. "The trace worm was uploaded from her servers a few seconds ago."

"Back on her feet so soon? Break the encryption on those files now, and let me know as soon as you have any identification on the site she's downloading from."

"Yes, sir. I'm sending the files to the Puzzle Palace now."

After twenty minutes, Mochyn called out, "Sir, we've tracked the trace file through a SatNet downlink site in Herndon and from there to a server bank in the same area. The owner records took some time to crack. The owner of that site she's downloading from is Willem Hallowell. File coming up now."

Downs watched a photo appear on the Wall. "So the good Dr. Hallowell is Paparazzo? I should have guessed," he said to himself. "As you were so fond of saying, old man – was it the reality of your illusions that drove you mad, or was it the illusions of your reality?"

The decrypted files began to play on another screen, and Downs decided this was enough evidence to redact him. "Cochon, tag this and send this up as our Paparazzo suspect. Notify Cheyn that I'm also taking the initiative of issuing an immediate redaction order, highest priority. Having said that, though, I have no idea what hole the man is hiding in. Input?"

"We've had sporadic acquisitions over the years, sir," Buta said. "Usually at the Constitution Avenue tunnels or the Seventeenth Street culverts, although he's always gone when the Executives get there."

A map of Washington's storm sewer system flickered onto the Wall before Downs could command it. "That suggests he's accessing the sewer network via the western overflow lateral," Cochon said. Blue lines appeared on the map, and then a red line overlaid them. "The tunnels in blue are still flooded from Hurricane Xena, though, and they'll remain flooded for at least sixteen more hours. He must be hiding in the lateral sewer shown in red unless he has extended-immersion capability."

"Good work, Cochon. Hogue, send an Executive team in and instruct them to make this redaction messy. Dispose of the remains in a public place. I want Warner to know that amateurs shouldn't play the spying game while the professionals are on the field, at least for the brief time she remains alive. Cochon, request a lethal endorsement on her now."

The staff scrambled to execute his orders, and Downs smiled for the first time in three months. At last, Paparazzo had been found, and he'd be able to sleep.

TROPE HAD REQUESTED A DAY to get to West Virginia, and by Krista's calculations, it was only a few hours short of that. Deciding he was long gone, she uploaded the video files to her website. She also asked for a lip reader to discover the identities of those in the video and what they were discussing.

After the attack in the alley, it was dangerous keep this story to herself and hope to release a blockbuster exposé. Something bigger than her career was underway, and the world needed to hear it.

She hit 'send' and stumbled to her bedroom, happy to end the day.

MOCHYN WASN'T MERELY MONITORING Krista's server activity; he was reading every keystroke on her tablet as she typed.

"Sir, Warner is about to upload a large encrypted file to her website. It could be the Paparazzo videos from the size of it. She's also writing a post asking for a lip reader."

Downs grimaced and turned on the podium. "Cochon, what's the status of her lethal endorsement?"

"I just sent it up, sir, but Cheyn and Grimes are on a bus tour across the South through late Tuesday and are unlikely to respond promptly."

"We can't redact an MRC journalist without Executive Branch approval, so we need to block this post without raising her suspicions. If we spook her and get her running, she'll be hard to find. Mochyn, can you intercept that post and make it unreadable? Make it seem like a computer error?"

"No sweat," Mochyn said, adding quickly, "sir."

"And scramble those videos on her computers too. They're dangerous."

"I can't do that, sir," said Mochyn. "She downloaded them to her tablet and not her servers. I can read what her tablet sends, but I can't get into it."

DISPATCHES

District Update
NewsHub NewsChannel
Broadcast Transcript of September 14, 2043

"HHS spokespersons confirm that the death toll from the New York virus is two thousand one hundred as of nine this morning, and it's expected to rise among the unvaccinated inside the Ring.

"The spokespersons also say the Containment Ring is slowing the disease's spread, with only isolated cases reported outside it. A few cases have been confirmed in the National Capital Area, as well as Baltimore and Boston. Department of Health and Human Services spokespersons caution that there's no cause for concern among those outside the Ring.

"While the supply of Recombin is being expanded, the HHS says, the amount of vaccine remains limited. Patience, not panic, is the best response to this crisis.

"They won't comment on unconfirmed reports from hospitals and doctors across the East indicating a widespread epidemic, stating that unconfirmed reports are unreliable and merely serve to spread fear throughout an already frightened populace.

"The mayor and council of Butler, Pennsylvania, are meeting with HHS officials today to brief them on suspected cases in the Pittsburgh area and to request more resources to fight the disease.

"In other news, the body of Willem Hallowell was found in the Tidal Basin this morning, the victim of an apparent mugging. Dr. Hallowell was best known as the driving force of Advanced Heuristics in the 1990's, where he was the lead development engineer. He held over three hundred patents, including several for the Anisotropic Electro-Optical Membrane, also known as the synthetic retina, for which he received a Nobel Prize. It's widely believed to be a key component of the high-resolution cameras used on the Blackeye surveillance airships. In 2024, Dr. Hallowell left the world of private industry and joined the National Reconnaissance Research Center at Fort Meade, Maryland, moving to the National Security Forces in 2025. He resigned in protest in 2027."

Midnight Sun
News Post of September 14, 2043

CONDITIONS DECAY INSIDE THE CONTAINMENT RING

New York Emergency Services representatives say riots are flaring up inside the city as civilians vie for the limited supply of vaccine. In all, seventy-two deaths have been blamed on civil disturbances to date.

The situation in the city remains dire and unstable, and Emergency Services personnel say Federal assessments of progress are grossly exaggerated. The city is descending into a state of open chaos, and officials fear that order may be difficult to maintain even with the deployment of the National Guard. They expect the sporadic incidents of violence to become more serious as the disease continues to decimate urban populations.

LAW ENFORCEMENT ABANDONS NORTHERN NEW JERSEY

Civil disturbances in New Jersey are rapidly increasing. Our Witness in West Orange has just completed a road tour of Northern New Jersey:

"The cities of Newark, Paterson, and Elizabeth have been totally abandoned by police. The streets are filled with looters and rioters, and nobody's trying to stop them.

"I talked to a few gang members who were looting a shopping center in Clifton. They said they were trying to grab as much as possible since they might survive the virus, and they wanted to have the spoils if they did. I guess I can see that. Forward thinking.

"Everything's on fire too. There's a rumor that a firefighter in Newark was killed responding to a fire, and they're refusing to leave the firehouses unless police come along for security. Of course, there are no cops, so the fires just burn and burn, and keep spreading.

"I was driving west on Route 280, trying to get back home, and the entire west side of the city's burning. I couldn't see the highway for all the smoke. It's worse than the fug.

"My family isn't safe here anymore, so I'm packing it in and heading west while we still can. I never thought something like this could happen.

"This is my last report. Sorry."

WAKING IN RUINS

Day 27
Monday morning, September 14, 2043
3120 L Street NW, Washington, DC

Krista sat in her chair and glared at the trees across the canal. Her sleep had been fitful, and she'd awakened more tired than she'd been before going to bed. Also, a headache pulsed in one temple and the pain relievers weren't working. She rubbed the spot again, but the pain returned when she stopped.

It had blossomed a minute after she'd climbed out of bed. Memories of the mugging returned with so much force that she lost her balance, and she stumbled to the toilet to get off her feet. However, just as she felt capable of standing again, another memory surfaced – she'd been lying in a pool of infected blood for five hours yesterday. A panic attack hit her hard after that, but it was mercifully brief. A few minutes later, she could breathe normally again, and her pulse stopped pounding – except in her temple.

None of her usual remedies had worked. Slapping an ice pack on the dull throb turned it into a cold, piercing stiletto, and rubbing coffee paste over it just made her hair sticky. After an hour, she decided to suffer until the headache went away or she died.

Death was close; she felt it more than ever. She'd lived longer than her parents and didn't expect to see her twenty-eighth birthday. However, she'd always thought her death would be sudden and gory, as was her family's fashion, and a virus eating her organs didn't seem like her destiny.

She needed to get the vaccine. Even if she hadn't caught Neovirus yet, she didn't have enough food in her apartment to carry her through a months-long epidemic. Although she'd only been four during the New York coronavirus lockdown, she remembered that her mother had nearly run out of food – and their pantry had been fully stocked when it started.

Krista's shelves were completely bare, though. She'd expose herself to the bug by getting meals from restaurants, so she needed to scrounge up a vaccine shot somehow unless she wanted to starve.

Ed had already gotten his shot, as he was a nurse, and she'd called him to ask if he could arrange one for her. Georgetown Hospital only had a small supply, though, and he'd heard that armed guards were watching it. He promised to ask if she could get it, but since they were still cooling off over the Bleaker's dung-eating episode, she suspected he wouldn't. She rubbed her temple again and unfolded her tablet. If she wanted to live, she'd have to find the vaccine herself.

The newsfeeds talked about a shortage, but she found a doctor with Recombin on her first call. Dr. Abramovitz's office said they'd received a shipment the previous night and that she should come in, although she'd have to wait.

She hurried to the elevator and stabbed the button, dabbing Alkaliniment on her face and strapping on her mask as she waited. As she rode down, she thought about the inconsistent way the vaccine was being distributed. Her internist had more than a regional hospital, which made no sense. It would make a good subject for an article on government ineptitude, and she was composing snippets of it when she stepped onto Felony Lane.

The temperature topped a hundred degrees, and the fug stank of rotting meat. She glanced into the weeds to see if any stiffers were sprawled and decomposing there, but none were – the fug was the source of the stink. "By Jaysus, is the wind coming in from Jersey?" she muttered, tightening her mask's straps.

The two-block walk took twenty long minutes of bumping and jostling along M Street, but she finally spotted Dr. Abramowitz's gleaming white office at the base of the Key Bridge. A line of people stood at the door.

She sweated in the queue for two long hours. Once she squeezed into the packed reception room, she realized that many patients weren't getting the vaccine. They'd give their name to the nurse at the counter, who would check her computer monitor and shake her head, and then they were dragged through a side exit by guards. An NSF officer wearing an 'A5' stood calmly behind the reception counter and watched the nurse's every move.

This guy's on the A-list, like Bob Downs, she thought. *Why do they have the brass here? And why's he watching the receptionist and not the patients?*

As she crept to the head of the line, she detected a pattern – the door to the treatment rooms only opened for the well-dressed, while the poorly-dressed were shown to the exit. She looked down at her sweat-soaked shirt and tried to scrape off the coffee dribbles.

Her turn came forty-five minutes later. The receptionist, a young thing fresh out of school, dismissed the patient before Krista. After wiping her flushed face with a wet cloth, she asked for the spelling of her name, tapped it into the monitor, and then looked up with the same worn look of commiseration she'd been dispensing all day. "I'm sorry, Miss Warner, but you aren't authorized to receive the vaccine."

"Why not?"

The nurse glanced over her shoulder, and the Federal man stepped forward. "Ma'am, you aren't authorized to receive the vaccine –"

"I just heard that, boyo. I want to know why not."

"Please move on," he said.

"Right. Let's move on to why I can't get the vaccine when other people are. I'd like to know what –" A guard grabbed her arm and tugged her away, but she spun from his grasp. "Hey, watch the merchandise, Adolf!" she snarled.

A sharp-faced woman walked to the reception desk and read the data on the monitor; she then looked up at the NSF officer, and an unspoken communication took place between them. He nodded slightly. "Miss Warner? May I have a word?" she asked.

Krista turned around, but the woman had left the counter already. A moment later, a nearby door opened and she beckoned to her. They walked to a small, windowless room, where she sat behind a meticulously organized desk and gave Krista a smile thin enough to slice an atom. "Miss Warner, we have a small supply of unassigned vaccine. They send extra to account for breakage, spoilage, and other kinds of losses. I could set some aside for you," she said.

"Please do. I can't afford an illness," Krista said.

"The cost isn't covered by Wellness Corp or any government program, you understand, because we shouldn't be doing this." She squared a stack of paper with the desk edge. "The fee is twelve tenpez."

"What! I could buy a new server bank for that!"

"And we'd ask that you keep this confidential to avoid any fuss out there. We'd prefer that you didn't stir up any controversies."

"Because only the rich will be getting the shot, right? That's the controversy you want to hide. Well, I'm rich, so why didn't you just vaccinate me along with the rest?" Her face twisted into a scowl. "Downs. I bet that fuckwad Downs blocked me."

"Who?"

"But you can get around the block if I cross your palms with gold. Money talks and the poor walk, is that the deal?"

"Here's the only deal you need to be concerned with – this virus will digest your internal organs, and within days, you won't even have the energy to wipe off the blood. And bleed you will – through your eyes, through your nose, and when you go to the bathroom, you'll excrete your intestines and then it's a matter of minutes –"

"Hey, you're good at this! You must be a big hit at the Halloween party!"

She shot Krista a glare so piercing that she flinched. "Listen, Missy, the HHS gave you such a low priority that you'll be lucky to ever get it! If you want to live…" She looked down at her desk, corralling a wayward pencil and aligning it with the papers. "I advise you to consider your personal interests in light of this deadly disease. If you wish to receive the vaccine, you can't turn this into one of your muckraking crusades, or I'll withdraw the offer. This is a time to make wise and practical choices."

"That's a significant sum. I'll need to think this over," Krista said.

"Certainly," she said. "We're open until nine this evening if you decide to proceed. I'll make a note in your file to authorize the vaccination upon receipt of payment. If you wish to receive the vaccine, please come to the back door off the alley and knock. I'll show you where it is."

She hustled Krista through a door that opened onto the alley. Outside, she stomped around and kicked some boxes, but she got over her indignation fast when she found a stiffer behind a trash container. Another boy in his teens lay in a pool of gritty blood and wore the same blood tears and shocked grimace as the one she'd seen yesterday.

Everybody seemed to be coughing and hacking on the walk back to her apartment, and she tightened her mask and tried to avoid touching anybody. By the time she turned onto Felony Lane, she'd decided to get the shot despite Abramovitz's extortion.

She strode down the lane, palmed open the door to her garage, and pulled twelve gold pieces from a leather bag under her car seat.

FOR TWELVE TENPEZ, she didn't get much service. She realized why Ed was such a success as a nurse – he delivered warmth and humanity along with medical care, which was why the wealthy showed up for their treatments at a tenpez a day, every day. The nurse at Abramovitz's treatment desk wasn't warm, though, and Krista wondered if she was human or some replicant skin job with defective emotional software. She simply took the gold without a word, tapped a few keystrokes into her monitor, and handed her a keycard for Unit Two.

Krista turned for the door and drew a shaky breath. *Crap, I hate sitting in the Stainless Maiden. Why don't they put this stuff in a pill? Does it always have to be needles?*

However, she'd done this before and knew to walk to the treatment room, which held an array of machines specialized for different treatments, each shaped strangely and purposefully. The place was as mystifying as the fitness center she once strolled into, having overdosed on resolve and determination one New Year's Day – a sea of strange and frightening machines built only for the torture of a human body.

She opened the door. In Unit One, a man was being digested inside the immense stainless-steel arachnid, or at least it sounded that way; the device gurgled and burped, while the man inside remained deathly still. She continued to Unit Two and sat.

Wrist and ankle cuffs engaged, and a restraint clamped her chest and shoulders, squishing her breasts and constricting her breathing. As she tried to find a comfortable position, the monitor slid down in front of her face and parked two inches from her nose. The blood pressure cuff inflated, and the ads started:

YOUR TREATMENT WILL BEGIN IN FIVE MINUTES
TAP BELOW TO SKIP THIS ADVERTISEMENT

She'd once tried to tap the SKIP button on the screen with her nose, and all she'd gotten was a stiff neck. After that, she'd given in and just watched them.

An advertisement for an asthma medication flicked onto the screen. Everybody she knew had asthma, so the medications sold well, and competition between the drug companies for a slice of the wheezer market was intense. The ads always showed kids running through green fields under blue skies, so they had to have been filmed on another planet. She resolved to visit there someday if she could divine where the place was.

She started to organize a snarky article but gave up, not feeling the wit and lightheartedness that compelling satire needed. Instead, she watched kids cavort and frolic across the screen celebrating their newly relaxed airways. Then the machine whirred and the crawl under the ad said ...ADMINISTERING RECOMBIN 4CC LOT NUMBER 2335G MFD 12APR43 MFR CHALYS PHARM PLEASE MAKE A NOTE OF THIS NUMBER FOR YOUR RECORDS... She smelled antiseptic and prayed the damned thing wouldn't prick her in the same spot it had two months ago, or she'd have a permanent hole in her arm. The machine whirred again, hissed, and then whirred at a higher pitch. The needle pierced her skin, and her arm muscles tried to flinch and shudder but couldn't, and then she felt coldness spread through her arm and shoulder as if the thing were injecting liquid ice into her.

"At least Mengele's research didn't go to waste," she muttered.

The needle withdrew, and the smell of antiseptic and glue rose from her arm. The restraints snapped open and the screen read:

THANK YOU
PLEASE PATRONIZE OUR SPONSORS
HAVE A NICE DAY

She checked her arm – it was the same spot again, but that was okay. Her existential crisis was over.

KRISTA STOOD IN THE ALLEY and watched as the Key Bridge's lights powered up and their yellow auras bloomed. She was usually entranced when the streetlight's golden orbs set the hazy fug aglow, but tonight she hardly noticed. Her mind was elsewhere.

Something was wrong. Abramovitz was extorting patients with government collusion, but beyond the greed was a larger pattern that made sense. However, she couldn't get a grasp on it.

She walked down M Street in a daze, seeing none of the shop windows she usually did. Twice, she walked straight into other pedestrians. Mumbling apologies, she stumbled through the darkening fug until the alley for the farmers' market appeared on the right.

The square was deserted, which was unusual even for a weeknight; without life, the place was unsettling, like a dark and forbidding Gothic ghost town. She shuddered and told herself that she was safe, since nothing, not even a supernatural beast, could find her in this miasma.

She sat on the canal wall and lit a cigarette. She took a puff and allowed her intuition some space, and soon, the thoughts began to flow.

A historic event...too few resources and too many people...and the HHS has a list...

Images swirled in her mind, randomly at first, and then a few took shape: the blood-streaked stiffer in the alley, the working-class families walking away from the counter while the doors opened for the wealthy, the NSF officer nodding.

They can only live if they have the gold.

She shivered in the sweltering gloom as the images connected to thoughts in her mind. It didn't take long for the pieces to come together – and the picture that formed in her mind was devastating.

That was Cheyn's plan to avoid a financial apocalypse: He'd let a natural apocalypse solve his problem of too many people and too few resources. To save America, he was planning to kill it.

And if some family wasn't on his list and couldn't buy the vaccine, it was fine with him if they all died an agonizing, bloody death. The higher the body bags were stacked, the better his plan worked.

She jumped to her feet and walked through the deserted market. She swore to herself, kicked a cardboard box, and then swore some more; she paced, smoked, and turned the possibility over in her mind, but whichever way she looked at it, the conclusion was solid.

Someone needed to raise the alarm. She sat on the wall again, pulled out her tablet, and began to type. When she finished, she posted her article and left the market.

DISPATCHES

District Update
NewsHub NewsChannel
Broadcast Transcript of September 15, 2043

"HHS officials note that the number of new confirmed cases of Neovirus has diminished in the last day. Spokespersons hint that the Containment Ring might be lifted soon if all indications remain positive.

"Supply of the vaccine remains low, although multiple pharmaceutical companies are working day and night to replenish it. Spokespersons say as the virus wanes, the demand for the vaccine should diminish, although production will continue at an accelerated rate until all citizens are vaccinated.

"I, for one, am relieved that this crisis is finally abating, and I can get back to a normal life. I plan to celebrate tonight by curling up on the sofa with the wife to watch the Director's Cut of *The World's Tiniest Violin* in 3D, on our new Hitashi Plasmoid 3D Three Hundred Incher…"

Midnight Sun
News Post of September 15, 2043

CITIZENS FLEE MANHATTAN STREET WARFARE

Our Witness from the Upper West Side of Manhattan describes a city gripped by chaos:

"When they say the number of new cases is droppin, it's bullshit. It's the doctors that are droppin – from exhaustion. They can't diagnose new cases cuz half of 'em are sleepwalkin. And anybody who could get the virus has already got it, or they're dead already or hidin in the woods. There's no one left to get sick except me and the wife, and I'm lucky I've got a friend in banking. He's a Class One, and he'll help us get the shots tomorrow. He charged me for it, but hey, he's a banker. He probably charged his mom too.

"You can't trust the news anymore. I saw dump trucks at the Brooklyn piers yesterday fillin trash barges with long white body bags, so they're takin bodies out to sea and just dumpin 'em. Nobody's got any fuckin clue how many people died. I hear rumors of twenty thousand, thirty thousand, and any number can be right. Sure as hell, it's not two thousand like they say on TV. That barge alone had two thousand body bags on it.

"The crime's gone down lately cuz there's nothin left to steal. That's bad, cuz when they were lootin, they weren't shootin. Now that the street sharks got nothin to do, they're leaving their turf and shootin up the place. We still have cops on the Upper West Side, but I don't know how long they can hold.

"I'm gettin outta here before we get zotzed. Tomorrow, after we get the shots, me and the wife are buggin out. We got a friend who's a survivalist, way out in Connecticut, and we're going there. I always thought he was a nut, and now I'm gonna run like hell to get to his little hole in the ground. We're that desperate. It makes me nostalgic for the good ole coronavirus days, y'know?

"He was right all along. Who knew the city would go down the shitter so fast?"

We haven't received reports from our other Witnesses in the New York Area for almost two days now, and we fear the worst. Please remember them in your prayers tonight.

Witnesses living near the Containment Ring report that it has collapsed in some areas. National Guardsmen have abandoned their posts in large numbers in recent days, convinced that their efforts are futile. Many are returning home to care for loved ones in their final days or fleeing to areas that haven't reported an outbreak.

NEOVIRUS INFECTS VACCINATED PHILADELPHIA

Neovirus has taken hold in Philadelphia, despite the citywide vaccination program, with over one hundred cases reported in the past day.

Our Witness in Philadelphia City Hall reports that the government is in disarray:

"Obviously, a carrier from inside the Ring brought the virus into the city. A few of the councilmen argued that since the vaccine was available to everyone in the city, it should be enough to ban the unvaccinated from coming in and let the police enforce the ban with spot checks.

"That wasn't enough. Not everyone got the vaccine in the city, although most did. The only policy that would have made sense, in retrospect, was an absolute cordon. And now we're outta Recombin, so whoever didn't get it last week is screwed.

"Three councilmen resigned today because they opposed the absolute cordon. The mayor's office is decimated, what with resignations and staffers bugging out. I'm just a city manager, and now I'm running all of South Philadelphia like my own kingdom. There's nobody else left in City Hall to do it.

"All we can do now is tell the unvaccinated to stay indoors till the virus passes through. We're working with Southeastern Pennsylvania Emergency Services to deliver food and water to the homebound.

"We'll be imposing food rationing in the city tomorrow to try to prevent food hoarding. Sometimes a crisis brings out the worst in people."

Our Witness in York describes an exodus of vehicles traveling west. Public health agencies ask that citizens remain in the metropolitan area and not undermine the containment effort.

AUTHORITIES FEAR SPREAD OF NEOVIRUS

Health authorities fear that the massive flight from Philadelphia and its suburbs may spread the virus to the west and south. While most of the refugees are uninfected, some may carry the disease.

Many experts agree that the Containment Ring has broken. With Neovirus possibly present in a mobile refugee population, they now recommend other measures to control its spread.

Legislators in Illinois are considering a statewide police-enforced absolute closure of the border, as Vermont did, although it is doubtful that the police have enough resources to maintain an effective cordon.

Most nations have responded to the prospect of a pandemic by banning entry to aircraft or ships that have visited the United States. As a result, most international airports on the East Coast are now closed. Flights to Asia from the West Coast continue.

Officials from the Canadian Border Authority and the Québec *Police aux Frontières* say they have closed the border between the United States, Canada, and Québec. Both authorities state that a *Cordon Sanitaire* is now in place along the entire border, and forces are being mobilized to man every crossing. Canadian citizens and Québécois living in or visiting the United States are cautioned not to attempt a return as they will be denied entry. Here in Vancouver, the mobilization of Canadian troops for enforcement of the border closure is complete, and several convoys have already left the city and headed south.

The Mexican government is sending armed troops to secure the Unity Wall from Texas to California.

Similarly, the California legislature, in emergency session, is discussing the imposition of an absolute closure of its borders as Vermont did. Governor Rodriguez declared a state of emergency today, enabling him to activate the state's National Guard and enforce a future Health Cordon.

Washington, Oregon, and Idaho are considering California's example as their plans for a Health Cordon are finalized. A state of emergency has already been declared in Idaho, and private militias have offered their assistance in enforcing any border closure edict.

DEATH AND TRANSFIGURATION

Day 28
Tuesday morning, September 15, 2043
3120 L Street NW, Washington, DC

Krista ran her fingers through her hair and tried to wake up. She'd slept badly, if semi-conscious exhaustion could even be called sleep. She shifted in her chair on the balcony but was uncomfortable no matter what position she chose.

The nurse had said she might get a mild fever in reaction to the vaccine. If she ran a high fever, though, that meant she'd already been infected by the virus – and the higher the fever, the more dangerous the infection had been. She didn't take her temperature, but she was broiling all night long.

And she'd tossed her MRC credentials out the window last night with her post accusing Cheyn of premeditated murder, which also helped wreck her sleep. Everything was happening at once; trying to get her bearings was impossible when her world was constantly changing.

She tapped on her tablet and checked her site to see what damage she'd wrought, but the page was taking forever to load. While she was waiting, she pulled out her notebook and made a list of things to do on her faulty servers once the current crisis blew over.

Five minutes later, her homepage appeared – and every post from Sunday night onward was scrambled. Worse, the video files had vanished. She tried every trick she knew, but nothing brought the posts back.

She sat back in her chair and puckered her lips. *Something's different out there now, Miss Kellen. Something's changed and it feels bad.*

SHE HAD TO TAKE PRECAUTIONS, so she switched her phone to satellite mode to keep her communications from being monitored. After a few minutes of fiddling, she confirmed that the tablet's geolocation tracking was off like the salesman promised when she bought it. The world was changing in strange ways, and she needed to become hard to find.

When this was done, she logged on to her *Midnight Sun* account. For years, the editor had been nagging her to be a full-time correspondent for his site and not a mere Witness, and he'd given her a page for *The Rake* in case she ever accepted the offer. Today, she would.

It only took a few minutes to transfer her site to *Midnight Sun*. After her page appeared, she reposted the warning she'd written in the farmer's market.

The Rake
September 15, 2043

HE'S CHECKING IT TWICE
Break the glass. Pull the lever. Run like hell

Gabriel Cheyn has a list of those who will survive this epidemic and those who won't.

Are you ex-employed, disabled, or elderly? If so, you're not on Gabriel's List, and he'll let you die an agonizing death. You're on your own.

There won't be a new supply of vaccine. If you haven't gotten it already, you won't. Don't wait for it. You won't be waiting for salvation but waiting to die. The only one who can save you, your parents, your children, and all you love and hold dear, is you. All you can do to survive this virus is to stay inside, seal your doors and windows, and avoid other people. Trust our leaders, and they'll put you in a grave.

Isn't that a simple proposition? But many will not believe me, and it gives me no comfort to know that those doubters and cynics will be in, and not on, this earth in the coming weeks.

I can do nothing about that. This is the price of incredulity and cynicism, and some will discover how steep that price is soon.

If I can offer proof later, I will. For now, I only offer this warning: You're on your own. Protect what you love because you're the only one who will.

-KLW

SHE DECIDED TO BEGIN HER RESEARCH and prove her hypothesis to the world. She was confident because her intuition was so insistent, but nobody would believe her gut feelings. Hard evidence was the only currency in a world of cynics.

She knew who might help her gain access to the vaccinee list, and with any luck, she'd post some evidence on *Midnight Sun* tonight along with the Trope videos. The MRC crone would slap a fine on her, but she'd happily pay that price to save lives and expose the truth.

However, she needed to save the lives of those she knew first, so she threw on some clothes and headed downstairs. Even though it was only 6:00 AM, they wouldn't mind being awakened. Not for this.

In the gray dawn-light of her garage, she reached into a leather bag and removed twenty-four tenpez.

KRISTA STUMBLED ALONG BLUES ALLEY, the road that paralleled her alley on the north side of the canal. Trash filled the curbs, along with a thick crust of soot. Like the farmers' market and Felony Lane, the paving on Blues Alley was a patchy hodgepodge of asphalt and loose cobblestones, a surface the street sweepers wouldn't touch for fear of damaging their brushes.

She walked along the alley looking for the BoHo village entrance. At the end, she found an empty lot where a narrow building once stood. A chain-link fence surrounded it, but it was pulled back on one end and a beaten dirt path wound into the scrubby gray-green undergrowth. She edged through and followed the path carefully, unable to see far in the blinding fug. Keeping her head bowed, she stumbled through the stands of struggling, sickly red oak that punctuated the viney undergrowth. A moist, earthy funk infused the air, almost neutralizing the fug's pervasive rotten-egg smell.

From somewhere ahead, she heard a sound, a faint and regular *shick-shicking*. After a few more steps, she kicked something on the path that skittered away with a tinkle, and she knelt and patted the grass. Her hand brushed a soft object, and she pulled it toward her.

It was Spring's hat covered in dust. She picked it up, blew the dust off, and continued walking until she bumped into a large oak tree. With a hand on the trunk, she looked around it and saw the outlines of people far away in the fug. She started to move, intending to call out her presence to avoid startling them, but then she stopped when a deep voice began intoning words she couldn't make out.

They gathered around a patch of bright pink lying on the ground. The pink form rose, glided sideways, and then descended slowly into the ground. After a time, the slow and solemn *shick-shick* resumed – and then she recognized the sound of a shovel digging in the earth. The BoHos were burying a body.

She glanced at the pink hat in her hands, and the terrible realization slammed her so hard that she couldn't breathe. Gasping, she staggered backward, and then her foot caught a loose vine and she fell into the underbrush, the hat landing on her chest. She lay there for a few long minutes and stared unseeing at the tree branches. Once she could breathe normally again, she grabbed Spring's hat and ran through the undergrowth toward Blues Alley.

KRISTA WAS STANDING ON THE CANAL WALL at the farmer's market. She couldn't recall how she'd gotten there; she'd been in the BoHo village and then she was here, sweating and trying to catch her breath, clutching Spring's hat with both hands.

Her tablet said it was 6:49 AM. Twenty minutes of her life had vanished.

She had to have imagined that scene in the BoHo village, and only finding Spring would banish the nightmare from her mind. She stumbled through every corner and stall of the market and prayed to every deity she knew and begged to be proven wrong, but Spring wasn't there.

Exhausted, and feeling emptier than ever, she laid the hat on the stone wall. Then she sagged to the bricks and cried until she ran out of tears.

SHE RAMMED A CLEANING BRUSH into the baristomat and scrubbed the coffee grime out of it. She rinsed it, stood back, and assessed her work – it was so clean that it could be fired up in an operating room, but that wasn't clean enough for her. She blew the sweat off her forehead and scoured it again, grunting as she shoved the small brush into every crevice.

The effort helped her concentrate. Researching the vaccine exposé was now more urgent than ever, but beyond that, it would help banish the haunting image of a pink hat lying in the dirt.

"I'll nail that cryptofascist fucker's wrinkled ass to the wall," she said to the tortured coffeemaker and to whatever microphones the Federals had planted. "The cure for this depression is a good cold shot of vendetta. Go ahead and raise my Irish, Cheyn. You'll see what you get."

She grinned and grabbed a scouring pad, and then she shoved her hand into the coffeemaker again.

AFTER SHOWERING, Krista walked to the table by the elevator and daubed her face with Alkaliniment. As she put the tube away, she glanced at the thermometer, which said it was 107 degrees outside. "So why'd I take a shower?" she asked as she punched the button.

She turned off Wisconsin into the canyon of M Street and was carried off with the flow of people, which was going in her direction for once. Once past the Key Bridge, she crossed the street and climbed the stairs rising to the bluffs of upper Georgetown. The exertion felt great, but she immediately began sweating and fighting for air in the claustrophobic heat.

She arrived at the top and trudged across the university grounds with her arms spread, hoping to cool her sweltering armpits. After a few minutes, she spotted the large white Respiratory Care Center, turned in to the main lobby, and took the elevator.

The fourth-floor lobby was lovely, with a floor-to-ceiling window that had a park view on clear days, but an ominous blanket of swirling yellow-gray fug pressed against the window today. She passed through the lobby and walked into the Continuing Care Unit.

It was a new, sparkling suite that looked more like a hotel than a hospital. The walls were paneled with black oak, the white maple plank floors gleamed, and the corridors glowed softly from discreet lighting. Leather furniture, not medical equipment, filled the hall's alcoves.

A short, round-faced man stood in the patient lounge, a space further down the hall with large, comfortable chairs. Ed was dressed in a gray double-breasted suit with his shirt open at the neck – dignified yet casual – and was wiping his reddened face with a wet cloth and schmoozing an older woman. "…treatment, Sylvia, don't disappoint me, I hold you on such a high pedestal!" Ed was saying.

When he saw Krista, he broke into his widest smile, held his arms wide, and cried, "*Caramia!* I must say, you look like shit this fine day! What brings you to my menagerie? Such a surprise! Welcome…" He looked at her breasts; she'd forgotten to put on her bra and had soaked her shirt on the walk here, so few details were left to his imagination, "…to the three of you, a most hearty welcome! We both stand and salute your feminine abundance! Can we do lunch? I'm starving! You know what they say – feed a fever and all." He wiped his face again and fingered the lapel of his suit. "I hope I don't spontaneously combust. This suit is bespoke."

"Ed…"

"I know, I know, I have so much to atone for after that debacle at Bleaker's." He motioned to a large, unibrowed orderly passing by and hooked an arm around the man's shoulder. "Hérman, I took the lovely Krista to dinner, and I admit that I did, in fact, eat shit. She thinks it's because I didn't have the balls to tell the chef, but it's really because I don't read Eritrean, and I didn't know what I was ordering." He grabbed the orderly by both shoulders and shook him. "But thence, I discovered an unsavory truth! Shit tastes like shit, my friend, and it lingers on the palate for days! The world must be told, Hérman! Spread the word! Fly, my herald, fly!" He shooed the man away, who shambled down the corridor, puzzled and smiling uncertainly.

"Really, that wasn't the point, Ed, I don't –"

"It's all right. He doesn't understand a word of English. We communicate using grunts and hand gestures. He's actually very primitive.

We sometimes find him drawing pictures of mammoths on the walls in charcoal, they're so –"

"Ed!"

"Mmm?"

"I just need your professional help today," she said.

With a quivering effort, he assumed his sober medico persona. "I'll help any way I can, you know that."

She pulled him into an alcove. "The HHS has a list of who can get the vaccine and who can't."

He nodded slowly. "It's up in Administration. I heard there's a dozen Federal Fiends up there watching every keystroke the admins make. Everybody's spooked."

"Those pests are up there too?"

He nodded. "They're scaring everybody out of their wits. I swear, sometimes I think we're becoming a police state."

"I know, right? It's like we're in some Orwellian dystopia." She waited until a wheelchair-bound patient rolled past. "I could tell you some horror stories from my trip to the NTC, boyo. They'd turn your hair white as a sheet."

"Hmm. White hair might impart that air of *gravitas* I need to get promoted to Nursing Director…"

"You'll look thirty years older by the time I'm done jabbering, Ed. Guaranteed."

"Okay! Tell me over lunch?" he asked.

"Sure, if you'll do me a little favor."

"Ask, *caramia!* I am but your slave!"

"Ed, I really, *really* need to see who's on the vaccinee list. I need at least a half hour with it."

"You must be joking!"

"I am not."

He sagged against the wall and loosened his collar. "A kidney, perhaps, can I talk you into that instead? A matched pair? It'd be easier."

"Really, if you'd do this for me, lover, I'd appreciate it."

"Why is it so important? Are you on another crusade?"

"I'm doing research for an article I'm writing. I've got to confirm something, that's all."

"A crusade, yes, I knew it. Raking muck again today, are we? And in this heat!"

She nodded.

"Then it's best you tell me no more. Plausible deniability." He ran his fingers through his hair. "Okay, it's not a matter of whether I'll help, but whether I can. I could sneak you into the Admin office, but how do I get you on a computer with a Federal watching? That's the problem." He puffed out his cheeks, and for the first time since she'd known him, his eyebrows seamed in concentration. After checking the corridor in both directions, he slipped a Cannabliss inhaler from his pocket and toked hard. "Don't tell anybody about this," he said in a squeaky voice as he held the vapor in his chest.

"You get high at work?"

"High? Most of the time I'm dodging satellites in orbit, Krista. If I'm not Mr. Jingles all day long, I'm back to emptying bedpans. Okay, it's kicking in, lemme think…the Administrator's office isn't a good place. We could never distract the officers long enough for more than a peek." He toyed with his hair as he thought, and then his eyes livened. "Bunny…there's always Bunny. She might be able to do it."

"Bunny?"

"She practically lives in the sub-basement and tries to hack the network all day long. She tests the security, I think. I don't understand that stuff, but I know she can get into everything from there. She says so, at least. She has a backdoor into everything, so she might have a backdoor into the list."

"Where do I find her?"

"Oh, I'll have to take you. You couldn't find it on your own." He bit his lower lip and then said, "This is a huge risk for me."

She hugged him. "I appreciate it."

"I may have to give her something that was meant for you. Please don't be offended."

"I won't. I promise."

He checked his tablet's clock. "She should be there now. After you?"

She smiled. "Why, thank you, sir."

The elevator lobby was crowded, so they waited near the window wall. "We're licensed for nine hundred beds, and we must have three thousand patients," Ed said. "We just can't handle this traffic. The elevators are crowded, the kitchen can't make enough meals, and every system is stressed." He shook his head. "We can't work with this overcrowding. It's hard to even move around in the patient rooms, and we aren't providing any real care. And half of our equipment is contaminated too."

"It's the virus, isn't it?"

"A third of my patients have it. We put them all at the north end of the unit, but that isn't proper isolation. I'm afraid it'll spread to my regular patients no matter what precautions we take. And from the rumors we hear from the Connecticut hospitals, it'll get even worse." He wiped his face with a wet cloth. "I broil on my shift already. How do I stay cool? Wear a bespoke thong to work?"

She was starting to feel warm as well and fluffed her shirt. "I can't understand why they'd put virus patients up here. I mean, most of your patients are elderly. Aren't the elderly the most vulnerable?"

"Of course! That's what I don't get!" He shook his head again. "This bug is gonna tear through my regular respiratory patients, and once this blows over, my unit will be totally empty." He looked through the window at the fug. "It'll take years for our patient volume to recover. I guess I can forget about that promotion."

ED AND KRISTA RODE THE PASSENGER ELEVATOR to the basement, walked through a long tunnel to a fire door, descended a flight of stairs to another level, and then entered a long, dimly lit corridor of concrete block painted in the previous century. After another five minutes, they found a steel door with a sign that said INFORMATION SYSTEMS INTEGRITY and below that KNOCK BEFORE ENTERING. Ed grabbed the knob, prompting her to ask, "Aren't you going to knock?"

"Go ahead, take all the fun out of this." He swung the door wide and cried, "Bunny!"

A clatter and a curse came from the room beyond, and a woman's voice growled, "Can't you read the sign, fool?"

They walked into the room, a tall concrete-walled space illuminated only by dozens of monitors. A U-shaped workstation cluttered with monitors occupied the space beside the door, and inside it sat a large, middle-aged woman with enormous breasts. If tugboats had figureheads,

Krista thought, she'd be the model. "Ed, of course. Knew it was a fool." She removed her glasses and pushed two monitors aside to get a better look.

"A Fool of Medicine, of course. A noble profession. And I'm paid well to be one, Bunny."

"More'n me, as I recall," Bunny said. She snorted and sat back.

"I keep telling you, Bunny, presentation pays and sobriety doesn't. The only true fools these days are the serious ones." He clasped his hands together and leaned forward. "Bunny, Bunny, Bunny. How are you? This is my friend Krista. Krista, Bunny Masters. Is life in the dungeon treating you well?"

They continued an inane stream of parry-and-thrust that lasted ten minutes. Krista tried to make sense of the printouts on the wall, and her attention returned to the conversation when she heard Ed say, "Y'know, Bun, I can get a table for two at Cravendish next Friday evening."

Her eyebrows rose. "Wow, *that's* a hard table to get. I know some people that had to wait a year just to get turned down."

"They only seat sixteen tables a day. That's all they can do because the entire menu is on the endangered species list! Even the vegetable dishes! It's the hardest table to get in this town and believe me, I'd know." He leaned over her workstation. "And I'm inviting you to come and experience this splendor with me."

"Just like that?"

"Just like that!" He stood and snapped his fingers high in the air. *"Voila!"*

Her eyes narrowed. "And...?"

"And we dine under the rainforest canopy, monkeys swinging from the palms above, two adventurers lost in the epicurean wilderness..."

"This isn't free, Edify. Don't you bullshit me."

"Bullshit you? Have I ever bullshitted –" He noticed her arched eyebrows and cleared his throat. "Don't be a slave to the past, Bunny. Live in the now."

She tapped her pencil on the desk.

"There *is* a small favor I'd ask, now that you've offered," he said. "My friend here needs half an hour alone with the HHS vaccinee list."

She barked a short laugh and pinned him with a piercing look. "You serious?"

"If you can get in, of course," Ed said as he studied his fingernails. "It's supposed to be ultra-secure, hush-hush, uncrackable by the finest minds of science."

She laughed again. "You're *so* obvious! Look, I cracked it last week. Broke like a dry twig in three minutes. You want security, try hacking our accounting system." She leaned back in her chair. "But it's illegal, y'know."

"So's dining on Andean Snow Leopard. Anywhere else in the world except at Cravendish, that is."

She gazed back at him, tapped on her keyboard for a minute, and then lifted her bulk out of the chair. "I'm going up to the surface for a smoke. Prob'ly two. I'll be back in a half hour."

COCHON SPOTTED THE FLASHING ICON on his monitor and tapped it. "We've received the redaction endorsement on Warner, sir."

Downs walked to his station. "Excellent. What teams are available, Hogue?"

Hogue tapped her monitor a few times. "All we have in the near term is Executives Seventeen again, sir. They're up in Butler, Pennsylvania. They can be down here by this evening."

He grimaced. "Seventeen is messy and crude. They're unsuited for urban work, and they nearly botched the Warner snatch. What if Sanitation had picked up that deceased indigent? She might have been revived too early. It was unprofessional."

"I know, sir, but they're all that's available. Our other teams are committed to higher-priority targets."

Downs paced the podium a few times. "There are positives to using Seventeen. A messy and crude team will deliver a messy and crude kill, and this woman deserves one. Schedule them for a late evening redaction, Hogue."

THE DOOR CLICKED CLOSED and Krista hugged him. "Thanks for Cravendish, although eating endangered species...never mind. Were you going to surprise me?"

"Mmm-hmm. A last-minute call and off to the wilds we were to go. Now I'm going with the delightful Bunny Masters." He looked comically glum.

"She'll be a good dinner companion. I'm sure you'll find something about her you like."

"Ah, yes, she has that special *avoirdupois...*" He kissed his fingers.

"Try pretending she's me."

He laughed. "She's three of you!"

"Triple bonus day for Ed, then."

"It won't be the same. I wanted to go with you." He sighed. "What I do for love."

She kissed him on the cheek, and he wrapped his arms around her and stroked her back.

"I appreciate the sacrifice. I really do," she said, resting her head against his chest. "Ed, will we ever have a normal life?"

"But *this* is normal."

"No, it isn't. Trust me, this is a bizarre time."

"Krista, things will never be any more normal than they are now. You can't wait for everything to be perfect before you allow yourself to be happy. Enjoy the ride now."

"I wish I could believe that. I want to. I really do."

"Just believe and it'll all fall into place for you. Trust me, that's what I do and it works. I don't fight happiness, and I don't try to fix the world. This is the normal world and I accept it. Your problem is that you don't."

"My problem." She stiffened and pulled away from him.

He pulled her back and tried to kiss her, but she turned away. "What's wrong?" he asked.

"Just distracted," she said, avoiding his eyes. "I've got to do some work. I'm sorry."

"As do I. Alas, my intubated audience awaits. Remember – lunch when you're done?"

She smiled and pecked him on the cheek. After he left, she ran around the desk and sat in Bunny's chair. The page on the monitor said:

VACCINE ADMINISTRATION PRIORITIZATION

NATIONAL CAPITAL REGION

Underneath it was threatening legal language over a ghosted HHS logo, with three search boxes below that: last and first names, and middle initials. She typed in her name to see what came up.

Two Krista L. Warners lived in the Washington area, and a number was beside each name – the other Warner's number was a green 2, while Krista's was an orange 4. She frowned and right-clicked the numbers. An information window popped up:

CLASS 1: MANDATORY
CLASS 2: UPON REQUEST
CLASS 3: CLASS 1 SPONSORSHIP REQUIRED
CLASS 4: AT DISCRETION OF PROVIDER IF AVAILABLE
CLASS 5: CM49FJMF23FN34J143BF947FO48FP39M

She scrolled through the list and found a pattern – almost everyone in the corporate world or the Archangelist church was assigned a Class 1, and first responders and critical government personnel were assigned a Class 2. Most of the population was assigned a Class 3, which allowed them to receive the vaccine with the recommendation of an employer. The self-employed were assigned a Class 4, so they'd have to pay for the shot. Everyone else's name had a red 5 next to it, but no matter how much she clicked, the gibberish next to the Class 5 description remained.

She scrolled through the list, and recalling the pastel artist's unique last name, she searched for Spring. Her real name had been Livia de Almeida, which also had a red 5 next to it. Nothing happened when she clicked the number again, and she began pressing keys at random. Suddenly, another information window popped up:

CLASS 5: CONTACT NSF FOR CASE DISPOSITION

She sat back and let her breath out; asking the NSF to dispose of a case sounded like a euphemism for burying a body.

Her hands trembled as she realized what she'd found – the list didn't just name those who would live but also those selected for death. More than that, Cheyn was having his Fascist thugs enforce it. That meant she couldn't have saved Spring even if she'd gotten to the village earlier. Cheyn had already decided her fate.

She balled her hands into fists, aching to punch the accursed page through the screen, but she needed to remain calm if she was going to accomplish anything. Closing her eyes, she repeated her mantras and practiced her yogic breathing, but she was even angrier when she was done. She tried to channel her frustration into composing a post but found her fingers stabbing the tablet screen so hard that they went numb.

Growling under her breath, she squeezed her head between her palms, incapable of converting thoughts into words, frustrated that she could find nothing to do, tormented by a mental picture of a pink hat lying in the dust. Seconds later, though, the answer came to her: All she needed to do was publish the list, and Americans would then rise in rage and topple Cheyn's government. The UN would send in peacekeepers and doctors and medicines. The world community would draw a wounded America into its embrace and comfort it.

She tried every trick she knew to download or print the screen, but the page wouldn't allow it, so she took photographs of the search results and the information window with her tablet. The quality was poor, but the pictures were readable. As a precaution, she saved everything to the tablet's disk and then reread the list.

A piece was still missing, though; it felt like much more of this story was just beyond her grasp. As she was staring sightlessly into a corner of the room searching for the answer, the screen flickered. She checked to see what changed – and then she gasped and covered her mouth.

A bright red '5' was blinking next to her name. Cheyn had sentenced her to death.

KRISTA HAD MADE A PROMISE to Ed and wouldn't break it, death sentence or not. Besides, their conversation in the sub-basement had convinced her that their relationship was likewise stuck in the sub-basement, and it would never rise higher. Sitting across from him in the cafeteria and pushing greens around on her plate, she tried to find a way to say goodbye.

And it might be a permanent goodbye. Lingering in Washington and becoming an easy target for Federal assassins was lunacy. Trope had gone to West Virginia, and so would she; she'd pack tonight and leave in the morning, perhaps never to return.

Her stomach turned at the thought of eating her salad, so she reached across the table and sliced a piece of bread from the rubbery loaf there. She scanned the room for Federal thugs, half-expecting them to spring from behind a table. A plate fell off a nearby table with a clatter, and she flinched and dropped her bread.

"I'm so glad you're enjoying our meal, darling," said Ed.

She looked at him with swollen red eyes. "I'm not even trying to enjoy this."

"I guess you found more than you expected?"

She wiped her face with a wet towel, and the moisture evaporated instantly. Her misery reached panic levels: She felt like she was on fire, too many people clogged the room, and all she wanted was to return to her apartment and weld the door shut.

"You're scaring me, Krista. This isn't just some article, is it?"

She shook her head and scanned the room for assassins again.

"You have to let this go, whatever you're working on, relax awhile. Why can't you just go with the flow like the rest of us?"

"Because the flow goes over a waterfall!" She looked down at her plate. "There's no way back for me anymore, Ed. There's no way back for anyone."

"Never say that. Listen, I've gotta tell you this, and it's for your own good: You're heading for a psychotic break, Krista. You're losing touch with reality."

"Hey, boyo, I *wish* I could lose touch with reality, but it won't let me be."

"Why do you always have to fight? Take my advice and just let go. You'll find out everything's just wonderful."

"If everything's so wonderful, why are you doing so much pot? If you pissed on a tree, it'd spout marijuana buds. You do that because everything is all so feckin wonderful?"

"It's a coping mechanism, that's all. Everybody does it." His eyes brightened, and he leaned over the table and whispered. "*There's* your answer! Cannabliss will burn away that antsy part of your mind, and you'll never miss it, trust me. You've only gotta toke for two, maybe three weeks to get a solid addiction. Once you're hooked, you'll be getting baked so regularly, that crazy part of you won't even be a distant memory."

She began to speak, but no words would pass her lips.

"Whaddaya say? Buy you a toke and get you started tonight?" He wiggled his eyebrows.

"I give up. You're bloody hopeless."

"No, I'm hopeful, doll, and I'm happy. And you can be if you give Cannabliss a try."

"Ahh, so you not only got your brain washed, you gave it a wax too? I thought I smelled carnauba!"

"Krista, Krista," he said, and then he let out an exaggerated sigh. "You have such a beautiful mouth, but so much ugly comes out of it."

"Don't be going on about *my* ugly, Ed. I'm just calling things the way they really are, and if you don't like that –"

"I *don't* like it. I don't like hearing you tear down all the good things. I wish you'd just shut up sometimes and learn how to adapt, for chrissakes. I'm happy with the way things are, and I don't understand why you won't be."

She threw her napkin on the table. "You're feckin dense, boyo. You're living in a happy delusion. Take my advice and never leave it." She stood and walked toward the door.

"Once you cool off, can I call you for dinner?" he called.

"Sure. I just won't answer," she said over her shoulder.

DOWNS LOOKED UP AT THE WALL: It was approaching 2100 hours, and half the population of Georgetown was still on the streets. Couples even strolled the battleground of L Street, perhaps savoring the noxious night air or the thrill that they could be slaughtered any second.

Whatever their reasons, redacting a target in such a witness-rich environment was risky. A talented Executive might pull it off, but the crew for this operation couldn't redact a wheelchair-bound octogenarian on a remote farmstead without attracting attention. He was tempted to send them back to MMU to teach new Executives what not to do.

"Executives Seventeen is briefed and in place, sir," said Cochon. "Target is inside, event perimeter believed to be clean, and we're waiting for a Go order."

"How's our surveillance, Buta?" Downs asked.

"Pea soup fug, sir. Even the mini-drones are fugged out now."

"Then we can't confirm the perimeter is clear. This isn't our best team, and I want as much space around this event as we can get. If visual surveillance can't confirm it, then we'll just wait till we're sure everyone's gone. Take a break if you want. We're staying here tonight till this target is bagged."

KRISTA SLUMPED IN HER BALCONY CHAIR, bathed in the glow from her apartment windows. The fug was so thick that she couldn't see more than six feet, but that felt comforting for once. Being wrapped in the murk isolated her from the insane reality beyond her door, and she urgently needed relief from it.

She'd tried to pack her bags earlier, but her doubts about leaving grew with each one she filled. Every option was terrible, and she didn't want the only one that made sense: run to West Virginia and fight the battle from there. That wouldn't stop the HHS from using their list and deciding who would live and die. All it would accomplish was to destroy what minuscule chance for normalcy she had left.

On the other hand, staying was insanely risky; the full moon was approaching, and her luck hit low tide at this time of the month. She'd be weak and vulnerable for the next few days, and even life's mildest challenges would be daunting. Standing up to a government conspiracy wasn't going to happen.

As she thought about her choices, Ed's last words bubbled up in her mind, and she realized he was right. She didn't have to choose between bad and worse options – she just needed to silence that restive and discontented part of her mind that was driving her crazy. That was the piece she needed to break off to fit into life's puzzle. Cannabliss would burn it away painlessly, granting her the baked and hazy happiness of Ed and Liza.

She just needed to destroy her mind to find contentment. It was senseless. It was selfish. She loved it.

Three weeks was all it would take to kill it, Ed had said. Suddenly, she felt an electric tingle, and then she gasped as she realized that she was going to do it – she'd free herself from the shackles of reason and responsibility, and nothing would stop her. Her pulse pounding, she picked up her tablet and dialed Ed's number. She apologized for her meanness in the cafeteria and asked him to bring over a Cannabliss toke as soon as he could. He promised to be there the second his shift was over.

After she clicked off, she sat back in her chair, relieved. Soon, Ed would show her how to toke her way to contentment. Soon, she'd take the blue pill of oblivion, and battles would become somebody else's problem.

KRISTA CHECKED THE TIME on her tablet: It was twenty minutes to midnight, and Ed's shift was over in fifty minutes. Her torment would end in an hour.

However, the more she thought about taking up Cannabliss, the worse she felt. She recalled Ed's dull and distant eyes on that night he'd eaten the breaded dung, and she shivered as she imagined herself wearing the same bovine expression.

The Black Dog lived down that path; the despair and ruin waiting there were as clear to her as a Trope video. And Cannabliss wouldn't only wreck her mind; the habit would kill what remained of the little girl in her heart. The restlessness that maddened her was also all that remained of Miss Kellen, and too many children had been laid to rest that day. Not only that, Bob Downs and his goons wouldn't hesitate to kill her just because she was mellow and wasted. Indulging a drug addiction would only make their job easier.

She desperately needed to focus. Hoping that thinking of something else for a few minutes would clear her mind, she opened her tablet and clicked the first icon she saw.

The Trope videos began to play in chronological order. She watched the soldiers walk across the screen, this time not caring what they were doing, but then she noticed Trope's data ticker along the bottom – and her subconscious mind jolted her so hard that she sat upright in her seat.

She checked the dates on the screen again, and then she gasped and covered her mouth: The videos had been recorded in February and March, but nobody had seen Neovirus before August – and the Recombin shot she'd gotten had been made in April. Cheyn and his cronies had known that an epidemic would ravage the country before anybody else.

"The bastard unleashed that bloody bug himself," she muttered to herself as she sagged into the chair. "Neovirus isn't some random act of nature. It's a feckin biological weapon."

AFTER A FEW MINUTES OF SHOCKED STILLNESS, Krista stood, and her muscles responded as if she were swimming through jelly. She paced the perimeter of her balcony, angry with herself and angry at everything, but she couldn't feel anything else.

I'm wrecked, she thought, walking to her chair. *I can't handle this*. The light from the apartment windows blinded her, and its glow felt as if it was devouring her life force, so she pulled the chair away into the darkness. She collapsed into it and lit a cigarette.

Her consciousness clipped and darkened around the edges, her senses faded, and the external world receded – but this time she let the emotional withdrawal pull her into its uncomfortable but safe womb.

THE RUNGS OF PERDITION

Day 28
Tuesday night, September 15, 2043
3120 L Street NW, Washington, DC

The Executives were sitting in a Silverback off the alley when the Go signal came in. They walked to the trunk and pulled out their equipment bags; dressed in dark gray T-shirts and black camouflage pants, they were invisible in the deep fug and night. Each strapped a holster and a combat knife to his upper thigh, donned night-vision goggles, and voice-checked his comm headset. The leader motioned to his partner, and they walked to the loading bay door.

KRISTA WAS STARING SIGHTLESSLY INTO THE FUG when the red light illuminated over the elevator door. She gasped and dropped her cigarette, and then she stumbled away from the penthouse window. As soon as the door scissored open, a man in gray clothes and wielding a knife jumped through and ran to her writing studio. A second man ran up to her bedroom.

They were dressed like the man she'd met at the NTC – black camouflage pants, gray T-shirts, and black nylon boots. The assassins searched the apartment in under a minute and then met at the bottom of the bedroom stairs.

One talked into his headset and pointed to the balcony. Adrenaline cleared the fog in her mind, and she threw the chair over the railing and ran the other way.

EXECUTIVE TEAM SEVENTEEN WAS CONFUSED. The target should have been in the apartment, but they'd checked everywhere, and it was empty. Seventeen Alpha asked Hogue for new location data, but the answer was negative. They decided to search the exterior.

As they opened the glass door, something splashed into the canal. They switched their night-vision optics to forward-looking infrared and searched the fug.

Seventeen Alpha pointed to a smoldering cigarette on the patio and walked to the rail. He told Hogue that she might have jumped into the canal, but Hogue said that she wouldn't have survived the seventy-foot drop.

They pointed their flashlights over the edge of the roof and checked the balconies below. Finding nothing there, they split up to check the roof.

KRISTA STUMBLED TO THE AIR SHAFT'S HATCH and stepped in, dogging the latches behind her. After groping around in the dark, she found her respirator and strapped it on.

She shuffled across the metal grate floor to the ladder, taking careful steps and feeling for the floor opening with her foot. After six steps, her foot found open air. She reached out and felt for the rung, and then she placed one foot on the ladder. However, as she swung her other leg onto the rung, her hands lost their grip and she fell on her rear. A black cloud of fine soot rose into the air.

Sitting on the edge of the opening, she reached for the ladder again and grasped it. Rung by rung, whimpering quietly, she descended into her nightmares.

THE ROOF WAS EMPTY TOO. Hogue had said there was only one way in or out, but Seventeen Alpha decided that couldn't be true. She'd either jumped into the canal or used an escape route Intelligence hadn't identified.

As he walked back to the penthouse door, he noticed a rusted wall hatch. He twisted the latches and opened the door. His flashlight illuminated a metal grate in a concrete shaft, with a black ladder at the far end descending to a lower floor.

A fine cloud of soot swirled in the flashlight beam, so someone had passed through recently. He shined his light through the hole in the floor, but the beam disappeared after two feet. His forward-looking infrared showed something warm below on the ladder, though, which had to be Warner.

He placed his hands on the rung and felt fine, slippery soot. It would be dangerous to follow her down this ladder, but he didn't need to because his mission was to kill, not capture. He pulled his pistol from his holster and aimed down the ladder.

He started to squeeze the trigger, but then he noticed the concrete walls and realized that the shot could ricochet and hit him like the Executive at St. Elizabeth's. As he returned the pistol to the holster, though, he lost his grip, and the weapon dropped through the grate.

Two seconds later, he heard a muffled cry from below and smiled: Target location confirmed. He stepped outside, tapped his headset, and told Seventeen Beta to cut off any escape from the loading dock. He'd climb down the shaft and flush the prey into his sights.

KRISTA WAS PASSING THE FOURTH FLOOR when she heard the door open above, and she froze as light filtered through the grate and illuminated the fine black soot. Hoping it would obscure her from the light above, she rubbed her hand on the wall and filled the air with more fine black grit.

She was moving her hands to the next rung when something hard hit her left shoulder, and she cried out and peered into the darkness. A second later, she heard the rattle of the old air filters far below as a heavy object landed on them.

The light turned away. She resumed her descent, but she was too tired to control her muscles and couldn't stay on the ladder much longer. She'd descended as far as the third floor when she heard him cough and felt a vibration in the rungs. Her pursuer knew she was there, and he'd climbed onto the ladder. She needed to hurry.

Grasping the rungs was difficult because the soot formed a thick, slippery crust on her sweaty hands. After wiping as much off as she could, she continued down to the second-floor hatch. She pushed the door open, waited a few seconds, and then slammed it shut without going through.

The diversion might not deceive her stalker for long, but at least it would force him to try every hatch and buy her more time.

SEVENTEEN ALPHA CHOKED ON EACH BREATH. The atmosphere was more soot than air, and to make things worse, it was getting into his eyes and causing intense pain. He'd closed them keep the soot out, but that only made him disoriented. With his free hand, he flipped down his night-vision optics to cover his eyes. However, they were coated with dust and he couldn't see heat signatures below even with the sensitivity dialed up to maximum.

He moved one rung down and his right foot slipped off, followed by the left foot and his left hand. Hanging from one hand, he swung over the void and groped for the ladder.

A FALL OF FINE SOOT blanketed Krista, covering her mask faceplate and making the rungs even more slippery. She looped an elbow around the nearest rung until her sore hands found a firmer grip. She didn't have far to go – she'd just passed the first floor, and the next door would be her last.

SEVENTEEN ALPHA REGAINED HIS GRIP on the ladder, but he'd lost his headset when he'd slipped. He felt the outline of a door and tried it, but the handles were stuck. He banged on it, but it wouldn't budge, and he began descending to the next floor.

KRISTA REACHED FOR THE LOADING DOCK HATCH. With her arm looped around the rung, she turned the rusted latches and pushed the door outward, and then she swung through the opening and onto a concrete floor.

Everything was black, and she felt a flash of panic until she remembered she was wearing a grime-covered mask. She yanked it off and saw the loading dock lights filtering through gaps in the garage door. As her eyes adjusted to the low light, she spotted the outline of her car.

She shook the soot off her clothes and then slammed the hatch. There was nothing in the garage to jam it with, so her only choice was to get far away fast. She walked to the door control and palmed the rolling door open, and then she unplugged the charging cord and climbed into the driver's seat.

She thumbed the ignition on and pulled the shifter into drive, but the only sound the hybrid electric car made was the soft whir of the ventilation fan. Her foot reached for the accelerator, but then a shadow flitted across the windshield.

Noiselessly, she slipped the transmission back into neutral as a man walked past the garage and shook the grille opening onto Felony Lane. He talked into his headset but received no reply, and then he walked back to the elevator past the dark opening of the garage doorway.

She was trapped, with one killer behind her and another blocking her escape. Her self-control shattered, and a shudder rippled throughout her body – and then her right foot twitched and tapped the brake pedal, bathing the rear of the garage in bright red light. The man turned toward the garage door and their eyes met. He reached for his pistol.

Krista yanked the shifter back and jammed the accelerator to the floor. The engine's turbines screamed and the front tires squealed, and then the tires found traction. The car leaped forward, hitting him in the knees and throwing him back into the concrete wall. She slammed the brakes, and the car squealed to a stop.

She opened her eyes and screamed – his shattered body slid down the concrete wall, and he looked into the headlights, his lips forming silent words. She opened the door and ran to the wall. "I'm sorry, I'm so sorry..." she said, and he collapsed to his knees as if in prayer.

As she bent to help him up, he lunged and grabbed her shin, reaching for his knife with his free hand. She kicked and twisted but couldn't break loose. She spotted the black combat knife in his free hand, and she drew back her other foot and kicked him hard in his jaw, knocking him off balance and breaking his grip. As he fell back to the wall, though, he whipped his knife from behind him and slashed the top of her left shoe and her ankle.

She stumbled for the car and then fell hard to the floor, pain radiating up her leg from the wound. She rolled across the concrete and tried to rise, but the killer crawled toward her, knife in his teeth, dragging the dead weight of his legs behind him.

He swung the knife again at the same time she climbed to one knee, slashing the back of her leg and sending her sprawling back on the concrete. She rolled to one side and then crawled to the bloody front bumper of her car.

When she turned around, his knife flashed, missing her feet only by inches. She pulled her legs up to her chest and away from the knife's arc, but he kept crawling closer. When his knife was just a few inches from her legs, she uncoiled and kicked his shoulders with all the strength left in her tired legs.

She drew a breath to scream, but the Life Force must have been floating in the air; the breath erased her weariness and new strength surged into her muscles. Her legs felt more powerful than ever, and she pulled them back and kicked his shoulders as hard as she could. Something inside him cracked, and his face twisted in agony.

"Fuck you!" she yelled, once, twice, a dozen times, and with each word, she kicked his neck, his shoulders, his head, ripping his ears and bloodying his face. When he finally sagged to the floor, she pulled herself up and leaned on the car's hood. "Enough, already," she said, panting. "Give it up, wouldja? You're a bloody stump."

The man rolled over and pulled his broken body toward her again. She limped to the open door of the idling car and fell in – and when she looked through the windshield, she saw the killer leaning on the hood. He'd found his pistol and was aiming it at her head.

She jammed the shifter into drive, closed her eyes, and punched the accelerator pedal. The car slammed him into the concrete wall, but she pressed on with her front tires spinning and smoking and trying to gain one more inch. After a few seconds, she realized that the car had stopped and lifted her foot off the gas pedal.

She opened her eyes but couldn't see through the gloppy red mess on the windshield. When she tapped the wipers, though, what she saw made her recoil and retch.

Before she could vomit, she backed up and drove to the grille. She climbed out, and holding one hand over her queasy stomach, she limped to the palmpad and laid her hand on it. The grille started to rise.

As she was climbing back in, though, she was shoved sideways into the driver's seat. She turned to see what had happened – and an inch from her face, a black knife in a gray hand sliced at the air.

She yanked her head back and tried to block the hand at the same time, struggling to stay away from the knife. She slammed the door on the assassin's arm, but the blade swung even closer. She pulled the handle with both hands and then saw what was outside: a black, soot-coated golem with glowing green eyes.

She screamed and pulled on the door, banging it against the arm while trying to avoid the blade, but the soot-golem's knife still slashed the air. With no options left, she let go of the door, aimed for the grille, and stomped the gas pedal.

The car leaped forward and ground along the brick wall, leaving behind a spray of sparks, and then it slammed into the solid steel jamb of the grille.

Glancing sideways, she saw that the golem's arm and the knife were gone, and she stepped on the gas. Free at last, she roared down Felony Lane at sixty miles an hour.

SEVENTEEN ALPHA LAY BESIDE THE BRICK WALL and looked down the alley, his head ringing and every body alarm screaming red alert. The taillights moved away, and he tried to reach for his holster, but his right arm wouldn't move. He couldn't feel his left arm at all. The taillights diffused and grew larger until he couldn't distinguish them from the fug.

He remembered that he'd lost his sidearm, but that didn't matter; he couldn't redact Warner anymore. Groaning, he rolled onto his back and decided to rest.

Directly above him, the heavy steel grille whined and began its automatic descent. He watched it rattle toward him, but he was too tired to move out of its way. It continued down, slowly crushed his windpipe, and then it rose and began the cycle again.

The loading bay grew quieter. After a time, even the sound of ragged breathing ceased, leaving only the rattling of the grille.

"Seventeen Beta is on cutoff in the loading bay, sir," said Hogue. "He reports that he lost contact with Alpha. Alpha took an air shaft and believes Warner used it to escape."

"Contact lost due to interference?" asked Downs.

"Could be, sir," said Hogue. "The plans show the shaft is concrete, and it's difficult to transmit through that."

"Buta?" he asked.

"Seven-foot visibility, sir."

"I've just lost contact with Beta, sir," Hogue said, stabbing icons on her screen. "No signal."

Downs tensed. "Send in the backup now. This feels wrong. Buta, I hate being blind."

"There's nothing I can do, sir!"

The room was quiet as the managers scrutinized their monitors for any indication of Team Seventeen's status. "Executives Six ETA is nine minutes, sir," Hogue said.

Buta sat upright. "I have something, sir!" The screen on the Wall showed a blotch of orange yellow that darkened briefly and changed back.

"What was that?" asked Downs.

"I think it was a car, sir. I'm enhancing it now." Lines scrolled down the screen and sharpened the image, but it remained a blotch. "A large dark object, sir. Possibly a car, given its speed."

"Warner doesn't own a car, correct, Cochon?"

"No ownership records we know of, sir," replied Cochon.

"The Executives reported no vehicles in the loading bay when they entered, sir," offered Hogue.

"Show me the plans of the ground floor," said Downs. "It came from somewhere."

KRISTA'S CAR ROARED UP M STREET at full speed. Trembling and still standing on the accelerator, she drove into the dark tunnel of trees that covered the river road heading north. She turned on the headlights, only to be blinded by the glowing fug, and shut them off again.

As she drove, she felt her mind withdrawing again; a tunnel formed around her vision, and the world became softly surreal and dreamlike. She knew she was traveling at high speed and making turns, but with each mile, she became aware of less. When she turned onto a highway, she tapped on the car's self-driving system to engage the road's magtrack in case she sank into a stupor.

Seconds later, she did.

"Executives Six reports two fatalities, sir," Hogue said. "Both ours. No evidence of Warner yet."

"Dead?" Downs asked. "Both of them? Warner killed two Executives?"

"Appears so, sir. It's a mess in there."

Downs stood silently on the podium, a muscle twitching in his jaw, and then he turned to Cochon. "Prepare a Citizen's Apprehension Directive and send in an evidence team and a media team." He pulled his glasses off and rubbed his eyes as he paced the podium's circumference. Stopping at Intelligence, he noticed the building plans on the Wall, which showed a room that could hide a car. "Cochon, Warner has a trust. Does that trust own a car?"

Cochon's hands tapped on his monitor. "Yes, sir, or at least the records show it did. A '40 Bicep D4, purchased November '39, color slate blue, Pennsylvania tags AC9-DD5-VG5. Registration expired November 2040, never renewed." He tapped a few more times. "No record of a sale."

"That's what she's driving, and that's good. The Bicep's onboard communication module is easy to hack. Find the IP address of that vehicle and have the NSA tap into the hands-free mikes and navigation cameras. Maybe we'll hear her talk about where she's going, or we'll see a road sign or a landmark."

Cochon worked his monitor again. "Sir, the vehicle has no IP locator. Records show she had the comm data module disabled after purchasing the car. Remote monitoring is impossible."

"Why would she do that? Her satnav system wouldn't work without data."

"Unknown, sir."

Downs stared at the Wall, deep in thought. "Okay, we'll do it the old-fashioned way. Put out a bulletin on that vehicle. Hogue, she'll probably go for West Virginia, so move our off-duty SAGs from the west side to the east. I don't want her getting even a seven-day sanctuary."

THE HALLOWEEN COUNTRY

Day 29
Wednesday morning, September 16, 2043
Eleven miles west of Cadiz, Ohio

The Freaks decided Ada wasn't ready to eat and sat by the glass door to stare her to death. Sitting on the dirty red tile floor of the rest stop lobby a few feet away, she death-stared them right back. After a few tense moments, they found something else to watch.

It was after midnight, and she'd been working on the tobacco machine's lock for two hours already. She pushed a pin forward with shaking fingers and tried to turn the barrel, but it still wouldn't move.

It had taken her most of last Friday to pick the snack machine's lock, but she hadn't eaten for four days and was hungry and motivated. Because of the Freaks, she couldn't walk to a nearby town and grab some grub. Unless she wanted to eat the beetles littering the tiles near the men's room, cracking open the snack machine was the only way to get food. And now that she was out of cigarettes, it was the tobacco machine's turn.

The crooner warbled through the speakers. "Only twenty tracks, twenty-four / seven, over and over and freakin over," she muttered. "This is some demented oldie form of torture!" Ole Blue Eyes started singing about doing it His Way for the millionth time. "All right, I'll talk already!" she yelled. "What have I gotta say to get this crap turned off?"

The Freaks, ever attentive, sat up and cocked their heads. However, she didn't appear any closer to death, so they curled up by the door and waited.

She tried to turn the lock, but it still wouldn't move. A growl of frustration arose, and with it rose the temptation to kick the crap out of something. But she reminded herself to be patient; the lock was merely a machine, and she could make any device do her bidding. Besides, she'd have to start again from scratch tomorrow if she gave up, and her cravings were getting seismic already.

Her last one had been this morning. "This is inhuman! What made me get addicted to this? Right, thanks for the advice, Frida Armstrong, you were so freakin right when you said cravings are fun. You stupid, butterface prostatot. Some friend. I hope you get lung cancer."

The cravings were her fault, though. She'd had nine packs in her bookbag, which should have lasted for weeks, but she'd been so nervous that she'd burned through them in record time. That was shortsighted, but she hadn't expected to be stranded here, alone, for over a week.

"This is the rest stop of Hell. No, this is the rest stop on the side road to Hell, the one nobody stops at anymore." Another craving rippled through her. "Fantastic. Like I need to be a chain-smoker. Mom's going to obliterate me when she finds out. She won't even ground me. She'll underground me."

She turned her lock pick again, but the lock still wouldn't budge. Squinting in the sickly greenish fluorescent light, she pushed the next pin forward a millimeter. "Freakin Freaks," she muttered. "Like I need mutants stalking me on top of everything else. If I only had that big black gun."

She was still tempted to run for Cadiz, which was about ten miles away, but the creatures were built for speed and she wasn't. On top of that, she wasn't sure she could outrun a turtle after smoking so much, especially since she was still wearing her prostiboots. They hurt her feet even just standing still. She couldn't imagine sprinting in them.

The lobby was safe, at least. The janitor's closet lock had been easy to pick, and she'd found keys inside that locked the lobby doors. The Freaks weren't interested in breaking the glass and devouring her; they were content to show up in the evening, stare at her, and wait. Nevertheless, she was getting desperate for a way out. The snacks in the machine could only feed her for another week, and once that was gone, what would she do? What would the Freaks do?

They'd eat her, of course. If she was lucky, they'd kill her first.

She turned the pick again, but the lock still refused to budge. An intense tickle grew at the back of her skull, one warning that a kill-me-now craving was about to tap dance on her brainstem. She gritted her teeth and concentrated on the lock, but then her nerves snapped.

"Stop looking at me!" she screamed at the Freaks. "I'm having a bad enough day!" She closed her eyes and breathed a few deep breaths; if she didn't calm down, she'd never pick this lock.

Her thoughts drifted back to the first day, before she'd known about the Freaks. She started to walk to Cadiz, but the plan fell apart when she heard a large animal tracking her from behind the roadside shrubs. She walked faster, and so did the creature, and her composure was shredded by the time she spotted a beige car ahead. She ran for it and then hopped in and slammed the door behind her.

A nauseating smell struck her so hard that she gagged, and she turned to see what was causing it – and looked directly into the silently screaming face of a dead woman, her mouth and eyes crawling with flies. Turning away, she saw a fly-coated lump of a man in the driver's seat, whose ears and nose had already been chewed away by some creature. She jumped out of the car, screaming madly and convinced she'd have a heart attack.

Nobody came to see why she was wailing. She was standing alone on a deserted highway with two dead people and a mysterious animal that wanted to eat her, like a Halloween where every effect was real, all trick and no treat. She wouldn't stand around at night in that Halloween country, so she ran back to the rest stop.

That evening, the two Freaks appeared at the window. They had bodies like German shepherds – long, gray, and muscular – but they also had the blunt face of a mountain lion. Their alert, yellowish eyes looked more like a cat's than a dog's but not exactly either.

In the past week, their eyes had become increasingly hungry, and sometimes their stare was so intense that she felt the pressure of their gaze on the small hairs on her arms. They stared at her all night with their heads on their paws; only their eyes moved, and they never blinked.

She turned the lock pick yet again and moved another pin forward.

The Freaks were so patient that they were almost giving her nightmares. And they were smart; they knew she'd make a delicious meal if they waited long enough. What they didn't know was that she planned to smoke so much that they'd die of nicotine poisoning on the first bite.

Panic would do no good, so she tried to think constructive thoughts. She could learn to drive the car and get out of this hellhole, except that she couldn't find the keys. And she couldn't find any tools to hotwire it with, either.

She could wait until the Freaks went off prowling at daybreak, and then walk to the beige car and push the two old stinking stiffers out. After eight days, though, they'd be even riper. It might be better to be eaten by the Freaks than to deal with that stink – and what if she couldn't get them out? What if they fell apart like human piñatas when she pushed them? Although she'd been vaccinated for Neovirus, she hadn't been vaccinated for projectile vomiting.

She had no decent options. With a frown, she turned the lock pick – and this time the lock turned with it. She slid her fingernail under the latch, pulled it out and twisted it, and the door edged open.

With the solemnity of Carter opening Tut's tomb, she peered around the edge. Her eyes opened wide, and she yelped "Woo-hoo! Kamelles, baby!" and then pumped her fists in Olympian victory. She juked and jigged to the janitor's closet so abruptly that the Freaks blinked, and then she grabbed her bookbag from a shelf inside, emptied the contents on the floor, and stuffed the bag with as many packs as it would hold.

When it was full, she grabbed a pack of Reapers, the ones only juvenile delinquents and cowboys could smoke without contemplating their mortality, and walked to the far side of the liquor machine where the Freaks couldn't see her.

She lit up, sighed, and leaned back against the liquor machine as the nicotine untied the knots in her back muscles. Tomorrow, she'd have to break into it – not so she could drink the stuff, but to find alcohol to dry up the pincushion of zits colonizing her face. Eating greasy food for a week had wrecked her skin.

"Talk about food issues," she whispered to the empty room. "Potato chips are eating my face, and my life's been ruined by sauerkraut. Freakin sauerkraut did me in! How embarrassing is that?"

She'd found the water heater hidden behind a bale of toilet paper in the janitor's closet. It had taken all of five minutes to get it working again, so now she could wash up with hot brown goo instead of cold brown goo. However, her face still looked like it had been whacked with a football shoe cleat.

The crooner's voice slithered from the overhead speakers yet again, singing the awful love song about moons and eyes and pizza pies. She pointed a finger at the ceiling speaker. "Listen, chump, I've put up with you for a whole freakin week, and I've had enough! I'll need years of therapy to get over that song. Your voice is greasier than potato chips. It's giving me zits. I'll probably be disfigured for life, thanks to you, and all my friends will point at me and laugh. No, they won't – I only have one friend and she's probably dead, so I don't have to worry! Akkhh! This is all so totally…it's all so…oh, hell. I'll never get over this!"

The crooner started singing about strangers in the night.

"I might as well be dead," she said, thumping her head against the liquor machine. "I oughta open the door and let the Freaks have me. As long as they start with my face, I'm fine. I'll make good dog food, at least. Virgin dog food. I'll be a freakin *pure* meal." She scowled through the window. "It's official – I'll be a virgin till I die. The boys don't hang with Scary Ada Lang, right? But why worry anymore? I'll be dead soon."

She shook the thought from her head and wished for the thousandth time that her mother was here. The Commander would slap a zombie patch on her, and within seconds, she'd have all the emotional range of a doorknob. Maybe not even that. Her mother was always right, which usually infuriated Ada, but this time she'd happily admit that if she got the chance. She'd even apologize for Baby Bang Bang and stop cutting classes just to get her back.

"All I want is another chance," she whispered. "This time I won't blow it. I know I'm hard to live with, but I'll try to be better. Bring her back and give me another chance, just bring her back, please." Her eyes filled with tears and she began to sniffle as she remembered all the horrid things she'd said and done to her mother. "Please, oh, please…I hate being alone. I can't take it anymore. I didn't do anything to deserve this, and I'm sorry. I'm so sorry." The crooner felt her pain, singing that he had a few regrets too, and she broke into a soggy bawl.

EXHAUSTED AND DRAINED, she stared at her reflection in the glass and saw a small and vulnerable girl, one who was incapable of rising to this challenge and would likely be dead soon. All she'd leave behind in this world was a chalk outline.

This mood's probably just from PMS, she thought. Her eyes opened wide, and she thumped her head against the liquor machine again. "Aww, freakin hell! The Crimson Tide comes in six days!"

She lit another and glared through the window at the orange fug. Even if she picked the tampon machine lock, it would be empty. The damned things always were, according to some universal law. She pulled a lock of hair forward and chewed on it, wishing she had a Not Now button.

In a deepening funk, she stared through the window and thought of nothing until her black mood lifted. Out beyond the line of thin trees, the highway was still empty and quiet. She twirled a lock of hair in her fingers and wondered what had happened out there in the past week. It seemed like she was the last person on Earth.

She took a big puff and barked a harsh, hacking cough. Her mom was right about this too: She'd be on oxygen by the time she was a senior if she kept this up. She'd have to quit someday, if the mutant wolf-lion beasties didn't eat her first, or she didn't starve to death. She heard her mother's voice in her mind – one crisis at a time, Ada – and she laughed. *I'd love to have only one, Mom.*

She stubbed her cigarette out and lit another, her thoughts turning back to her mother. The Federals had to have gotten her because no civilian could; there would have been more blood in the parking lot if they'd tried.

Ada knew she hadn't been killed because Victoria Lang was a superhero when she turned into The Commander. When she was a kid, Ada once saw her beat the snot out of a Navy SEAL she'd been dating – and they'd just been playing with each other. If a mere civilian had tried to take her, there would have been pieces of them strewn across the parking lot, like the time a man tried to carjack her at St. Elizabeth's. He'd been hiding in the backseat with a knife, which he foolishly thought was enough to subdue her. The car was so messy when she was done that she'd just bought a new one.

But she still didn't know why the Federals wanted her. Maybe her briefcase really did hold the plans for a doomsday device, but she couldn't open it. Cracking the combination lock had become an obsession, and like a casino addict, she'd spent hours spinning the dials and hoping for the jackpot.

She reached for her cigarettes and then froze: What if the Federals hadn't kidnapped her mother? What if the Reds were targeting *her?* They might have arranged the entire weeklong nightmare as the deprivation phase of an intelligence operation, all so she couldn't resist when the extractor arrived. And they'd love to crack the mind of a Blue, especially a treasure chest like hers.

Pulling her hand back inch by inch, she searched with her peripheral vision for the concealed cameras and microphones the spies had planted. She couldn't see any, which meant her opponent was better than she thought – or she was losing her mind. Her pulse rose as another bubble of panic burst, and she closed her eyes and focused on controlling her breathing.

She was exhausted when her rational mind regained control. Paranoia was warping her sense of reason: If Red extractors were watching her, they wouldn't have waited so long. They would have known that her defenses collapsed a week ago and interrogated her then. Besides, this rest stop was too gruesome a setting even for them.

She closed her eyes and wondered why the Blues hadn't rescued her yet, but she started to fall asleep. She stood slowly and stretched; it was time for another uncomfortable night of napping in the janitor's closet. Yawning, she stumbled to the door between the cigarette and liquor machines, and as she was opening it, she noticed the Freaks. One was smaller than the other, but they appeared identical other than that. She'd named the larger Freak One and the smaller Freak Two.

They cocked their heads as their gazes met hers. After a few seconds of staredown, she reached into the snack machine and pulled out the greasiest potato chips it held. She turned it over in her hands and decided that she'd rather starve than eat chips again.

They stood and watched her walk to the door, but they padded a short distance away when she unlocked it and emptied the bag on the concrete walk.

Freak One sniffed the chips, and then Freak Two walked over and they began to eat. They ate the chips, the crumbs, and even the paper bag. When they finished, they returned to the window and stared expectantly at Ada again.

She opened another bag. As they were eating, she noticed a black tag on Freak Two's right ear. The letters 'OSU' were stamped on it in white.

"You belong to Ohio State, don't you? You're used to being fed by humans. Is that why you're hanging around?" Freak Two looked up at her with its odd, yellow cat's eyes. "We have a lot in common – sometimes I think I was a genetic experiment too, but at least you have each other. I think I'm the only one of my kind."

A shudder swept through her, and she leaned toward the glass. "We might be the only things alive anymore, so maybe you shouldn't eat me. I might be an endangered species now." She sat cross-legged on the floor and watched them devour the chips, thinking that if she fed them enough, they might get too fat to catch her if she had to run.

"Do you even know how to hunt? Well, I'm sorry, but I can't help you. I'm pretty pampered myself. You need to go back to Dr. Moreau or whoever or figure out how to get your own food. I don't have enough for everybody."

Freak Two turned around and pressed its hindquarters against the glass. "Okay, so you're a boy, but I won't sniff your damn butt. Put that thing away, all right?" She waved her hands at them, and Freak Two wiggled his rear in reply. "C'mon, get your damn balls out of my face!" She rapped her knuckles against the glass. "Go! Stop that! It's gross!"

The Freaks moved near the door and curled up together. After closing the vending machine doors, she opened the janitor's closet and arranged the cloth mop heads on the floor to make a bare mattress. She closed and locked the door, and in the darkness, she laid her head on her bookbag and tried to find sleep.

THE REST STOP

Day 29
Wednesday morning, September 16, 2043

Krista flinched as metal screeched across glass, and she blinked and tried to focus her eyes. The windshield wipers were still running, but the rubber had disintegrated on the dry windshield, allowing the metal arms to grate against the glass and carve thin white grooves. She tapped them off and blinked a few more times to relieve her dry and itchy eyes, and then she squinted at the clock: It was 2:07 AM.

She didn't know where she was or how she'd gotten here; her last memory was of driving on a highway shortly after midnight, but she couldn't remember which one. Once she activated self-driving, the car detected that it was on a major road and engaged the speed control, the automatic navigation, and hazard avoidance systems, and then it linked to the highway's embedded magtrack. She usually resented how the car mothered and nagged her, but tonight it had saved her life. Her mind had whitespaced for almost two hours.

After groping around the passenger seat, she found a crushed and empty cigarette pack. She'd been conscious enough to smoke but hadn't been lucid, like she'd suffered an absence seizure; however, she'd never had one for more than a few seconds. "Now where'd you go for two hours, kiddo?" she croaked through a dry throat, and then she looked at the speedometer and gasped – the car was speeding at 110 miles an hour.

She turned off the drive computer and stretched the blood back into her limbs. Her arms and shoulders were sore, her ankle stung, and her left leg was stiff. She didn't feel injured on her face and head, but her hair was damp and sticky on the left side. "Another episode, that's what this is. I didn't just run a man over. This is a reality vacation, that's all, kiddo."

The dried blood splattered across her hood and windshield were hard to explain away, though. "Right, and there's that too. Well, there's got to be another explanation. I need coffee. That'll fix me."

She had no clue where she was, though, or where she might find some hot brew. A few minutes later, she spotted a green sign ahead and pulled to the side of the road. It said:

DARLAGH
AGORA
1 MI.

"Agora. It figures." She barked a mirthless laugh. "I'll take a hard pass." She pulled the car back onto the road and passed the exit. After driving a few more miles, she spotted a blue sign advertising a service area ahead.

Shortly after, she glided off an exit ramp to the rest stop. The building was bland – two yellow brick octagons connected by a glass lobby – and the parking lot was deserted except for a small white car parked to one side. The place felt haunted, but the lights were on, and she spotted vending machines inside the lobby.

KRISTA PARKED NEAR THE ENTRANCE. Ghosts seemed to flit through the murky fug swirling around the front door, but they disappeared after she blinked a few times. After scanning the area for a minute and finding nothing ominous, she tried to open the car door.

It was stuck. She threw her weight at it, and her shoulder flared with shocking pain. Groaning and mewling at the same time, she laid her head back against the headrest.

The shove had opened the door, but as she tried to get out of the seat again, pain radiated up her spine. She sat back, gritting her teeth and vowing to make gentler movements next time. After a few ragged breaths, she turned slowly in the seat and swung her feet out; her body was stiff and sore in so many places that she couldn't tell which part was injured. She rose to her feet and felt a sudden sharp twinge behind her left leg, and then warm wetness trickled down her thigh. Clasping her hand over the pain, she leaned back against the door and groaned again. She held up her hand and saw clots of blood dripping from them.

Holding her hand over the wound, she limped to the trunk and pulled out her first-aid kit. After a few calming breaths, she closed the trunk and walked into the entrance's glow.

As she drew closer, she saw a spider web of cracks in the window roughly shaped like a human body. She opened the door and glanced around the lobby – vending machines with coffee, soda, snacks, and cigarettes lined one wall, and a faded map screwed to the opposite wall said YOU ARE HERE. But coffee would have to wait; so much blood was trickling down the back of her leg that her shoes squished as she walked.

She shuffled through a creaking metal door into a pink-tiled women's room even more decrepit than the lobby. However, hot and cold water ran from the faucets, and the stalls even had toilet paper.

She washed her hands and then opened the first-aid kit. Holding up a tube of antibiotic, she squinted to read the instructions – and then glimpsed her haggard face in the warped stainless-steel mirror. She dropped the tube and ran water across her face and through her hair, the stream swirling brown in the sink as she pulled clots and tangles out.

After stripping her clothes off, she cleaned her entire body. She checked her scalp but found no wounds there, meaning that someone else's blood was in her hair. The realization made her shiver, and she started washing again.

When she finished, she checked again for injuries. Her left torso was a tapestry of angry yellow bruises, and she had two cuts on her left leg, a deep one on the back of her thigh and a long scratch across her ankle. The bleeding slowed on the deep cut after a few minutes of pressing on it, and then she nearly emptied her can of antibiotic spray on the gash and dressed it with gauze. She had skinspray, but it wouldn't work on a bleeding wound, so she decided to wait until it stopped.

After drying off and dressing, she returned to the lobby and bought a bottle of water. She downed it in one quaff, and then she dribbled a few drops in her eyes and bent over, whimpering, as sudden cold stung them. She bought a cup of coffee from the vending machine and drank it in one searing gulp, and then she belched like a frat boy and walked to the wall map.

It showed that she was on Interstate 79 in western Pennsylvania, just a few miles south of Pittsburgh. Vertigo overtook her, and she steadied herself against the wall. When it passed, she bought another cup of coffee to steady her nerves.

After buying a few more things, she hobbled back to the car and walked around it a few times to loosen her muscles. Now that she knew her location, she had to decide where to go. She could continue into Pittsburgh, but the city was under quarantine. She wouldn't find anyone who would help; with her luck, she'd probably get caught and turned over to the Federals. Staying at the rest stop for the night was her best choice, even if it was spooky. If the virus was keeping everyone honest indoors, then maybe the creeps and criminals were staying in as well – at least, that's what she hoped.

She decided to sleep in the backseat, so she tossed her supplies on the passenger seat, opened the back door, and climbed in to lie down.

A BLOODY ARM LAY ON THE SEAT inches from her eyes. It clutched a knife in its dead gray fingers, with the point of the blade embedded in the seat leather – and then the hand twitched and the entire arm crept toward her.

She shrieked and backpedaled over a trash can, falling on her injured thigh. Still screaming, she rolled onto her hands and knees and backed away, afraid to turn her back on the thing. Between her screams, she thought she heard a scratching sound – was it coming after her, the dead hand planting the knife into the pavement, dragging itself inch by inch to complete the murder?

She kept moving backward. Once the car was invisible in the fug, her screaming subsided into shuddering breaths interrupted by moans. Her throat hurt so much that she could barely breathe, but she kept moving until she bumped against a curb. Dizzy from hyperventilation and exhaustion, she sat and wrapped her arms around her knees, crying and rocking herself slowly. Every so often, she looked into the fug for the arm and listened for a knife scratching across the asphalt.

"It's the spent wrapper of a human being, that's all…oh bloody hell, it's not a feckin wrapper, it's an arm! There's a feckin amputated arm in my backseat! I am *not* supposed to feel okay with this!" Her head sank into her hands and she muttered, "This is *not* okay. This is *not* normal. This is bizarre, that's what it is, it's all so bloody bizarre…"

She rocked for a while longer, and her sobbing quieted and stopped. After a few minutes, she fell asleep.

NINETY MINUTES LATER, she awoke stiff and sore, still sitting curled up by the curb. She rubbed her eyes and rolled to one side to take the weight off her injured thigh, and then she stood and stretched her aching muscles. Staying clear of the car, she limped to the restroom and used the toilet again.

"Feckin scared the bejesus right out of me," she grumbled, drying her sodden underwear with a paper towel. The last thing she wanted was to return to her car, but she couldn't get anywhere if she didn't. The arm had to go.

As she walked back, she snatched a broken glass bottle from the upended trash can and crept to the passenger side door holding it like a sword. The arm was still resting on the seat, but it also wasn't moving anymore.

Her stomach turned as more details became clear: It was the soot-golem's arm, or at least it had been until she hit the wall and slammed the door on it. Another wave of nausea rippled through her.

After a few calming breaths, she looked again. The arm was wearing a gray T-shirt from the shoulder to the elbow, and she might be able to slide a stick into it and lift the foul thing out and away.

She stumbled into the fug, keeping the lobby's glow behind her. A few hundred feet from the building, she found a stand of feeble trees that had dropped their branches near a row of silently bobbing oil pumpjacks. They'd startled her at first; backlit by some distant light, the nodding pumps appeared to be dinosaurs drinking from a stream, but soon she heard the creaking machinery and relaxed. "First bloody thing tonight that hasn't jumped out and gone boo," she muttered, groping through the piles of dead branches in the dim light. She found a few suitable sticks and walked back to the car.

She slipped the sturdiest stick into the open loop of the shirtsleeve and lifted, but nothing happened. With a strained grunt, she tried again, but the thing still didn't move; it was either far heavier than she thought, or it was glued to the seat. Looking closer, she saw that the shirt was lying in a pool of sticky, congealed blood. She'd have to push it out.

She shoved the stick into the bloody meat of the shoulder and pushed hard, but the arm remained stuck. Suppressing the rising urge to vomit all she'd ever eaten, she walked to the other side of the car, slipped the stick into the sleeve again, and lifted with all the muscle she had. The arm rose, pulling the seat's leather with it. It came free with a wet pop, and she almost had it out of the car when the sleeve ripped and the arm fell onto the seat.

It bounced toward her, fingers wiggling, and she ran deep into the fug again and hyperventilated until calm returned.

Holding the stick out, she returned to the car and saw the thing hanging out of the door. She shoved it hard, and the arm tumbled onto the pavement with a nauseatingly wet thud. Whooping anemically, she reached across and pulled the door shut.

She climbed into the driver's seat, ready to burn rubber and get far away. When she tried to thumb the car to life, though, it refused to start. The console screen said:

PRIMARY BATTERY DEPLETED
SWITCH TO RESERVE BATTERY?

She'd left the car on all night, and it had killed the battery. Swearing, she stabbed the YES button a dozen times. The car started, and she sat dumbfounded behind the wheel; she'd never read the manual and hadn't known the thing even had reserve batteries. The night's events had proven that she possessed no survival skills whatsoever, not even basic abilities like how to operate the getaway car. She needed to hide in the remotest hollow West Virginia could offer.

She stomped the gas, and leaving some tire rubber and a dismembered arm behind, she returned to the highway and headed north to Pittsburgh. The city and its suburbs were quarantined, so she took the eastern bypass around the town hoping to get past while the sky was still dark. She couldn't drive safely for much longer anyway; the clock showed that it was 4:43 AM, so she'd been awake for nearly an entire day. She needed to rest soon.

Pittsburgh was smaller than she expected: Just an hour later, she'd passed the city and was cruising through a forest. It was the ideal place to pull off and get some sleep.

She took the next exit for a place with the improbable name of Beaver and snorted as silly images came to mind. With a name like that, it had to be a rustic, funky, out-of-the-way place full of disinterested gomers, a place of log cabins with pelts nailed to the walls.

Beaver wasn't a bucolic backwater, but a city that looked like a ghost town, with no human activity anywhere. She switched the drive to batteries and glided silently down the main street, masked by the fug and the still-dark dawn.

Driving in fug was exhausting, and she was getting so woozy that she drove through a few stop signs. She decided to pull over and rest, but then she spotted a pair of young men that appeared to be patrolling on a sidewalk ahead. She turned off the main street and took a smaller one paralleling it, driving slowly and praying nobody would notice her. This part of town was a quilt of modest homes stitched together with rusted fences, a place where people didn't ask much, didn't get much, and didn't wonder if there should be more.

Down an alley, she saw a moonsuited man leaving a white van with 'Allegheny Emergency Preparedness' painted on the side. She glided quietly past it. Shortly after, she left the town and pressed the accelerator to the floor.

IT WAS ALMOST 7:30 IN THE MORNING, the sun had risen, and Krista still hadn't found a safe place to stop. She was driving on a two-lane road high above a broad river, with dense forest on one side and a sharp drop to the water on the other.

However, her vision was getting blurry. She couldn't drive another second more, so she slowed to pull onto the shoulder for a nap. She stopped in front of a road sign that said:

NEWTON, WV
TOLL BRIDGE
10 MI

Nailed to the post below, a hand-lettered cardboard sign read:

VACINATED
ONLY
(BULLSEYE OK)

On the river bluff ahead, she spotted a long, low building with a neon sign blinking 'MOTEL.' She pulled back onto the road, turned into the parking lot, and stopped at a restaurant above the far end of a strip of rooms. The motel wasn't large – the last room was Number 12, and only one other car was parked in the lot.

She climbed out and walked up the steps to the front door. Above it, a painted wood sign said 'Welcome to Ohio! The River Rest Motel.' She opened the door with a jingle and entered a room draped in old, mildewed shower curtains.

After a moment, an unseen door slammed and the curtains billowed, and then a small woman wearing long yellow gloves pulled the curtains apart and stepped up to the counter. A respirator covered her face, much like the one Krista had flung off a few hours earlier. Through the faceplate, she saw the face of a young woman in her mid-twenties with straight brown hair pulled back in a ponytail. The woman asked in a muffled voice, "Help yew?"

Krista replied, "I need a room tonight. Do you have any vacancies?"

The woman's expression hardened. "You making a joke? The place is empty. Epidemic, y'know? You got your shots?"

"I have," Krista answered.

"Got the health travel clearance?"

"Sorry, I don't." She raised her arm and showed her the vaccination bump.

The woman nodded and scrutinized Krista's face. "You seen trouble."

"Husband loves the bottle more'n me, some nights."

"Yeah, that so?" She stared at her for a long, uncomfortable moment and then looked away. "Okay. Two hunnert a night, then."

Krista slid a tenpez across the plastic, and the woman glanced at it as if it was diseased. She disappeared through the curtains and returned a few seconds later. "I can only give you four hunnert ten in change. That's all the cash I got."

"That's fine," said Krista.

The woman arched an eyebrow under the mask. "Well, then you get three nights, dinner and breakfast included. Got a restaurant behind the curtain." She sprayed the tenpez with a bottle of bleach, and Krista coughed and backed away from the desk. The woman disappeared beyond the curtains and returned with a keycard, a plastic bag with two earplugs, and a bundle of dollar bills.

"Room 1, just down below." She picked up a spray can and filled the air with mist as Krista left.

KRISTA WALKED DOWN A WOODEN STAIR and found her room at the end of a breezeway running beneath the restaurant. Just past it, she saw a small gravel parking lot. One side dropped off to the river, and the other rose to the upper parking lot. Nobody would see her car from the road if she parked it there. She drove around the restaurant into the lot, parked under a tree and plugged the recharging cord into a wall outlet, and then she pulled the first-aid kit from the trunk and limped to her room.

It was a surprise: The room was clean, the furniture was new, and the bed was soft and plush. A window wall faced the river, opening onto a small balcony with a spectacular view of the river valley. A plastic chair sat in a corner, the same kind she'd had in Washington.

She looked over the railing at a pair of railroad tracks below. The hotel sat atop the bluff, and the tracks ran directly below the balcony and along the river. They shone in the soft sunlight, extending as far as she could see up and down the river, so she figured that trains still used them. That explained the earplugs.

She returned inside and removed her clothes carefully, hoping she wouldn't reopen a wound. Looking in the mirror, she checked for more injuries. She found none, but bruises were surfacing where they hadn't last night.

She stepped into the shower and spent a half hour in the stream stretching her sore muscles. After drying off gingerly, she examined the thigh wound again in the bathroom mirror.

The cut wasn't bleeding anymore, but yellowish liquid oozed down her leg and gray speckled meat bulged from it. She sprayed antibiotic and anesthetic on the wound and then uncapped the can of skinspray. With a painful contortion, she reached behind her and gave the cut a generous coat.

A stinging pain bit into it, and she yelped through gritted teeth while thumping the bathroom wall with her fist. After a few minutes, the pain eased enough that she could work on her ankle; she was pleased to see that she still had a toenail, a pretty purple one that would match the rest of her once the bruises ripened.

She'd just finished covering the cuts with gauze when someone knocked on the door. With a towel wrapped around her chest, she walked to the foyer, looked through the peephole, and saw the masked woman from the reception desk. She opened the door, and the woman said, "I see you showered. Gotcher clothes?"

Krista nodded to the pile beside the bathroom door. The woman pulled a spray can from her bag and filled the foyer and bathroom with a choking mist of pine cleaner, and Krista backed up to the window to find oxygen. The woman eyed the room as the mist fell, and satisfied with her work, she picked up the clothes and walked to the door. "I'll wash these."

"Thanks, but you don't have to do that," Krista said.

"Yeah, I do. Virus all over it, I bet." She turned the clothes over in her gloved hands and studied them. "Pissed your pants, looks like. And lotsa blood. Not yours either." She dropped them into a plastic bag and tied it, and then set it down outside the door and doused it with bleach.

When she was done, she walked back into the room and glared at Krista, her hands on her hips. "Well? Whatcha got to say?"

"You see, my husband..." Krista started.

"Oh, stuff it. Your type don't marry drunks. Ladies get to choose better." She closed the door behind her. "You're the one the Fucks want, yeah? I saw your picture on the Internet. You were younger then, but it was you, I bet." She looked at the red bump on Krista's right arm and pulled off her respirator, revealing a girl-next-door face marred by hard and wary brown eyes. "They say you killed two Federals."

"Two?" Krista blurted.

"Thought it was only the one, huh?" Her gaze became distant. "So you're her. Wow. The rebel Krista Warner here..."

"I don't want any trouble. Look, I'll just be leaving now if it's a problem. I can be in West Virginia in ten minutes and be out of your hair. I won't say –"

"The fuck you wanna do that for? Dumbfuck Wevvies will kill you soon's you get over the bridge. You gone as far along the river as you can." Krista sat back on the bed, stunned into silence, and the woman sat in the chair next to the desk. "I'm not gonna do the Fucks' dirty work if that's what you're worrying over. I hate the Fuckin Fucks. They can do it themself. Long as you're here, you're safe." She pulled off her gloves and held out her hand. "Name's Sue McConnell."

"Krista Warner," she said, taking her hand weakly.

"Pleasure. It true what you wrote, that they're picking who gets the shot and who don't?"

"It is. I saw it myself yesterday, and I've got pictures of the list."

"Figures," she scowled. "Shitheads. That's gold-collar thinking for you – just croak the rank-and-file cuz they can't find no work. Hell, they always wanted to kill us off."

Sue gazed through the window, her eyes hard and cold, until Krista interrupted her trance. "So you read my posts?" she asked.

"Yeah. I read *Midnight Sun* all the time. I was surprised when you showed up there yesterday. Read you when you were on the Internet too." She reached down for a plastic bag at her feet. "I saw that you come in with nothing, so I brought some stuff for you, case you need it, y'know, toothbrush, toothpaste, comb, all that."

Krista smiled and pulled the towel from her hair. "Thanks. I need to get a comb through this mop when it's still damp, or it'll look like a Halloween wig." She pulled a comb from the bag and started running it through her hair.

"Whatcha gonna do? Can't stay here long. The Fucks got squads only a few miles downriver, and they're gonna bump into you sooner or later. You gotta get far away."

"I know," Krista said. "I thought West Virginia would be safe."

Sue snorted, frowning. "Ain't safe. They want people to think that. They make a lot of money robbing and cheating the fugees. It's a business over there." She looked through the window at West Virginia. "They do what they want with 'em, and then the Fucks get 'em when they're done. The Wevvies and the Fucks got some sorta deal, is what I hear. Every few weeks, they catch a fugee over here trying to make a break. I don't think anyone ever made it past 'em."

"I thought it was a haven," Krista said. "I'm glad I met you before I walked into a trap."

"Yeah, it's a trap."

"Well, I guess I'll be going to Canada, then."

"Can't."

"I can't? Why not?"

"Border's closed. Closed it day before yesterday, tighter'n a nun is what I hear. Guess you were too busy killing Fuckin Fucks to notice." Sue glanced at the alarm clock on the nightstand. "What happened? Was it a big fight or something? The news didn't say nothin, but the Fucks are pissed. Say you got mental problems and you're Public Enemy Number One.

They put that Snuff Order out on you too. It musta been something nasty you did."

"A Snuff Order. Huh. I guess I got under their skin." She gazed into the distance for a few moments. "What happened? I'm not sure, but there was no big gunfight or anything dramatic like that. Two guys broke into my apartment and tried to kill me. They…well, they failed."

"They did a number on you, all them bruises and cuts. They beat you bad. You make 'em hurt at least?"

Krista remembered the wipers and the arm, and she nodded slowly.

"Okay, guess I shouldn't bring that up." Sue glanced at the alarm clock again as a distant whistle sounded. "Need to be quiet now. Empty's coming down. Won't be able to hear anything for a few." She jammed her fingers in her ears as the air outside the window filled with black-and-white smoke. A steam train engine roared past on the tracks below, shaking the floor.

After a few minutes, the sound and vibration faded. "Comes free with the room." Sue said. "Empty coal train, hits a mile a minute coming down the hill from up past Wellfleet. Damn things are all run by computers, so no point going out and yelling at the engineer. Think it's bad here, it shakes the restaurant stupid. Speaking of that, when you want dinner? Gotta be after eight, got visiting hours before, but any time after, come up to the restaurant and I'll make you what you want."

"Thanks, but I'll just be getting some sleep now, Sue. I can't even remember when I slept last. I'll let you know when I wake up."

"Okay. Dial nine on your room phone. I'll be gone from six to eight tonight." She stood and smiled. "See you later. Get some sleep."

DISPATCHES

District Update
NewsHub NewsChannel
Broadcast Transcript of September 16, 2043

"We repeat this message. The National Security Forces issued a Citizen's Apprehension Directive early this morning. Citizens are directed to apprehend the following individual, and the use of deadly force is authorized.

"The fugitive is Krista Warner, formerly a resident of Washington, DC. She is 27 years old, 5 feet 10 inches tall, 150 pounds, Caucasian, with waist-length red hair and blue eyes. She was last seen in the Georgetown area of Washington at approximately midnight last night.

"The fugitive may be driving a blue four-door 2040 Bicep D4 bearing Pennsylvania license plates. The license plate number is AC9-DD5-VG5. The front end of the vehicle may be heavily damaged.

"Citizens are advised to use extreme caution approaching the fugitive. She is mentally unstable and may be armed. If the fugitive cannot be killed or disabled, citizens should contact the National Security Forces at the toll-free number at the bottom of the screen.

"The fugitive is wanted for the premeditated murder of two National Security Forces officers on September 15. A reward of one thousand tenpez will be paid for her identifiable remains."

Midnight Sun
News Post of September 16, 2043

The infamous Snuff Order has been issued by the National Security Forces of the United States for one of our correspondents, the dissident journalist Krista Warner.

A Snuff Order hasn't been issued since the United Nations banned the practice in 2027. With today's order, the United States has contravened the ban and placed itself in direct opposition to the values of the world community.

Midnight Sun doesn't editorialize, but at this juncture, we must suspend that policy.

Clearly, Krista Warner possesses information that could damage the administration of President William Gibbon, making this order an act of political self-defense and retribution. We urge the government of the United States to withdraw this Snuff Order and allow justice to be served in a fair and open hearing of the facts.

Such an order is not the act of a modern democracy. By this act, reasonable people may well wonder whether the United States is returning to the fascism that tainted it twenty years ago and destabilized much of the industrialized world.

Midnight Sun urges all United States citizens to disregard this Snuff Order and refuse to participate in the apprehension of Warner.

TIP THE HANGMAN

Day 29
Wednesday evening, September 16, 2043
River Rest Motel, Wellfleet, Ohio

Krista awoke at 7:30 that evening and stretched her sore muscles, and then she climbed out of bed slowly and showered again. After what she'd seen at the rest stop, she couldn't get clean enough. She dried off and looked in the full-length mirror – the bruises were blossoming into large, livid purplish-yellow blotches along her left side.

I need pain relievers. She looked in the mirror again. *Crap, I haven't got any clothes!*

She searched the room in a panic, but Sue hadn't gotten around to cleaning them; she couldn't find her clothes anywhere, inside or out. On the way back into the bathroom, though, she found a plastic bag on the toilet tank with new sweats, socks, shoes, and underwear. Smiling and shaking her head, she slipped into the clothes and then limped up to the restaurant. The door was locked, so she strolled along the river bluff and watched the faint lights of West Virginia.

JUST AFTER 8:00 PM, car headlights flashed across the parking lot. Sue rustled up to the lobby door wearing a fiber jumpsuit, respirator, and gloves.

"Sorry, hospital was busy," she said in a muffled voice. She unlocked the doors and parted the curtains for Krista, revealing a small dining room. "Have a seat, anywhere you want. Back in a minute."

Krista sat and looked around the room: It had six tables, knotty pine paneling and ceiling, and a U-shaped banquette made from the skin of red vinyl alligators. A few minutes later, Sue returned and dropped the wet respirator and gloves on the next table. "Sorry, after a hospital visit, I gotta hose down. The place is scary, especially with the virus around, and I get the creeps that it's all over me. Whatcha want for dinner?"

"First, I want to thank you for the clothes. That was sweet of you."

Sue waved it off. "I got time, it's okay. For what you're paying, it's the least I could do. I gotcher other clothes drying now, but some of the stuff was too ripped, y'know, the pants, the shoes. Yeah, so dinner? What?"

"Anything with protein," she said. "Make it the chef's choice."

"Chef?" She threw her head back and sniffed. "You're getting burgers, the chef says." She walked to a small kitchen behind the reception counter. "The pop machine's over there 'round the corner. We're outta cola, so other'n that, help yourself!"

"You enjoy that burger?"

"That was great, Sue. I don't remember tasting one that good in my life." Krista leaned back on the banquette. "It's like a totally different food. How do you do it?"

"It's just the meat, not my cooking. It's fresh, not that frozen shit you get in the cities. Tastes good cuz you're eating real beef for the first time."

"Now, I've eaten a meal from just about every country on the planet, and that was the best. Really, it was."

"Thanks. You were just hungry, I think," said Sue. "Glad you liked it. That was the last delivery of fresh beef I might see for a while."

They sat at the table closest to the large window, one with a panoramic view of the river. They lit cigarettes, sat back, and gazed out into the mists; a barge strained upriver against the flow and the puddles from its lights made kaleidoscopes of color in the fug. "I'll bet this is a beautiful view on a clear day," Krista said.

"Don't get clear days no more, so it don't matter. I remember when I was little, though, you could see all the way up and down the river," Sue said. "I guess you'll be staying the night?"

"Definitely. I'm whipped. I still have some sleep to make up." She patted her stomach. "I think your burger's knocking me out too."

"In the morning, I'm back at the hospital from eleven to one, so if you want breakfast, you gotta be in here by ten, okay?"

"Who are you visiting in the hospital?" Krista asked.

"My dad," said Sue. "Been there a few weeks."

"What's wrong with him?"

"Nothin serious. He got beat up bad last month. Him and a few of his friends headed down to Wevvie, figgerin on bagging a deer, but they got rolled instead. Beat my dad up real bad."

"Wow. I'm sorry."

"You didn't do it. Nothin you oughta be sorry for."

"Will he be all right?"

Sue nodded. "There's some pins in his leg that won't take, and he can't get out just yet. Biggest problem is that a lotta people there got that virus. It's starting to hit here, and I hope he don't get it. People there are always coughing up blood now, you see it all over the hospital, and he hasn't got his shot yet."

"What class are you?"

"We're Class Four. I don't know what that means, but we're prob'ly on our own."

Krista sighed. "You never know. Maybe you will. You shouldn't give up hope, Sue."

"Fuck Hope. It just makes you weak. When you see that river of shit coming, best to take a deep breath. Don't *hope* it ain't coming or you'll drown." Sue glared through the window as she sipped her water. "Naw, he won't get the shot. Just the Lords and Ladies got it, is what I hear, but a gimpy Rank ain't gonna." She took a puff and watched the plume rise to the ceiling. "I better get used to running this place all alone. Usually my dad does, and all I do is just cook and clean the rooms after school. It's crap work, but I'm lucky to have it. Dad was going on about buying them cleaning 'bots a few years ago, but they cost too much. If he got 'em, I don't know where I'd be going after graduation. Sure as hell ain't no jobs 'round here."

"What college do you go to?" Krista asked.

Sue snickered. "Wellfleet High."

"You're in high school? How old are you?"

"Turned seventeen last month," Sue said. "Few days before my dad got beat up. Been working like a railroad Chinaman ever since." She took a long, hard pull on the cigarette and gazed through the window with tired and unfocused eyes. "Running this place all alone is hard work. Two weeks ago, the place was filled up for a whole week. People leaving the Pittsburgh lockdown, y'know, getting out before they starved. Most of 'em never stayed more'n a night, so I was cleaning rooms and cooking meals on six hours sleep. We live upstairs, so I was working from the minute I got outta bed to the minute I got back in.

"Then it all stopped a week back, and the only guests we had were four days ago. Family from North Philly. They had their shots, but things got messed up in the city, and they got out. Once they got to Harrisburg, they all got beat up. Y'know, it's dangerous to wear targets in a place where nobody else can get the shot. And they said they were always burning up, cuz when you get exposed to the virus, you get real hot."

"You do. A few minutes after you're exposed, you start to get warm, and sometimes you get a high fever a few hours later."

"Yeah, that's what they said too."

Krista lit another and imagined refugees scurrying for the West; she'd also be doing that because she had nowhere else to go except the haven of California. "By the way, you said they were wearing targets?"

"Where you get the shot. You get a red bump that don't go away, and you get a red ring 'round it a few days later."

Krista lifted her right sleeve and looked at the red bump, and a faint ring was rising around it. "Oh, splendid. Like I need to be wearing a bull's eye too."

They sipped their drinks quietly for a few minutes, lost in thought. "Well, at least you're getting a break from all that traffic now, Sue. But if it was too much for you, why didn't you hire help or close the motel?"

"We need the money. My dad's bills are gonna be huge, and I gotta save up. That's why I been taking everybody in, shots or no."

"Wellness Corp should cover the bills, shouldn't it? They cover nearly anything."

"Naw, they said he was engaging in a hazardous sport, so they're covering zip."

Krista shook her head. "Those heartless bastards."

"That your name for 'em? I got a few better ones."

Krista laughed bitterly. "I do too, but I can't say them in polite company."

"Who you calling polite? You gotta watch that kind of talk 'round here. Folks'll think I'm getting uppity!"

"Sorry," Krista said. "Sue the bastards, then. They should pay the bills even if it was an accident. That's just not fair."

"Naw, those corporations got their own laws, those gold-collar types. Regular folk like me can't do nothin. All I can do is work my tail off and try to hold it all together till my dad's back on his feet. I just gotta be tough awhile." She sighed. "Just can't be tough forever, y'know?"

"Nobody can, really. After a while, it makes you weird. You've got to get some relief or it'll destroy you."

"Oh, it'll get normal again, once this virus thing goes away and Dad gets out. Then I'll just forget about it all till another river of shit comes at me." She laughed. "And I'm not real smart, so I'll forget about that one too."

"Well, there's nothing wrong about forgetting the bad stuff." Krista pushed her cigarette around in the ashtray and made patterns in the ash. "Remembering everything can make you so afraid that you just can't function anymore, and you can trust me on that." She crushed her cigarette out slowly. "Forgetting keeps you sane. Forgetting helps you cope."

"Cope with a shit life, yeah." Sue walked to the dispenser to get another drink and then sat on the banquette beside her. "But I can cope. I'm strong, Krista, a lot stronger'n I look."

"I know you are, Sue. You're tough. You'll get through this."

"Yeah, we McConnells, nothing keeps us down for long." She looked up at Krista, her eyes glistening. "We're tough as old hickory, and that's the truth."

Krista wrapped an arm around her shoulder and hugged her tight. "You don't have to be tough, not for me. This is hard, and this is unfair, and it's okay to feel scared and hurt."

Sue nodded, and then she sobbed and buried her face in Krista's shoulder. "I'm only seventeen," she said in a muffled voice.

"It's hard, I know, having everything come at you all at once. Being a grown-up totally blows."

"I don't think I'm old enough to handle this, not yet, it's too much..."

Krista ran her fingers through Sue's hair. "I know what you mean. I don't think I'm old enough, either."

SUE WALKED TO A CABINET over the drink dispenser, unlocked it, and pulled out a brown bottle and two small tumblers. She set them on the table and then gave Krista a questioning look.

Krista picked up the bottle and turned it over in her hands. The crude label said 'Bud's Liquid Hug.' "If this is alcohol, then no thanks. I don't drink alcohol."

"Gave it up, huh?"

"No, I never drank."

Sue's eyebrows rose. "For real, never? Not once? Not at all?"

Krista shook her head.

"Never heard that before, not from someone over the age of twelve at least." She poured a finger of the amber liquid into her tumbler. "Just don't lecture me, then. I really need to get fit-shaced right now." She took a small sip.

"I'm not a temperance lady, Sue."

"Then what's your problem?"

"I don't have a problem. It's just that when I was eleven…" Krista stopped and stared into the distance beyond the window. "My mother was killed by a drunk driver, and I've always despised alcohol because of that."

"Yeah, heroin took my mom away, so I know what you're feeling, and I'm real sorry." She wrapped her fingers around Krista's hand.

"I'm sorry for you too."

"It's okay. Been nine years, and it's all sorta gone away. That's good cuz I carried a big angry 'round for a long time. It hurt so much."

"You forgot about her?"

"Naw, I couldn't never do that. That'd be an awful thing. But the anger and the hurt just wandered off after a while, found a shady spot in my head to chill and all. I just leave it there, and I figger that's okay. My mom wouldn't expect me to bleed forever, y'know?"

"Mine wouldn't, either. In fact, she'd be pissed that I'm teetotaling. The girl always had a throat on her for a cold pint, that she did." Krista grabbed the tumbler and banged it down on the table. "Screw it. Fill me up. I just won't drive."

"Attagirl! Let's pop that cherry right now!" She smiled and held up the bottle. "This is my Uncle Bud's apricot brandy. Makes it himself, down Cadiz way. Best you ever tasted."

Krista laughed. "I guarantee that."

Sue poured her a splash. "Give it a try, just a little. It's par'ful stuff."

Krista sniffed the sweet liquid and took a tentative sip. "Mmm." A second later, her tongue and nasal passages started to sting as if she'd just swallowed a glass of flame. "Wow," she gasped. "That was a little…intense."

"Isn't it smooth?"

"It's…umm…going to take some getting used to." It tasted awful, and she still felt the hot trail of the brandy from the tip of her tongue to the pit of her stomach. She imagined pissing fire when the stuff hit her bladder. "Boy, I bet that'll hurt."

"Naw, it don't hurt a bit. Just sip it and you'll have a nice buzz in a few minutes, and you need a buzz more'n anything else right now, lemme tell you."

As they drank, they talked of Krista's life in Washington, and Sue gaped as if Krista were giving the crop report from Mars. "That's fucked up. It's hard to believe how bad it got for you."

"I became all numb and weird, Sue. I thought they were all normal, and there was something wrong with me."

"Nothin wrong with you." Sue shook her head and poured more booze. "At least you didn't stand for it. Y'know, you didn't say it was all okay and go along."

"Sure, I didn't, and now they all want to kill me." She smiled and shrugged. "Ta-da! What an achievement!"

"At least you got 'em scared of you. Nobody's scared of me. I gotta take shit all day long, and I can't do nothing about it. Can't get worked up over it neither, or pretty soon I'll be out at the road yelling at cars. At least you fought back, even if you didn't win. At least you still got your pride."

"And that's all I've got, kiddo." Krista leaned back on the banquette. "Ahh, this sure is nice. I haven't been this relaxed for weeks."

"Hitting you now? Well, that's where you stop. Stuff's like five hundred proof. More'n that and you'll get drunk fast."

They sat quietly and savored the sensation and the moment. Krista glanced outside; the barge lightshow had ended, and the fug had turned lifeless again. Sue lit the candle at the center of the table, and they watched the flame dance. "My dad's gonna be thrilled, he finds out we had Krista Warner in the house. A real live rebel and all. That'll give him something to think about in the hospital."

Krista rested her head back on the banquette and looked at the wood ceiling. "I'm no rebel. What happened last night was an accident." She shuddered. "And what did I really do in Washington? I wrote some snarky stuff, I was Miss Witty and Miss Glib, but my writing sucked mud and I didn't change one feckin thing. Not one feckin thing in five long, miserable years. I just made fun of people like the bloody bitter gossip columnist I was."

"Hey, you need to slow down on that stuff. You're turning Irish and moody."

"The accent comes and goes." She sipped some brandy and sighed. "Like everything else in my sorry life."

"You just cut that sorry shit out. I read your stuff, and I thought it was great."

"You did?"

"Yeah. I like the wiseass stuff, like with that rangatang and the congress lady. The people there sound interesting, not like what you get 'round here. Everyone 'round here's stoned solid or drunk the whole time or both. They're boring as all hell. I been tempted sometimes to go hit up Mother Johnson just to shake things up."

"It's the same in Washington. Everybody there's high or drunk all the time too. The only way we could live in that madhouse was to delude ourselves that everything was normal. Or hit the Cannabliss." She shivered and took a sip of brandy. "Things aren't that much different –"

Flashing lights invaded the room, followed by a distant screech of tires, and the sound of slamming doors and angry voices filtered into the restaurant. They crept to the window facing the road, pulled the curtain back an inch, and saw flashing yellow, red, and blue orbs of light outside. Somebody yelled, but it was cut short by a crack and a pop, and then an engine roared. Many of the lights moved away, leaving only two white puddles setting the fug weakly aglow.

"Frickin Fucks at it again," said Sue.

"Okay." Krista sighed. "I can't stay any longer. They're closer than I thought. I'll leave tomorrow night."

"Better to leave during the day." She looked through the window, scowling. "Bastards feed at night."

KRISTA POURED A DOLLOP OF BRANDY in her coffee and gazed across the water. She'd tried to open her soul to the Life Force's infinite goodness and recharge her battered spirit, but that was impossible with the threatening hulk of West Virginia looming across the river.

It was impossible with the wreckage of her life looming over her, too. Everything she'd known and all she'd assumed to be permanent had been ripped away. And the loss wasn't only shocking and sudden; it was also brutally final.

Following Sue's advice, she tried to let the anger and hurt wander away and leave her be, but she could still feel the killer's cold blade slicing through her skin. It would take time to forget that sensation, but she felt that she might someday. It just wouldn't be today.

Taking a slow sip, she tried to focus less on the past and more on the future. Now that she'd been set free, now that she had so little to lose, what would she do?

She still had a bag of gold in her car, which would be enough to live off the grid. That's what she'd do: She'd build a new life, free of striving and abundant with peace, even if the existence was small and austere.

Suddenly, she felt a jolt inside her skull as if a spark had sizzled from ear to ear. A thought popped into her mind, as clear as if she'd heard it: *You're the only one who can stop this tragedy, Miss Kellen, but you must escape this trap first.*

She sat back, her eyes wide as saucers, and looked from left to right, top to bottom, and even under the chair. Not finding the source of the words, she examined her doctored coffee. "Whoa, this stuff *is* five hundred proof. Well, I've got every phobia and neurosis. Might as well go full-on schizo too." She laughed and reached for the Liquid Hug. "I've almost got the complete set of baggage! All I need now is amnesia, and I'll have every condition in the book!" She splashed more brandy into her coffee and swirled it around. "Jaysus, a hit of amnesia would go down nice, that it would."

You must get out of this.

"Ah, there you are!"

You're responsible for lives other than yours now.

"So tell me – is this what a buzz feels like? I've never had one before." She took a long swig of her brandy coffee. "Bit of a bottle virgin, I am."

Pay attention. It's time to grow up and be serious, Miss Kellen. You're not a little girl anymore.

Krista sat up as if she'd been slapped. "Now you be nice. I don't like mean people."

Does anyone care what you like?

"They don't, not at all."

So grow up and get over it.

"Why should I listen to you? You're just a voice in my head, that's all, some figment of my schizophrenic imagination. Well, listen up, Figment. Being a grown-up sucks monkey ass, and I won't get used to it. Now shove off."

But this is what you always wanted – a chance to stand up and make the world right and fair.

"Ah, but that was before they all tried to kill me, boyo. That makes a huge difference in my book."

It should make no difference because you can't run away from this fight. Your only choice is to die on your feet or live on your knees.

"Well, I guess I shouldn't be worrying about that. I'll be dead in a few months anyway. Knees, feet, whatever, it doesn't matter to the cosmic flyswatter, now does it?"

Be pragmatic and stop putting so much belief in unseen forces.

"Says the unseen voice in my head, right. Isn't that like a lawyer calling a politician a liar?" She lit a cigarette. "Now I said shove off, and I meant it. I don't need your brand of nuts. I've got a whole tree to pick from."

If you hide from this, you'll regret it the rest of your life. You'll die slowly inside even if you survive. Your time of slacking off and moping is over, and you must stand and face this challenge.

"Wow." She took a drag and exhaled a long plume over the river. "You've got a mean-ass mouth on you, boyo."

Get used to it.

KRISTA SAUNTERED ALONG THE EDGE OF THE BLUFF hoping to silence her mind. She savored the sharp, oily funk of the river and its moist chill for a few minutes and then walked up to the road. The car that the Federal goons stopped earlier was still there; the headlights burned weakly, and sad Spanish music played softly inside the cabin. In the backseat, a plush unicorn sat atop a bundle of neatly folded clothes.

The lights of the car flickered, and she thought of the things in her life that brightened and darkened it, about how temporary and transient they'd ended up. Inside her heart, she felt a gentle tug, as if something delicate had parted from it. Images of her Washington life lost their hues and faded into tones of sepia; the story of that life emptied of meaning and became a stranger's story. All that remained of her past was the omnipresent and suffocating fug surrounding her, which was nothing to remember.

At that moment, she understood that her past had just wandered away, and she wouldn't chase it and bring it back. Turning to the breeze from the river, she filled her chest with moist air and let it go slowly.

Then an image flashed into her mind of a pink hat lying in the dust, and she strode to her room to get her tablet.

The Rake
September 16, 2043

BE SURE TO TIP THE HANGMAN

You might want to practice your Spandau Ballet, Cheyn. That's a Nazi's traditional last dance

I killed two officers of the NSF this morning. I admit it freely. I acted in self-defense, and I believe it was justified.

In a land governed by the rule of law, the facts of my case would be examined to determine whether I'm a hazard to society. But this land is no longer governed by the rule of law. It's governed by Gabriel Cheyn.

If I'm captured, I won't get a trial. I'll get a bullet – not for the crime of killing two Federal agents but for knowing what Cheyn is really doing.

Gabriel Cheyn has unleashed a deadly virus on America and is allowing the vaccine to be given to only those he's chosen: the wealthy and their employed minions. He's consigned the rest to luck or the mass grave.

I have evidence on my tablet that proves his guilt, and I will deliver this to a court that will arrest and try Gabriel Cheyn as well as numerous other high officials in the HHS, the NSF, and the United States Army.

It will be difficult, and the NSF will try to stop me, but I guarantee you this: I will live to see good and righteous people hang Cheyn.

-KLW

DISPATCHES

Midnight Sun
News Post of September 17, 2043

A CHAIN HANGS IN PHILADELPHIA

Our Witness in South Philadelphia reports the local reaction to the Warner revelations:

"Warner's accusations are on everyone's mind, and most people think she's right. I haven't met a single soul who says she isn't. Everyone hopes she makes it to wherever she's going.

"There's little pieces of chain hanging over doors all over South Philly. Everyone here thinks Cheyn's guilty, that he's definitely behind this epidemic. But nobody's too surprised. Indignant, yeah. Angry, yeah. Surprised, no way. They say the government and the corporations have been trying to crush them for years, so that's no big news.

"But they're angry. I feel it in everyone I talk to. The anger's under control, but it might not be for long. We lost too many folks to the virus to be calm about this. The news has only been out for a day, and the anger hasn't had a chance to build, but it might boil over soon. I bet it does, now that there's someone to focus it on.

"Forget about anyone here cooperating with the Snuff Order. Krista Warner, if you're reading this, then c'mon down to South Philly. It's the safest place.

"I was talking to a guy, runs a T-shirt shop down on Pattison Avenue, and he said he's selling shirts left and right today. One of them says AIN'T SEEN NO KRISTA WARNER. Another says RUN KRISTA RUN.

"But his biggest seller says HANG SOME CHEYN. Now that says it all."

A BOMB TICKS IN SOUTHEAST WASHINGTON

Our Witness in Anacostia reports that the population of Southeast Washington is unsettled:

"Everywhere I walk downtown, I see a piece of chain hanging from something. Rusty or shiny, hanging from a window or a door, they're everywhere. So most people here believe Warner's accusations against Cheyn.

"Folks are voicing a lot of resentment toward the government, even more than usual, and some of it sounds pretty racial. Cheyn is white, and so is everyone else at the top, and I hear a lot of talk about the white man trying to kill us all off. I think he's trying to kill everyone he doesn't like – white, black, or yellow. This is the perfect time to achieve racial equality, isn't it?

"I know a lot of the civic leaders are concerned about this thing with Cheyn blowing up into a racial conflict. They're trying to put the genie back in the bottle because racial tensions here are like an atom bomb. Once they get triggered, all you can do is try to save your own ass.

"This won't get defused, no way. There's too much pain here, too much poverty and neglect, and it's been going on too long. I think there'll be a war, and it'll be ugly. I'm clearing out before the riots start. There'll be blood in the streets, and I'll be damned if it'll be mine or my family's."

ACROSS THE RUBICON

Day 30
Thursday afternoon, September 17, 2043
River Rest Motel, Wellfleet, Ohio

Krista woke in the early afternoon and stretched fourteen hours of sleep from her muscles, although she hadn't rested well. She'd awakened at 4 AM burning with a high fever and had to shower in cool water for an hour.

As she dried off, she looked at her thigh wound, and the skin around the cut had become an angry, swollen red. It needed a doctor's care, but a hospital might turn her in to the Federals. She sprayed more skinspray on it, hoping the glop worked this time, and then closed the cut with adhesive tape.

After packing her few things, she reread her post from last night. The thoughts still seemed alien, although they were her words and she remembered writing them.

She folded her tablet and slid it into her pocket. It was time to move on, and perhaps somewhere along the way, she'd learn if she'd just written her epitaph.

KRISTA OPENED THE RECEPTION ROOM DOOR, and Sue peeked through the curtain wearing her respirator. When she saw Krista, she removed it and said with forced cheer, "Checking out so soon? You got three nights here, y'know, and we don't give refunds, neither."

"It's time to move on, Sue. I wish I could stay, that I do."

"Maybe you'll come back. Maybe this'll all be over someday and you can." She took the key from Krista with a smile. "You remember the directions?"

"Got it. I've got the maps and everything. I'm all set."

"You better get a move-on, but before you go…" She reached behind her and then dropped a pink backpack on the counter with 'Suzy McC.' printed on it in purple glittery letters. "Sorry. Only one I could find was from seventh grade. I was a kid once, I shit you not. I put your clean clothes in it, a few other things you might need, some sandwiches, a thermos, drinks, and some other stuff. Umm…don't bang it around a whole lot."

"Thanks." Krista cleared her throat. "And I've got something for you. Here." She slid an envelope across the plastic-covered counter.

Sue picked it up and weighed it in her hand, her eyebrows furrowed. She ripped it open, and thirty tenpez spilled out.

"Get the vaccine, you and your dad," Krista said.

"You can buy it?"

"That's what I did. That should be more than enough."

Sue was quiet for a few moments, looking down at the gold pieces. Tears fell on her hand, and she sniffed softly. "You don't need to do this. This is a lot –"

"I've got to, more than you know." She picked up the backpack from the counter. "And do it right now. Please. Trust me, you haven't got time to waste."

She looked up quickly. "You been getting hot?" she asked in a voice barely above a whisper.

Krista nodded. Sue's eyes widened and lost their focus for a moment, and then she picked up the respirator and ran around the counter. She gave Krista a quick, hard hug. "Thanks," she said in a small voice, avoiding her eyes. "We both gotta get moving, so go. C'mon, scoot."

They left the motel, and Krista hobbled down the steps to her car while Sue locked the front door. "Hey, Krista," she said. Krista turned at the bottom of the steps; Sue's brown eyes were moist, and their bitter hardness was gone. "I read what you wrote. You take those videos of yours and go take that SOB Cheyn down. We're counting on you."

Krista looked down at the ground. "I'm terrified, Sue. I'm no hero."

Sue walked down the steps and raised Krista's face to hers. "You listen – real heroes keep going *even when* they're scared, not cuz they *ain't* scared. You remember that."

THE HAND OF FATE

Day 30
Thursday afternoon, September 17, 2043
River Rest Motel, Wellfleet, Ohio

Krista thumbed her car on, pulled onto the road, and drove slowly along the river looking for a turnoff just before the creek. After a longer time than she'd expected, a small ribbon of blacktop appeared on the right, and she turned onto it. Clutching the wheel with both hands, she climbed a one-lane road crowded by dense pines on both sides that blocked what little sunlight penetrated the fug. She smelled the sweet, moist scent of the forest floor, and off to one side, a small creek murmured.

The road ended at an intersection with a two-lane highway. She turned left, wound along it for a few minutes, and then stopped in a small graveled turnoff beside an open field. She pulled an atlas from the backpack and tried to find her location.

Maps. She hated maps; they made her feel like a small and insignificant speck in an immense world. The car had come with a satnav display, but she'd had the system removed so the little map wouldn't remind her how puny she was.

She drew a deep breath and opened the atlas. Sacramento, California was her ultimate destination, but how she'd get there wasn't clear. Route 22 went the right way, but it wound through urban areas after twenty or thirty miles. She'd need to find a different road somewhere before she got to the Columbus area.

It would be safest to avoid main roads and urban centers on the way to Sacramento, which would make the trip long and arduous. She memorized the route to take for the rest of the day and stuffed the atlas into the pack.

She felt something warm inside, and a smile spread across her face when she saw a bottle of fresh coffee. She unscrewed the cup, poured some hot brew into it, and took a sip. After another, she felt the familiar shiver of the caffeine hit.

Sipping the coffee, she looked at the fields surrounding the car. Here on the ridge, the fug was much lighter than down in the valley, and she could see hundreds of yards in each direction. Over a wooden fence to one side, she saw a field that wasn't planted in corn, unlike every square foot of open land she'd seen so far. Trees bordered the far side, broken by a small clearing; two deer stood in it and stretched for the low-hanging maple leaves, a doe and her fawn.

"I'll build a little cottage over there," she said to the empty car. "With a feckin huge veranda and a big comfy chair. *Two* big comfy chairs so Sue can come and visit. I'll cuddle in a soft, fluffy blanket to chase the chill away, and I'll sit there and read real books made from real paper, and I'll throw my tablet away and forget about the world. I'll make a coffee fountain that'll bubble all day long with rich, dark stuff that'll make Achtung taste like water. I'll feed the little fawns and I'll have a small garden and grow all my own food and nobody will know except Sue. I'll build my world of peace instead of trying to escape a world of pain, and I'll tell that feckin Black Dog to head on back to Hell."

With a small quiver of joy, she sipped coffee and relaxed into her seat, dreaming of her woodland home, of peace and happiness and safety.

Miss Kellen, you can't indulge in comfort and evasion. You've been summoned to something greater, and you must answer the call.

She sat up and blinked her eyes. "Jaysus! Bloody well knock, wouldja? You've got to barge in like you own the joint?"

You can't stop yet.

"I know! I was just having a moment, for the love of God! Couldja give me a little privacy?" The voice didn't answer, so she poured another cup and sighed. "Right, what the hell, it'll be a long trip. I can use company." She held up her cup and made a toast. "To madness, the only true freedom! It's my year of endings anyway, so why worry if I'm nuts? I won't be making it to the finish line."

But you must try.

Unbidden, the image of a pink hat lying in the dust materialized in her mind. "Right. I don't need motivation to score payback on Cheyn, Figment. Blow off and leave me be." She listened in her mind, but the voice was gone.

She looked through the windows at the distant glade, where the fawn stood shakily on its hind legs and reached for the leaves on a lower branch. Over the trees, the sky yellowed and thickened, and the leaves shivered; a sheet of rain crossed the trees and dashed across the field, the grasses quivering with its progress, and the deer bolted into the forest.

It came on her fast. The downpour shook the car and sent rivers of rain down the windshield. It was clean in seconds; the water had either dissolved the bloodstains or blasted them off.

She reached around the steering wheel and tapped the wiper lever, and a sudden screech filled the car as the metal arms tortured the glass. She dropped the cup and covered her ears, and then tapped the wipers off with a shaking hand.

Swearing under her breath, she picked up the cup from the floor with one hand and tried to wriggle the tingle from her ears with the other. Rivulets of rain meandered down the windshield, and she watched them, envying their aimlessness, until the rain stopped a few minutes later.

THE FUG THICKENED as the road descended back into the valley, and Krista's gloom deepened the further she traveled from the field. It felt wrong to leave peace for conflict whether she had a calling or not.

She glimpsed a flash of green to her right – a road sign, perhaps – and searched for an entrance to the highway. Soon after, she saw a ramp and turned onto a four-lane road empty of traffic for as far as she could see. She picked up speed even though the visibility was poor.

The car hit a bump in the pavement and she groaned. "Three cups of coffee…" She looked for a place to pull off and relieve her bladder, a shoulder or a turnout, but the shoulder was barely wide enough for a thin man.

However, it widened a few miles later, and she slowed the car and pulled off. She crawled forward and noticed a car in the fug ahead; her foot hovered over the gas pedal in case she needed to flee.

It wasn't the police cruiser she'd feared. As she drew closer, she saw a sedan, a big beige one, with soot coating the trunk. The left rear door was open, and a dark cloud of smoke hovered beside it.

She looked at the cloud coming from the door, but it didn't rise to the sky as smoke usually did; it just hung in the air and changed shape. Rolling the car forward a few more feet, she saw that the cloud was a swarm of flies hovering around the back door.

She pulled onto the highway and stopped next to the driver's door. A mound of flies sat in the front seat, a huge, man-sized mound that rippled and boiled – and then she caught the rank smell of rotting meat. She gagged and pinched her nose, her eyes watering, and stomped the accelerator to the floor.

Her bladder felt like it was being squeezed hard by a bony hand, though. She whimpered and peered into the fug ahead, trying to avoid more potholes, but she saw no way to get off the road. The narrow shoulder had disappeared, replaced by a muddy verge that ended in the trees.

She let out a relieved whoop when, a minute later, she spotted a blue sign advertising a rest area in two miles.

DISPATCHES

Molle's Hill
NewsHub Political Affairs Channel
Broadcast Transcript of September 17, 2043

Molle: We're chatting again with Surgeon General Esteban. Mae, what's the update on your war against this terrible Hemorrhoid Virus?

Esteban: Recombin, the vaccine for this *hemorrhagic* virus, is being produced at much lower rates than we'd initially been told. The situation is confusing, to be honest, and I'm frustrated by the lack of cooperation I'm getting from our fellow Federal agencies. It looks like the only facility that can produce it, right now, is Chalys Pharmaceuticals of Fort Washington, Maryland.

Molle: Are you sure no one else can make the vaccine?

Esteban: Damned if I know. I'm just the Surgeon General, Arista, so why should anybody tell me? Maybe you ought to ask Cheyn or Grimes.

Molle: I know we're all under stress, but let's try to keep this on an even keel, General.

Esteban: It's Dr. Esteban. I'm not in the damn…oh, never mind. Call me whatever you want (expletive deleted).

Molle: Great, General! So tell me, since we can't make more, how much vaccine do we have available at this point?

Esteban: Only a limited number of doses were produced, and most of them have already been administered. I hear stories that more vaccine is in production, but none has entered the pipeline yet.

Molle: I understand that other companies are producing it, though, and that we'll be getting more soon.

Esteban: I'm not sure that's true. From what I can tell – and no one will just come out and tell me – there's a special bioreactor system and a secret proprietary process that grows the vaccine. Nobody knows what that process is except for selected executives at Chalys, and I can't get through to any of them. Until we know how to make it, I don't think any other facility can do it. As I said, it's frustrating to be blocked at a time like this. I'm starting an investigation into this debacle, and that'll start right after I come back from Chalys this afternoon.

Molle: I'm glad you're on the case, General, and I hope your investigation produces results.

Esteban: Yeah, a lotta butts in this town will be sporting my bootprint, I guarantee it.

Midnight Sun
News Post of September 17, 2043

NEOVIRUS SPREADS TO AMERICAN MIDWEST AND SOUTH

While the American newsfeeds have stopped describing the epidemic's extent, our Witnesses report that Neovirus continues to spread to the south and west. The virus is reported in Columbus, Ohio; Lexington, Kentucky; Knoxville, Tennessee; and Athens, Georgia.

The spread of Neovirus to the north has stalled, and experts cannot explain why. Neovirus hasn't spread past Duchess County in New York, which has given authorities in the Albany area time to deploy a health cordon.

One Witness in Columbus, Ohio says the behavior of the virus seems to have changed:

"I went down to the plant this morning to pick up my equipment. I talked to my supervisor, and then I left and did field work all day. When I got back at five, I saw him walkin across the shop floor, cryin blood, stumblin into things like he was blind. I wanted to help him, but then I thought, he's got that damned bug. So I just stood back and he collapsed. Some other people came to help him, but I just bolted out of there. I feel like shit for that.

"This isn't going the way they said. The virus killed him in hours, not the days or weeks like they say on the newsfeeds. This must be a different bug, or maybe it changed somehow. Whatever it is, it's fast. Real fast.

"Now I'm gettin a fever and my joints are aching. I hope that's just my imagination, but I guess I'll know real soon if it isn't. I'm keepin my pistol handy just in case. I ain't going down like my boss."

BEATING BUSHES

Day 30
Thursday evening, September 17, 2043
National Tranquility Center, Fort Belvoir, Virginia

It was approaching 2100 hours, and Downs was ready to hand the Watch to Raphael. They stood on the podium as Raphael scanned the monitors.

"Keep an eye open for anything on Warner. She's still deep in the landscape somewhere, but she'll pop up on our screens soon," Downs said. "I want her and that tablet as soon as possible."

Raphael laughed. "I don't think it'll work out between you and the lovely rebel. There's just so much competition in your relationship." Downs glowered at him, and Raphael looked up nervously at the Wall. "But, of course, I meant that as levity."

"If she doesn't leave a signature somewhere on our net, though, we'll have to flush her out. We're nearly ready to do that," Downs said.

"I was talking to Kopelli down in the cafeteria. Do you think his method has a chance? It seems like a stretch, like making something out of nothing."

"The dwarf thinks it'll work. What's uncertain is the degree of success, but there'll be some."

"Why the bigoted language, Bob? Is it really essential?"

"He's a dwarf. I can't call him a dwarf?"

Raphael sighed. "No. It's crude and coarse." He glanced up at the screens and then grinned and turned to Downs. "Did you know that he has a booster seat in his car?"

Downs snickered. "Probably has a little rubber horn that goes beep-beep."

Raphael stifled a laugh. "That's why I like you. You're so delightfully evil."

"Still, he's good at his job, and I think he can pin down her location."

"Okay, fine, but I want to be there. I'm curious to see it in action."

"Absolutely. We'll do it before the Watch change some evening. The equipment Kopelli needs should be installed in the next few days, and his assistant should be here by then."

"Mmm. And Lang? Any more progress on the extraction today?"

Downs crossed his arms and shook his head. "None. She's a tough problem. We can't get a readable cognitive map from her, and we have the Mapper dialed in as tight as we can without cooking her brain. Partly it's because she sustained head injuries during the apprehension, despite my explicit order to avoid them."

Raphael brightened. "Well, at least SAG Four won't be making that mistake again. By the way, I sent flowers to the widows and signed your name to them. They think you're a caring boss."

Downs snorted.

"Y'know, Bob, you lack a certain sense of style about these things. You can't just terminate an employee without sugar-coating it."

"Lang blinded one, and the other was a total incompetent. They were useless to us, and that's a fact. Why get sentimental about cleaning house?"

"C'mon, you can't say that out loud. You need to work it a little, make it seem like an accident. A regrettable tragedy."

"It *is* a regrettable tragedy. I have a lump of meat in Suite Seven, and I can't find out where her package is, and that's all because SAG Four bungled things."

"We need to talk sometime about your directness of mission. Style matters, Bob. It's not only the art of the thing, but it gives us the freedom to do what we want. We need to come off as friendly and benign, so lighten up. We'll get Warner. We'll crack Lang. We always win, so have fun. You'll get a heart attack if you keep this up. Really, it's a fun game. Enjoy it."

"I *am* enjoying it."

Raphael looked at Downs, an eyebrow cocked. "This is you having fun? Oh, brother, now you really scare me."

Downs smiled. "By the way, I have an idea on the Lang extraction. Dr. Timmons says there's some minor brain injury, but she could also be in a voluntary theta state. He said it was a kind of meditation, something about a thalamus and theta wave activity."

"He's hard to understand once he's gets going on that stuff."

"Anyway, she could be keeping her cognition out of the Mapper's reach. He thinks we might be able to map her if we induce a cognitive disturbance and motivate her to rise to a beta state."

"Yes, yes," Raphael said, grinning and nodding. "I love motivation. It's one of my favorite things, right after schnitzel with noodles. What's your idea?"

"We snatch her daughter and bring her here. She's at a Science Camp at the Naval Academy till next week. If we haven't cracked Lang before then, we can use the girl as an incentive. What do you think?"

"Ah, the old-school method! I have a pair of antique thumbscrews we can use too. They're a boffo icebreaker at parties."

"And you say *I'm* crude and coarse," Downs said.

"It's good, clean fun, though. But since we're in a hurry, why shouldn't we just go take the girl now?"

"You know how uncooperative the Navy is. We can't get into their computers or their facilities. If we tried to snatch her off the Naval Academy grounds, we'd have high personnel losses and a low success probability. Not to mention a battalion of Marines outside our front door, which I'd like to avoid. The best approach is a public snatch away from the Academy grounds."

"Mmm. Good point," Raphael said.

"Although I wouldn't mind the challenge of an Academy snatch just to break the tedium," he said. "Well, the Watch is yours, Raf. See you in twelve."

CONVERGENCE

Day 30
Thursday evening, September 17, 2043
Eleven miles west of Cadiz, Ohio

Krista was trying to drive with one leg crossed over the other as she looked for the rest stop. She'd just decided to stop in the middle of the road and unload on the yellow line when she spotted the exit ramp.

As she rolled up to the building, she saw a white car in the lot and two brick octagons connected by a glass lobby, exactly like the Pittsburgh rest area. However, she knew she was in Ohio. Shaking her head, she stopped in front of the lobby and peered inside.

Otherworldliness permeated the place; a figure seemed to be standing inside the lobby, but when she looked closer, it vanished as if a shy haunting spirit possessed the building. She was tempted to find some remote part of the lot to attend to her business but then chided herself for being timid. Right now, even ghosts couldn't stop her from finding the toilet.

She climbed from the car and limped to the entrance. The door opened with a creak, and she wondered why keys were hanging from the lock, but then she choked on the reek that assaulted her nose – the place stank of stale cigarette smoke, body odor, and cheese. She pinched her nose and hurried into the women's room.

It smelled even worse than the lobby. She pinched her nose tighter, found a stall with a door, and jettisoned her used coffee while humming *Duck and Cover* under her breath. When she finished, she reached for the toilet paper, but the dispenser was empty; frowning, she checked the pockets of her hoodie for a napkin or a paper towel. They were empty too.

The door hinges creaked. She heard the scuffle of a footstep, and then a small hand reached under the toilet partition holding a roll of toilet paper. "You'll need this," said a girl's voice.

"Thanks," said Krista. "There's none in here."

"Yeah, don't I know it."

Krista finished and opened the door. A blonde girl leaned against the wall by the sinks with her arms crossed; she was a foot or so shorter than Krista and wearing a smudged black satin blouse, too-tight black jeans, and knee-high black suede boots. She had a perky blonde's face marred by a bad case of measles.

Krista walked to the sink. "Thanks again."

The girl nodded. "So I guess not everybody's dead."

"From the virus? Not yet, but it's spreading fast. I didn't see anyone from the Pennsylvania border to here." Talking about the virus made her recall the stinking stiffer in the beige car, and her stomach heaved. She leaned over the sink and turned on the taps, which sputtered a diarrhea-like fluid into the bowl, and her lunch threatened to make a reappearance.

"The water's okay," said the girl. "It just looks bad, but it's safe to wash up in."

Krista washed her hands, and her nostrils twitched – the low-tide lobby stench was back, and it was coming from the girl. She flicked water from her fingers and looked for paper towels, but then she saw the girl beside her holding out another roll of toilet paper. She peeled off a handful and sneaked a look at her as she dried her hands: She just had severe acne and not the measles, and she was filthy. She'd been living in her clothes too. The blouse was dirty and wrinkled, and the knees of her jeans were stained. "Again, thanks," Krista said. "You're a lifesaver."

She nodded again, leaned back against the wall, and crossed her arms. "So, are you heading west?" she asked.

"That I am."

"Could you drive me to the next town? I'm stranded here."

"Stranded? How'd you get stranded?"

The girl looked away. "My dad's car broke down a few miles down the road."

"And he just left you here?"

"Well, it's…complicated. I don't know where he went," the girl said.

Krista imagined a faint whiff of rotting meat. "Was he driving a beige car, by any chance?" she asked nonchalantly. The girl nodded, and the smell of week-old chicken hit Krista full strength. She turned away and forced her voice to be casual. "Sure, I can give you a lift. Just to the next town, right?"

"Thanks. The next town, I think. I need to get to my mom's house, and I think it's in the next town, but I'm not sure."

"You don't know where your mom lives? You don't even know the name of the town?" Krista asked.

"I'm not from here, so I don't know the area. I live near Washington."

Krista stiffened. "I hear it's lovely," she said.

"Four or five days out of the year it is, yeah. The rest of the time, it's like living inside a smokestack. They should call it the Nation's Tailpipe. So where are you from?" the girl asked.

"Beaver," Krista replied. "A small town outside Pittsburgh."

"Beaver." The girl's eyes glittered and the corners of her mouth rose. She cleared her throat and said, "Well, that's an interesting name."

"Speaking of names…" Krista held out her hand. "I'm Sue McConnell."

Ada smiled and shook it. "Amy Lichtblau."

KRISTA WANDERED AROUND THE LOBBY while Ada opened a closet door and rummaged inside. Trash was mounded by the men's room door – bent cans, wrappers, and cigarette butts, all pushed to one side. The stink was even stronger here.

"Help yourself," Ada said from inside the closet. "There's soda, snacks, cigarettes, even booze if you want it."

Krista pulled open the cigarette machine door. "How'd these get open?"

"I needed some stuff."

"Well, I wouldn't want to steal."

"It's okay. I've been doing it all week long. Nobody comes here. You're the first person I've seen in ten days."

Krista shivered, despite the sweltering heat; the girl didn't know that her father never got away but had been rotting in his car for ten long, hot days. Her nose twitched as the stink of death threatened to return. "Well,

I'm not hungry, but I'm running low on cigarettes. You're sure this is all right?" An annoyed grunt came from the closet, which she took as a yes, and she reached into the machine and stuffed her pockets with Breathless Menthols.

Ada walked out of the closet, a brown leather bookbag over her shoulder and a metal briefcase in her hand. "Ready whenever you are."

Krista nodded and walked to the door. "Wait," Ada said, holding up a hand and scanning the parking lot for some unseen threat. "Did you see any Freaks out there?"

"Not outside, I haven't," Krista replied.

Ada looked at her sharply. "I don't always look like this! Spend ten days in this hellhole and see what you look like!"

"I'm sorry, that just came out wrong. I didn't mean to imply anything."

Ada looked through the window as if she hadn't been listening. "We're clear. They wander off sometimes. Okay, let's go."

Krista started through the door, but Ada stopped her again. "What is it now, Amy?"

Ada propped the briefcase against the open door and ran back to the snack machine. "Just something I have to do. It'll only take a minute." She reached into a machine and came out holding an armful of bagged snacks. Outside the door, she poured a mound of chips a foot high and then returned inside for more.

Krista watched the girl shuttle back and forth, intent on performing the strange ritual. "So, umm, just what would you be doing?" she asked.

"Freaks like potato chips," Ada replied. She emptied the last bag and then wiped her hands on her jeans. "Okay. We can go now." She picked up the briefcase and strode to Krista's car, still scanning the fug for threats unseen.

Krista puffed out her cheeks and followed. Ada threw her bags into the backseat and jumped in, slammed the door behind her, and ran her hand across the dashboard. "A Bicep, thank god. By the way, you have some sorta goo back there," Ada said.

"Umm...I spilled coffee on the seat," Krista said, thumbing the car on.

"It doesn't look like coffee," Ada said as she turned in her seat and glanced into the back. "It looks more like –" She stopped, and her nostrils flared. "Do I smell turkey?"

"There's food in my backpack. That might be what you..." she started, but Ada already had a foil-wrapped package in her hands and was opening it.

"Omigod," she breathed. She bit into the sandwich, and soon, her cheeks were full and her eyelids at half-staff to ecstasy. She devoured it in seconds, horsed in the last mouthful, and then noticed Krista staring at her. After one more chew, she swallowed with a gulp. "Sorry. That was profundo Jurassic of me."

"It's all right. I guess you were hungry."

"I haven't had protein in, like, forever. I've been eating all that damn carbage for ten freakin days." She looked up quickly at Krista. "Sorry, I have a foul mouth," she mumbled.

Krista laughed. "That's all right. I swear like a sailor myself sometimes."

"We'll get along pretty well, then." She smiled and sat back in her seat.

NINETY MINUTES LATER, the fug was darkening as they sped west on Route 22 looking for Ada's exit. Krista lowered the passenger window a little, and Ada raised it.

"Why do you keep opening my window?" Ada asked.

"I like fresh air," said Krista.

Ada pointed through the windshield at the blanket of fug. "You should move to Mars, then. There isn't any here."

Krista lowered the window again.

"Look, do I stink or something? If I have BO, just tell me, all right?" Ada raised the window, and Krista lowered it. "Jeez, Sue, would you just spit it out?"

"Okay, you're really whiffy! The angels are holding their noses, all right?"

"Wow. Savage."

"You told me to spit it out, Amy. Don't be so sensitive."

Ada scowled, lit a cigarette, and glared through the window. "You didn't have to napalm me."

"Sorry. Hey, there's an exit coming up. Is this the one for your mom's house?"

"No. Maybe it's the next one."

"That's what you said for the last ten exits. I'm starting to think you're lying about this."

Ada pointed to the dashboard. "You left your blinker on."

"Oh, sorry."

"Don't apologize. Old people do that sorta thing."

Krista tapped her fingers against the steering wheel.

"Do you yell at kids to stop stealing your newspaper?"

"What?"

"My mom does, and she's old too," Ada said. "You oughta start practicing."

Krista's tapping became an irritated drumming, and she looked straight through the windshield, her lips thin and tight.

"I can tell you're mad," Ada said. "Don't be. Senescence is a normal phase of the human life cycle."

"Not in yours if you keep sliming me," Krista muttered.

"So you handle uncomfortable facts by pounding them down? That's how the deniers –"

Krista yanked the wheel and pulled off the road, sliding to a stop in a cloud of dust. She reached across Ada and pushed open the door. "That's it. Take a hike."

"What?"

"I've had enough of you. You're pissing me off royally and I'm going through a rough time and I can't take it, okay?" She nodded toward the door. "Hit the road, kiddo."

Ada pulled the door closed. "I'm really sorry."

"Too late."

"Could you give me another chance? Please? They don't let me out much and I never learned how to get along with people and…look, I'm a social retard, and I sometimes say things that piss people off, but I'm not mean. I'm a good person with a smartass mouth. Please, I need somebody to give me a break for once."

Krista sagged in her seat and sighed. "Splendid. Like I need more pathos."

"I'm going through a rough time too, but I'll try to keep my mouth shut. I'll try to be nice. I promise."

"Okay. I'll give you one more chance if you promise to curb your mouth." Krista slipped the car into gear and pulled back onto the road. "So who doesn't let you out much?"

Ada paused for a second and then asked, "Why do you want to know?"

"Let's see…because I'm curious? Is that a good enough reason?"

"Not for me."

"Why not?"

Ada crossed her arms and stared through the windshield. "I know nothing. I'm everything I appear to be, okay? Can we drop it now?"

"Hunh? What are you talking about?"

"Are you hungry? I'm famished!"

"Stop changing the subject, wouldja? You're making me dizzy."

"If you'll stop interrogating me, I'll stop changing the subject." Ada settled into her seat and said no more. They continued for another half hour and passed two more exits; night fell, and it became hard for Krista to see far. Another exit came up, and the fug glowed brightly ahead.

"Okay, we've got to pull over and talk," she said. "I can't drive in this soup anymore, and I think you'll be having me drive all night looking for an exit that doesn't exist. I'm getting off, and we'll get some food." She pulled onto the ramp.

"I don't have any money."

"The meal's my treat. You can pay me back in straight talk. We have a deal?"

Ada nodded. "Some things I can't talk about, okay?"

Krista spotted the exit sign and turned onto the ramp. "All right, I don't need your origin story. I just want to know what the hell's going on right now."

They pulled into a truck stop right off the exit. Beyond the pumps, Krista spotted a clock in the distance. As she approached it, she saw that it was mounted atop a long, low building, with neon letters beside the clock shouting TIME TO EAT HEAVY. "I'm thinking that's a restaurant," she said, and she drove through the gravel parking lot and stopped at the entrance.

They climbed the steps to a yellowed glass door with a sign taped on it declaring NO SHOT? NO SERVICE! Krista pulled it open, and they walked into a greasy dining room with booths along the windows. Red stools lined a long plastic counter, and overweight men sat on half of them.

A short woman bounced from behind the counter holding two menus and wearing a bright smile. "Welcome!" she said.

"A booth for two, please," Krista said.

"Y'all gotcher shots?"

Krista and Ada raised their sleeves and showed her their vaccination bumps. Her nostrils twitched a few times, and she fanned the menus at Ada. "Whew. Hon, you been rollin in butt mud or somethin?" The woman leaned forward and whispered. "It's okay, y'ain't the first stinker we got in here. You oughta smell some of these guys when they get offa the highway." They walked down the aisle, and she elbowed a fat man on a stool. "Right, Ron?" Ron either burped or grunted in assent. "Before they take a shower, they can knock a buzzard offa gutwagon. Shower's only a buck, and we got one open."

"Thanks, but not now."

"Okay, hon. Long as your mom here can take it, I can too." She dropped the menus on their table and hustled away to get drinks, and they slid into a booth with seats that were more tape than vinyl. When the server returned, they ordered half-pound burger platters with all the fixings. The server told Krista that the price had quadrupled because beef was in short supply.

They sat in awkward silence for a few minutes, listening to country music and looking out at the parking lot. Krista sipped her water, and then she slammed the glass down like a judge banging a gavel. "Now it's time to tell the truth, Amy. Where's your mom's house? Is it anywhere around here? Are we on the right road, or even in the right feckin state? You're going to tell me what's really going on, or I'm dropping you off at the firehouse. Where they can hose you off, at least."

Ada raised her glass to her lips, her eyes twinkling over the rim. "We don't have to find my mom's house anymore. *You're* my mom now."

"What!"

"Sure. Didn't you hear the lady? Mom? Mama? Which do you prefer?"

Krista's eyes narrowed. "You're either a flaming asshole, or you're barking mad."

"Nah, I just have mommy issues."

The server returned with a huge platter of food and set it before them. Ada scowled at her basket of French fries. "These are pretty greasy," she said.

"Makes 'em go down easier. Ya don't want 'em, don't eat 'em, hon."

She pushed it away with one finger and looked up at Krista, the twinkle back in her eyes. "Want my fries, Mommy?" Krista glared at her, and Ada grinned back.

"Y'all okay here?" asked the server.

Krista forced a smile to her lips. "We're fine, thanks. We'll let you know if we need anything."

The server walked back to the counter. Krista bit into her burger, glaring darkly at Ada, who had closed her eyes and was savoring each mouthful. They finished the meal in silence.

Ada wiped her lips. "Thanks a lot. I actually had a burgasm!"

"You're welcome."

After they pushed the plates away, Krista lit a cigarette and eyed Ada narrowly. "I've got your number now, Amy. You're a tricky little one, aren't you?"

"Golly gosh, I don't understand. Tricky in what way?"

"You're an evasive, manipulative little liar. I've seen your type before. I *was* your type. The last thing I'll get from you is the truth."

Ada pulled a cigarette from her pack and tapped it against the table a few times, avoiding Krista's eyes. "That's a little insulting."

"It's after nine o'clock. I'm not driving much further tonight, so I'm giving you a choice. Tell me the truth and you can stay with me. And take a shower. Keep lying and you can go to the firehouse, where abandoned kids belong. Which do you want?"

Ada took a long, slow puff and looked at the bug corpses glued to the greasy glass. "All right, but you have to promise you won't tell anyone, and you won't dump me somewhere."

Krista nodded.

"My dad's a cop in Steubenville. I can't stand him, and I want to go live with my mom. She moves around a lot, and the last I heard, she moved in with some guy, and they're living in a trailer up this road somewhere. They don't have a phone, so I can't call. I was trying to walk there, but I got tired. I can't go to a firehouse cuz they'll call my dad and send me back."

"So you were lying when you said you live in Washington? You're actually a backwoods hick?"

Ada nodded and looked outside again.

"Listen, I'll tell you something you obviously don't know – a well-crafted lie needs a germ of truth in it. Now look at you, wearing thousand-dollar boots and designer jeans and carrying around a spy briefcase. You expect me to believe you're a hick?"

"My dad makes good money, okay?"

"Let it go already, wouldja? You're busted. Why don't you try the truth?"

"I can't tell you that! All right? I just can't."

"Right. What happened to the straight talk you promised?"

Ada looked into the parking lot, her eyes glistening with tears. She blinked them away and took a savage puff.

"Are you in trouble?" Krista asked gently.

She stubbed out her cigarette and sat back. "Look, I don't know who you are. You could be a Red spy. Why should I trust you?"

"I'm not a spy!"

"Yeah? How do I know that?"

"Because I just said I wasn't!"

"Which is exactly what a spy would say, right?" she asked, crossing her arms. "Okay, you want the truth? I think you could be an extractor. This whole episode is way too freakin suspicious. I think the Reds let me marinate in that rest stop for ten days till my defenses cracked and I'd trust anybody. That's when they send an operative in to rescue me, and then this operative asks a lot of innocent questions that get more and more personal, and if I don't answer them, she'll give me the pinprick and I'll wake up the next day in some freakin gulag in bumfuck Siberia."

"Hunh?"

"Well, borscht turns my ass into a firehose, so I'll make you a deal, *tovarisch*. I'll tell you everything I know if you let me go free after." She leaned forward and examined Krista's face. "And I know *everything*. I'm a Q-Level Blue."

"Hunh?"

She studied Krista's blank expression a second longer and then sat back. "Nah, you're pretty clueless. If you were a Red extractor, your head woulda just exploded. Forget everything I just said."

"You're in that QAnon thingie?"

Ada laughed. "You're *totally* clueless! Perfect!"

Krista massaged her temples to ward off the tension headache this conversation was brewing. "Jaysus, are you nuts?"

"I'm practicing identity hygiene, that's all. It drives me up the wall too."

Krista rubbed her temples even harder. "What the hell is that? I'm so lost."

"We're all lost, sister," Ada said. "Look, I'm just an ordinary girl with no extraordinary talents, okay?"

"Did I say you weren't?"

"That's all I'm saying," Ada said. "Here's the thing – you don't trust me. I don't trust you. That's not changing anytime soon."

Krista took a deep breath and let it out slowly. "All right, but you still need to give me a reason why I just shouldn't drop you off at the firehouse and make you their problem."

Ada's eyes widened. "You just promised you wouldn't!"

"And you lied, so the deal's off!" Krista slipped the tablet into her hoodie and picked up the check. "Let's find the firehouse. I'm tired of this game."

Ada didn't move. Instead, she took her time lighting another cigarette.

"I said *let's go*, Amy."

Ada glared at her and made no effort to move. "Some mother you are. No wonder I'm so screwed up."

Krista rolled her eyes. "Oh, Jaysus, Mary, and Joseph! All right, fine, I'll just leave you here then. Have fun. Hitch a ride or something."

She edged out of the booth, but Ada's hand shot across the table and grabbed her arm. "Sue, look, okay, I'll tell you what I can, but not everything. You have to trust me. Please, don't leave me here." Krista looked across the table, where Ada was blinking back tears. "I can't be alone again, not in the middle of nowhere. Please?"

Krista's shoulders sagged, and then she slid back into the booth.

"But I can't tell you here. It's too public."

Krista rolled her eyes. "The walls have ears? How coldwar of you."

Ada pinned her with a sharp glance. "Do *not* joke about things you don't understand."

Krista assessed the girl for a few moments and then said, "Okay. Let's go find a place to stay tonight, and then you'll tell me everything."

KRISTA FOUND A SMALL MOTEL called Brasser's across the road from the truck stop. They charged by the hour, and the sheets and blankets cost extra, but they didn't ask for her identification.

The room was appalling: It had no TV, but it did have an elderly carpet that had seen its share of bodily fluids and walls painted a mottled yellow. Looking closer, Krista hoped the blotches were only paint. However, it had a big soft bed and a shower, which was all they needed.

While Ada showered, Krista surfed the SatNet but learned nothing new: The virus was still eating the country, and the survivors still wanted her dead. It was just another boring news day.

She wrote another post asking for a lip reader, attached the Trope videos, and then propped her tablet on the windowsill to find a satellite. The files were large, and it took ten minutes to upload the entire message.

Ada stepped from the steamy bathroom, wrapped in a towel and as red as an overripe tomato. She smiled as she combed her hair.

"You're looking happy," Krista said.

"Oh, yeah! I dropped a dumposaurus and wiped up with real toilet paper! And all before my shower! I love a clean finish!"

"Right. I needed to know that."

"*And* I cured my terminal grungitis." She grabbed a cotton swab and inserted it deep into her ear canal, and she closed her eyes and smiled. "Mmm, I could do this for hours. It's as good as sex."

"Aha! You're a virgin!"

Ada flicked the waxy swab at her head and picked up her panties with her fingernail. "I'm not putting these on again." She waved the underpants in Krista's face. "You think if I wash them, they'll be dry by tomorrow?"

Krista curled her lip and recoiled. "Probably. So when will we be having that talk?"

"After you shower. I need to figure out how to explain my weird life first. And I *really* need to clean these." She walked to the sink and started washing the panties. "Gross, gross, gross."

Krista stepped into the shower and washed while singing a piece from *Madame Ovary*. She dried off, and then she felt her thigh wound and swore, remembering that she'd left the first-aid kit in the car. She called through the door and asked Ada to get it, but she said she couldn't because she was still naked. Krista wrapped a towel around her shoulders and decided to get it herself later.

She walked to the mirror, started combing her hair, and then looked closer at her face – maybe it was the light, but she thought she saw a wrinkle. "Do I really look old enough to be your mom?" Krista asked.

"Yeah, if you were a teen mother," said Ada as she hung her wet bra over the back of a chair.

Krista thought she saw a white hair and pulled a lock down in front of her eyes to scrutinize it. "Splendid, just splendid. I'm already turning into a hag," she said to her reflection. She leaned over the sink to comb back through her hair. "Okay, I'm out. Time to talk."

Ada sat on the bed and crossed her legs. "Here goes. First, my name isn't Amy Lichtblau. It's Ada Lang."

"Lang, Lang, now where have I heard that lately?" Krista leaned into the sink even further, and the towel rose up her thighs. "Oh, well, it'll come back to me. Keep going, Ada Lang."

"Second thing is, that briefcase…holy shit! What's that?"

"What's what?" Krista started to turn, but Ada was already kneeling behind her, swearing and pressing the skin around the cut on her thigh. "Get on the bed and lie down on your stomach. I need to get some light on this."

Krista limped to the bed. Ada pulled a table lamp over and prodded at the wound. "How'd this happen? Why didn't you get this treated? This is going septic, for chrissakes! Look at this!"

"I *can't* look at it, Amy, I mean Ada. It's on my ass."

"It's infected, and the infection's spreading up your leg." She sat back on the bed. "You're going to the emergency room right now. You get your clothes on, and I'll go up to the office and get directions to the hospital." She stood and started pulling her jeans on.

"We're not going to any hospital," Krista said.

"That's bullshit! You could lose the leg. You could die! If you won't go, I'll just call an ambulance. One way or another, that's getting attention." She pulled her jeans up and buttoned them.

"I can't see a doctor and I won't and if you call an ambulance I'll just get in my car and drive away!"

Ada buttoned her blouse and sat with a puzzled expression on her face.

"I'll leave you here," Krista said. "Alone. No doctors."

Ada tapped her foot a few times and pursed her lips. "Okay. We'll circle back to that. In the meantime, you said you have a first-aid kit?"

"In my trunk." Krista began to sit up. "I'll go –"

"Don't move. I'll get it." She picked up the keys, ran to the car, and returned a few minutes later holding a large white plastic case. She laid it on the bed. "This is very pro," she said, running her fingers over the tubes and bottles. "This is almost a medikit."

"A nurse gave it to me for my birthday," Krista said. "There should be a can of spray antibiotic in there, but there's probably not much left."

"Spray antibiotics don't work on systemic infections." She reached into the kit and pulled out a yellow can. "You have polyfloxacin nanopowder. Why didn't you use that?"

"Because I've got no idea what it is?"

"It's a broad-spectrum topical antibiotic. It'll buy you another day, maybe. Okay, let's get to work." Ada reached for her supplies and then bent over the wound.

"Jesus, you're such a weenie!"

"Crap, Ada, that hurt! I nearly passed out!"

"I wish you did, I mean, you scream like a banshee! Look, it was a mess. What did you do, stop the bleeding by stuffing dirt in it?" She wrapped gauze around Krista's leg, taped down the free end, and then sat back on the bed. "That'll last you till tomorrow, but you need to get an oral antibiotic, and you definitely need to get that wound sutured. It's right at a joint. It'll just keep opening up and getting infected."

Krista started to roll over.

"No, no, no," Ada said. "I'll tell you when you can get up. You need to let that polyfloxacin work."

"Try to remember who's the adult here, all right?" She lay back down, though, and rested her head on the pillow.

"Adult. Right." Ada sat in a plastic chair by the head of the bed and reached for her cigarettes.

Krista turned her head. "Gimme one."

"You shouldn't smoke in bed. Besides, you can't do it lying down."

"Sure I can. C'mon, hand it over."

Ada's dark eyes sparkled like black diamonds as she exhaled a lazy cloud of smoke. "Wow, that hit the spot. I had a huge craving, I mean, two whole hours."

Krista groaned.

"I'm sorry, is my smoke bothering you? I hope I'm being inconsiderate."

Krista buried her face in the pillow, while Ada took another slow puff and smiled. "Sue, Sue, Sue. You haven't been completely honest with me, have you? Wow, it's amazing how the tables have turned, huh?"

"Like yer some feckin great fountain a'truth."

Ada broke into a laugh, her eyes tearing.

"What's so damn funny?" Krista asked.

Ada wiped her eyes and started giggling again. "You sounded like an angry little leprechaun for a minute. Go ahead and say it – they're always after me Lucky –"

Krista screamed into the pillow, "You! You annoying little bitch!"

"Aww, c'mon. Just say it."

Krista spewed a sizzling blue cloud of epithets. Ada sat back, wide-eyed and stunned into silence, and then lit a cigarette and handed it over. "You know, that's no way to talk to a child. You could stunt my development. I could get Issues."

Krista glared back, but Ada just smiled and settled into the chair. "What do we have here, Susie pie? You have a knife wound, not self-inflicted, not accidental, made with a really sharp knife. A really dirty knife. And it went into you with enough force to expose the muscle. And you're bruised all over. So you were assaulted by someone who wanted to kill you and not just knock you around. Am I right so far?"

Krista nodded. "But that's all I'm telling you."

"That's okay. I won't push you to talk, unlike some people I know. But it doesn't matter whether you tell me or not. Either way, you have to get that sutured."

"I'm not seeing how that's going to happen. I'm not going where they'll report me. I'll take my chances."

"You're staying below the radar, huh?"

Krista nodded. They were silent for a minute, each lost in their thoughts, and then Ada said, "I can suture that, y'know."

"You? What are you, thirteen?"

Ada's face soured. "Almost sixteen, thank you. I'm just a little short for my age. And my mom's a physician, so I know how to do it."

"Well, it's your mom that's the physician, not you. Why can't she do it when I get to her house?"

Ada stubbed her cigarette out and slowly pushed it through the ash.

"Because you're not going to her house, right?"

Ada looked away and nodded.

"Your dad's house?"

She shook her head. "I haven't seen him since I was two."

"He wasn't the one in that beige car?"

"I never saw those people in my life," Ada said. "And I seriously *do not* want to talk about that."

Krista sighed. "We're a mysterious pair, aren't we?"

"But we need each other." Ada picked up some paper and a pen from the table. "Let's make a shopping list. Do you have any money?"

Krista nodded and then laid her head on the pillow. "Money I've got. However much you need."

"Good. Tomorrow, we'll go to a pharmacy and pick up the supplies I need, and then I'll suture that wound."

MAGEE'S DRUG STORE

Day 31
Friday morning, September 18, 2043
Brasser's Low-Tel Motel, Oxford, Ohio

Krista awoke and stared at the flaking paint of the ceiling, unsure where she was or why a blonde girl was lying beside her. She rolled over and saw the clock. It was 7:14 AM.

She slipped out of bed and walked to the desk; her limp wasn't as bad, and the pain in her thigh was much less than it had been yesterday. After feeling the gauze over her wound, memories of Ada's ministrations returned.

Shaking her head, she picked up her tablet and opened the door. The fug outside was as thick as it had been for days, but the smell was even more biting, and her cheeks were already stinging. She reminded herself to buy a tube of Alkaliniment at the pharmacy.

She turned from the breeze, lit up, and then checked her tablet: She'd received a message from Aaron Birnie, the executive editor of *Midnight Sun*, and all it said was 'Call Me.' She checked his site, and her post from last night wasn't there.

"Is this feckin post cursed? Why can't I ever get the damned thing up?" She tossed her cigarette away and dialed Aaron, and then she endured five minutes of mild swearing because it was only 4:30 AM in Vancouver. "Aaron, all right already, I'll try to keep the time zones in mind from now on."

"Just don't call at this barbaric hour. It wakes up the whole family, and the dog won't stop barking for hours."

"I said I'll try. So what happened to my post?"

"Diplomacy happened to it. Do you realize that I'm in Canada? That white splotch north of the United States? It's actually a foreign country, Krista."

"I know, but what's that have to do with my post?"

"Well, ever since you started posting on my site, I've been having these nice little chats with this sub-minister or that. What you say has significant international implications, Krista. They're concerned about the role you're taking."

"What role? What am I doing?"

"Pay attention to your press. You're becoming an icon. You're the face of a growing revolution."

"What revolution?"

"Your last two posts stirred up discontent on the SatNet and burst a blister of resentment against the American government. Suddenly, everyone on the Net is anti-Washington and believes you're being persecuted. These are the seeds of revolution."

"I *am* being persecuted, but I'm not trying to topple the government, Aaron."

"Intentions matter not in political physics, Krista, only the momentum of power. And Ottawa is troubled by your momentum. When they heard you had videotaped evidence and a death list, they confiscated the server it was on. They're politicians, and they're suspicious of grassroots power and instinctively want to crush it. They're scared catatonic of what you could do."

She swore and kicked a rock across the parking lot. "Got a testicle shortage up there, boyo? Maybe you guys should get implants. It'll help you pretend you're men."

"Krista, please –"

"What have you got to lose by trying? A bra size?"

"You've been through a lot, I know, but understand that I'm not your enemy, please."

"I know, I know." She mussed her hair and paced up and down the walk. "It's not your fault, Aaron."

"I know it's been brutal for you. How are you handling all this?"

"I'm fine."

"Yes, yes, you may be fine now, but you *do* understand what you're up against? There's a Snuff Order out on you."

"I'm aware of that, Aaron. I read the news."

"However, I'm in a position where I may be of help. Some of our Witnesses – practically all of them, to be precise – are sympathetic to you and your cause. I can contact them if you need help. We may be able to fashion an Underground Railroad of a sort."

"Could they get me into Canada? I'm not far from the border, maybe only a days' drive away."

"I don't think that would be possible. Ottawa's apoplectic about me just sponsoring you. How do you think they'd feel about harboring you? They wouldn't be greatly cheered, I assure you. I'll ask, but don't count on it."

"Thanks. Now about these Witnesses – do you have any in Ohio?"

"Less every day, sadly, but there are still a few. Tell me what town you're in, and I'll point you to the nearest one. Where are you now?"

"Oxford. Would any of your Witnesses be doctors, by any chance?"

"I don't believe so. Why? Do you need medical attention?"

"I don't need any help right now. I just wanted to know if there was help around. Thanks, Aaron. I feel much better knowing I'm not alone."

"And in that regard, I just sent you the name of the closest Witness. Check your mail."

She opened the message. "Okay, got it, thanks. Maybe I'll get in touch with him." An engine roared and a truck gunned into the lot. "Gotta go, Aaron. Thanks."

She knelt in front of a car and peeked over the hood as the sound came closer. A gray truck took shape in the fug that appeared to have men with guns clustered in the back. When it passed, though, she saw that it was just a pickup truck with rakes sticking out of the bed.

She drew a relieved breath and then walked off to find coffee.

ADA DIDN'T SUFFER MORNING GLADLY; she was sprawled across the mattress as if she'd fallen into it from three stories up. Krista pounded her with a pillow and shook the bed, but the girl showed no signs of waking, so she lifted the sheet and tickled the bottoms of her feet until she stirred. Ada groaned and threw the pillow at her.

KRISTA LOCKED THE ROOM DOOR just as the timer ran out, and the light on the lock blinked red. "It's ten o'clock already. Listen, you've got to get moving quicker after you wake up. You should drink coffee. It's a magic elixir, and it'll jumpstart your morning."

"I can't stand that stuff. It tastes like ass water," said Ada.

"You've tasted ass water?"

Ada groaned. "It's too early for this abuse. I'm just not a morning person. Is that okay with you? Besides, I haven't slept in a bed for ten days. I was getting good sleep."

Krista reached the driver's door and clicked her remote to unlock it, but the door locks seemed stuck. While she jiggled the handle, Ada stood by the front of the car and squinted at the bumper. "Did you hit something?" She crouched in front of the grille. "Some short-haired animal?"

Krista pulled on the sticky door. "I don't recall –" She froze and saw Ada scrutinizing a piece of fur.

"A fox squirrel, maybe, it's large enough for that, except this fur is blonde. But, wow, you really smeared the thing. It's packed into the grille. Blammo! Instant squirrel purée!"

Krista's face went pale. "Umm…just put that down and get into the car. Please?"

"C'mon, don't be squeamish. It's dead. It's not like it'll jump up and bite me or something." She examined the dangling shred again and shook it. "Maybe it wasn't a squirrel. Maybe a dog –"

"Put the feckin thing down!"

Ada dropped it and walked to the passenger door. "Okay, but you oughta clean that off. It'll stink if you don't."

"I'll take it through a carwash later."

"You expect a carwash to clean *that* mess? You have to scrape all that meat off first –"

"Ada?"

Ada looked over at her. "Shut the ole piehole?"

"Please."

KRISTA PULLED INTO A PARKING SPOT on Oxford's main street. The old town was crossed by wide boulevards and lined with sidewalks for crowds of townsfolk, but from the decrepit condition of the buildings, they'd left a hundred years before. The main street had plenty of parking spaces, but few were taken.

They found a pharmacy on the main street called Magee Drugs, which was the only business with its lights on. They parked and walked into the small store.

It looked a hundred years old, with ornate cast-iron columns holding up a high, painted tin ceiling. However, only a few bare shelves filled the mostly empty space. Dents in the carpet showed where furniture had been removed recently.

Krista grabbed a basket from a rack and started filling it, now and then referring to the list while Ada wandered around and picked up a few things for herself. They met back near the entrance.

"Did you see any bras?" asked Krista.

"Training bras, that's all," said Ada. "I thought you were the nature girl type."

"Not with these baloobas. I just forgot to put on my bra, and now I'm paying for it." Krista pointed to a few items on the list. "Okay, we just need these."

"Those are behind the counter. You'll have to ask."

"Wouldn't this one be a prescription drug?"

"So ask nicely. You need it," Ada said, and she wandered to an alcove at the end of the counter where a TV was playing.

Krista walked to the counter and rang the bell. A man with thinning gray hair shuffled from behind a row of racks and gave her a joyless yellow grin, or perhaps it was a grimace of pain. "Help you?"

She flashed him a bright smile. "Hi. Do you have these?" She circled the things she needed and handed him the list.

He slipped on a pair of glasses and read it. He was painfully thin, a pound shy of a skeleton, and wore a mustache so thin that it had to be one hair high. After frowning and harrumphing for a few seconds, he walked to the back and picked boxes from the shelves.

Krista looked around the old store, but there wasn't much to see, and she turned back to see how the man was doing. On the counter, she spotted a small cardboard sign that said SIGN IN FOR VACCINE with an arrow pointing down.

A few minutes later, he returned with a handful of boxes and rested them on a shelf behind the counter. "I have everything, but some of this is unusual. Why do you need a field surgery kit, may I ask?"

"Oh, my daughter's doing a science fair project." She leaned toward him and shook her head. "I really don't understand it all. I'm not the sciency type."

"Her school is open? All the schools around here closed last week for the health emergency."

"Umm...she's homeschooled."

"A homeschooled science fair?" He shrugged. "Guess she'll win, then. Fine, you want to pay for it, I have no problem, but these other two are regulated substances. You have a prescription?"

"I didn't know I needed one."

He nodded and studied her face over the top of his glasses, and Krista patted her hoodie pockets. "Well, I'm sure it's in here somewhere. You know how women are. Oh, here it is!" She held out a tenpez on her palm.

"Yep, there it is." He took the coin, dropped her boxes on the counter, and started ringing up the rest of her purchases.

"You gave out the vaccine here?" Krista asked.

"A few weeks ago, yeah."

"Do you mind if I ask you a few questions?"

"As a matter of fact, I mind a lot. Why do I have to talk about that? I did what I was supposed to, that's all." He picked another item from the basket and scanned it.

"I'm just writing a story, and I'm doing background research. I'd appreciate it." She batted her eyes and flashed her best pretty-girl smile again, but he scowled and turned back to the register. "And I'm willing to pay for your time."

He cupped his hand over his ear. "Sorry, my hearing's not so good anymore. You say there's two tenpez in it for me?"

"You must have misheard me. I only offered one." She rummaged in her pockets again, pulled out another gold coin, and dropped it on the counter. He reached for it, but she quickly covered it with her hand. "*After* you answer my questions, friend."

"All right. Take your hand off and leave it where I can see it." He sat on a stool, glanced at the tenpez, and then crossed his arms and looked at Krista. "Go ahead. Fire away."

ADA WAS COMPLETELY TUNED IN. She'd been starved of electronic entertainment for two weeks, and she skipped across the channels, watching a few seconds of her favorite shows and then switching again to find more.

"What's this? A rerun?" She snorted and punched up another channel, which was a newsfeed – and a picture of Sue was on the screen. Ada blinked a few times and looked closer: It was definitely Sue, perhaps a few years younger, but those deep-blue eyes were the same. The chyron under the picture said KRISTA WARNER - FUGITIVE.

She sat back in the chair and turned up the sound:

> "...Citizen's Apprehension Order is still in effect, and the reward for the identifiable remains of the fugitive has been increased to two thousand tenpez. We repeat, the fugitive may be driving a blue four-door '40 Bicep D4 bearing Pennsylvania tags AC9-DD5-VG5. The front of the vehicle may be damaged.
>
> "The fugitive is mentally unstable and dangerous. Citizens are advised to use all necessary force to detain or disable..."

She looked at the picture on the screen and then at the woman standing stiffly at the counter. Chewing on a strand of hair, she watched the scene change to a loading dock.

Blood streaked across a brick wall and puddled on the floor. A body bag was being loaded on a stretcher – a limp, almost empty bag. Crime scene technicians measured, plucked, and dusted everywhere, and dropped small yellow flags on the floor. The camera then zoomed in on the brick wall: Chunks of bloody flesh and fabric were ground into it, and the gate at the end was twisted and scraped. The announcer was still talking:

> "...premeditated vehicular homicide of unsuspecting Federal agents. The fugitive fled the scene immediately after the murders and has not been seen since. We repeat..."

She shut off the TV and sat back in the chair. Being rescued by a wanted murderer fit her bizarre life perfectly. She always took the tunnel at the end of the light, and every silver lining had a storm cloud.

Suddenly, she remembered crouching in front of the murder vehicle and looked at her hands. She jumped to her feet and stalked to the counter.

KRISTA HATED INTERVIEWING HIM. This man and his so-called values repulsed her, and she had to struggle to remain objective. However, she was paying for the monster's time and wanted to get something quotable.

Ada stormed to the counter and grabbed a bottle of hand sanitizer. She pumped the little dispenser furiously and squirted the glop all over the countertop and the floor.

"Easy there, young miss. You only need to use a little. That stuff costs money."

She pumped it a few more times and spritzed the counter and the floor again, all the time glaring at the man. He ignored her look and wiped the counter with a paper towel, and then he sat back on the stool, wearing a smug smile. He crossed his arms, looked down at the counter, and then back up at Krista.

She glanced at the countertop, and the tenpez was gone. "You greasy little nickum!"

"I just wanted to be sure I got paid. I'll still answer your questions, though, so don't worry. I'm an honest businessman, and a deal's a deal." Krista stamped her foot and balled her fists.

Ada pulled the arm of her hoodie. "Sue, we need to talk."

"Later."

"No, we really need to talk *right now*, Sue."

Krista turned to deliver both barrels, but then she saw the anger in Ada's eyes and held her fire.

"When you get a moment, Sue."

"We can talk *later*," she hissed.

"As soon as you can. Susie, Susarama, Suzapalooza..."

"Just go sit down and shut your feckin gob..." Krista noticed the shopkeeper's eyebrows rise in surprise, "...my darling little angel?" She patted her head, and Ada fumed off to the alcove.

ADA SAT IN FRONT OF THE TV again and surfed the news channels. The news moved onto other topics, but the Snuff Order crept across the bottom of each show she found.

She stopped surfing when she found a talking head show. A shiny-faced little guy with a mane of recently bleached white hair was on, and he was nervous as hell:

> Molle: You can relax, Dr. Stanton. I won't bite...unless you want me to!
>
> Stanton: I've never been on TV before, Arista. Thanks for understanding. I must say, I'm delighted to be on your show. I'm a huge fan of yours. By the way, I'm a nurse, not a doctor. And I'd love if you called me Ed.
>
> Molle: Great, Dr. Stanton. I love kudos! So I understand that for the past year you were romantically involved with the murderess Warner.
>
> Stanton: Oh, it wasn't romance. She had an adventurous appetite, and we went out for dinner a few times. She was just an engaging dinner companion, but I suppose the insane can be charming when they want. Sometimes it was hard to enjoy dinner, though, what with her eyes rolling back into her head. Sometimes she could see in two directions at once! And she was always talking to herself, and did I mention those weird facial tics? It was all so bizarre.
>
> Molle: You knew she was mentally unstable when you were dating her?
>
> Stanton: I suspected she was, of course. I didn't realize how dangerous she could be, though. I would've alerted the authorities if I had.
>
> Molle: Were you frightened? You didn't feel that you were in danger being in the company of a murderess?

Stanton: No, but then, I didn't know that she was capable of murder. I was completely in the dark, I'm sorry to say. I didn't know that I could be rubbed out at any moment. I get nightmares about that now.

Molle: What do you think brought her to commit such gruesome murders, Dr. Stanton?

Stanton: She was under so much pressure. She'd developed some wacky delusion about a dark government conspiracy, and it sent her over the edge into raving madness. Did I mention that the last time I met her, she was actually foaming at the mouth? And she was barking –

Molle: (coughs) Some low-information types say she's right about a conspiracy.

Stanton: They shouldn't believe a word she says. She's completely insane. The sooner she's dead, the better off civilized society will be.

Molle: We can take your word on that because you're an upstanding member of our fine medical community. I understand you've just been promoted to Nursing Director at Georgetown Hospital. That sounds like quite a responsibility!

Stanton: It is, Arista, but it's a responsibility I'm proud to shoulder.

Molle: Thank you for being on my show today, Dr. Stanton. Maybe we can meet again. I also have an adventurous appetite!

Stanton: I'd love that, Arista, I really would! More than you know!

"Oh, c'mon, I could come up with better bullshit than that." Ada was about to switch channels when she heard the tap of footsteps from the store. She looked up and saw Krista, her face tight and her eyes burning with anger.

"I guess it's time to go?" Ada asked, but she turned without a sound and stormed out of the store. Ada ran to catch up. They walked to the car and Krista opened the trunk, threw the bag inside, and slammed the trunk lid so hard that it bounced open again. She closed it more gently and climbed into the front seat.

"You're a little pissed," Ada said.

"The bastard needs a good pizzlin." She slammed the car into gear and then squealed onto the street.

"Find a place to pull over and cool off, okay? This is a little dangerous. You could run somebody over."

Krista nodded once and turned onto a side road.

"So is this a '40 model?" Ada asked.

"What?" Krista looked at her with furrowed eyebrows. "Oh, the car. It is." She pulled into a small park beside a railroad siding cluttered with trash.

"All right. This looks like a good place to chill," Ada said.

Krista unfolded her tablet and tapped on it furiously.

"You look busy. I'll go walk around," Ada said. Krista muttered an unintelligible reply.

She pulled her bookbag and briefcase from the backseat and wandered into the park. At the far end, she climbed a gravel embankment and found a weathered wooden bench a few feet from the railroad tracks.

She sat on the gravel in front of the bench and squinted down the tracks, which headed west. They were pitted with rust and hadn't seen a train wheel in decades.

All she needed to do was to get on them and walk to California. *Right, I can walk two thousand miles in these boots. And watch out for Freaks and bears and a million other things that want to kill me the whole time. Just a few small wrinkles in that plan. On the other hand, I could go back to that freakin warwagon with the damn scalps dangling off it and hang out with the homicidal maniac. Just to see how well that works out. But on the bright side, at least she's not a Red extractor!*

She closed her eyes and rubbed her temples. Her mother had told her she'd face some tough decisions when she became an adult, and the best thing to do was to remain calm, weigh the pros and cons of each choice, and decide only then.

She snorted a laugh. *Shall I behead you with the ax today, madam, or would you prefer the broadsword?*

Oh, I don't know, good sir. What are the pros and cons of each?

She banged her head against the bench a few times, but nothing made any more sense after she stopped.

My best choice is to get abducted by the aliens. All right with me. Just a few fingers up the ass, and I get a free ride. That sounds like a square deal right now.

She turned her face to the sky and spread her arms. "Okay, you little bastards! I'm waiting!"

The Rake
September 18, 2043

MEDICINE MANIKIN
Our lives are in the hands of men with less soul than department store dummies

"Life's all about money, getting as much as you can and keeping it. Everyone wants money," says the manikin. "So I'm not a bad person. I'm just a small businessman trying to survive in a competitive climate."

"You weren't motivated completely by money. You said you denied the vaccine to a few Class Fours even though they could pay. And for those who didn't have enough, you wouldn't lower your price despite having plenty of vaccine left over. You made life-or-death judgments for some other reason, Mr. Magee."

The manikin shakes its head. "Look, I worked in this damned burg for forty years, building this business, listening to these people wheedle and whine. And what happens when the Mal-Mart opens in the next town? They go there instead, and my sales drop thirty-seven percent. That hurt me, right here." It thumps its chest, where a human would have a heart. "Why should I be loyal to them? They weren't loyal to me."

"So you let them die."

"I'm only an instrument of Fate," says the manikin. "Why did Fate pick me? To make the choices I did, that's why."

"How many died because you denied them the vaccine?"

"None of my regular customers." The manikin smiles a yellow death's-head grimace. "A lot of the Mal-Mart customers did, though. Their sales volume will drop now, almost as much as mine did when they moved in. Turnabout is fair play. It says so in the Bible."

"Wrong. The Bible says vengeance is for God and not man."

The manikin raises an eyebrow. "Whatever."

"I'd like to thank you for being so brutally candid. But I can't bring myself to do it."

"I don't care. I don't need you or these swine. I have all the money I need now," says the manikin. "At the end of business today, I'm closing this store. Some other sucker can have it. As for me, I'm moving to California. My sister has a house across from the State Fairgrounds in Sacramento, and I'm going to sit on her lawn all day and soak up the rays.

"I don't care what people think of me anymore because pretty soon I'll be history. It'll just be me and the rays, sweetcakes, just me and the rays."

-KLW

ADA OPENED THE CAR DOOR, set her bookbag and briefcase outside, and then climbed into the passenger seat. Krista was rubbing her nose and staring through the windshield. "Back at last. Where were you?"

"I was waiting for the aliens, but they never came. It took a while to settle on Plan B."

"Whatever. Close the door and let's get going."

"I'm not ready to go yet."

"At least close the door, then. You're letting the fug in."

"No. I like fresh air, *Krista Warner.*"

Krista's head hit the headrest with a thump. "Jaysus, can this day get any worse?"

"Oh, yeah, it can get a lot worse. They have a Snuff Order out on you."

"Right, I know. Everybody's trying to kill me. That's old news."

"Two thousand tenpez for your body. It's all over the newsfeeds right now."

"Two grand now?" She lit a cigarette and glowered through the windshield. "The most anybody's ever offered for my body was a good dinner. I'm moving up in the world, kiddo."

"Why aren't you even trying to hide, then?"

"I've got a face people forget," Krista said. "I'm kinda invisible, really. I blend in."

"Right. Movie star looks and red hair down to your ass, and you just blend in." Ada scowled and looked through the window. "Maybe they're right. Maybe you *are* crazy."

"Please don't believe what they say. It's just not true." Her lips rose in a faint smile. "You really think I've got movie star looks?"

Ada glared at her. "Can you focus? Look, why do they want you so bad? What's the real reason?"

"Didn't the newsfeeds say why?"

"No. They just said you're insane and you murdered two Federals, and that's all. But why offer a two-thousand-tenpez reward just for a crazy lady? That's over two million bucks. That's the kinda money you pay to eliminate a real and imminent danger, not a demented chick with a lead foot. So I'm keeping an open mind. Tell me your side."

Krista massaged the bridge of her nose again. "It's a little hard to swallow, but here goes. I found out that the vice president spread this virus on purpose, I think to kill off the ex-workers, or the underclass, or maybe just the folks he doesn't like. I don't know why." She tapped the tablet lying on the console. "But he's behind this pandemic, and the proof is right here. Originals, admissible in court. They want to get this before I give it to someone who'll prosecute Cheyn. Me? They just want to whack me around like a Memorial Day melon. They couldn't care less about me."

"I saw those bruises. It looks like they already got a few whacks in," Ada said. "You're saying that this pandemic was intentional? That this is some kinda biowar?"

"It is. I know it's hard to believe, and I refused to believe it myself at first. I mean, it sounds like the plot of a sci-fi thriller, not some real-world thing, and it's hard to accept. But trust me, Cheyn really *is* killing off people."

"You're right. I'm having trouble believing that."

"I can show you the proof. I'd have to explain a few things, but it proves that this whole thing was planned."

"Maybe later. That two grand reward says whatever proof you have scares the government, so it's gotta be real," Ada said. "Okay, so you're telling the truth. What I need to know, right now, is if you're nuts. Are you?"

"*That's* for sure," Krista said. "Okay, that came out wrong. I've got a bunch of…maladjustment issues that come and go." She drew a slow, deep breath and gazed through the windshield with unfocused eyes. "When I get into bad cycles, though, it's just self-destructive. I never harm anyone else. I'm not an insane, raving lunatic. I mean, I'm not violent or anything."

Ada snorted. "Bullshit. I saw the pictures of that garage on the newsfeeds. There were little bitty chunks of Federals all over the place like freakin human confetti. And you have faceprints in your front bumper. You don't call that violent?"

"Okay, well, I'm not *normally* violent, but when you've got two feckin gorillas with knives chasing you around your bloody apartment in the middle of the night, things stop being normal in a goddamn hurry!"

"So you're a murderer?"

"I'm not! I mean, technically, maybe..." She banged the steering wheel and turned in her seat. "Look, it was the only way to stop them! What was I supposed to do? What would *you* do?"

Ada was silent for a few breaths and then spoke quietly. "I woulda killed them too."

"You would?"

"Yes." She pulled in her bookbag and laid her briefcase on her lap, and then she closed the door with a quiet click. "Okay. Let's go."

"Go where?"

"Wherever you're going."

"I'm going to California."

"Good. So am I."

Krista shook her head. "You might get hurt. The Federals want me dead, Ada."

"No prob. They'll want to kill me too when they find out I have this." She tapped the briefcase.

"Whoa!" Krista jerked her head around. "What?"

"Carrying this briefcase around is a death sentence. It might have been for my mom, but I don't..." She looked away, stroking its smooth side as if to release its secrets. After a few moments, she found her voice again. "I don't know what's in here, but it's gotta be some wicked bad shit. She knew they were coming to get her, and that's why she left it with me. And once the Federals figure that out, I'll be getting a Snuff put out on me too."

She glared through the window with her teeth clenched and then pounded the briefcase with her fist. "Screw it. The Feds wanna go nuclear? Fine, I can go nuclear too. I'm playing by Ada Rules now." She turned to

Krista, her eyes wet and fierce. "And you know what else? I'm really freakin glad you smeared those bastards! Okay? I wish you were here at the rest stop to squash the rest of them when it mighta done some good! It mighta…it mighta saved…" A tear escaped her eye and ran down her cheek, and she buried her face in her hands. "Oh, God, my mom," she whispered.

Krista wrapped her arm around her shoulder and held her to her chest. "They just took her…she just disappeared like that, and I was alone for so long and maybe I'll be alone forever now –"

"It'll be okay."

"Nothing will ever be okay again, everything's just so fucked up…"

Krista held her tight and stroked her arm until she calmed down. Soon after, she fell asleep.

ADA AWOKE IN EARLY AFTERNOON as they were approaching another small town on Route 22. She blinked a few times, and then she noticed the clock and swore. "Is that the right time?"

Krista grinned. "You were out for two hours."

Ada lit a cigarette and looked through the window, suddenly quiet. "I'm really sorry for that outburst. I'll try to keep it under control from now on."

"What the living hell are you talking about?"

Ada still stared at something in the distance. "This is the wrong time to break down like I just did."

"There's nothing wrong with that. You had to let it out, Ada. What are you supposed to be, a robot or something?"

"Yeah. Yeah, I am." Still looking away, she slid her hand gently into Krista's. "But we can't go soft. We need to remain completely aware of our situation. We'll have to be careful, and that means we need to stay sharp and plan every move."

"We'll come up with a plan, then." Krista squeezed her hand.

"Yeah. We can break down when this is all over, and we're safe and sound."

"We can get through this together," Krista said, and Ada laced her fingers into hers.

CENTERING THE CROSSHAIRS

Day 31
Friday evening, September 18, 2043
National Tranquility Center, Fort Belvoir, Virginia

An hour remained in the watch and Downs' feet were getting tired, so he did a few laps around the podium. It had been a slow Friday – usually the busiest redaction day of the week except for Saturday – and he wondered if the boredom had settled to his toes and numbed them.

"Sir, I've received a report from Fort Wayne." Cochon looked up from his monitor. "Someone called in with a probable sighting on Warner."

"Specifics?"

"A pharmacist in Oxford, Ohio, reported this afternoon that a woman matching Warner's description entered his store just before eleven this morning. She asked questions about the vaccine, purchased some items, and then left in a blue Bicep with a dented front bumper. The officer pressed him for more information, but he refused until he was paid the reward. He attached a copy of her receipt, along with a bank account number where we can send the money."

"He's a little premature, isn't he? He shows me her head, I'll show him the gold," Downs said. "Put Oxford on a highway map. Let's see where this place is."

Cochon tapped at his monitor a few times, and the map appeared on the Wall.

"She hasn't gone too far, then. Buta, do we have any surveillance in the area?"

"None, sir. Not even ATM's. The town's a backwater."

Downs pursed his lips. "Cochon, what did she buy?"

Cochon read off the list. "A field surgery kit, face cream, acne ointment, deodorant, pain relievers, antiseptic cream, surgical gauze, tampons, two toothbrushes, toothpaste…"

"So she's wounded. A serious wound too. But why two toothbrushes? She only has one mouth. Unfortunately, I can confirm that."

"I don't know, sir. Perhaps as a spare?"

"But she only bought one of everything else. That makes no sense. Does she have someone with her?"

"Unknown, sir."

Downs tapped his foot on the podium. "Find this pharmacist and bring him in. We need to know more."

"Fort Wayne has two officers in Oxford right now. His store is locked and closed, as is his house. His neighbors report he's been packing his van all week, and this afternoon he loaded suitcases in it and left. They don't know where he went."

Downs paced for a minute and then snapped his fingers. "He's going to Sacramento. Warner told us herself – she was writing about this pharmacist. Put up her post from today."

The post appeared on the Wall. "Well, sir, the fugitive herself confirms the sighting," Cochon said. "This is unusual."

"It's a gift." Downs calculated for a few moments. "Draw a ten-hour travel radius from Oxford. Use speed limits to approximate the length of travel."

Cochon tapped on his monitor for a few minutes and then asked Mochyn to help. They worked a few minutes more, and then a ragged red splotch, shaped like a ketchup stain, appeared on the Wall.

"Clip off everything east of Oxford along a north-south axis." Downs looked at the shape on the screen, which extended to Illinois, western New York, and Tennessee. "She's in there somewhere. Hogue, move the Special Activity Groups from West Virginia into this area. Go in through Oxford and have them follow all the roads out of town heading north, west, and south. Get Fort Wayne to do the same from the other direction with all the personnel they can assign.

"Buta, launch two Blackwings from Dayton. Put them into an arc-search pattern working out from Oxford. I want two more Blackwings and two assault drones on ready standby.

"Cochon, put out a bulletin on the pharmacist's van. He'll be driving west on I-70. Let's see if we can talk to him. And send this map to the Media Department and instruct them to release it to the newsfeeds. I want every hick with a gun to know that a two thousand tenpez reward is in their backyard."

STITCHES

Day 31
Friday evening, September 18, 2043
Brasser's Low-Tel Motel, Thornacre, Ohio

They found another Brasser's outside Columbus. Ada rented the room, and like the previous night, the desk clerk asked no questions. They settled in, and then Ada walked to a fast-food restaurant to get burgers; with Krista's face being broadcast all over the newsfeeds – and with a two-million-dollar reward – they'd decided that she needed to stay out of the public eye. Since nobody was looking for Ada, she could forage without attracting attention.

After finishing the greasy sandwiches, Ada laid out her surgery supplies on the desk. Krista watched her warily, and her eyes grew wide when Ada opened the kit and pulled out a cellophane envelope filled with curved needles. "This is really going to hurt, isn't it?" she asked. "Those are feckin huge. They look like fishhooks. For whales."

"Oh, don't be a wimp. It'll just be a few pinches, all over before you know it."

"I just don't like needles."

"Now who's the grown-up here? Huh?"

Krista sat on the bed and mumbled, "I don't need two legs. I'll buy a fake one or use a crutch or something."

"Whiny-ass. Look, that's why you bought Spectracain." She held up a vial. "You won't feel a thing, take my word on it." She pulled a long, shining syringe from the kit.

"That's another needle! Doesn't it come in a pill?"

"No. I have to do it this way." Ada sighed. "This'll be hard. Maybe I should knock you out first, like with a freakin baseball bat."

Krista pouted for a few moments, and then her eyes brightened. "Sue!" she cried, and she limped to her backpack.

"I thought we were done with the code names," Ada said.

Krista sank her hands deep in the backpack, muttering to herself, "Don't bang it around, of course she put some in here, the little alkie darling...Aha!" She pulled out a jug of Liquid Hug and kissed it. "I love you, Sue!"

"You named the bottle Sue?"

"The real Sue gave it to me, moron." She twisted off the cap, and a sweet scent wafted through the room.

Ada sniffed the air. "Ahh. Do I smell booze? Hooch? Firewater?"

"The best." Krista walked to the sink and picked up a plastic cup. "Hope this doesn't melt."

Ada sniffed again. "Brandy. Peach...no, apricot. Mmm, apricot's my favorite. Gimme some too. It might help me handle your endless whining."

Krista brought another cup to the desk and poured a splash into each. "It tastes terrible. Drink it slowly or you'll explode." She took a sip and shuddered.

Ada gulped from her cup and smiled. "Hey! This is good!"

"You actually like it?"

"Mmm." Ada took another sip, larger this time, and then she smiled again. "Oh, yeah."

KRISTA WAS WEARING ONLY A SHIRT and lying facedown on the bed, clutching the bars of the headboard with both hands. "All right, get on with it. Just look at the cut and not my outback."

"Like I wanna look at your ass," Ada grumbled as she tore open an alcohol swab. When she touched the swab to her skin, Krista's leg and cheek quivered violently.

"Damn! Are you trying to kill me, girl? What'd I ever do to you?"

"I haven't even done anything yet! I just swabbed your leg, that's all!" Ada ran her fingers through her hair. "Have another slug of that stuff already. You're driving me nuts."

Krista took a large sip of brandy and rested the cup on the nightstand. Ada had the syringe ready, and when Krista's fingers let go of the cup, she slapped her hard on the rear. Krista filled the air with colorful oaths, and Ada injected the anesthetic while she was busy swearing. "There. Done!"

ADA SAT ON THE FLOOR and reached for her cup. "We have to wait ten minutes for the anesthetic to work, so we might as well get comfy." She took a sip. "I love this stuff. It goes down easy."

Krista grinned. "Doesn't it? You get a sweet buzz."

Ada took a sip and giggled.

"What's so funny?"

"I don't know!" She giggled again.

Krista snorted a soggy laugh. "Wow. We need to slow down."

KRISTA SCREAMED INTO THE PILLOW. "I can feel that! It hurts! It really hurts!"

"I gave you the entire freakin syringe! That was enough for two people. Now there's none left." She tried to tie the suture, but her vision was becoming blurry. "Try to be good. Try to be brave or something. Sixteen down. Only two more, 'kay?" She shook her head and tried to clear her vision, but it made her dizzy.

She threaded the next suture, and again Krista shuddered and swore as Ada pulled it through her skin. The racket frayed her nerves, so she piled all the pillows over Krista's head and finished suturing as fast as her numb fingers would allow.

KRISTA POURED MORE BRANDY and lay back against the headboard. "It's Fate that I ended up with the evidence to bring down Cheyn," she said blearily. "Fate wants me dead. It's telling me my number's up, dropping this time bomb in my lap." She swigged the brandy and then looked into the cup with a scowl. "Well, that was one feckin miserable life."

"You're a depressing drunk," said Ada, sitting cross-legged on the bed.

"I won't live out the year. I should be depressed." She made a sloppy toast with her cup. "To Fate, that cold-titted whore."

"Fate," Ada grumbled. "That's superstition. It's for people who don't understand science, that's all. Gimme a break."

"You think science can explain everything? Like intuition, magick, the Life Force…?"

"Oh, don't gimme that mystical bending-spoons-with-your-mind crap."

"Mystical? There's a Life Force. It's a part of all of us, we're a part of it. It makes all living things grow. I feel it in me, so I know it's real. Don't you feel it when you smell sweet flowers on a soft breeze, or when you stand next to a grand ole tree and feel its Entish power? That's the Life Force rewarding and blessing –"

Ada snorted and shook her head. "Gah! Stop it! What is, is. What isn't, isn't. End of inquiry."

"Right. You sciency types, you're all the bloody same. You act like the universe has got the cuddliness of some feckin cosmic machine. And only you guys can twiddle the dials and make it do stuff."

"Basically, yeah. Show me the machine. I'll make it work."

Krista took a sip and rested her head against the wall, looking up at the ceiling. "Aren't you just the Mistress of the Bloody Universe?"

"Not really. Anybody can understand the cosmos, Krista. Even *you* could. You're almost as smart as me."

"Oh, so you think you're smarter than me?"

"Well, I *am* one of the top ten…" said Ada.

"Good for you. I graduated in the top ten of my class too."

"Good for you. I'm one of the top ten geniuses of all time."

"Oh." Krista found something interesting to study in her cup.

"I have the eighth-highest IQ ever recorded. If DaVinci was on the list, I'd be ninth." She gazed softly at the wall and smiled. "Ahhh, Leonardo. Is it sick to love a dead man? Is that necrophilia? Anyway, I'm not on his level. I can split an atom, but I can't even drive a car. If Leonardo was alive today, I bet *he* could drive."

"Still, that's something to be proud of."

Ada snorted a soggy laugh and covered her mouth.

"C'mon. It's good to be smart."

"It's freakin awful! It's a prison sentence! Everybody wants to get in my head! But I have a heart, y'know, but forget about that. They won't let me date anybody else 'cept another Blue." She emptied her drink in one gulp and licked her lips. "And why would I bang a kemmy…a kemmery…?"

"Chemistry?"

"Yeah! Why would I bang a chemistry geek? The sweet nothings he'd whisper in my ear." She shuddered violently. "Eww. Might as well get used to twirling my trackball. That's all the sex freaks get."

"I don't think you're a freak."

"My mom does. She keeps beating me over the head to act like a *normal person.*" Ada hooked quote marks in the air and made a face. "Like I can pretend to be normal. She didn't even try, y'know. She graduated at sixteen, but she expects *me* to fake the last two freakin years."

"Hey, everybody fakes the last two years of high school."

"Not like me. I already have a degree in quantum chromodynamics." Ada looked into her cup and grinned. "I said that while I was lit. Wow, I'm good."

"You studied about color?"

"Sorta. I studied the color force of sub-nucleonic particles."

"Ah, and that is…?"

"…impossible to understand unless you have a degree in it." Ada licked droplets off the cup's rim. "Sub-nucleons, they're itty-bitty things that make the universe happen. You probably heard 'em called quarks. I'm spooky good at what they do in transuranic metal alloys."

"Sounds a bit boring, to be honest."

"Amen, sister. Total snoredom."

"So you've already got a bachelor's in that whatsis color stuff–"

"No, my bachelor's is in energic chemistry. I have a Ph.D. in that whatsis color stuff."

Krista touched a finger to her nose to see if she was drunk, but she hit the tip on the first try. "I guess I heard that right, then. You're already a doctor, and you're still going to high school?"

"Yeah! That's what's so freakin sick! That's serious suckage!"

"I'll say. Wow, this is hard to believe."

"Well, trust me. I clock in at thirty-four IQ points over Einstein."

Krista knocked back a slug of brandy and gasped as the heat bloomed in her stomach. "I'll take your word on that, Doctor."

"Don't call me that! My mom's Dr. Lang, not me!"

"All right, chill," Krista said. "So once you graduate from high school, you're done with the whole education gig. That's not bad at all."

"Oh, no, I don't get off the hook with just any ole Ph.D. I gotta get one in engineering physics too. I finished the dissertation this summer, but I'm holding off on submitting it."

"Hunh? And why would you do that?"

"Cuz I'm allergic to the sun, and dry weather gets me *so* itchy. My skin gets so dry, it flakes off like I'm molting or something." She scratched her arm. "I'll bet my dad was an iguana."

Krista shook her head and looked into her cup. "This stuff is killing off brain cells fast. I don't get that at all."

"I'm with you, sister. I don't get it either, but that's my life."

"I mean, I don't understand," Krista said. "I'm a little polluted. You've got to make it simple."

"Okay. All Blues go to the Land of Disenchantment. It's so sunny there, you catch a tan even two hundred feet underground." She belched softly. "I start sneezing and itching the second I get off the plane."

"I'm still not getting it. Who are these Blues? Where's this Land of Disenchantment?" Krista asked.

"I can't tell you. I have enough felonies on my record." She wiggled her cup in Krista's face. "More mother's milk?"

"Jaysus girl! You took down half the jug already!"

KRISTA SHIFTED ON THE BED. "I was in love with my bodyguard. Wanted to nug-a-nug him in the worst way."

"You had a bodyguard?" Ada rested her head on Krista's stomach.

"My mom did. Seth. Big, handsome, quiet, ex-Marine. Not too bright, but that's a plus for hunky guys. Had a huge-big crush on him. Sometimes I can still remember his scent." Krista looked up at the ceiling dreamily. "After Dowdie died, he was practically my dad, teaching me how to watch out for myself and stay out of trouble. He was a good friend. He always knew when I was troubled, and he set me right every time. Dumb as a stone, but wise as a..."

"Dowdie?"

"That's what I called my dad."

“…think I’d scream if I saw one of those things coming at me. I mean, don’t you think they’re a little scary?”

“True. Weenies are like l’il hairy one-eyed pirates.” Krista squinted and made a face.

“Arrrh, matey!” Ada squinted too, pretending to peer into a vagina. “It’s r-r-real dark in there! Caution be called for!”

Krista grabbed an imaginary penis at her crotch. “I’m Pubic Enemy Number One!”

Ada laughed. “Come and get me, coppers!”

Krista machine-gunned a crowd of imaginary cops with sticky stuff. “Splatta-splatta-splatta! Toppa the world, ma!”

Ada covered her head with a pillow and howled. “Stop it! You’ll make me wet the –” She giggled. “Oopsie!”

Krista snorted. “You’re sleeping on that side tonight.”

“…and in the backseat – a severed human arm!”

Ada shrieked and covered her mouth.

“You sure this is okay? This isn’t too scary?”

“Nonono!” Ada’s dark eyes glittered like shining neutrinos in the blackness of sub-nucleonic space. “And then what happened?”

“And in the backseat – a severed human arm, gray and bloody! Its hand clutched a knife, the black instrument of my demise! And as I reached for it…it reached for me! The hand twitched, digging the deadly blade into the seat, dragging itself forward – inch by bloody inch – seeing only my death, hungry only for my flesh…”

“I read some of your stuff.” Ada belched and lay back on the bed. “I liked *Bingo’s Happy Ending*. Now that was a classic.”

“Splendid. For however long I live, people will say, ‘Oh, she wrote about that monkey getting his pipes cleaned.’ That was my worst shitepost ever, which is saying something given my body of work. And what sucks is I meant to raise drug-abuse awareness, not screw over Representative Rosen.”

“At least they’ll remember you for something.”

Krista swirled brandy in her mouth and swallowed with a small gasp. "But everybody missed the point. Nobody read the part about a staffer tricking Rosen into taking a rock of Base-M earlier that night. That's really why she blew Bingo. Base-M makes you want sex wherever you can get it. It wasn't her fault."

"Yeah, I'm sure Bingo woulda stood up for her. What happened to him?"

"The National Zoo sent him back to Borneo," Krista said. "He probably told all the guy orangutans and became a celebrity. You know how they talk."

"Yeah, but who can blame him? He had sex with a creature at the top of the food chain. That's something we'll never do." Ada stretched languidly and then burst into a sputtering laugh. "That'd be pissin! What if the aliens finally show up, and instead of saying they come in peace, they ask us to drop our drawers so they can tickle the Little Man in the Boat?"

Krista laughed and clinked her cup against Ada's, as much as plastic could clink. "Now that's the sign of an advanced civilization. What a way to say hello."

"...she freezes me out, like I'm a freakin leopard or something."

"You mean leper?" Krista asked.

"Yeah, leper, thassit. Brandy messes up my mouth. S'okay, I'll black out in a few minutes. So I was saying?"

"You're a leper."

"Yeah! She won't come near me 'less she's slapping on a zombie patch. I wear more patches than a girl scout sometimes." Ada leaned back against the headboard, her head on Krista's shoulder. "Still, I miss her. It's so off-planet, her not being around. I keep expecting her to show up any minute and tell me off."

"I know that feeling. I'd run to the door because I always thought the person knocking was my mom. Or that the person calling on the phone was my mom. And you know what's weird? I knew she was dead. I went to her funeral, saw her in the casket and all, but I was sure she'd come back."

Ada gazed softly at the ceiling. "I'll see her again someday. Someday's gotta be good 'nuff, I guess." She looked up Krista. "Sorry you won't have a someday. Thasso horrible."

"It is. Nobody deserves that." Krista ran her fingers through Ada's hair. "But you'll see her again. Once we get to…whassit? Where we going again?"

"California."

"Right, forgot. Once we get to California, I'll hire someone to find her. You 'n me, we'll hire a private dick, eh?"

"Man the rubbers, me hearties! The wenches need a r-r-righteous bonin!"

"I said 'private', not 'pirate.'"

"I want a pirate. One of those Crabby…Carby…"

"Caribbean?"

"Yeah, a Caribbean pirate with long hair and earrings and eyeliner and stuff."

Krista poured the last drops of brandy into her cup and tossed the bottle on the floor. "Mmm. Awright, change of plan. We'll get a pirate for me, one for you, and another one to go look for your mom."

"I just hope he can find her."

"Long as she's alive, he will."

Ada snorted. "She's definitely alive. My mom's a superhero. She was a physician for the SEALs."

"Seals? So she's a vet?"

"Yeah, signed up in college 'n all," Ada said. "Back in Coronado, thass where she learned how to fight so good. One time I saw her beat the crap out of a SEAL."

"She beat up a seal?"

"Yeah. They really smacked each other 'round. Shoulda seen it."

Krista tried to picture that, but her brain felt too dusty. "Poor things. Sorry, but thass just wrong."

"No, they love it. I mean, they're trained to do it."

"They actually train seals to do this?"

"Well, natch. They train all the SEALs."

"Not every one. There's wild seals too."

"Oh, yeah. All the SEALs are wild."

"Except the trained seals."

"No, they're *all* trained." Ada yawned. "You're stupid. I like you." Her head grew heavy on Krista's shoulder, and she began snoring soon after.

Krista lay back against the headboard, her mind spinning as fast as the carousel she imagined, with angry and malevolent seals bobbing up and down on their poles, barking and trying to smack each other with their flippers, and then the carousel spun faster and faster until she couldn't see it anymore, and she gave up trying to stay awake.

THE DOCTOR IS OUT

Day 32
Saturday morning, September 19, 2043
National Tranquility Center, Fort Belvoir, Virginia

Downs pulled his robe tight around his waist because the Mapping Suites corridor was chilly. He'd run from his house across The Green wearing thin pajamas, and now he regretted it. "Who has the night Watch?" he asked.

"Ari," Raphael answered. "It'll be all right. He can handle it. Not much happens at three in the morning."

"Is that so?"

"Except for the present situation, of course."

"What's our clock?"

"No idea. I'd guess this happened anywhere from one to two hours ago."

Downs walked into Suite Seven, where a limp figure in a white lab coat lay facedown across a narrow table. Blood dripped from behind the bed, and a trickle was already spreading toward Downs' feet. He reached around the bed, silenced the alarm on the Mapper, and then picked up the headpiece from the floor; all the wires were pulled out of it, and some looked chewed. "This is Dr. Timmons?" he asked, and Raphael nodded.

"It looks like he was taken by surprise. She gave him the Glasgow Grin, ear to ear," Raphael said. He pulled up Timmons's head and examined the cut. "And did a professional job."

Downs appraised the doctor's slit throat. "She nicked the trachea. A seasoned professional would know that much force is unnecessary."

"So she was in a hurry." He let the head fall back to the mattress.

"He's still bleeding out," Downs said. "This didn't happen two hours ago. At the most, fifty minutes. Did we pick up her escape on camera?"

"No, there's nothing at all. I watched the replay myself, at least on the cameras that were still working."

"She wouldn't know which cameras were offline unless somebody told her. She had an accomplice." Downs walked to where Jake Stiver was sprawled against the wall. His head was turned sideways, his forehead touching the shoulder, and his tongue stuck out as if he were trying to lick his collar. A round white bone protruded under his ear. His holster and his knife sheath were empty, but blood coated his hands.

Another officer sat upright against a cabinet with his legs splayed out, wearing a surprised expression. He was in excellent condition except for being dead. Downs crouched in front of him; he knew this man, Don somebody, a new guy. He examined his misshapen head and tried to imagine the kind of blow that could bend a man's skull like that.

"The way I see this unfolding was that Don was first on the scene, and she rearranged his head all by herself. She didn't have a weapon then." Raphael looked around the room. "Then Stiver showed up. She broke Jake's neck after a struggle and took his pistol and knife. Timmons was third. From the cleanness of the cut, he walked right into it." Raphael crouched down in the aisle behind the table. He looked up into the face of the dripping doctor and then scanned the floor. "Hey, Bob. Does everyone have their ears?"

Downs, on the other side of the table, stood and counted. "I count six ears."

Raphael smiled and picked up a bloody object. "I guess Jake lopped one off the industrious Dr. Lang." He held it next to his ear and wiggled it. "Hey, I can hear the ocean!"

"Raf, be serious." Downs pointed to a camera dome. "Facilities Security wasn't even suspicious?"

"They thought it was just solar flares," Raphael said, tossing the ear into a trash can. "They reported sporadic signal loss all over the building. Happened last night too."

"We had no problems with the cameras during the day. I wonder if somebody scrambled the signal last night so they could talk to Lang unseen and make arrangements for tonight's breakout."

"Bob, be serious. This was an equipment malfunction and that's all. Don't start connecting dots that aren't there."

Downs leaned against the table. "Okay, maybe there isn't a conspiracy here. If that's the case, Facilities Security let the camera outage happen, and a prize target escaped. They should answer for that."

"Keep the sword in the sheath, all right? These aren't a grimy Special Activity Group. These are the homeboys."

"Failure is a disease to be cut out wherever found, Raf. The Profit says so himself."

"Sure, but The Profit won't mind if you chill just this once."

Downs shot a hard warning glare at Raphael. "So you speak for The Profit now?"

"Relax." Raphael laughed. "You really need to get laid, Mr. Downs. You're screwed down way too tight. Hey, I know a gal, she's clean –"

"No, thank you."

"Are you sure?" Raphael bounced his hands a foot from his chest, nestling imaginary breasts.

"I said no."

"Well, your loss," Raphael said. "Listen, we're over budget on death benefits already, so I won't sign off on a staff redaction this time. Find another punishment."

"All right. Transfer the entire Facilities shift to Tonopah. Let the Nevada sun bake discipline into them."

Raphael chuckled. "Okay, fine with me. That's a good compromise."

They walked into the small corridor as the custodians arrived for the cleanup. Downs leaned against the wall with his arms crossed. "Weren't you the one who said we'd catch Warner and crack Lang? That I should just relax and go with the flow or something?"

Raphael looked at the floor and smeared a drop of blood with the toe of his shoe. "So I was wrong. Everybody's wrong sometimes."

"This is the wrong time to be wrong. Not now, not so close to the end."

Raphael sighed and puffed out his cheeks. "I know. At the Elder's Synod this afternoon, Noah Hayborn was talking about how critical the timing is right now. You know, you should go to the meetings instead of getting it secondhand from me. Noah keeps asking for you."

"I can't take time off for a social tea with the other Elders. I'll settle for the secondhand report from you."

"Okay. Well, the bad news is that Noah won't be ready for ten weeks at least."

Downs stiffened. "What? That's another four weeks added to the schedule!"

"It's bad, I know, but Noah's having a problem finding general officers for the Navy and the Air Force. He's already got most Army generals on our side, but they're mostly Others in the Navy and the Air Force, and it's hard to find good candidates. He needs the general staff in place on Day Zero so he has consistent military readiness during the transition. Noah thinks there's a real chance of a Soviet Bloc first strike if they see an opportunity while we're assuming government control. Since the Navy and Air Force are our strategic forces, it's important that they're publicly on board."

"I agree. The Soviet Bloc would nuke us if they got the chance. Once those *Patrick Henry* subs are fully deployed, they'll have to do our bidding." Downs looked down the corridor. "We don't need nukes popping off all over the country. The environmental damage would be incredible."

"Not to mention the loss of life."

"Don't worry, the population would recover. Remember, the first Eden started out with only two people. The planet, though, that might never recover from a nuclear war."

Raphael rolled his eyes. "I won't care what happens to this friggin rock if I'm dead."

Men in overalls pushed three stretchers into the corridor. Downs waited until the door to Suite Seven closed behind them. "Why can't Noah find somebody else? He just needs any officer who'll do what he says."

"It's not that easy. He chairs the Armed Services Committee, and he knows how they work. This isn't a plug-and-play deal, not with the technology both the Navy and Air Force use. We need people who can manage those systems and be loyal to our mission at the same time. And it's wearing him out – he looks like he hasn't slept in a month. Everybody in the Transition Group is looking kinda hollowed out already."

Downs paced the corridor. "Well, that's grim news for us too. How can we keep the lid on the Transition for ten weeks with both Warner and Lang loose?"

"He wants us to redact Warner as soon as possible, of course. But if we can't, then we need to keep her out of California for only six more weeks.

After that, he'd actually like her to publicize those videos. It'll turn public opinion against Gibbon and Cheyn and make it easier to remove both simultaneously. She's the perfect mouthpiece to make everyone believe that the RVE Initiative was Cheyn's idea. But if she gets to California too soon, there's a chance that idiot Gibbon will just remove Cheyn and replace him with someone else."

Downs rubbed his temples and groaned. "And there goes our scapegoat."

"And Cheyn will tell everyone we were involved in the RVE release too, because he'd have no reason to stay quiet if he was ousted. He'd take us down with him. It'd be a disaster."

"We'd have to redact him before he did that. We'll have to do that anyway, no matter how this turns out. We can't let him reveal our role in the Initiative." Downs sighed and looked at the floor. "I wouldn't want to be in Noah's shoes, though. I'm glad I'm just a soldier in this war."

"So am I, brother, so am I." Raphael pointed at the door to Suite Seven. "So what do we do about this? I'm thinking this deserves a Snuff Order."

"It certainly does," Downs said. "But I don't think that's wise tactically. We just issued a Snuff on Warner, and it'll make us look desperate if we do it again. Besides, it's unnecessary – unlike Warner, we know exactly what Lang will do."

Raphael gave him a questioning look.

"It's simple. Lang's out in the wild now searching for two things: the Recombin package and her daughter. We know where she'll be in five days, Raf. She'll be at the Naval Academy picking up her daughter from the Science Camp, or her intermediary will be. She'll need to surface for that, and we might get her then."

"I'm not sitting on this for five days, Bob. We'd look like we've got our head up our ass."

"There's a lot to do in the next five days. Her biggest leverage against us is that package, so she'll go for that first. It has to be somewhere between DC and Cadiz, Ohio. If we flood that zone with assets, there's a good chance we'll find both her and the Recombin pretty quickly. And if we don't find her, we can snag the girl outside Annapolis and use her as collateral, or we'll catch Lang trying to make contact. We can't lose."

"Sure we can. Look at what just happened here. Every plan can fail," Raphael said. "We can't even confirm where the girl is. Our Blackeyes haven't picked her up at the Naval Academy. Lang's an ex-Navy commander, and she might have a Navy contact keeping the girl somewhere else, or on the Academy grounds in protective custody out of view."

"Then if she doesn't come out, we go in and find out if she's there. And if that doesn't flush Lang out, we'll just keep her desperate and off-balance for six weeks. After that, who cares what she does with her package? We'll have the government under Archangelist control, and none of that will matter."

Raphael shook his head as he watched the stretchers being rolled down the corridor. "Keeping her running is problematic, and by that I mean it's a TOTAL FUCKING NIGHTMARE. She's already killed eight of our guys – while unarmed – and we're gonna just let this death princess traipse around? Maybe even find weapons? We'll have to get the warehouse pack of body bags then cuz she'll –"

"Raf, relax."

"I'll relax when they tag her and bag her. Dude, this chick is *way* too dangerous to futz around with. We've gotta order up a juicy Snuff and finish this."

"But a Snuff doesn't only make us look weak and desperate, it also cuts off our only conduit to that package of hers, which could blow the Transition out of the water. We can put out an apprehension bulletin, we can hound her and hunt her, but a Snuff is out of the equation. Quiet and relentless is the only way to pursue Lang, Raf."

Raphael snorted and rubbed the back of his neck. "All right. I'll trust you on this one. So you really think you can catch her?"

Downs smiled. "Hey, the odds are on my side. You know me, Raf. I was built for the hunt."

TERMS COMMONLY USED IN 2043

Aluminati: Pejorative slang for members of the Second Creation movement, an extremist group within the Archangelists. The term implies that they wore tin-foil hats, although there is no evidence this actually occurred.

Archangelist: a member of the Archangelic Church of the Son of Christ.

Arkie: Popular term for an Archangelist.

Base-M: A hallucinogenic street drug that was growing in popularity in the early 2040's. Due to eradication efforts, the drug disappeared by mid-century and is unknown today.

BoHo: Bohemian Homeless, itinerant urban artists of the working class.

Corporate-Americans: Corporations. The 31st Amendment provided them all the rights and protections of human citizens, as well as exemption from taxation.

Elders: Leaders of the Second Creation movement. See *Aluminati.*

Federals: Popular term for the National Security Forces.

Fug: A mixture of acidic coal smoke and ground fog, primarily affecting the eastern two-thirds of the country. It is believed to be a contraction of the F-word and Fog.

Great Correction, The: A prolonged recession that decimated the American middle class and placed all economic power in the hands of corporations.

MRC: The Media Regulatory Corporation, a public monopoly formed to control the dissemination of news and information on the Internet and other electronic media.

NSF: National Security Forces, whose primary mission is to uncover and suppress domestic dissent. See *Federals.*

PRC: The Persian Regional Conflict, a naval and aerial war in which the United States sought to prevent the unification of Persian and Arab populations into one nation. It ended in a stalemate and an embargo on the shipment of Persian Gulf oil to the United States.

Ranks: The rank and file. This group once comprised semi-skilled laborers but after the Great Correction came to include most of the surviving middle class as well. Also known as Breeders, Naggers, Mullets, or Working Class.

Soviet Bloc: Also known as the Group of Sixteen, those nations allied with Russia to achieve nuclear parity with the United States.

Stiffer: A person who has died on the street from an untreated illness.

Tenpez: A coin containing ten grams of gold issued by the State of California in the 2020's. In 2043, its value was approximately one thousand dollars. The name is believed to be inspired by a candy popular in the mid-20's.

Transportation, The: The forced resettlement of the urban poor from Detroit and Cleveland after a period of rioting and urban warfare in those cities. See *The Troubles.*

Troubles, The: A period marked by the broad repeal of civil liberties and repression of public dissent, spanning from early 2024 to late 2027. See *The Transportation.*

www.ingramcontent.com/pod-product-compliance
Lightning Source LLC
LaVergne TN
LVHW091022080826
845145LV00002B/324

* 9 7 8 1 9 4 6 8 4 3 0 1 2 *